DISTANT TURNS

A Novel about Abuse Survival

MARIE HAMMERLING

AuthorHouse™
1663 Liberty Drive
Bloomington, IN 47403
www.authorhouse.com
Phone: 833-262-8899

This is a work of fiction and while it contains many realistic scenarios, any resemblance to persons
alive or dead is purely a coincidence. I was myself a victim of narcissism in the past, but this
is not my story. Weather conditions depicted in this story are realistic but largely fictitious.

Published by AuthorHouse 10/19/2021

ISBN: 978-1-6655-4009-4 (sc)
ISBN: 978-1-6655-4019-3 (e)

Library of Congress Control Number: 2021920362

Cover art by Phoebe Chatham

Print information available on the last page.

This book is printed on acid-free paper.

AUGUST 2014

Distance. It was all about distance for Tina, and as she drove on Route 10, she wondered whether Florida would be far enough away to protect her from her ex-husband Artie.

Her hands clutched the steering wheel. Their California life behind them, Tina and her youngest daughter Sarah had loaded the SUV with suitcases, their two cats and pet dachshund.

They departed before dawn while the dew was still fresh on the leaves, preceded by nights where fear kept Tina awake as she wondered what would happen next. When they finally left the lights of Los Angeles behind, Tina took a deep breath. It was still two hours until daybreak. Sarah slept; their dachshund Hans lay cradled in her lap. She slept through the sunrise that cast a rosy light on the desert and mountains. They passed Chirico Summit, where signs pointed to the General George S. Patton Museum. Tina began to breathe easier. When they crossed into Arizona, Tina wanted to whoop for joy with blissful relief.

She saw happiness as if she met it for the first time. Florida promised a new start, and Tina's dormant adventurous spirit hoped this new experience would provide some long-needed peace and comfort. She would deal with her anxiety, as long as *he* stayed away.

Sarah yawned and stretched. Still half asleep, she pushed her long dark curls away from her face. Tina was always struck by her daughter's looks, her long dark lashes and hazel eyes. She often wondered how she produced such a beautiful child.

"Did you two have a nice nap?"

"Um." The girl yawned again as she pulled out her phone and surfed for a few moments.

"Are we there yet?"

"Right, silly girl. We have a long way to go. Are you hungry, sweetie?"

Sarah shrugged her shoulders. "Kinda."

"Okay, let's go get some food."

They stopped at a cozy little café in Quartzsite for breakfast, which had an outdoor-covered patio, so they were able to eat outside with the pets; it was already too warm to leave the animals in the car. After the restaurant hostess seated them, Tina walked Hans in the restaurant parking lot, as Sarah took the cat carriers out of the car and set them next to the table.

It was windy and desolate; barren desert framed with jagged grey mountains surrounded them as they ate. In the distance, numerous recreational vehicles huddled together in what appeared to be an RV park. Tina repeatedly brushed her blonde hair away from her face, which stung from flying sand. A cheery server stepped outside to take their orders. Tina ordered tea, eggs, and bacon; she had never kept kosher. Sarah asked for pancakes and a coke.

A loud chirp sprang from Tina's phone. Startled, her breath caught in her throat when she saw a message, but it was just Adam texting to make sure his mother and sister had gotten a good head start on their trip. Tina sighed with relief, but a second later, her eyes filled with worry, and she turned to Sarah.

"Did you make sure your GPS is turned off on your phone?"

Sarah nodded and took another sip of her coke through her straw.

"Don't turn it on."

"I don't talk to him."

"You don't have to talk to him. He can track us if your GPS is turned on."

"I'm aware."

"So why are you drinking Coke in the morning?"

"Sorry. Not sorry. I like it."

"It's not good for you."

"He let me drink it when I stayed at his house."

"That's the most you've ever told me about your visit last spring."

The server brought their orders to the table.

Sarah poured syrup on her pancakes. "Nothing to tell."

"Did you spend time together?"

"You know the dude is always busy. Too busy for me."

"Didn't you do anything together?"

"We ate out."

"Nice places?"

"Mostly buffets."

"Anything else?"

"I saw him play."

"Where?"

"Starlight Theater."

"Where's that?"

"Burbank."

"Oh yeah. I remember it now. What did he play?"

"'Elvira Madigan'."

"That's the Andante from Mozart's C major piano concerto. Your father played that a lot. It was originally used as a theme for the movie *Elvira Madigan* from back in the 60s."

Sarah shrugged her shoulders and sipped her coke. Silence.

"We always went to his concerts. Anything else? Any problems during your visit?"

Sarah hesitated and took another forkful of pancake.

Tina's eyes widened and a serious look spread across her face. She and Sarah locked eyes. "Your father is unpredictable, so let me ask again. Any problems?"

"Sorta."

"What does that mean, Sarah? 'Sorta'?"

"Asshat. Hashtag CrudeAndRudeDude. Embarrassing." Sarah fell silent as she continued to eat her breakfast. "Up all night. Gross. Broken junk all over the place."

Tina was silent for a moment and set down her fork. "He wasn't nice to you, huh?"

Sarah wiped her mouth with a napkin. "The dude was only real nice to me around other people. He would hug me and say what a great kid I was. Otherwise, he ignored me as usual. I don't want to go back there again."

"Hopefully not, now that we have a restraining order," said Tina. "I don't think it would have done much good if we'd stayed," she added. "I hope Florida is too far away for him to find us."

After breakfast, they fed the pets and walked Hans again before they drove on their way.

The journey presented an endless highway interrupted only by nightfall and sleep in nondescript budget motels. The little SUV swallowed mile after mile under the brilliant hot August sun. A scorched incandescence raged over the entire country late that summer and left a drought in the West. The Southeast offered even less relief. As Tina drove further east, the intense humidity caused sweat to pour over both mother and daughter as soon as they stepped outside.

4

The trip continued, mostly in silence permeated with blower noise pushing the air conditioning throughout the vehicle interrupted occasionally by music from Sarah's games. She fumed as she ran her fingers through her hair or fidgeted as she stared at the road or her feet. Most of the time, Sarah played with her phone. She frequently sighed to herself in between long silences and stayed busy as she texted or chatted with her friends or sister, scrolled through Facebook, or played games. She interacted minimally with her mother during the trip.

Tina's anxiety leaped through her chest whenever she saw her daughter texting others. She asked Sarah again if she heard from her father.

"I'm not talking to him. I hate him." Sarah sounded irritated. She and her older sister Leli were so direct. "It's all his fault that we're moving. I can't even."

"Sorry, but we had to leave."

"I hate him," she said again. "Sorry, not sorry. He's a narcist."

Tina burst into laughter. "Where did you hear that?"

"Leli said so. She said he is narcistic." Sarah paused. "What's that mean?"

"Your sister doesn't mince words, does she?" Tina continued to laugh so hard that tears ran down her cheeks. "The word is 'narcissist' and means a manipulative, self-centered person."

Sarah laughed aloud. "That's Señor Asshat for sure."

"Oh gosh. I haven't laughed like this in ages." Tina whooped again with laughter as she enjoyed a momentary break from fear and stress.

Tina's mind flashed back a few weeks when Sarah returned from that vacation with her older sister, soon after the house sold. Sarah had a meltdown when she heard the news. Tears ran down her red face as she screamed in anger. This was the only home she ever had. She wanted to stay in her neighborhood and choking between tears, recited several other reasons.

Tina stayed firm. She knew they had to get away from the past and the fear of the future. Artie had almost destroyed the family. His lightning-swift violent moods frightened her enough to make the big decision to move away from Los Angeles. Yet, she worried that nowhere could be far enough from this abusive man. She hoped he would never find out their whereabouts, but she knew Artie's impulsivity too well; it was only a matter of time.

Sarah would adjust. She was going to be a high school freshman. The girl made friends easily and was a good student. Sarah's dramatic exterior camouflaged her inner strength.

Tina's mind flashed back to 1988, the year she had driven the same route to Florida with Artie, shortly after their marriage to retrieve her things from storage. Bittersweet memories floated in front of her. Things had been different. She pushed it out of her mind and concentrated on the road. As the sole driver, she found the trip especially tiring, compounded by Sarah's obvious resentment. This current move was a big change for them both, and to cheer Sarah up, Tina had planned some special stops on their trip. They overnighted in El Paso, and stayed an extra day in San Antonio, where they visited the Alamo and an old mission church. New Orleans not only offered Bourbon Street and Café du Monde beignets near Jackson Square, but Sarah actually fell in love with the city and its quirkiness. That was the last stop; Tina drove the last 640 mile stretch in one day.

They arrived in downtown Winter Park just before dusk. Tina parked the car, and she and Sarah got out to walk Hans. Heat and humidity stifled them; a sauna was probably cooler. The song of cicadas rang through the air, surrounded by green palmettos and tall palm trees. However, although the town's quaintness and charm had undergone little change, the stores were different and the busy traffic startled Tina. She took a deep breath. When they returned to the car, Tina started up the engine again and cranked up the air to maximum power.

The apartment complex was easy to find. Old oaks weighed down with gray Spanish moss lined the streets nearby. The two-story vintage 1940s Spanish-style buildings stood on a lake near the charming downtown district. Alas, there was a downside: not much parking space. Tina edged the SUV into a tight corner at the last building by the lake, thankful she already activated the utilities. She pulled out the apartment key, which had been mailed to her. Both mother and daughter wearily ascended the outside wrought-iron staircase with their pets to the second floor.

Tina unlocked the front door to a hot musty blast; nobody had aired out the stuffy apartment before they arrived. As they stepped inside, they wiped their foreheads. The new place had two small bedrooms and one bathroom along with nondescript beige walls and carpet. The old-fashioned white kitchen opened to the living room and dining area with a beautiful lake view.

Then she saw the disappointment on Sarah's face.

"I hate this place. It's a dump, plus it's hot in here."

"I know it doesn't look like anything special now. Once we fix it up, it will be home." Tina sounded optimistic. "Let's turn on the AC. Which bedroom do you want?"

"I don't care."

"Pick one out, please."

Sarah hesitated for a moment before she chose the bedroom on the right. A neighbor's noisy window air conditioner sounded through the closed windows in both bedrooms.

"I want to sleep at night without that shitty noise," said Sarah in an irritated tone. "I can't even."

"Honey, you'll get used to it."

"And, like, I don't have my clothes, my stuff. When are we gonna get our stuff?"

"The truck will be here Wednesday."

"We need other stuff too."

"We'll go and shop tomorrow, okay?"

"I hate to sleep on an airbed, like, the struggle is real. I want my own bed. Can't we go to a motel?"

"Sarah, this is only temporary."

"I hate this place. It's flat and too hot. I wanna go home."

"This is our home, honey."

"Not for me. I'm a California girl."

The battle was hopeless.

"Let's get a bite to eat. Then, we'll unpack."

Tina thought the place definitely had potential, and she hoped to win Sarah over. After Tina fed the animals and gave them water, the hungry travelers drove to a small nearby Chinese restaurant. Sarah was a vegetarian; she could get her favorite Ma Po Tofu or Buddha's Delight there.

Decorated in typical Chinese style, the restaurant had red booths, Chinese prints on the walls and lanterns, which hung from the ceiling. The hostess seated Tina and Sarah right away and brought them dried noodles with duck sauce. Mother and daughter perused the menu and placed their orders.

"School starts Monday. It'll be a whole new experience for you. Are you excited at all?"

Sarah shook her head.

"Sometimes we all have to make changes. This is one of those times. By the way, I promised you voice lessons when we moved, right? I didn't forget. We'll look for a good teacher."

"Why again did we move here?"

"It's a fresh start," said Tina in a calm tone, "for both of us. I read Winter Park is a good place to raise kids, better than LA. I want you to do well, graduate, become a strong woman and go to college. I want you to get a good foundation to make you successful in your chosen career one day. You need a positive environment to do that."

"Geez. You sound the principal giving a pep talk at school, Mom."

"Please have an open mind and give it a chance."

"This isn't California. Why didn't we stay out West?"

"You know why we couldn't stay there. You know what, Sarah? It was bad, but I don't want to talk about it right now. I really just want to eat dinner, relax, and go to bed. We drove over 2500 miles this week. I'm tired. Besides, Leli said she explained it to you. When you turn 18, you can move or go to school wherever you want. In the meantime, you live with me and we live here, in Winter Park, Florida, USA. *Fertig.*"

Sarah stabbed her spring roll with her fork. "I don't understand what happened, just that we had to move and get away."

"It's because of your father."

Sarah interrupted. "You mean my sperm donor."

"Your sister definitely spoke to you. She is always straightforward and doesn't mince words."

The girl paused. "Leli said he tried to rape you, and that he's scary dangerous." She stopped and looked at her mother. "Did the dude really hurt you, Mom?"

Tina took a sip of tea and looked at her daughter. "He was drunk and maybe under the influence of who-knows-what. I got lucky, but

9

I still got nightmares. Yes, he's dangerous. That's why we're here. The end."

"I miss Leli already." Sarah sighed. "She's so far away now."

"I miss her too. So, did you have fun during your visit together?"

"She had to work, but it was awesome."

"What kind of stuff did you do together?"

"We went to Sacramento and San Francisco. The sea lions and seals are so cute. I love them."

"They're cute. Smelly too. Anything else?"

"We ate chocolate and went to Forever 21."

"You went to that store all the time in LA."

"My fave. Leli bought me the cutest lace top and torn jeans. I also got new earrings."

"How nice of her. What else did you do together?"

"We drove to Oregon. We went up to Newport. We tried to see whales, but we didn't see any. Somebody told us it was too late in the year."

"Gosh, that's far. I remember when we all drove to Oregon years ago. Do you remember how you and Leli danced together in the woods at Crater Lake?"

"Yeah. Didn't Adam almost fall off a cliff?"

"That boy was always into something. Tried to take pictures and leaned over too far."

"You told me. I don't remember too well cuz I was young."

"You were about four. We drove up there, because your father played in a music festival."

"Leli and me, we had fun on this Oregon trip. It was too cold to swim, but we ate good seafood. She treated me great."

"And why wouldn't she? Leli is such a good person, right?"

"She's 100 percent. Best sister ever."

"I'm glad you enjoyed your visit, because I took care of everything while you were gone. Thanks for sharing stuff with me." Tina knew that Sarah chatted most of the time with her friends and sister but was not verbal with other adults.

They ate the rest of their meal in silence.

When they returned home, they both went downstairs, unloaded the SUV and brought everything up to their new apartment. Tina pulled out and inflated the airbeds. After she and Sarah dragged one into each bedroom, Tina opened the box with linens, pulled out sheets, pillows, and pillowcases. Sarah made her bed, undressed, put on her nightshirt, brushed her teeth, and sank down on the air mattress. Soon the girl slept; Tina, however, lay awake in the dark as thoughts raced through her head, and she watched the lights peering through the drawn blinds, as they flickered and danced on the ceiling. For the first time in almost 30 years, she had made a major independent move with a new job and a new home, entirely on her own. Yet, she regretted the stress she had caused Sarah, but there was no alternative. Tina's thoughts jarred when a thunderclap echoed in the distance, and she remembered daily rain was typical during the Florida summer. For a moment, her anxiety intensified as she doubted her decision to move such a distance, but finally, as she assured herself that things would fall into place, she relaxed and drifted off to a dreamless sleep.

That Monday, Sarah dressed for her first day at school in a blue mini skirt, her new white lace blouse, and beige sandals along with a delicate silver necklace and hoop earrings. In contrast, Tina stayed casual; she wore shorts, flip-flops and for the first time, a new T-shirt which said *Sexy, Single, Lovin' it* with a big martini glass, a goodbye present from her friend Sydney. Sarah's eyes paused when she saw the shirt but said nothing.

After Tina registered Sarah at Winter Park High School and drove her to the Ninth Grade Center building, they hugged goodbye and Tina returned home. It was then that she remembered there were no more clean clothes. The full laundry bag from their days on the road contained several sweaty clothing changes, and yellowed sheets with dog pee, compliments of an annoyed dachshund. Tina had time to do wash that morning, so she sorted the clothes and dragged the heavy bag downstairs to the laundry room in the adjacent building. The only two washers and dryers were both in use, so Tina decided to go somewhere else, because she did not want to sit around all day and wait for her laundry. Besides, the machines clanged and banged, so Tina questioned their efficiency. She threw the bag in the back seat and drove to Bob's Wash-O-Matic down the block.

The laundromat sat in an old shopping center. Dryers lined the walls, and the washers stood in the center of the large business. The dingy pink walls needed a repaint. The torn-up linoleum floor had seen better days. An old bulletin board full of business cards hung on one wall near the door.

Tina saw that besides her and the attendant, there was only one other person present. The woman sat on a chair by the window reading the *Orlando Sentinel*. The blonde had a pretty face, was probably in her 60s and somewhat overweight. She wore typical Floridian attire, white shorts, a peach flowered short-sleeved shirt and sandals.

Tina loaded her clothes and poured soap into three washers before she realized she did not have enough quarters. *Shit.* A bored young woman sat by the front desk. "Do you have change for the machines?" Tina set down a five-dollar bill. The attendant got up, reached over and took the money, made change and plunked down the quarters on the counter without a word, her sour expression unchanged. Tina said a hasty thank you, stepped over to the washers, slid the quarters into the slots, and started the machines.

When she finished, she walked over to one of the orange plastic chairs by the window before she realized she had nothing to read, so she turned around and walked over to the bulletin board. Tacked business cards advertised auto repair, housecleaning, pyramid schemes, pet spas, and churches. *Whatever,* she thought as she saw two magazines on the seat next to the other woman. Tina walked over to her. "Excuse me," she said. "Are you going to read these magazines?"

The woman looked up with a bright smile. Her striking blue eyes peered through her cat-eye reading glasses. "Hi, there," she said. "Please take 'em. Boy, isn't it a bitch to sit around and wait for laundry?" She spoke with a strong Southern drawl.

Tina smiled back. "It sure is. Nothing like a waste of a morning to get laundry done." She sat down two chairs away from the other woman to give some space between them.

"Yup and it's frustrating," said the woman "My washer died this morning. It made horrible noises, and then nothing more. The fucking thing is so old, that it's not worthwhile getting it fixed." She laughed. "The clunker came over in the Ice Age, I swear, so I'm getting a new one this week." The woman stopped to wipe sweat off her forehead with her bare hand. Tina pulled a tissue out of her purse and gave it to her. "Thanks, hon. Oh, my name is Cheryl."

"Nice to meet you. I'm Tina."

"Nice to meet you. Y'all live around here?"

"We just moved back from LA, but I used to live here."

"Wow, quite a far move, that's for sure. I'm sure you've seen how much the Orlando area has grown. It's gotten pretty big."

"It's amazing. I've been gone so long, and back when I left in 1987, it wasn't like this. It's a bit shocking. Still, I'm glad to be back, especially since my son already lives here, and I start my new job Thursday."

"Where's work?"

"I'm going back to being a social worker at my old job, now in Orlando. They tore the old Winter Park office down."

"No kidding. I was a hospital social worker for 30 years. I just retired."

Tina smiled. "Good for you. I retired from the state of California three months ago as a case manager supervisor."

"So why work? Why not take it easy?"

"I still have my kid at home, plus I'm single." Tina scowled as her mind raced. *'A single parent.' I never wanted it to be this way."*

"Y'all be fine. I'm sure things will work out. Welcome back to Florida. What brought your son here, all the way from California?"

"Adam followed his girlfriend here. She's from Orlando. They met three years ago in California, but she got so homesick, they both decided to move here."

"Sounds like true love."

"It seems so. I hope they get married soon, but no plans yet."

"I have one daughter, who just turned 30. She's single and is a bit shy, but she rocks as a concert pianist."

"No kidding. She must be very talented."

"She was such a pretty kid with red hair and blue eyes, who became a child prodigy with a busy career. She's been playing for years. It's on hold though. She's home with me right now."

"Oh, is everything okay?" Tina caught herself and stopped. She told herself she sounded too nosy, so she rose from her chair. "Excuse me. I have to check on my stuff. I think the wash cycle is done."

"Sure." Cheryl smiled and picked up the newspaper again.

Tina pulled her laundry out of the washers, quickly sorted the items and threw them into the dryers. She threw in two quarters each, returned to her seat and began to squirm. "You know, this plastic seat is hard on my rear end."

Cheryl laughed. "Same here. I also got an achy ass from this hard chair. My butt hurts."

Tina laughed. "When Sarah gets upset, she sometimes says she doesn't like to get butt hurt. I don't get this teenage slang stuff sometimes, but it sounds crazier than when we were kids."

"Oh, I don't know about that, Tina. We said cool crazy stuff like shindig, groovy, and far out, but hey, I started to tell you about my daughter Maggie. I don't know how long she'll be living at home, but it's not good for her to be living by herself right now. She done tried to kill herself, and thank the Lord, she got saved in time."

Tina shook her head in sympathy.

"Things aren't great right now," Cheryl continued. "It's been rough for Maggie. She wrecked her car and injured her hand, which has permanent nerve damage. Then, she tried to drown herself over at Daytona, but a lifeguard saved her, so she ended up in the hospital. Now she has fibromyalgia on top of her hand problem. She may never perform again, and that's really hard for her to deal with. You know, Maggie had quite a career. In fact, about five years ago, she played a concert with the Los Angeles City Symphony. Did you ever hear of Margaret Ann Miller?"

Tina's eyes opened wide in astonishment. "Oh, my goodness. I was there and saw her play with my ex-husband. We were still married, and the kids and I went to all his concerts. I remember Maggie's beautiful red hair and how they each played a Liszt duet together on their separate pianos. Artie used to be the official symphony pianist, before he got fired for misogyny and other nasty stuff."

15

Cheryl startled. "Really? I remember him. Artie, right? A big Spanish guy with a bushy beard and hair. He cracked jokes all the time. However, I gotta tell you. Maggie had mixed feelings about him. He was a great pianist, but kinda fresh with her plus, he had dirty pictures in his piano bench. If you were still married to him, I wouldn't say nothing, but since he's gone, I'm glad you're rid of him. Small world. Now, tell me about your kids."

"First of all, I'm stunned that you know my ex."

"I don't know him. I just heard about him from Maggie and saw him on stage. I've never met him."

"Let's change the subject, so I can tell you about my kids. Adam just got his master's degree. My middle child Leli works as an ER nurse in California. Sarah just started high school." She heard the dryer chime which signaled the end of the cycle. "Oh, well, I guess my stuff is dry."

"I didn't hear any chime, but it's been so long, I guess mine is ready too."

The women got up and folded their laundry.

"You know, Tina, it's been great to meet you. It's also so nice of you that you let me share Maggie's problems."

"Oh, I was afraid I was being too nosy," said Tina. "I'm sorry that both of you have to go through this tough time."

"Let's stay in touch, okay?"

"Sure. Glad to." The women exchanged phone numbers.

They planned to meet for lunch the following week near Tina's office.

★   ★   ★

Wednesday, the movers brought the furniture and other items. Even with boxes galore, the small apartment began to feel like home.

Tina liked being back at her old job. The friendly boss and casual office atmosphere in the new location made her feel at home. She stayed confident and focused at the office. Yet when alone at home, her inner fears, doubt, and anxiety, which had haunted her since childhood, still clung to her like large menacing creatures.

After so many years, Florida felt familiar again yet strange. so different from California. She found much of the changing Central Florida landscape stressful and unrecognizable, but the thought of a new friend here already brought her some feeling of peace and familiarity.

★　★　★

The following Tuesday, the two women met for lunch at a Vietnamese eatery. They glanced over the extensive menu, ordered summer rolls and pho. Tina ordered water while Cheryl ordered sweet tea and mentioned that this was her favorite drink.

"So how long have you lived here, Cheryl?"

"Since the 1970s. I moved from South Carolina."

"You must have been a kid."

"Actually, I had just finished college. I got a job down here, because I wanted a change from Columbia. Love the city. I grew up there, but I was ready for something new."

Tina laughed. "I love your Southern accent."

"I never lost it, did I?" laughed Cheryl.

"People still tease me about my New York accent. What's your family like?"

"Well, we had it rough. My daddy was a country boy from Sumter and a drunk to boot. My mama was a schoolteacher. She worked hard to raise me and my two brothers, because Daddy was always out cold somewhere."

"My mom was a drunk too. I understand."

"Cheryl shook her head. "Bad parents, bad marriages. I assume yours was bad, right? Jerks for husbands. Problems with kids. Life isn't always smooth."

"Have you been divorced a long time?"

"Since '86. We split when Maggie was a year old. Joey was always good to her, though, and they adored each other. Maggie was Daddy's girl, so his death in 1995 from prostate cancer devastated her; she was only 11." Cheryl paused. "How about you?"

"My divorce was finalized last January after 25 years of a horrible marriage. I was so glad to get rid of that asshole."

"Did he give you a rough time during your divorce?"

"Yeah, but I came out okay. I got the house plus no restrictions where to live with my daughter. I can take her to Tucson or Timbuktu, so that's good." Tina took another sip of her water as she dipped part of her summer roll into the side of peanut sauce. "I don't know if I can count on child support. Artie is a dickhead. We'll be okay, though. I have my California pension and my new job. I'm glad the other kids are adults."

"California is so beautiful. I have been there several times, and I know I would find it hard to move from a place like that." Cheryl tasted her soup as she poured Vietnamese chili sauce into the bowl. "I like to spice things up," she joked. "I make bad puns too. Go on."

"I loved living there, but we had to move far away for various reasons. Besides, the taxes kill you. It's too expensive. Florida is more cost-effective for us right now. I did my research. I believe Winter Park is a better place to raise a child anyway."

"Sounds like y'all had it rough for sure."

"I can't talk about it. It's too traumatic right now. I try to block him out of my mind, so I can function."

"I also went through a horrible time after my divorce," said Cheryl. She took a bite of her summer roll. "I was only married to Joey a couple of years but it felt like a hundred." She laughed. "We'll share one of these days."

"I don't know what got into me," mused Tina as she ate her entrée. She paused a moment. "I often wondered what I ever saw in him, and then how he almost totally had me under his control in so many ways."

"Don't beat yourself up, okay? We all make mistakes."

"I don't know. I look back at my childhood and try to figure out what fucked me up. I think it was my parents, especially my mother. They were German Holocaust survivors."

"So, you're Jewish?" Cheryl picked up some noodles with her chopsticks.

"More traditional and privately spiritual. My family raised me without any religion. In fact, they wanted me to grow up as gentile as possible. Why do you think my name is Tina? Most people think I'm a *shiksa*. Look, I'll talk about my stuff another time. It would probably bore you anyway. Besides, I have to get back to work. I only get an hour for lunch."

"No sweat. What's a *shiksa*?"

"It means a non–Jewish female in Yiddish."

"Thanks."

They paid the bill and gave each other a hug before they left. Tina returned to her vehicle and noticed her shirt already covered with sweat. She had forgotten how bad the heat was during a Florida summer. The car's cool air conditioning provided a temporary respite, before she had to venture outside again.

★   ★   ★

SEPTEMBER 2014

Tina and Cheryl met again for lunch the following Tuesday. This time they drove to an Italian restaurant in Winter Park.

"You know what, Cheryl? After we met for lunch last time and spoke about our families, my mind flashed back to the past."

"Same here," said Cheryl. "I suppose it's good for us to talk about this stuff in a way. Still, it does conjure up bad memories. Flashbacks."

"Yup. PTSD, I'm afraid. I hope you meet a nice guy one day who will love and respect you."

"They're all horse's asses, Tina. I'd rather stay single."

"It sounds like you were married to a jerk," said Tina.

"Joey wasn't a bad person, bless his heart, just in the closet. In those days, they never spoke about that kind of stuff. I was so naïve; I never heard about gay people before. Of course, he hid it and cheated on me. I came home from work early one day and found him in our bed with a guy. It's still tough for me to talk about it."

"Mine was just an insincere, lying, cheating asshole. It wasn't that way at first, but he evolved into a horrible creature. I've blocked a lot of it out."

"I hope you don't think I'm rude, but have y'all thought about therapy to deal with this monster? You sound very stressed."

"My best therapy, Cheryl, is that we're now far away from him."

Cheryl stared off into space for a minute as she twirled spaghetti on her fork. "I think about my marriage. I had trouble moving forward, even though everything happened years ago. My life has centered on Maggie. It's always been about her."

"I've also stayed focused on my kids. I ran interference for years to protect them from their father." Tina took a sip of her soft drink. "I see things more in perspective since we split up." She paused for a minute and closed her eyes.

"Just relax, Tina. You'll be fine."

★   ★   ★

Back at work, Tina tried to concentrate, but past memories clouded her thoughts. Flashbacks returned and brought pain. Her heart raced, and she could not catch her breath. Her hands shook so violently, she could not pick up a pencil off the floor. Tina panicked. The world appeared to swirl quickly around her. She was out of control and broke into a sweat. Finally unable to work for the rest of the day, she stared at the wall.

After work, a terrible headache clamped down on Tina's brain like a vice as she drove home. Sarah was already in her room doing her homework. Tina checked on her daughter, took two ibuprofen and lay down; hoping her headache would go away by dinnertime. However, as she lay on her bed, bad childhood memories, which surfaced at lunch, now returned stronger than ever. Tina's denied emotional pain for years and silent suffering beneath her cheery exterior rose to the surface. She remembered how she once resolved never to get married because of her parents' terrible relationship. Her thoughts now drifted back to her youth, her childhood in New York, and her family. She could not escape from the vivid recollections flashing before her as chronological milestones and events paraded through her head.

★   ★   ★

MARCH 1977

"Tina."

Tina awoke from a deep sleep. She saw her mother standing in the bedroom doorway. Cars and trucks rumbled down the street as usual six stories below.

"Ma, what is it?" Tina sat up and looked at the alarm clock. It was 2:00 AM.

"Liebchen," Eva's speech was slurred. She swayed unsteadily and spoke to Tina in German. "I have to talk to you now."

She staggered and sat down on Tina's bed. Tina could smell the alcohol on her mother's breath.

"I don't know why I married your father." Eva switched to English. "He is such a shit, a crumbum. I hate him, Tina. Did you know I hate him?"

Tina sighed. Her mother got drunk and fought with her father on a regular basis, especially on weekends. Tina had heard a big argument before she fell asleep. Many times, when in a drunken angry state, Eva woke her up in the middle of the night.

Before Tina could answer, Eva began to cry. "A bastard. Your father Max is a rotten disgusting man."

Tina did not respond immediately. She rubbed her eyes. Her mind blanked as she was still half asleep. She could not think straight,

23

but she was used to this behavior from her mother. "Ma, I gotta get some sleep. I have to study this weekend for my test on Monday."

"You know what? You're fresh. You're a rotten daughter," shouted Eva as she broke into loud sobs. "Go back to bed. Ignore me and just worry about your test."

Tina closed her eyes. Exhausted, she did not respond and ignored her mother, who finally gave up and returned to the living room.

Eva drank off and on throughout most of the day. At night, she often got intoxicated and fought with Max. Tina tried to stay out of their way after dinner to avoid these vicious and verbally abusive fights, so she usually locked herself in her room, watched TV and did her homework. She was thankful that the old two-bedroom apartment was rather large. The building where they lived was built in the 1920s. The back windows looked out upon 34th Avenue, a wide boulevard lined with old cookie-cutter brick buildings. It passed through the heart of Jackson Heights, one of the oldest sections in Queens.

The Perry's nondescript apartment resembled their neighbors' homes without any special style. An old upright piano stood against the living room back wall. It came to life years ago when Tina took piano lessons; now it was silent. The plain brown curtains blended in with the beige walls. In the summer, old air conditioners huffed in the living room and bedroom windows. The scuffed wooden floors needed a refinish, while the walls required new paint.

Often, when she afforded herself liberty to daydream, Tina wondered if things in life would ever change, or if things would stay disappointingly the same.

Monday morning, Tina woke up to a cold bedroom. She pulled herself out from under her warm covers and shivered. March had begun like a lion indeed with its cold and gray weather. A chill fell throughout the apartment. The super must have turned off the heat already for the building; He always did that too early in the spring. Tina would tell her father to please call the super and tell him to turn the furnace back on.

She dressed, peered out the window and saw scores of snowflakes fall to the ground. 34th Avenue, and the roofs of the parked cars were already covered with a layer of fine white powder. The bleak gray sky showed no evidence of sunshine. Schools would close for sure; New York City could never handle heavy snow.

Tina pulled on her red sweater to ward off the cold. It was the warmest thing she owned besides her gray wool coat. She walked into the 1940s old white kitchen. Max sat at the table with the morning newspaper. Short and balding, he wiped his mustache with a napkin between cups of coffee as he read the *New York Times.* When he saw his daughter, he stood up and greeted her with a quick kiss on the cheek. Then, he put his index finger to his lips in a motion for silence.

"Your mother is still asleep," he said. "She has a bad headache."

"Probably hung over, right?"

Max nodded.

"I'll make some breakfast." Tina got up and looked through the refrigerator. There was nothing she could use, so she took a box of oatmeal from the cupboard. She heated some water in the kettle on the old gas stove and after completion, she set the steaming bowl in front of him before she made a bowl for herself. In the meantime, Max brewed some more coffee, smiled and thanked Tina for fixing breakfast, which made her happy. It was a rare moment when he acknowledged his daughter; he was usually too wrapped up with his work or fights with his wife.

This was Tina's existence, a passive bystander to her dysfunctional parents' self-absorption. Unadorned, unassuming without makeup and plain shoulder-length hair, Tina blended into her environment. Music was the one true joy in her life, something she and her parents shared. Max had studied violin as a child, and Eva enjoyed a brief opera career in Germany after the War. Their radio or phonograph often resounded with classical music and opera. In fact, on Saturday afternoons, announcer Peter Allen presided over the Texaco Metropolitan Opera live broadcasts, which echoed through the apartment. Sometimes, the family would go to concerts or the New York City Opera or even the Met. Tina lived for those moments.

"Did you know the Blumfelds' nephew is visiting them?" Max asked her. Hyman and Esther Blumfeld lived next door. "I'm going to introduce you. He seems like a nice boy."

"Oh, I don't know, Daddy."

"Liebchen, you haven't dated at all. It's time already for you to meet someone nice."

"Nobody likes me. Besides, I have to study."

"You're a pretty girl with blonde hair and blue eyes, just like your mother when she was young," he smiled. "Let me call Hyman."

"No, please. Don't fix me up."

Max drank more coffee and wiped his mustache again. "As you wish," he said. "Oh, I heard on the radio that there's a blizzard forecast, and all schools are closed."

"Good. I can study here at home."

"I can't go into the office today either, so I'll work at home. Keep yourself busy, liebchen." He walked over to the old cream-colored dial phone on the table "I'm calling the super now."

Eva got up about noon. She sat at the kitchen table with cup after cup of coffee and smoked several cigarettes, her usual routine, as she held her forehead and complained of a terrible headache; other than that, she ignored her husband and daughter. Tina was secretly thankful. A conversation with her mother usually turned into an argument.

The telephone rang; Eva's friend Helene Goldberg was on the other line. She was a wealthy widow, a tall aristocratic woman with high cheekbones and beautiful silver hair pulled into a French knot. A born and bred New Yorker, Helene peppered her speech with Yiddish expressions and words. She never hesitated to speak her mind and could tell off-color jokes or swear with the best of them. Helene liked to compare herself to the famed Yiddish risqué comedienne of the 50s and 60s, Belle Barth.

Tina loved Helene, who treated her more like a daughter than Eva did.

"Hello, maidele," said Helene cheerfully. "I just wanted to check on you during this bad weather to make sure you're okay."

"We're freezing and need some heat."

"Why is there no heat?"

"The super turned off the heat already for the season."

"Tell that schmuck to turn it back on," snapped Helene sharply. "So, what else is new?"

"Nothing. Same old stuff," sighed Tina.

"How's your mom?"

"Fighting and drinking as usual."

"Oy, that's a tough situation, maidele. You know, I've known your mother for over 30 years. It's gotten worse. What can I say?"

Tina did not want to hear any more. There was nothing she could do at the moment about her family situation. "Can I say hi to Stevie. Is he home?"

"So where else would he be in this kind of weather? Just a moment." Helene handed the phone to her son.

"Hey, cuzzie!" Stevie and Tina, both only children, treated each other like family.

"Hi, sweet Stevie," said Tina. "No heat here today."

"Stay warm, cuzzie darling," he said. "I miss you."

"Me too. See you soon." They said their goodbyes and hung up. Soon the apartment began to get warm; the super had finally lit the furnace.

By early afternoon, the kitchen trash can was full, so Tina gathered up the bag and took it down the hall to the incinerator. She was deep in thought about her math homework, when she suddenly collided with a body. "Sorry."

She looked up to see a young man about her age smiling at her. His blue eyes, dark hair, sideburns and mustache accented his looks. "That's okay."

She walked to the incinerator, pulled open the door, and threw the bag into the chute, listening to the bag slide down the hatch all the way to the basement. She felt the man's eyes on her.

"Do you live here?" he asked.

Tina nodded. "Are you visiting? I've never seen you before."

"The furnace broke down in my Manhattan apartment. That's why I'm staying with the Blumfelds, my aunt and uncle, for a few days."

"They're our neighbors."

He laughed. "My name's Gary Blumfeld."

"Tina Perry." All of a sudden, she felt painfully shy.

Gary paused a minute. "Say, do you want to grab a bite later?"

Surprised, Tina hesitated for a second. "Okay."

"Good. How about that Chinese restaurant down on 37th? It's called Dragon Head or something like that. I heard they're open in spite of the weather."

"You mean Dragon Seed. We eat there sometimes. Even Louis Armstrong ate there before he died."

"No kidding. So, it's a deal?"

"Sure. I don't even know you, but okay."

"See you at 5. I'll pick you up."

Tina returned to the apartment. Max still sat at the kitchen table, as he reviewed some budget ledgers.

"Guess what, Daddy. I met the Blumfeld's nephew Gary, and we have a date."

"Good. Where are you going?"

"Dragon Seed."

Max looked distracted. "Your mother is very upset. She's out of wine." He turned to her. "You know Abe's Liquors next door to the restaurant? If it's open, please get her what she likes. I'll give you money."

"Daddy!"

"I just want to keep her happy."

"Then get it yourself. I'm not buying her any booze."

Before he could respond, Tina walked into her room and got ready for the first date in her life. She signed with relief, because Eva had left to visit a neighbor, probably to get a drink. As Tina slipped into her best jeans and sweater, she thought to herself how she would never enable her mother's alcoholism. Ever.

During dinner, Gary told her about himself and his family. He studied business at NYU. His father was a Wall Street stockbroker. His family lived in Manhattan with a summer house in the Hamptons, and Tina immediately understood they possessed immense wealth.

At the end of the evening, Gary kissed her good night, which thrilled her with a strange warm feeling; she had never been kissed before.

A few days later, Gary returned home, called Tina and told her that although he was very busy most of the time, he wanted to see her during the week. Tina began to date him, but they never went out. Once or twice a week after school, Tina took a subway to Gary's apartment. There, between cuddles, they ate takeout, and watched TV together.

Meanwhile, Gary promised her he would not force her to have sex for the first time; however, Tina lost her virginity one night after a heavy petting session, and Gary became her whole life. However, it frustrated her, that they only visited during the week, because she wanted to see him more often, so she decided to show up and surprise him one Saturday night with some dinner. It was bitterly cold outside. Tina decided soup was appropriate, but since she did not know how to cook, she walked to Northern Boulevard and bought a container of matzo ball soup from Waldbaum's supermarket.

Surrounded by chilly wind, Tina walked the several blocks to the 82nd Street and Roosevelt train station, where she took the #7 subway into Manhattan. Gary's doorman already knew her well. Tina greeted him, took the elevator up to Gary's apartment and rang the bell.

He opened the door, dressed in a suit.

"Hi, sweetie. Surprise! Wow. You're all dressed up." Tina grinned and cheerfully held out the soup, but Gary stared at her blankly with his arms at his sides.

"This is not a good time."

At that moment, she heard a woman's voice. "Who are you talking to, baby? We're going to be late for the show." A beautiful woman with dark Farah Fawcett hair, dressed in a pink satin halter cocktail gown appeared behind Gary and spotted Tina. "Who are you?" She turned to Gary with an indignant expression.

Devastated, Tina turned around and headed for the elevator, never looking back She left of the building in shock, and when she saw a payphone down the street, she pulled out two dimes and dialed Helene's number. She could barely see the phone as tears flooded down her face.

"H-h-hi, Helene," Tina sobbed.

"What's wrong, maidele?" Helene sounded alarmed.

"May I come over? I can't go home."

"Is your mom having problems again?" Helene knew Eva too well.

"It's something else. Please. I can't go home right now."

"Come on over, maidele. We're home."

Still carrying the soup, Tina took the subway to her friends' beautiful co-op in a high-rise near Central Park. Helene had designed it herself; black marble floors accented the large rooms with their floor-length glass windows, state-of-the-art kitchen, and white carpeting, offset by a red, white and black contemporary look. Fresh flowers adorned the tables. Modern art decorated the stark white walls. A pillow that said 'Everyone is entitled to my Opinion' sat on a chair in Helene's bedroom. The towering New York City skyline accented by Central Park below, dominated the view in almost every room.

Helene and Stevie greeted Tina in the doorway. When they each gave Tina a hug, the girl burst again into tears. Tina clung to Stevie, who was only a bit taller than her and slightly built, with dark hair.

"What happened, baby?" Stevie took her hand and led her to the couch.

She recounted the event with Gary.

"That asshole doesn't deserve you," said Stevie. "How dare he treat you like that?" He brought Tina a box of tissues.

Tina wept. "I thought we would be together forever. I loved him. I mean we got together twice a week."

"Tina, my dear girl, I'm sorry. That putz can go fuck himself," said Helene. "He's now ancient history for you. How are things otherwise, darling?"

"Not that good."

"Still problems with your parents?"

Tina nodded.

"And your dad?"

"He makes sure mom has her booze, so she's happy."

"You know," said Helene, "your mom and I became friends when she arrived in this country. She was fine then. Beautiful, elegant. She had a gorgeous operatic voice. I tried to encourage her to audition, but she declined. I think her life in the camps messed her up."

"Mom never speaks about her life in the concentration camps, so I don't know anything, except she always wears long-sleeved blouses to keep that tattoo on her arm covered."

"I first met her when she worked for that big stockbroker firm, Farswell & Pryne."

"She told me she was a secretary there," said Tina.

"I remember how your parents tried so hard to have a baby and their joy when you came along. Of course, your mom quit work and stayed home."

"They don't care about me now, but that's okay. I accept that I'm just there, that's all."

"Honey, I just don't understand." Stevie was beside himself. "How could anyone treat you so badly? We love you so much. I just don't get it." He put his arm around her. "You're going to graduate in two months, right?"

Tina nodded. "Did I tell you I just got accepted at Hunter College? I'll start in fall. I want to become a social worker."

"*Mazel Tov*. So, you'll still be living at home and going to school?" said Stevie.

"I guess so until I graduate. No other options."

"How about a dorm?" asked Stevie

"Can't afford it."

Stevie and Helene glanced at each other.

Helene paused. "Let's go get something to eat." She put Tina's soup in the refrigerator.

They walked to a nearby cozy Italian restaurant for dinner. The company and the delicious food warmed her up and comforted her. Afterward, they returned to the apartment.

Helene spoke first. "Tina, would you like to live with us while you attend college?"

"Thanks, but I can't. It's too generous an offer."

"Maidele, we want you to stay with us for free. We know you're on a budget. It's rough for you at home. Besides, we love you and enjoy your company."

Tina hesitated before she spoke. "Oh, that would make me so happy. I'll get a job and pay you rent."

"No," said Stevie firmly. "No rent. It's not necessary."

"We don't want any money from you," said Helene. "We just want you to go to school, study, and feel peace. Hunter is close to us. Besides, we have extra room."

Tina hesitated. "Come on, say yes," said Stevie. "Please say yes."

"If you're sure it won't be a problem, I'd love to stay with you." Her relief was obvious as she envisioned her next four years.

Tina's excitement grew as her graduation day approached in mid-June, and she bought a lovely green jersey dress for the occasion. To her surprise, the school had asked her to give a commencement speech at the ceremony. Eva and Max seemed happy for their daughter. They planned a dinner at the Luigi Ristorante with Helene and Stevie.

On graduation day however, Tina woke up feeling sick with nausea and vomited. At first, she crawled back into bed, angry that she was ill at such a time as this, but then decided nothing on this day would stop her. She attended the ceremony, gave her commencement speech, and graduated. The nausea continued, so she visited Helene's doctor a few days later. He took blood and a few days later told her she was eight weeks pregnant.

Tina called Gary and told him the news, but he sounded cold and distant. Finally, he responded, "I'm not going to marry you," and hung up the phone. Two days later, Helene took Tina to end her pregnancy, and afterwards, Tina never mentioned the situation again.

Meanwhile, Eva accused Helene of meddling with the family and stopped speaking to her when Tina moved in with them and wondered what lay ahead in the next chapter of her life.

★　★　★

MARCH 1985

Tina's one desire after graduation was to leave New York, so she found a job as a case manager near Orlando. The new start elated her and seemed a continuation of her happiness in recent years when she lived with Helene and Stevie in spite of tragedy and a change in family dynamics. Tina purposely limited her contact with her parents during the years she lived away from home. Yet, her life remained in turmoil. Two years earlier, Max had suddenly died of a heart attack, and a year later, Eva found herself a new husband, Irving Weinstein, a tall overweight older Bronx native, whose gold chains and white chest hair protruded though his partially buttoned shirts, which stretched over his belly. Irving owned a garment manufacturing business. He was friendly to Tina, but his clothing reeked of cigar smoke, which permeated her nostrils and nauseated her.

A few months after they met, Eva and Irving celebrated their opulent wedding at Leonard's of Great Neck with a reform rabbi, hundreds of guests and a fabulous dinner. Flowers were everywhere. Eva wore a gorgeous cream colored formal beaded dress with padded shoulders, and her perfect bouffant hair and makeup brought forth her once faded beauty.

Neither Helene nor Stevie had been invited to the wedding. They told Tina it didn't bother them, but it hurt Tina's feelings and filled her with guilt. She attended the wedding in a pretty teal formal dress, but remained a bystander, since Eva's girlfriend was the matron of honor. The wedding celebration flew by in a haze, and the couple soon jetted off to the Caribbean for a honeymoon. When they returned, they announced they were moving to South Florida, since Irving loved nothing more than a year-round good game of golf, and bought a two-story condominium with its own elevator in Boynton Beach. Eva seemed happier and told Tina she had stopped drinking and attended AA meetings.

Helene also moved to Florida and bought herself a Palm Beach oceanfront condo. Stevie stayed in New York with his new partner Mark.

Tina recalled her life with Stevie and Helene as blissful, without arguments, drinking or fighting. She realized that her goal was to continue on this path to happiness and peace. She still had no boyfriend but hoped that the ideal partner would manifest himself in her life one day.

Right now, she focused on her new life and career. She loved her small one-bedroom apartment in Orlando, five miles from her job in Winter Park. She adopted a black and an orange cat and named them Tiger and Lily. Her windowless office where she spent most of her days had its challenges, but she didn't care. Located in a pseudo-modernistic neglected 1960s turquoise and white building, the worn floors and walls needed paint. The women's bathroom had female urinals, which Tina had never seen before. The sinks leaked and needed an update. Sometimes the air conditioning worked, sometimes it broke, but her friendly coworkers more than compensated for the lack of comfort. None of this bothered Tina, who realized how happy she was to be on her own in a new place.

Florida fascinated her with the striking deep blue lakes and skies flanked with fluffy white clouds and striking green foliage, accented by palm trees, southern pine trees and oaks hung with Spanish moss. On weekends, she sometimes drove by herself to New Smyrna Beach and walked along the white sand by the roaring ocean waves. Often, she ran barefoot into the ocean, enjoying the cool salty water on her skin and trying to avoid the undertow. She scoured garage sales and thrift shops to furnish her new apartment and found some Victorian furniture and accessories. At night, she watched TV and read novels from the local library.

One day at work, Tina turned toward her office door to see Alice, her boss. Next to her stood a tall striking woman with skin the color of café au lait and beaded cornrows.

"Tina, this is Sydney Birnbaum. She is our new case manager."

Sydney greeted Tina, who smiled back, and they began to chat.

"Can't talk now," said Alice, before she nudged the new employee down the hall. "I have to introduce you to the other folks."

At lunch, Tina closed her office door, pulled out her sandwich and her book. A sudden knock startled her. She looked up to see Sydney in the doorway.

Tina smiled. "Welcome." "Thanks."

Sydney plopped in the chair near the door and stretched out her legs. She smiled at Tina. "Whew. First day, and I'm already wore out." She spoke with an obvious New York accent.

Tina laughed. "You're also from New York, just like me, right? What brought you here?"

"A long story. After college, I worked at Willoughbrook, and it was a nightmare. You should have seen how they neglected and abused disabled people. I had nightmares, plus I was sick of standing in freezing weather waiting for the bus to go to work. It was time for me to move." She smiled. "Where are you from?"

"Queens," said Tina. "Jackson Heights. Home of many German Jewish refugees in case you didn't know."

"That's right. So, you're Jewish? My dad is Jewish and my mom is black. They met during civil rights protests in the 60s." She stopped. "Do you have siblings or family here? Is that why you came to Florida? I'm an only child, so there's just me."

"Hey, same here. I'm also an only child." Sydney and Tina gave each other a high-five.

Over the next few months, they quickly became close friends, driven together by their common bonds.

Sydney announced one evening that she had met a new boyfriend. "Rick is so cool," she said. "He even plays the trumpet." A pang combined with slight envy surged through Tina. She still hadn't met anyone.

"I'm happy for you," Tina sighed. "I hope I meet someone nice one day. I'm just not as pretty as you. You look tall and elegant like a model. Me? Dirty blonde hair, big nose, don't like my face. I am not fat, but I feel dumpy."

"You look fine," said Sydney. "You're so sweet and cute with curves and big boobs. I'm too tall, skinny and flat-chested. You just haven't met the right guy."

Tina paused. "I may never meet anyone. Whatever."

Sydney chuckled. "You think. You never know what life has in store for you."

★ ★ ★

MAY 1987

Tina worked now as a supervisor and Sydney continued in case management. Still close friends, they often ate lunch together. Sydney now lived with Rick, and they were so busy together, that she had little time for much else.

One day, Sydney phoned Tina in the early evening, right after work. "Guess what? Rick just got a job in Los Angeles; I am sorry, but I need to tell you we're moving there at the end of the month. I just turned in my resignation."

Shocked, Tina felt a pit drop into her stomach. "That's exciting, but you're moving so far away. You're not only my best friend but like a sister to me. I'll miss you terribly."

"And you're also the sister I also never had," said Sydney. "We'll always stay in touch. I promise."

Tina helped her pack, and they said goodbye. A few weeks later, the two women had a joyous reunion by telephone.

"Do you like living in LA?" asked Tina. "What's it like?"

"Well, it's big and bustling with lots of celebrities, and Hollywood is amazing. Rick has so many gigs that we're barely home. We're close to mountains and beaches. The weather is great, and I hope you visit us soon."

"Sounds like fun. I've never been there."

"You'd love it, and–I almost forgot–my boss told me last week that they're going to be hiring experienced case managers soon. Would you be interested?"

Tina paused. "Oh, I don't know. I haven't thought about moving."

"They pay better. Sure, it's more expensive out here, but it all works out."

"If you hear of something, let me know, okay? I'll think about it."

Sydney called early on Saturday morning. "Hey Tina, hold your breath for a minute."

"You want me to turn blue?"

"Seriously. We just started hiring. If you're interested, I'll recommend you. My boss Mary likes me and she'll listen."

Tina hesitated for a second. "Okay. Why not?"

"I bet you'd love the job," said Sydney. "It's so different from Florida. I can't wait for you to move out here."

"Wait. Nobody has offered me a job yet."

"You're so experienced and such a hard worker. I bet Mary will hire you."

"I won't hold my breath."

A few days later, Tina returned home to a message on her answering machine. She rewound the tape. Mary had called from Los Angeles. Tina returned her call the next day, and Mary asked her if she was interested in a caseworker position. After they spoke, Tina drove to the local office store to receive a faxed application Mary had sent her. The next day, Tina faxed the completed application back along with her résumé.

In truth, Tina did not expect any success. Self-doubt cast a dark shadow on her cautious optimism. For privacy, Tina stayed home the day she, Mary and another manager held a conference call interview.

However, Mary called back two weeks later, much to Tina's surprise. Would Tina be available to start in early August? That was in two weeks. Quickly without much thought, Tina accepted the offer and called Sydney as thoughts whirled through her head about the move, breaking her lease and making sure her cats stayed safe on the trip.

"Oh, that's great, Congratulations. We'll celebrate when you get here."

"I start in two weeks. Can you help me find a reasonable furnished apartment? Everything is moving so quickly."

"I'll begin looking tomorrow. What are you going to do with all your stuff?"

"I'll rent a storage unit. I have more crap than I reckoned, including furniture, books, boxes of clothes and my old teddy bear Charlie."

"Oh, don't forget Charlie." Sydney laughed.

At 28, Tina knew her new venture would change her whole life, but what lay ahead both excited and frightened her.

AUGUST 1987

Thanks to Sydney and a rental agent's help, Tina found a small reasonable furnished apartment in Encino. The large old three-story house was divided into four apartments, and the second-floor one-bedroom unit was just right for her. Besides, her new landlady was an avid cat lover with several felines of her own and welcomed Tina's cats.

Before Tina left for California, she drove to Boynton Beach for a weekend to visit her mother and stepfather. Irving was pleasant and wished Tina good luck, but Eva frowned on her daughter's move. On Sunday, when Tina got ready to return to Orlando, her mother looked at her sadly. "I want to try again to discourage you, liebchen, but you don't know anyone out there except your friend."

"Ma, I told you I need a real change. New York hasn't offered me much. After thinking about it, I don't think Florida offers me the best opportunities either. I'm willing to try California. I can always come back. My boss said she'd rehire me in a heartbeat."

"I don't understand how you can move so far from your parents. I really don't. I thought you were a more caring child."

Tina sighed, more annoyed than anything else. "Have I ever acted as if I didn't care?"

"This move is certainly selfish on your part, Tina. Now I worry about you in that dangerous strange city. Who knows what might happen?"

"Ma, we lived in New York City, remember? All cities can be dangerous, but don't worry. I will be fine."

"Liebchen, you really should concentrate on one thing."

"What?"

"You should make it a priority to find yourself a good Jewish husband."

"Oy vey, Ma. This is 1987, not 1900. Besides, not much luck yet. Maybe I will, and maybe I won't, and why do you care about his religion? You never raised me religiously."

"It matters. They tried to annihilate us, our people. We survived," Eva paused. "Liebchen, please promise me to come back home to Florida if it doesn't work out."

Tina sighed in desperation. "Please understand how much I need this opportunity."

The following week, Tina loaded her car until it was packed. Tiger and Lily sat in their carriers on the back seat. When Tina started the engine, she never looked back as she headed out on 441 to the Florida Turnpike, which turned into I-75 after Wildwood. When Interstate 75 crossed Interstate 10, Tina headed west. The highway would take her straight to LA with nightly stopovers. As Tina drove along the endless stretch of highway, anticipation of a happy future energized her.

Her optimism peaked when she reached Los Angeles. Lost at first, she struggled with a roadmap until she arrived in Encino. Tina carefully followed handwritten directions, until she found the apartment.

The landlady greeted her upon her arrival and handed her the key. Tina thanked her, brought the cats upstairs, and unlocked the door. The apartment was clean and pleasant. The yellow walls lent a cheery air to the place despite the somewhat worn beige carpet. The living room held a couch, a recliner with a coffee table, a small bookcase, and an end table with a white ceramic lamp. The kitchen had basic white appliances along with a kitchen table and chairs. In the small bedroom, there was a full-sized bed and double dresser, plus a nightstand. The window beside her bed looked out onto the garden.

Tina fed her cats and made sure they knew their litter pan's new location. She carried her boxes upstairs one by one, then unpacked, taking her time. She owned two sets of 200-count queen-sized tropical floral sheets. Although a bit large, they would fit the full-sized bed. Tina hung her dresses, slacks, and blouses in the small closet. The rest of the clothing she carefully folded and placed in the dresser, unpacked her shoes and lined them up in the closet. After she finished, she set up her small television set on the bookcase across from the recliner. Proudly, she hooked the rabbit ears into the back of the set by herself.

Finally, Tina set her small jewelry box on her dresser. There was nothing valuable in her collection. She owned a few nice post earrings, but her favorite item was her cat and mouse watch. The little mouse second-hand scurried around a white cartoon feline once every 60 seconds.

Exhausted but hungry, Tina walked to the corner, where she found a sandwich shop and ordered the House Special Healthy Sprouts Tofu Sandwich with Bean Sprouts. She was not impressed with her flavorless first taste of LA. After her meal, Tina found a nearby payphone, plucked the quarters out of her purse and dialed her parents' number.

The robotic voice said, *please add one dollar and twenty-five cents for three minutes.*

Tina hurriedly pushed the quarters into the phone slot. The payphone swallowed each coin with a distinctive clang.

"Hi Irving, I made it."

"You did? That's great, kiddo. Wait a minute. Here is your mother. Hold on. Eva, it's Tina."

"Liebchen! Where are you?"

"I'm in Encino. The trip went well. Everything is fine. The kitties are doing great, and my apartment is cute."

"Good. I worried you would break down, have an accident, get sick."

"Ma, I'm fine. Honest."

"Do you need anything?"

"Ma, I said I'm fine."

"I worry."

"Ma, enough already. You sound like a stereotype of a Jewish mother. I expect to see you in a Woody Allen movie any day."

"Tina, really! Don't be fresh with me, young lady."

A robotic voice cut in. *Your three minutes are up. Please add an additional 50 cents to continue.*

"Goodbye, Ma. See ya." Tina blew a kiss into the phone. She heard Eva audibly sigh before she hung up. Drained from the conversation, Tina told herself she needed to stop her stressful interactions with her mother.

That night, she tumbled into bed exhausted. A dull ache begun in her lower abdomen, which meant her period would arrive in the next few days. She knew the impending signs, because she spent too many days in a darkened room with a heating pad on her stomach. The pill always helped relieve her awful cramps. Nothing else had worked as well, but when she read about potential blood clots related to the pill, she stopped taking the medication. Luckily for her, her menstrual pain lessened as she got older. She also did not need to worry about birth control; there had been no sex since Gary.

Tina could not sleep; she closed her eyes but was still wide awake. The street light outside her window cast a faint light on the ceiling through the thin shade. Tina rolled on her back away from the light and thought to herself how she craved peace, roots, a life, and most of all, love. Whether life in LA would fulfill her needs was uncertain. Part of her also wondered if she would be alone for the rest of her life. She could go back to New York if she still wanted to live in a big city. She was only 28, but as she looked back on her life, she remembered how she used to wonder whether opportunity had washed over her. It was always as if a wave blew over her head like a slap in the face as it passed by. Perhaps things would change, perhaps not.

Anxiety surfaced about new job, supervisor, and coworkers. These thoughts played around in her head and kept her awake, which stressed her even more. In a few days she would start her new position; she needed her rest.

Suddenly, there she was on a California beach. The full moon overhead cast light on the shore and made the waves sparkle like jewels. Tina walked along the shore naked with the sand between her toes and the salty air around her, until a huge man's shadow overpowered her and chased her. Tina ran for dear life toward the water which closed around her. She gasped and choked.

With a gasp, she woke up from her bad dream, glanced at the clock radio and saw it was 2:00 AM. It would be a long night indeed.

Two days later, her period cut through her like a sword. As Tina lay in bed and grimaced, hands on her abdomen, she knew she had to do something, because she would not be able to function at work with these cramps. Her concerns about the pill became secondary as later that day, Tina made an appointment at a local women's clinic for a new prescription.

Then, she could function again. Let life begin, she thought.

★　　★　　★

OCTOBER 1987

Tina became a case manager coordinator in a downtown state office, but her favorite part of the job was seeing Sydney again. The women helped needy clients obtain community benefits. It was a challenging job, especially for Tina who was not familiar with all the services in the area.

After hours, she could not get enough of Los Angeles and the surrounding areas. The large city rising out of the deep plateau fascinated her. Sometimes, she would rise early before dawn and drive to a point where she could see the sun rise like a brilliant gold flame over the bare brown San Gabriel mountains overlooking the city. Tina loved everything about the area. She loved Hollywood, the looming canyons, the active beaches and the Santa Monica pier, the desert and the mountains. Even the numerous pumpjacks delivering up the rich oil fascinated her.

At her job, she floated in a sea of cubicles surrounded by a large almost windowless space located in an old warehouse near downtown LA. The office itself, like the Florida office, had seen better days. The worn old carpet looked dirty even when clean. The paint chipped off the walls. The fluorescent ceiling fixtures glared down on the employees, and various old torn posters showed how to prevent work injuries, the importance of employee morale, and employee rights under the Equal Employment Opportunity Commission.

Tina's cubicle stood near the front entrance, where she overheard every conversation around her. Anxious clients, coworkers who busily chatted with each other, phone calls, and other distractions made it difficult for Tina to focus and write reports, especially when the case manager in the cubicle next to hers busily chatted on the phone with her husband about the grocery list. Sydney and Tina often went to lunch together but rarely saw each other after work due to Sydney's hectic schedule with Rick.

One day, Tina sat at her desk as usual completing caseload paperwork. As she reorganized her folders, Sydney popped her head into the cubicle.

"Are you busy Friday night?"

Tina looked up from her work. "Why? What's going on?"

"Rick is performing in the CATS orchestra. We thought maybe you'd like to see the show. We could all go out afterwards."

Tina smiled. "That sounds like fun. I love musicals."

"Great!" said Sydney. "Let's meet for dinner, just us. Rick has to get ready for the show. You'll follow me and...." She touched Tina's arm. "Let's get you a bit spiffed up with some new clothes. Do you have anything to wear besides work clothes? Sorry. No offense meant."

"None taken. I pick out clothes specially to hide the cat hair," Tina joked.

"Oh. Do you buy your clothes from Mr. Katz?"

"That's Mr. Garfield Katz to you," laughed Tina. "I also get my clothes from Monsieur LeChat. He's my Paris connection."

"Ooh la," laughed Sydney. "French for 'the cat'. Very clever."

"You buy your clothes from Poop le Fart, right?" laughed Tina.

49

"Oh gee, you're too much, gal pal." Sydney laughed so hard that she had to wipe tears from her eyes. "You gotta meet Artie."

"Who?"

"Artie. Argentine Artie, the Buenos Aires Boy."

"Who's that?"

"Oh, he's the pianist in the show. You'll meet him afterwards. Can't miss him. Besides, he's the best 15-minute friend ever."

"Huh?"

"Artie knows everyone, and everyone knows Artie. He dotes on you for a few minutes before he moves on, but during those few minutes, you're the best and greatest musician, artist, and nose picker, whatever. He flitters from person to person, but he's fun while he's around. He's a fabulous musician. When he plays, he'll take your breath away. He talks all the time how he was a finalist in a big Italian piano competition."

"Cool. I took piano for five years," said Tina. "My mother wanted me to pursue some kind of musical career. I suppose I disappointed her, because I wasn't very good." Tina filed her papers away. "It wasn't for me."

"I bet you'll find Artie hilarious, "continued Sydney. "Oh, one day, his mother came to a rehearsal and spoke about her little Arturito. His friends never let him forget that. Now, everyone razzes him and says 'Che Arturito'."

"What does 'che' mean? That sounds like a French word."

"It's an Argentine greeting or something."

Tina shrugged her shoulders. "Fine."

"So, when you meet him, Tina, don't forget. Say 'Che Arturito'."

"If I remember."

All week long, Tina looked forward to Friday. She splurged on a new pair of slacks and a boxy colorful appliqued sweater, perfect for a cool autumn evening. Tina paired her outfit with small patent leather pumps and a new black handbag.

Before the show, she met Sydney at a sushi bar. Fascinated by her first visit to such a restaurant, Tina watched as the chefs twirled, rolled, and designed miniature art embedded with rice and black sesame seeds wrapped in seaweed. She ordered the California Roll along with the Sashimi Tuna. "It's fishy, all right," she said, as she wrinkled her nose. "I guess it's part of the California experience, huh?"

"Sushi is not Californian. It's Japanese," said Sydney.

"Thanks for the heads up. I don't cook, so I could never make anything like this. The sushi looks so pretty. Nope. You know, my cats would love this stuff. I've never been to a restaurant like this before."

"Even when you lived in New York?"

"Nope, never. I guess that was too exotic for my parents."

Sydney laughed and paused a moment. "Say, isn't Tina a weird name for a Jewish girl?"

"My parents wanted me just to blend in."

"So, people would think you're gentile?"

"Yeah. As in not appearing Jewish." Tina turned to her friend. "They gave me a *shiksa* name. Remember, they were fearful Holocaust survivors, so when they came here, they wanted to avoid any identity with Judaism. They even changed their last name from Perlstein to Perry. I was raised as a vanilla gentile. So, how'd you get the name Sydney?"

"My grandfather's name was Seymour, so I got an 'S' name." She speared a piece of sushi with her chopsticks.

"Isn't Sydney a weird name for a girl? I thought it was a guy's name."

"Go fuck yourself, Tina."

"I have to. There's nobody else."

They both laughed aloud.

Cats promised to be a spectacular production. Even the composer, Andrew Lloyd Webber, was present along with various well-known celebrities. Tina caught her breath, as her heart fluttered with excitement. The cast, the costumes, and the music filled the theater with beauty and sound. At intermission, Tina noticed Rick with the other musicians in the orchestra pit. She waved to him, but he did not see her.

Afterward, Sydney grabbed Tina's arm. "We're all going to the Afternote." She laughed. "Rick and the other musicians will be there. It's an awesome place. All the artsy and musical people hang out there."

"Sounds like fun. I hope they won't find me too boring."

"Oh, just stop. You'll enjoy that place. Lighten up. Have fun."

When they arrived, noisy conversation pervaded the dark crowded restaurant. Clouds of smoke hung in the air, accompanied by the strong scent of burning tobacco. Tina gagged; she hated cigarette smoke. They joined Rick at an already crowded table. Tina managed a faint smile while nervously touching her hair, before she sat down next to Sydney.

Once seated, Tina glanced around and immediately noticed a heavyset man about her age at the end of their table. His domineering presence and personality were both larger than life and almost took over the entire room. He joked with everyone while his deep loud rapid voice with a slight Latino accent penetrated through the noisy establishment. His black t-shirt said in red letters, "Pianist Penist Organ."

Everyone seemed to know him. People ran over to greet him; women stopped to flirt with him. He laughed; they moved on.

Intermittently, he clowned around and made faces, which sent the table into hysterics every time.

The man's voice permeated her senses. She could not see him well in the semi-darkness, but she noted the dark halo of hair surrounding his sharply sculpted features, which aged his youthful face. Tina smiled to herself, because she could visualize him as an owl or a garden gnome with a big pointy red hat.

However, his loud mannerisms and attire began to irritate her, so she ignored him, drank a beer and spoke to Sydney and Rick instead. As the evening progressed, Tina's head began to spin, accompanied by a queasy stomach. She debated whether she should leave. If Sydney wanted to stay, Tina thought to herself, she would get a taxi.

Suddenly, the man turned toward her, stared and threw her a mischievous grin. Embarrassed, Tina blushed and quickly looked away.

"Oh, geez," whispered Sydney. "I forgot to introduce you. That's Artie and check out his shirt. Hey Artie, is that your new slogan?"

He laughed. "That's me. Can you imagine a pianist with a grand penis as he plays a grand piano?"

The whole table laughed. Tina's face turned beet red.

Sydney nudged her. "Tina, you need to get out more."

"I heard that." Artie turned to Tina with a mischievous grin and their eyes locked for a moment.

Sydney smiled. "Artie Diaz, meet my friend Tina Perry."

Tina smiled and nodded. He got up, reached over the table and shook her hand. "*Buenas noches,* señorita. Pleased to meet you. So how come I haven't seen you before?"

Tina smiled. "I just moved here from Florida."

He laughed but did not take his eyes off her. "That's pretty far. You've come a long way. Why?"

"A new job."

"You must be an actress or model."

She shook her head. "I work with Sydney."

"Oh, che?" He turned his full attention on her. "I thought you were a model."

Total bullshitter.

"Hardly. Is that a compliment or a joke?"

"Oh, a compliment," he said. "You're gorgeous."

Tina smiled. "I bet you say the same thing to all the ladies."

"Only when they have big tits," he answered.

The whole table roared with laughter. Tina, however, found him crude. The heavy smoke continued to burn her eyes. By the time she finished her second beer, nausea overwhelmed her. Artie's behavior and the alcohol almost made Tina want to vomit. She stood up and pushed her hair away from her face.

"Maybe I should leave," Tina whispered to Sydney.

"Excuse us," said Sydney. "We need to go the girls' room." She took Tina's arm and hurried to the ladies' restroom.

Tina bent over the sink and gagged.

"Hey, please use the toilet to barf," said Sydney.

Tina shook her head. "I'm okay. I just want to go home. The smoke gets to me. That guy is really crude."

"Please don't go," said Sydney. "I know Artie is a bit over the top at times, but if you get to know him better, I bet you'll really like him."

Tina hesitated. She stared at the sink for about a minute before her lips curved into a smile. "I can't decide whether he looks more like an owl or some kind of gnome. You know, the kind with a pointy hat you'd set up in your garden."

Sydney laughed. Tina turned to her. "You really want me to stay?"

"He didn't make a good first impression, did he? He's a bit of an oddball, but he's a cool guy and has done a lot of neat stuff. Get this. I told you he won a piano competition a few years ago. He once even acted in a movie about a gangster and played a Hassidic shopkeeper with the curls, fur hat, you name it. I forgot the name of the movie, but critics slammed it for stereotyping Jews. Maybe Artie looked Jewish to them, so that's why they offered him the role. I forgot what the movie was called, but Rich and I went to see it. Artie only had a few lines, but his acting was terrible. The whole time, he stared like a deer in the headlights. They should have had him play piano instead."

Tina laughed. "Is Artie Jewish?"

Sydney's brow furrowed. "I don't think so."

"Too bad. I might have liked him a bit better."

"He loves to talk about his movie part, but his big talent is music. He's in demand everywhere as a pianist. He plays for Broadway shows, movie stars, concerts, you name it. He's also a part-time piano teacher in a Chicago music school, and flies there once a month. He got that job when he won the piano contest. All this, and the guy is not even 30."

"Whoop de doo. Does he do bar mitzvahs?"

Sydney laughed. "I'm sure he would, if you paid him. You know, Tina, he's fun for the evening. Don't worry about any long-term friendship or anything. He's not into close intimate relationships, but he'll be the best 15-minute friend you ever had."

"Remind me to ask him about his movie and music gigs before my 15 minutes are up."

"Oh and, you forgot to say 'che Arturito'."

Artie greeted the women when they returned to the table. He locked eyes with Tina for a second.

"Che Arturito." Tina smiled at him politely.

He threw his head back and roared with laughter as he wagged his finger at Sydney before turning to converse with the man next to him. Embarrassed, Tina sat down and focused on finishing her chicken wings she had ordered. She noticed that Artie turned to her twice that evening and began to ask a question, but both times, passersby interrupted him. Sydney was correct; everyone knew Artie.

Tina looked at her watch; it was almost midnight. Still woozy from her beer, her clothing reeked of cigarette smoke. She wanted nothing more than to go home, shower, and go to bed. When Sydney and Rick got up to leave, so did Tina. Artie stopped his conversation, turned toward her and reached out his hand.

"Wait. I want to ask you about Florida, because I might get a gig there. Your name is Tina, right? What's your phone number?"

That surprised her. *What the hell, though.* She scribbled her number on a napkin and gave it to him. She decided to answer his questions as well as she could, tell him to have a nice day and hang up.

★ ★ ★

Sunday evening, Tina lay on her sofa. She got up and turned on the TV. Originally, she planned to watch the *Tracey Ullman Show*, but decided to watch *Married ... with Children* instead. The Bundy family was always good for a laugh. Showered and dressed in her nightgown and robe, Tina relaxed. Tomorrow, it was back to work.

The phone rang and interrupted her concentration on her show.

"*Hola,* señorita." She recognized his unmistakable voice immediately.

"How do you know I'm not a señora?" laughed Tina.

"Oh, I'm a know-it-all. I know everything," laughed Artie. "Now, what do you know about me?" Before Tina could respond, he began to talk about himself.

She interrupted him. "You asked me what I know about you. You're from Argentina, right? I heard you're a pianist, a professor, and a movie star."

"Si. I'm from Buenos Aires," he said. We call ourselves *porteños*. How old are you?"

"You first, señor. How old are you?"

"28."

"You're the same age as me."

"Now, let me tell you my story. "Do you know anything about Argentina?"

"I know Argentina is at the tip of South America, and the people dance tango and speak Spanish, but that's about it."

"It is a beautiful country. I grew up in Buenos Aires with my older sister Luisa and my parents. We lived in Palermo Viejo, a quiet lovely section. My mom Maria taught piano, and my dad Agustin was a journalist, who worked for the newspaper *Clarín*. I began piano lessons at seven, and I learned to play the bandoneon too, but I liked the piano better."

"What's a bandoneon?"

"A type of concertina used for tangos." Artie continued. "After the right-wing Isabel Peron and her Rasputin Prime Minister Lopez Raga were overthrown, the military government took over. There was terrible political upheaval before we left in 1978. During the *Guerra Sucia*, which we call in English the Dirty War, the military government arrested, tortured and killed anyone perceived as a threat, even clergy, teachers or kids, all gone."

"How terrible."

"My dad spoke out against the government. One day he too disappeared. Then, the military raided our house and tore everything apart. They took my father's books and papers. We lived in terror, afraid we would be next. Friends and relatives disappeared, one by one. Meanwhile, we were destitute. The peso had no value. The government took everything. Luisa took it especially hard and still has nightmares.

"How did you get to LA?"

"My dad's cousin sponsored us to come to the United States. Raoul lived in Beverly Hills and was a wealthy lawyer. We stayed with him when we arrived, because we owned nothing except the clothes on our back. Raoul and his family helped us get on our feet." He paused a second and continued. "A year after we arrived, he and his wife and kids died in a car accident."

"Oh, I'm sorry," Tina said. "It sounds like he helped your family a lot."

"He did. He got Luisa a job cleaning movie stars' homes. Now, she cleans offices. Mama worked in a factory, but when we could afford a piano, she gave piano lessons. Before we fled, I studied piano at the Buenos Aires Conservatory. Mama wanted me to go to Julliard, and I could have applied for a scholarship, but we still couldn't afford it. I finished school here in California, which was hard; I spoke almost no English when I arrived."

He charmed Tina with his friendly chat.

"Amazing story. You don't have an accent."

"Everyone has an accent. I can tell you are a New Yawker."

He started to mimic a New York accent. She countered with her corniest Spanish accent, "Ay, Caramba."

"That means 'surprise'. So, you are surprised to hear from me?"

"Well, you told me you were going to call me."

"Shucks. No surprise. Ay, Caramba."

They both laughed.

"You know, I can teach you lots of swear words in Spanish," he said. "For example, in Argentina, if you want to call a person a jerk or just say 'Hey Man,' you say *boludo*."

"I can teach you some Yiddish or German cusswords too."

"I think romantic chat is better. How about you?"

Tina was not sure how to respond. In the meantime, she realized the conversation had lasted two hours already, but Artie's charm and jokes mesmerized her.

Between giggles, Tina said, "Artie, I need to go to sleep. Gotta work tomorrow."

"Our conversation was fun. I hope we talk again soon."

"Sure."

"So, it's okay to call you again?"

"No problem."

They said good night.

It dawned on her after she hung up the phone that he never asked about Florida.

He called again three days later.

"How's your new job?"

"Going well." She told him about her case manager responsibilities, and how her agency assisted applicants with community resources. She also mentioned her recent promotion and the good benefits.

"I never met any social workers before you."

"Oh, we're low-key, nothing like your line of work. Your life sounds so exciting, playing for shows and celebrities."

Obviously flattered, Artie launched another uninterrupted monologue. He told her his parents named him after famed conductor

Arturo Toscanini. He also mentioned his mother Maria played piano, and how he had been a piano competition finalist at age 25, three years earlier.

"Wow. A finalist. You accomplished so much in a few short years."

Artie's voice sounded sad. "A finalist means nada. Agents only court the top winners. I got ignored. No contract."

"Don't give up. What you have accomplished at your age is amazing. You're been in a movie, a piano competition finalist, working in Hollywood and performing for stars. Not only that. Someone told me you're also a college teacher in Chicago."

Artie sighed loudly. "I'm done with competitions. I hate to audition anyway. I'd rather perform and teach. Now I play for Broadway shows, concerts, the Oscars, movie scores, you name it." He also told her how St. Cecelia Conservatory in Chicago had hired him a year ago to teach a few days a month, so he commuted to Chicago on a regular basis. After he spoke for almost two hours nonstop, Tina finally excused herself.

Artie called almost every night for a week. He would talk as much as Tina would allow. She just listened and ended the conversation when she went to sleep. Sometimes Tina shared her own childhood experiences with him. She told him how she wanted to learn more about her Jewish heritage. He told her he was raised Roman Catholic but was now an atheist.

"Che. I had no belief left after our terrible experiences. I saw hell, Tina. I really saw hell." He paused. "I can't talk about it anymore."

"Sorry," said Tina. "Let's talk about something else." She switched topic to the latest concert given by a local chamber music group. Tina's classical music and operatic knowledge surprised Artie. They spoke about music for the rest of the conversation.

Artie called again the next day just as Tina got home from work.

"Get ready, I'll be over in ten minutes. I'm sure you're hungry."

She laughed. "You don't even know where I live. How do you know I'm hungry?"

"I know everything."

"Maybe I'm fasting and gave up food forever."

"I'll make you eat," he joked. "Nobody starves around me. Where do you live, señorita?"

She gave him her address.

He showed up promptly and rang the doorbell. Tina walked downstairs to let him in.

Artie gave her a bear hug and a bouquet of red roses, and Tina saw him clearly for the first time. A shock of curly dark hair with a trimmed mustache and beard framed his round youthful face. His thick black eyebrows slanted downward over lively brown eyes, which shone with humor. His narrow smile showed small, slightly uneven white teeth. Tina noticed immediately his hawkish aquiline nose which curved almost to his upper lip and accented his very distinctive appearance. Nobody could forget Artie's face. He was a few inches short of six feet, with a large body over his proportionally shorter legs. His arms and hands were thick and muscular, presumably from his piano work. His almost too tight black T-shirt depicted a pen and a pencil and said, "My PEN IS Bigger than Your Pencil." Tina turned the corners of her mouth when she saw the shirt, but Artie's quick hug when he pressed her to his chest distracted her.

"Señorita." Artie hugged her again.

"Ay, Caramba, señor," laughed Tina. Delight surged through her and made her giddy. "Excuse me. Let me put the flowers in water. However, your t-shirt is gross." She turned and walked back up the stairs. "Excuse my place. It's very small. You're welcome to look around. It's too tiny for a real tour."

"I won't wear this shirt again. Don't worry. It was just for a sneak preview." Artie laughed, winked at Tina and walked quickly through the apartment, while she pulled a vase out from under the sink and set the roses up on her kitchen table. "Oh, those flowers are so beautiful. Thanks."

She found Artie staring into her bedroom. "Hey, cute place," he said. "Is your bed comfortable?"

"It's fine for me for right now," Tina answered. It quickly dawned on her what he probably meant. Tina could not think of a good comeback, so she did not respond. He just laughed.

They walked downstairs, and Artie drove to a 1950s style diner, which served the largest hamburgers Tina had ever seen. Artie insisted she order one, while he ordered two deluxe house double cheeseburgers and devoured them both before she even finished half her burger. During dinner, he chatted continuously with his mouth full and did not take his eyes off her.

"Why don't I take you to the Santa Monica beach this weekend?"

Tina agreed, but after he left, she flew into a panic. A beach outing meant a swimsuit and sunscreen. She hated her figure. Angry at herself now that she so readily consented to go to the beach, Tina reluctantly dug out her black and white swimsuit. She shaved her legs, bikini line and underarms. Artie picked her up Saturday morning.

"Oh look. It's going to be a great day." He laughed. They spent the rest of the trip making puns and cracking jokes with each other. Giddy with giggles, Tina's soul wanted to dance through her very being that day.

Dark curly hair crowned rows of fat on Artie's wide pale chest and large paunch belly. The mostly young and thin beachgoers stared at him, as he and Tina walked by, but Artie just smiled back. He obviously did not care how he appeared to others, and Tina no longer became self-conscious around him.

She remembered Eva's dislike of obese people, her snide remarks and comments about how these people should be eating less. Tina found her mother's unkind remarks prejudicial, and she knew Eva would dislike Artie, based solely on his appearance, because he weighed over 250 pounds, Tina did not mind Artie's weight, and in fact, she saw him as a cuddly teddy bear. He cheered her up and made her happy,

She soon forgot Eva and had fun in the waves with Artie. They splashed each other with water and afterward, they joked, giggled, and lay on the sand. Intermittently, they lathered each other's backs with sunscreen. Back at the apartment, Tina and Artie shared their first ardent kiss. They held other tightly and explored each other's mouths with their tongues. Tina's knees weakened. She could barely catch her breath. She ran her fingers through his hair. His beard caressed her face. After a few moments, Artie reluctantly released her.

"I'm sorry I can't take you to dinner, señorita. Che, Mama needs me. Oh, I forgot something. Wait a minute."

He went downstairs to his car and returned with a small box.

"For you, señorita."

She opened the box. Inside was a pair of silver heart post earrings with pearl centers.

"Thank you, Artie. I don't know what to say."

He bent over and kissed her again. "I'll call you," he said as he left.

★   ★   ★

Tina wanted to know more about Argentinean life, and one morning at work, when she ran into Roque, the friendly office janitor, she seized the opportunity. A short balding older man, he had told her once he was from Mendoza; everyone called him Rocky.

She greeted him. "Say, do you have a minute?"

Rocky set down the wastebasket he was in the process of emptying into the large trash bag attached to his cart. "Of course."

Tina explained she was seeing someone, who with his family were Buenos Aires refugees. "Can you tell me about your country? I don't know anything."

Rocky smiled. "Argentina has been through constant turmoil because of our government. Most of us, especially the people in Buenos Aires, descended from European immigrants. We're good people, friendly people, but we've suffered a lot."

"My friend's family escaped in the late 1970s."

"That must have been during the Guerra Sucia, the Dirty War. We had a terrible military government, which hurt so many people. They tortured others and many disappeared." He stopped and shook his head.

"My friend told me his father, who was a newspaper reporter, disappeared."

"I'm not surprised," said Rocky. "The government viewed most journalists as insurgents. He probably suffered a horrible death. I read that they would drug people, then drop them from a plane into the Andes or the ocean."

"How horrible." Tina shuddered. "And yet, my friend seems so happy, so cheery."

"That's good, and he's lucky," said Rocky. "So many people got seriously messed up because of what they went though."

"Really?"

"A lot of the survivors drink too much, have nightmares, act crazy. Some were nice but turned mean. I've been here since '76 and seen it all."

"That sounds a lot like my parents. They were Holocaust survivors, who went through a lot."

Rocky nodded in sympathy. "Many Holocaust survivors came to Argentina. Now, it has the highest Jewish population in Latin America. Unfortunately, many Nazis came too." He shook his head. "We went through so much. You know, Argentina is such a beautiful country. There is the desert, the Andes, unusual wild animals like guanacos and penguins."

"What's a guanaco?" asked Tina.

"It looks like a llama with a camel's face. You also must visit Buenos Aires sometime. It's the most beautiful city and looks like Paris. We even have the widest river in the world there, the Rio de la Plata."

"Sounds really nice. Did you work as a janitor back in Argentina"?

"I was a counselor, who worked in Buenos Aires for a year, before I came to California. I saw enough horrible things, and I have PTSD myself, Post Traumatic Stress Disorder, from seeing enough awful stuff. I'm 66 now, and like my job here. Now, I just want peace for the rest of my life."

NOVEMBER 1987

Tina and Artie saw each other almost constantly in the following weeks. The more time they spent together, the more he grew on her. She often studied his face with his mischievous eyes and found his features refined except for his beaked nose, which was a distractible to his face. Overall, Tina found him rather cute with his fair skin, and the thick curly texture of his dark brown hair. He was brilliant and quick-witted with a lightning-fast sense of humor. They matched wits, and he heightened her awareness and ability to engage in repartee; she found herself energetically alive and slowly realized she was not only strongly attracted to him, but she desired him more than anything else at that moment in her life. She wondered what sex with him was like and pictured his face when he was not around. She lovingly focused on each detail, so she could feel him with her, even in absentia.

They bonded together deeply over two things. First, Tina's knowledge of classical music amazed Artie; they spoke about the topic for hours. In spite of all his pop and show music performances, deep in his heart he was a classical pianist. Their families' refugee backgrounds also cemented the connection between them.

Artie overwhelmed her with attention; nobody ever doted on Tina like this in her entire life. He showered her with affection and sometimes with gifts. His happy-go-lucky infectious personality lifted her spirits. He wore silly T-shirts which made Tina laugh, although he never wore the original t-shirt from their first date again. He could be loud and boisterous around other people, but he was soft-spoken in private with a slightly goofy, singsong rapid baritone voice.

However, their relationship stayed nonsexual. Artie often joked about sex and kissed her passionately many times, but before they went further, he always excused himself and said he had to leave because of his mother; that action of his puzzled and disappointed Tina. On the other hand, she was thankful he did not pressure her too much; she did not mind a slow approach to the relationship and always looked forward to his company.

The couple's great sense of humor sparkled when they were together. Raucous and fun, Artie usually clowned around, made funny puns, and cracked jokes. Surprised at her own self and deliriously full of giggles, Tina would toss jokes back to him, and they would try to out-pun each other. Everywhere they went, they met someone who knew him. Artie basked in the attention; he loved it. Tina meanwhile discovered an aspect of her personality she never knew existed.

One evening during dinner at a Thai restaurant, they enjoyed a glass of wine before dinner, and Tina mentioned that she wanted to visit a local reform synagogue.

"I didn't know you're religious," he said.

"I didn't say I'm especially religious. I need more community."

"I don't give you community?"

"I didn't say that. I have a spiritual and cultural connection to Judaism, especially since my family hid their faith because of the Holocaust. I pray every day."

"Then you must think I'm a heathen since I'm an atheist."

"I don't care, Artie. You can be whoever you want to be."

"I'm a fat ugly porteño. Don't my looks scare you?"

"I think you're handsome. A little extra weight doesn't bother me. Stop it."

He became silent and obviously did not believe her.

"Okay. You could lose a few, but I don't judge people," she added.

He got up, bent over the table and kissed her before he sat back down.

"Tina, did I ever tell you how beautiful you are?"

"I'm like you. I don't take compliments about my appearance well."

"But you should. I adore everything about you. That day at the beach…" he trailed off. "Here is another gift for you." He brought out a large white box. "I want to see you in this bikini, but most of all, I really want to see what's underneath." He winked at her. "I can't wait. Let's go on Saturday. There is no concert this weekend, but I rehearse in the morning, so I will pick you up at two."

She opened the box. Inside was the skimpiest black bikini Tina had ever seen. She laughed and blushed in embarrassment.

"Is this even legal?" She joked. "How do you know it fits?"

He grinned. "I went into your closet and checked your dress size on a garment label."

"Well, aren't you sneaky," Tina giggled. "I'll wear it on Saturday."

Afterwards, he brought her home, kissed her and told her again he had to leave, because his mother needed him.

★   ★   ★

On Saturday, she got ready for the beach and slipped on the black bikini bottom and skimpy halter top, which barely covered her breasts. It laughed in the face of her previous modesty, but Tina swallowed and took a breath. *It's time for you to be cool, and maybe the bikini will turn him on, so he'll stay the night.* She slipped on a pair of shorts and a large T-shirt which doubled as a cover-up.

As soon as Artie arrived, they jumped into his car and headed to the beach. Tina took off her shorts and t-shirt as her self-consciousness evaporated.

It was unseasonably warm that afternoon. After they swam, they lay side by side on their towel, covered with sunscreen, and dozed off. Evening approached, and gradually the beach emptied. The air became a bit chilly. Tina sat up and shivered. She excused herself, put on her shirt cover-up and walked through the sand with her bare feet to the restroom. She returned to Artie, as he still lay on the towel. He pulled off her shirt, and they ardently kissed and necked as they lay on the beach.

By now, the sky was almost dark. Artie slipped his hand under her top and caressed her breasts. The cold hardened her nipples, and he relished touching them and kissing her. Tina began to get caught up in the heat of the moment; her hand wandered down to his swim trunks.

Suddenly a light shone on them. Startled, they both sat up. The flashlight made them squint; it was the beach patrol.

"Hey, you need to wrap it up," said the officer. "No sex on the beach. City ordinance."

"Oh, okay," said Tina. "Sorry." They both stopped to catch their breath for relief before they got up, rinsed the sand off under the small outdoor beach shower, and slipped on their clothes. They walked hand-in-hand to the car and stopped at an Italian restaurant for pizza.

When they returned to the car, they hugged and kissed once more. She lay her head on his chest. "Artie, why don't you stay over? Why do you run home every time we get a bit romantic?"

He said nothing but continued to caress her. "I can stay tomorrow night," he finally said.

"Oh, perfect." She threw her arms around him. "Monday is a holiday anyway."

They returned to her apartment, and Artie stopped at the door. They embraced and kissed again passionately, but he pulled away from her and gazed into her eyes.

"Señorita, you amaze me. I can talk to you better than anyone else. You understand me. I've met lots of people, even famous celebrities during my career, but never anyone quite like you. Frankly, I'm fascinated."

"I'm just an ordinary hard-working person. Good night, Artie."

"*Buenas noches,* señorita."

★   ★   ★

Their first night together began as a disaster.

After dinner, Tina and Artie drove to the Mulholland Drive overlook. Although a sign said the area was closed after dark, the road was still open. Artie drove up to the vista viewpoint and parked the car. They stood in silence as they watched the beautiful city lights. Tina caught her breath; the view of LA stunned her.

Artie put his arm around her and drew her to him. They threw their arms around each other and kissed passionately. Their tongues explored each other's mouths, and she ran her fingers through his thick curly hair. "Do you still want to let me stay over tonight?" He spoke in a low but excited tone.

Tina's voice was breathy. "You bet."

They walked hand-in-hand back to the car. They continued to embrace and kiss each other.

He pressed her body against the car seat while his hands wandered under her skirt. Tina gently moved his hand away. "Let's wait until we get back to my place."

When they got back to the apartment, Tina's trembling hands fumbled with her keys. After she unlocked the door, they walked inside, before she shut the door and turned the lock. The couple sat on the couch and resumed their ardent kisses while they ran their hands over each other's bodies. Artie awkwardly unbuttoned her blouse. He almost seemed like an inexperienced boy, as he fumbled with her bra. Tina felt his erection through his pants, told him to wait a minute and excused herself to go to the bathroom; she returned naked.

He reacted with delight and panic as his body shook in spite of his smiles. After he quickly undressed, they both slipped into the 200-count tropical-sheeted bed. Between ardent kisses, Artie's thick rough beard caressed her in a pleasant way. He doted on her breasts as he licked and sucked her nipples. He caressed the rest of her body and clasped her buttocks. Tina got very aroused. She turned her attention to his body, eagerly caressed him, but stopped and stared. Artie had grossly exaggerated his penis size. In fact, he was barely average. Suddenly things fizzled out; he became totally limp, pulled away from her and lay on his back as he sighed with closed eyes, so he could not see her. Tina climbed on top of him, her breasts firmly pressed against his chest.

"It's okay. Don't worry. Stuff happens, you know. Is this your first time?"

He laughed and opened his eyes to see her blue eyes face his own.

"Señorita," he closed his eyes again and paused. "I have to be honest with you, but you may not like me anymore."

"VD?" Tina sounded surprisingly calm but moved away from him. Artie winced and shook his head.

"Oh, che," He paused. "Sex is there for me whenever I want it. I just show my wallet. Sometimes, I want a girl and go to Nevada. Girls are legal there and don't have diseases. I enjoy all the fun I want without getting busted; that would kill Mama." He sat up and looked sad. "Sex is never a problem, so why now? Maybe I want to please you too much." He shook his head and said to himself. "I shouldn't have said anything."

Tina paused before she spoke. "Artie, if we're intimate, it has to be just you and me. Otherwise, we're through. Understood?"

"I promise. No other women."

"I mean it."

He nodded and looked at her nakedness. "I love your gorgeous breasts. I'm a boob man." He began to kiss her body again, his beard brushing against her skin, which gave her goosebumps.

Without words, she massaged his neck and shoulders and ran her fingers through his hair. Her other hand traveled down his chest and stroked his groin. Suddenly, the tide turned. They struggled for a workable missionary position, but right after he entered her, it was over in seconds.

Tina lay there, obviously disappointed. He lay his head against her face as he stroked her hair. "You excite me so much. I just couldn't control myself," he said. "Let's wait a bit."

Tina sighed with frustration, but just smiled at him.

About an hour later, they tried again. This time, intense passion overwhelmed them and satisfied them both. Afterward, they lay next to each other, covered with sweat. More sex followed that night without incident. Tina was also relieved that the squeaky bed did not break under their combined weight.

When they awoke, daylight streamed through the window. Damp sweaty sheets plus the smell of sex surrounded them. Tina and Artie shared a long passionate kiss. He clasped her tightly.

"Artie, I have to pee. I gotta get up."

"I will never let you get up," he said. "I could stay like this forever."

She wrestled loose from his grasp. "I'll fix breakfast."

"About last night…."

"Forget it. Everything worked out in the end, right?" She winked at him.

He sighed, "When you're with a hooker, the sooner you finish, the better. It goes by the hour."

"Artie, I don't want to hear about other women anymore. Now, it's just you and me."

He sat up and looked at his watch.

"Oh God, I must call Mama." He looked at Tina. "She worries so much."

"Where does she think you are?"

"At some all-night gig."

They both giggled. Tina gave Artie the phone as she went into the kitchen, her robe tied around her. As she fumbled in her refrigerator for breakfast, she heard him speak to his mother in a rapid sing-song voice. She listened for a moment and realized she only understood a few words of his Argentine Spanish.

Tina turned her attention back to the refrigerator as she just remembered how to make scrambled eggs. *Um, melt the margarine, break the eggs into the pan, and stir them with a fork. No, there was another step.* She remembered her mother's mantra to cook eggs only on low heat. *Wait. Mix the eggs in a bowl with some milk, salt, and pepper.*

The end result was fine, she thought. After breakfast, Tina and Artie took a long leisurely shower together before Artie reluctantly got dressed. He told her he needed to get home, but that she would hear from him.

Tina thought about their delicious night together after he left. Their level of intimacy seemed unreal to her. She felt light-headed as if she wanted to dance and never stop. This was the first time she had ever experienced such an intense sexual encounter, where she was relentless, free, and spontaneous during the experience. It was as if they were both one entity. Yet, when she remembered Sydney's words about Artie's fickleness, anxiety flew through her stomach and chest. In panic, Tina worried maybe he only saw her as a conquest after all, especially since his initial sexual hang-ups appeared resolved. Gary then floated into her head along with his painful abandonment after their intimacy and resultant pregnancy. Tina breathed rapidly and as she broke into a sweat, her hands trembled as she feared she might never hear from Artie again. She had to speak to someone.

Sydney was shocked; Tina had never told her about the relationship.

"You mean you have been dating Artie, of all people, nonstop, and you didn't tell me?"

"We only started to date about three weeks ago. Now, I'm scared."

"Why?"

"We had sex last night."

Sydney laughed out loud. "I thought he reminded you of some kind of creature when you first met him. Now you're fucking each other?"

"He's pretty hot."

"Aha. You must be in love. I doubt most women would find Artie hot." Sydney burst out laughing.

Tina responded in a rapid anxious voice. "Remember you said he was a great 15-minute friend? I still worry that my 15 minutes are up, even though he's been great to me. We get along so well. He takes me out to dinner. We went to a movie, to the beach. I went to one of his concerts. He buys me presents."

"That's certainly longer than 15 minutes. What kind of presents?"

"Last night, he bought me some Poison."

"Poison?"

"The perfume."

They both laughed.

"He has also given me flowers and earrings."

"He must really like you. In fact, that doesn't even sound like the Artie we all know. Things will work out, one way or the other," said Sydney in a light tone. "Oh, next week is Thanksgiving. I hope you have a nice holiday. We're going to New York."

Tina sighed. "My parents invited me to visit them in Florida, but I don't want to go see them. You've heard about my mother."

"How about Helene and Stevie?"

"They're going on a cruise. If worse comes to worst, I'll fix myself a turkey TV dinner and watch the Macy's Thanksgiving Day parade."

"Go shopping on Black Friday to make up for it," laughed Sydney. "Buy yourself something sexy. Maybe you'll hear from Artie and you can model it for him. If not, save it for the next guy."

★　★　★

THANKSGIVING 1987

Artie called Tina two days later.

"Señorita," his voice was quiet and breathy. "Sexy señorita, *Fantástica*. I'm replaying our love over and over in my mind. My sweet bombónita."

Tina laughed. "You weren't so bad yourself."

"I can't get you out of my mind. Our night was unforgettable." He enthusiastically proceeded to praise her body in detail.

"Artie, I don't know what to say," she laughed. "Nobody has ever waxed poetically over my boobs and vagina before."

"I can't help it," he laughed. "How about a pet name for me, my sweet bombónita."

"Doesn't that mean 'little chocolate candy or something like that'?"

"It means you're my beautiful stunning lady," he replied.

"You're my little piece of heaven," Tina responded.

"Then, I'm your cielito," he laughed.

"Okay, you're my sweet cielito."

He paused. "Do you have Thanksgiving plans?"

"Not yet."

"I want to invite you to my house to meet my family. We do an Argentine Thanksgiving."

"They celebrate Thanksgiving in Argentina?"

"They don't, but our family celebrates every year. I personally like our food better than the traditional stuff." He laughed. "Wait until you try our food, bombónita. You'll love it. And," he added, "I promise I won't grab you in front of my family."

"Artie."

He corrected her. "I'm your cielito now. Remember?"

She blushed and was glad he not around to tease her in person. They hung up, and she called Sydney.

"He's invited me to his house for Thanksgiving. I'm nervous about meeting his mom."

Sydney paused. "Rick met her and said she's nice. She sometimes brings homemade Argentinean cookies to the group at rehearsals or shows up with a meal for Artie. Rick also told me she talks to him like a baby in Spanish in front of everyone, and that his sister is weird. She came once to rehearsal, didn't say a thing and sat there, bobbing her head up and down like one of those dashboard dolls. Did you ever read or see the play *The Glass Menagerie*?"

"Once a long time ago," said Tina.

"A girl I know thought the sister was just like Laura Wingfield in the play. She's strange, a loner. Enough said. Just make up your own mind and don't contradict his mother, at least not on your first visit."

A few days later, Tina bought herself a lovely sapphire blue knee-length jacquard dress with padded shoulders and shoes to match. After a perm, her hair flowed in golden tufts around her face. Before Artie picked her up on Thanksgiving Day, Tina found an open grocery store and bought flowers for his mother. In the meantime, her hands trembled, and her heart pounded with panic, because she wanted to make a good impression. Downstairs, the doorbell rang.

"*Sos re linda*. That's how we say you're gorgeous in our country. You look simply beautiful." Artie seized her in his arms and gave her a long steamy kiss.

They drove to his home near downtown Los Angeles. The large somewhat dilapidated house obviously needed repairs. The paint had flaked off the windowsills and eaves. Several battered old cars stood in the driveway. Dead shrubbery and weeds littered the front lawn, yet beautiful pink and red climbing roses wound around the front gate.

He parked the car and smiled. "Welcome to Casita Diaz."

"Big house. How long have you lived here?"

"We bought it soon after we arrived."

Tina was about to respond, but the delicious smells which drifted toward them from the house distracted her.

Artie's sister Luisa and mother Maria greeted her in the doorway. Maria wore a blue dress with a white apron. Somewhat overweight, she had large dark eyes and full lips along with shoulder-length curly salt-and-pepper hair. She smiled and welcomed Tina, but her sharp eyes scrutinized the young woman.

Luisa looked slightly older than Artie. She wore a flowered housedress and thick old-fashioned glasses. Her hair was pulled back into an unflattering ponytail. She greeted Tina with averted eyes and a tightly closed mouth curved into a smile.

Artie introduced them, as Tina stepped forward into the bland beige living room with its old Victorian furniture. Various knick-knacks adorned shelves, curios and tables. Tina noticed little made-in-Japan figurines, vases, china cats, and Royal Copenhagen Christmas plates on the wall. A black Steinway grand piano stood in the corner and jutted out into the room. A faint musty odor wafted through the air.

Two black and brown Chihuahuas ran up to Tina and yapped loudly at her feet. Artie laughed. "Meet Pepito and Lucy. They bark around new people, but they won't hurt you." He looked at the dogs and put his index finger to his lips. They immediately quieted down before Artie picked them up, put them into another room, and shut the door.

Luisa sat down in the old tan living room chair with a book. Tina found her actually quite attractive, but her manner of dress detracted from her appearance.

Tina turned to Maria. "Thank you for inviting me into your home, Señora Diaz. I'm happy to meet both of you."

"Call me Maria," corrected his mother. "Do you speak Spanish?"

"Just a bit," smiled Tina, "*Pero no hablo ni entiendo el español argentino.*"

"That's okay if you don't understand our Spanish," said Maria and smiled at Tina. "It's quite unique. In any case, we're happy you're here. Any friend of Arturito is welcome. He brings people home all the time, and I cook for them. Whoever it is, I cook. Excuse me, but I need to tend to our food."

"May I help?"

"Not at all." Maria turned toward the kitchen and called out, "Arturito che, entertain your guest."

He did not answer as he was in the bathroom. Luisa stayed engrossed in her book.

Tina looked up and saw a large framed old photograph of two tango dancers on the wall, which hung over a table filled with family pictures including a large wedding photograph of Maria and her husband. Tina recognized Maria in both the tango and wedding photos. She looked stunningly beautiful with long dark hair, a small Roman nose and a heart-shaped face which framed her dark almond eyes. Tina immediately noticed Artie's resemblance to his father. They had the same eyes and mouth, and the father had a similar but smaller nose. Other photos showed Artie and Luisa as young children; in one photo, Artie, a toddler, sat on his sister's lap, but the photo which caught Tina's eye showed the teenaged Artie standing alone by a lake amid a mountainous landscape. Heavyset, he wore a coat and glasses, had long curly hair and a mustache.

"Bariloche." Tina heard Artie's voice behind her. "It was chilly there. When I was a kid, I performed all over Argentina, Bariloche, Cordoba, Mendoza, Buenos Aires. I even played once in Chile."

"Impressive, Cielito, and what a nice family you have," said Tina.

Artie pointed to the tango portrait. "When my parents were young, they danced tango every weekend."

"Beautiful photo. It looks like it was taken in the 1950s," said Tina. "Say, do you know how to dance the tango? I would like to learn if you show me how."

Artie laughed and shook his head.

Luisa looked up from her book, and Tina turned to her. "Is your book interesting?"

She nodded. "I like to read, but I really like to write poetry."

"You do? Really?"

Luisa smiled proudly. "My poem 'La Sombra del Corazon' was published last year in an Argentine poetry magazine."

"The heart's shadow. Interesting title. What did you write about?"

"Death. Destruction. Disappearance. Argentina during the Dirty War. I would write more, but I don't have much time. I clean offices. Then I come home, go to my room and write. That's my life."

Luisa's sudden openness surprised Tina. Before she could respond. She heard Artie's voice behind her.

"Let me show you the house. Welcome to Casita Diaz."

They walked through several rooms. The interior was as dilapidated as the exterior. Old plaster flaked off the wall, and a hallway ceiling stain indicated a roof leak.

Artie showed Tina his bedroom, which contained a messy unmade bed, clothes and musical scores all over the floor. That was no surprise, because his Datsun was always full of papers and debris. Tina found his room sexless, disorderly, and depressing. She wanted to leave it as soon as possible, but Artie shut the bedroom door behind them and kissed her ardently as he ran his hands along her body. She shook her head and pulled away from him. The last thing she wanted here was a quickie. Then, they heard Maria's voice call them. Tina opened the door and walked out of the room. He followed behind her.

In the dining room, a golden-brown turkey adorned the table next to plates of roasted meats, bowls of vegetables, and aromatic dishes which Tina could not identify.

"I just called you. Dinner is ready. Have you had Argentine food before?" asked his mother.

"This is my first time," said Tina.

Artie walked over to the table. "Here is *parrillada*, which are different grilled meats. We're especially proud of our beef. We know a real Argentine butcher here in LA. Guess what? I grilled the steak myself. Of course, there is *chimichurri* sauce plus salsa *criolla*." Artie pronounced the double Ls with a *sh* sound. He pointed toward two bowls and another dish. "Here are *empañadas* and *berejena en escabeche*, which is an eggplant dish." He smiled. "Of course, we have turkey."

They all sat down for dinner. Maria said grace. Artie poured the Malbec, and everyone got up and served themselves from the table.

When they returned with their plates, they seated themselves and began to eat. Maria smiled at Tina with an intense gaze.

"Are you Catholic?" she asked.

Tina was taken aback, unprepared for the question. "I'm Jewish," she answered.

"What is your family background?" Maria asked, not taking her eyes off Tina.

"They're German Jews. Holocaust survivors. My parents survived the camps. Mom was a former opera singer. Dad worked as an accountant for a garment manufacturer."

"Have you been married before? Any children?"

Tina shook her head.

"Are you a virgin?"

"Mama, *basta*." Artie interjected. "Enough questions."

Tina looked down and, having lost her appetite, picked at her food. Nobody spoke for the rest of the meal. Maria smiled. "I will get dessert," said his mother. "*Helado de Dulce de Leche Granizado* and of course, mate."

Tina looked puzzled.

"Oh," Artie laughed, "We love chocolate-covered ants." He quickly walked into the kitchen as Tina turned pale.

Maria brought out a gourd vessel with a metal straw, a bag of *yerba mate* and a teakettle. She carefully spooned some mate into the cup before she lifted the kettle and poured hot water into the cup. She let it steep a few moments, then drank from the metal straw and poured more water into the cup. She passed it to Luisa who added additional water and drank before she passed the cup to Artie. He added water and drank.

Tina looked a bit puzzled. "Is this tea?"

"It's *yerba mate*," Artie said. "You could call it the Argentine national drink. The straw, the *bombilla*, strains the leaves. It's a custom to share a cup of mate all with friends and family. He added water before he passed the cup to her.

She took a sip, but it tasted like watered down grass. She thought to herself that with so much water, the mate was diluted by now, and she wrinkled her nose in distaste

Artie laughed. "You get used to it." He picked up the gourd after Tina had finished her drink and returned to the kitchen to join Maria, who was preparing dessert.

Maria returned with cups of vanilla ice cream flaked with chocolate chips. Artie set a cup before Tina, who now laughed about the ant joke. When they finished dessert, Artie sat down at the piano and flawlessly played the Chopin *Fantasie Impromptu Op. 66.* His energetic performance lit the room on fire. Tina wondered to herself if Chopin himself could have played the piece any better.

"You must have been really young when you started to play," said Tina after Artie finished the piece with a flourish.

"I was five. I told you I also played the bandoneon as a kid."

Tina looked at him. "I'm learning more about Argentina every day. I read soccer is really popular there."

"I watch games sometimes, but I never played sports myself. Too fat and clumsy Now, tango music is different. When I was 16, I played piano with a tango hall orchestra. We needed money after my father disappeared."

Without a word, Artie returned to the piano and played Piazzolla's vivacious *Libertango.*

"I should kill you," joked Tina as he drove her home. "'Chocolate-covered ants. Yeah, right. You grossed me out until I saw the real dessert."

"Hey, you believed me, didn't you?" he laughed.

Tina nodded. "I won't take you so seriously next time."

When they got back to Tina's apartment, they made passionate love. Neither wanted to release the other and to them, it was as if they had started out as cocoons but merged together as butterflies. They both fell back afterwards as they caught their breath. Tina lay in a state of complete relaxation with Artie's arms wound tightly around her. She turned to him and touched his face.

"I have to go home, mi vida." Reluctantly, Artie released himself from her arms, stood up and got dressed. He shot Tina one final longing look before he left.

★   ★   ★

The next day, Tina wrote Maria a thank-you note and a little card of thanks to Artie. She signed his card *XOXO, Tina.*

When Artie stopped by the next day, she handed him the envelopes. As soon as he opened her card, he roared with laughter and could barely contain himself.

"What's the matter with you?" Tina looked puzzled.

He continued to laugh until he saw she was upset.

"I read it as cho-cho," he began to laugh again and winked at her "Slang for pussy."

"I guess for you that was appropriate."

He did not answer but hid something behind his back.

"Chocolate for my sweet bombónita."

He produced a rectangular box from a Beverly Hills chocolate shop, wrapped in gold foil paper. Tina carefully opened the lid. A heavenly aroma wafted from the expensive Swiss confections: champagne and liqueur truffles, pralines, and marzipan chocolates. Tina paused for a moment as she pondered which chocolate she should select. Before she could decide, Artie grabbed three chocolates and stuffed them in his mouth. At the end of the evening, the box was empty. Tina ate two; Artie finished off the rest.

★   ★   ★

It was late when he left, and Tina had to work the following day. As she slipped on her nightgown, she replayed their intimate moments often over in her mind. Sex had initially posed an aerobic challenge due to Artie's body size, but now, they had reached their mutual levels of comfort. Sometimes Tina straddled him as he lay on his back, sometimes, they did the missionary position or doggie-style. Regardless, the angle of his body against her naked flesh always drove her wild during their quick and magical sex, when the waves of orgasm washed over her, and her very being floated away and rendered her momentarily helpless, caught in the thralls of their lovemaking.

He certainly was not her idealized physical type, but because of her strong attraction for him, his physical appearance no longer mattered. The reality hit Tina like a smack in the face. She was now deeply in love. Yet her anxiety was like a dance over hot coals; a dull ache underneath her heart made her fear that her 15 minutes were over.

★   ★   ★

The relationship whirled like a tornado as it picked up speed. Music gigs and teaching occupied almost all of Artie's time, yet he always made time to be with Tina. He showed her something new on every date, and somehow, they managed to meet several times per week. He drove her everywhere. The aromatic scents of Chinatown penetrated Tina's nostrils. Her eyes absorbed the beauty of the surrounding mountains. Her skin breathed the warmth of the sun and the sea's inherent saltiness.

They spoke endlessly on the phone in between dates and when they were alone together, they had constant sex. Tina had never felt so loved before in her life.

★   ★   ★

DECEMBER 1987

Their whirlwind relationship was almost two months old, but Tina felt as if she had known Artie forever.

One cool Sunday morning in early December, they drove to Big Santa Anita Canyon to see Sturtevant Falls, where they hiked on the almost deserted dirt trail under shady trees. They passed cabins and small waterfalls cascading over rocks. A steep decline made Tina nervous, but Artie held her arm firmly, so she would not slip or fall. When they reached the falls, the roaring water sprayed a cool mist on their faces, and no other sound except the wind surrounded them.

"This is so beautiful, Cielito." said Tina as she inhaled the cool air.

Artie said nothing but pulled Tina close to him, as his arms around her tightened their grip. Transfixed, they lingered with a long kiss.

"Mi vida, you're the most unique person I have ever met." Artie pulled back to face her and touched her cheek. "Did you know I loved you from the moment we first met?" Tina just looked at him, as her face radiated with joy. "I never thought I could love anyone as much as I love you," he continued.

Tina threw her arms around his neck. "Cielito, you're my life. I love you more than anyone, anything. I feel we have known each other forever. I can't imagine life without you." They embraced and kissed again. The occasional passerby stared, but the couple ignored everyone around them.

Tina found this the perfect romantic moment and thought if Artie proposed marriage to her now, she would accept without hesitation. Indeed, Artie dropped to his knees on the forest floor. "Your shoelace is untied," he told Tina and tied it into a knot before he rose again. Tina said nothing as she reeled from disappointment.

Artie stayed silent on their return trip. He dropped her off at her front door with a light kiss, and after a quick goodbye, he left. Then, he dropped out of sight. One week, two weeks, no word.

Tina panicked. She called him twice and left messages, but he never called back. Silence. She was again alone, as he had abandoned her without any explanation. Yet, she had to confront the lingering shadow of his presence. At night, she embraced his pillow and cried until she fell asleep, exhausted from her tears. She barely made it through the workday. On the weekend, she stayed in her nightgown and lay in bed with her cats. Her loss and emptiness inside her stabbed her with pain throughout her being, while she continued to wonder what she had done to scare him away. Maybe it was also her fault that Gary had left her, she thought to herself.

She turned to her faith for comfort and prayed for inner peace, borrowed library books to learn more about her heritage and attended Friday night services at a local reform synagogue. Her religion and culture seemed so foreign to her, yet part of her being.

Tina attended the Hanukkah candle-lighting singles party at the local Jewish Community Center. She chatted with a few of the women, but she did not meet any appealing men.

A week later, she went to a young professional singles club holiday party at a local upscale restaurant. Tina wore her best blue dress, but she still felt out of place. The men wore expensive suits. The women wore designer clothing and high fashion jewelry. Some displayed obvious plastic surgery. One or two men spoke to Tina, but they walked off with no further interest. The women stuck in cliques and ignored her.

★   ★   ★

She told Helene, who responded, "It's his loss that he walked away from a pretty and smart lady like you. You can do better, maidele. Now, put your nose in the air, hold a mock funeral and sit Shiva for him. If he shows up again, tell him, 'I'm very sorry, but now you're a dead *putz* to me.' You can also give him a cantaloupe, put a hole in it and tell him to go *schtup* it." Those comments made Tina burst into laughter whenever she replayed the conversation in her head.

Two weeks after no word from Artie, Tina woke up with a headache and called in sick to work. After her headache had somewhat subsided, she lay in bed, stared at the ceiling and thought about life. *I need to move on. I can't let him upset me anymore. I must go on. Helene was right.* She decided to lock him away in her mind. "Focus, Tina, focus," she told herself. "What else did you expect? Didn't almost any person you ever loved screw you over? I don't deserve better. It must be my fault." Tina stretched her legs slowly as she got out of bed. "Fuck it." she told herself. "I refuse to grieve anymore for this schmuck. My 15 minutes were finally up, and I need to move on with my life."

She took a deep breath as she dressed in jeans and a sweatshirt and walked with her head held high to her car. She drove to downtown LA, treated herself to breakfast and visited department stores, adorned with holiday decorations. She bought some new clothes including a new red dress to wear to Sydney's and Rick's Christmas Eve dinner. Afterward, she got a new hairstyle, a manicure and pedicure.

At one point, she thought of Artie and told herself how she hated his guts.

★　　★　　★

"Stevie!" Tina was so happy to hear his voice when he called her the following evening.

"Cuzzie, talk to me."

"I'm feeling better. I really am. Fuck the asshole. I'm moving on."

"Come visit me, cuzzie," said Steve. "Come on. It's the holiday season. It will be fun."

She paused. "You know what? If my supervisor lets me take time off, I'll be there."

"Oh, fabulous," laughed Stevie. "I can hardly wait."

"Me too. It's been about four years!"

When they hung up, Tina jumped in the air and let out an exuberant shout. The cats looked up startled. Her boss let her take her earned leave, including some days in advance. Sydney forgave her for not coming to their dinner, and her neighbor agreed to take care of the cats. Tina booked a plane ticket for ten days. Stevie lived now in Greenwich Village and had recently also broken up with his partner, so she knew their presence together would comfort each other.

She arrived at LaGuardia airport to chilly weather, which froze the tip of her nose and turned her cheeks bright red. She bundled her scarf tighter around her head, also thankful she had kept her warm coat. Stevie picked her up, and they drove to his apartment, a lofty place in an older brownstone, furnished with the finest modern black furniture with contemporary accents. Tina thought he showed good taste in decorating his place.

The first two evenings, they complained and cried about their romantic losses over bottles of good chardonnay. Then, life for both became a whirlwind as they visited museums, enjoyed Broadway musicals which offered half-price tickets, shopped, admired 5th Avenue decorations and saw the Rockettes at Radio City Music Hall. They rode the subway all over Manhattan, ate at Katz's Delicatessen and several other ethnic restaurants. On Christmas Day, they dined in Chinatown. One evening, they went to Sammy's Romanian Steak House in Manhattan, where musicians played klezmer music at dinner. They celebrated New Year's Eve at Stevie's favorite gay bar with a hilarious drag queen party. Tina never had so much fun. With her now-improved mood, she prepared to move on with her life.

However, as she flew home to Los Angeles, Tina again thought of Artie and her emotions returned with a vengeance. Her heart pounded in her chest. Her stomach ached. Her hands trembled. She did not know if she could face her apartment again, where they spent so many hours together. Now that she had been away, she dreaded the place and decided to move when her lease was up.

Her delayed plane rerouted due to unexpected winter storms, so she arrived home late. Exhausted, she threw her suitcase on the floor, as her answering machine's flashing red light caught her attention. The thirty messages reached the end of the tape. *What the hell?* He called five times; there were twenty-five hang-ups.

Artie.

Numb with shock, Tina sat down on the bed with joy and anxiety at hearing his voice again. Tina could feel her heart pounding in her chest when the phone rang.

"Where have you been, señorita? I thought something happened to you."

"No kidding. I haven't heard from you in over a month."

"I will explain. I want to come over."

She hesitated, still overwhelmed. "I just arrived home. I need to go to bed."

"Let me tuck you in."

"Not tonight."

"Tomorrow then?"

She hesitated.

"I will be over tomorrow afternoon after my recording session."

Tina consented, but afterward, she thought she should have perhaps refused another emotional roller coaster. However, in spite of her misgivings, she took no further action, changed into her pajamas and slid under the covers.

He rang her doorbell at five minutes before six the next day and wore a navy T-shirt which said, "Cleverly Disguised as a Responsible Adult."

They locked eyes, and Tina quickly looked away. As Artie handed her a dozen roses along with a bottle of sparkling wine, he embraced her, but Tina stiffened.

"Mi vida." He took her face in his hands. His glance burned through her, as he kissed her. "Oh, how I missed those blue eyes."

Tina did not respond or smile. The intensity of his presence had weakened her to the point she could not respond. Artie walked over to a kitchen chair and sat down. Tina sat across from him with a downward glance and arms crossed over her chest. Expressionless, she looked up at him.

"So, what happened to you?"

"I was busy."

"That's B.S," said Tina. "You dumped me and never told me why."

"I never dumped you."

"Really? You never returned my calls and then disappeared for a month." Tina wrung her hands. Her feet nervously tapped the floor.

"It wasn't what you think," he said. "All I did for the past weeks was think about you."

He got up and walked over to the kitchen sink, pulled a glass from the kitchen cabinet and poured himself some water from the faucet, which he quickly guzzled down. He stared at the floor, as he ran his fingers through his hair. Silence. A flash of distress shone in his eyes. After a moment, he said, "I thought about what we told each other at our last date"

"That we loved each other?" asked Tina. "What's so terrible about that?"

He swallowed hard. "I thought everything over." Artie looked down again at the floor. He was the total opposite of his usual brash self.

"So, what I said scared you off?" said Tina slowly.

He said nothing.

"Anything else? I deserve the truth, Artie."

"Am I still your cielito?"

She ignored the question. "Tell me the truth. What is going on?"

He hesitated a moment and swallowed. "Mama has nightmares from the war. She remembers when my dad disappeared, and the police tore through our home. She wakes up terrified. She remembers how the government killed and tortured people. Did you know when pregnant prisoners had their babies, the torturers killed the mothers and adopted the babies out? Do you know what else they did?" Artie got up and walked back and forth. He was obviously agitated at the memories.

"Don't go on if it makes you uncomfortable," said Tina. "What does this have to do with us anyway?"

Artie ignored the question. "The torturers took their prisoners and dropped them out of airplanes. We think that's what happened to Papa. So many people disappeared. Mama only has me and Luisa now."

He got up once more, walked to the front window and was silent for several minutes before he spoke.

"I don't want to hurt Mama."

Tina's heart dropped in her stomach.

"She always finds something to say about any girl I bring home." He hesitated. "She really wants me to find a Catholic Latina."

"Do you blindly listen to everything Mommy says?"

"Tina, please try to understand what Mama went through. I want her happy."

"So where does that leave me?"

"I want to be happy too."

Tina stood up. Her eyes filled with tears. "So, you came over here to explain that it's over because of your mother?" Her face crumpled as her chest heaved with her bitter sobs and her eyes filled with tears. She turned away from Artie and wiped her cheek with her sleeve. Then, she turned to face him and yelled so loudly, her voice echoed throughout the apartment. "Why did you come here to tell me all this, Artie? Fuck you." She sat down, covered her eyes and sobbed loudly, as the raw wound inside her opened again. Artie leapt out of his chair, put his arms around her and held her tightly. Tina went limp, felt his embrace and stopped crying. Yet something was inconsistent. Tina saw Artie's eyes were vacant. She scanned his face for emotion, but saw none, but his soft sweet words lured her into a trance, and she forgot her misgivings, because she wanted to believe so badly that things would work out well.

"Oh, bombónita, how I love you. I love you more than anybody, anything. Let's move in together."

"What will Mommy say?"

"I don't care."

They shared a passionate kiss. She leaned her head against his chest as she smiled. "You know you can't get your piano into this small apartment."

"I'll practice at the studio."

"My closet is too small for your T-shirt collection."

"Oh shit, Tina. Is that a deal breaker?"

"I don't just live with guys," she said.

"I'm not just any guy. You still love me a little bit, don't you?"

"I love you to death. I adore you. I want your body. No, I take that back. Now, I'm jinxed. You'll take off again like a rocket."

He laughed as he whispered into her ear. "Now you'll never get rid of me. The only rocket you'll experience is between my legs. It's going to send you to heaven in ecstasy. I promise."

Tina laughed. "Oh, Cielito, you crack me up. You're so funny."

He wiped the tears off her face, pulled out a small gift box and whispered, "Surprise. Merry Christmas."

"Thank you, but for me it is Happy Hanukkah." Tina carefully opened the box which held a beautiful gold necklace with a pearl pendant. She lifted her hair up as he got behind her and fastened the necklace. His soft lips and rough beard brushed against her shoulder.

They went out for dinner. Later, they shared the wine, and Artie stayed the night. They made up for lost time, getting little sleep. At one point, Tina threw the blanket over their heads so they would not be too noisy and disturb the neighbors.

★ ★ ★

He was scheduled to perform Beethoven's *Emperor Concerto* with a local orchestra and insisted Tina be there.

Tina wore a new red dress to the performance, picked up her ticket at the box office and slid into her second-row seat. She saw Maria and Luisa seated nearby and waved to them. The theater was full. A large Steinway grand stood on stage. The orchestra gathered behind the piano and tuned their instruments. Artie wore a tuxedo with tails. He exuded charisma on stage as he played with his flawless technique. After the performance, the audience applauded wildly. The conductor stood aside as Artie walked up to the microphone and motioned the audience to be silent.

"Hey, thanks for coming to my concert tonight. And now, I've a special announcement to make." He smiled as he reached out to Tina and motioned for her to come up on stage. Bewildered, she excused herself as she stepped over two audience members' legs to walk up to the stage.

Artie took her hand and led her up to the microphone. "Everyone, this is Tina. Now, you're all witnesses."

As he spoke, he knelt before her on one knee as he took her left hand and slipped a diamond ring on her ring finger.

"Tina, will you marry me?"

Tina burst into tears. They kissed in front of the entire crowd, which cheered, clapped and congratulated the couple. The theater rang with deafening noise.

Afterward, still giddy from the experience, Tina called her friends to tell them the news. She still was in disbelief that Artie proposed to her in front of a crowd. It was too intense, too quick.

Finally, Tina called her mother, but Eva was not happy. "What kind of man is this, liebchen? You're going to marry an Argentine *shaygetz*?"

"I already told him we'll raise our kids Jewish."

"*Macht nichts*. Don't you know what Argentines are? Most of them are German Nazis, murderers and terrorists who escaped from Germany after the war."

"Ma, that's not true about all Argentineans, and Artie is not a Nazi. Artie is not even German. He told me he's Spanish and Italian."

Eva paused a moment.

"What kind of money can he make as a musician? Can he support a family? I want you to marry a man who can provide for you properly."

"Ma, that's sexist. We'll be fine. He makes enough money, and I have a good job."

"Send me a picture," she told her daughter. Tina chose a nice photo of the couple and sent a copy to Eva and also to Helene.

A few days later, Artie told her he had another surprise.

"Bombónita, since you told me you wanted to raise your children Jewish, I've started lessons with a local rabbi, and he'll convert me next week."

"How wonderful, but I would never force you, Cielito."

"I want to do it. Jewish ways, customs, and laws fascinate me. Plus, I found out I don't have to get circumcised."

Tina doubled over in laughter. "You said that to crack me up." Her mood became serious. "What did you tell your family?"

"Actually, I haven't told them yet. They're still in shock that we're getting married."

"You know this probably won't go over well, don't you?"

"I'll handle them. First, I will confess to Mama about my atheism, but tell her that I've have become religious through Judaism. That should make her happy."

"I doubt it. She'll blame me for sure." That night, Tina threw away her birth control pills. Since Artie had mentioned children, she hoped to get pregnant as soon as possible.

A week later, Eva called and sounded agitated. "I got the photo today. What kind of man is this? He is so fat. All that black hair and that beard…. Oy. He looks like Fidel Castro or that terrorist Che something. Can't you find somebody nicer?"

"My Artie does not look like Fidel Castro or Che Guevara or anyone else but himself. Artie is to me the handsomest and nicest man in the world. He's not a terrorist. Stop it."

"You could do better."

"I don't think so."

"So, you set the date?"

"April 23rd. We found a nice venue near the ocean, not too far away from LA."

"Why are you in such a rush? Are you pregnant?"

"Hell no, Ma. That was the only date open at the inn."

Eva signed audibly over the phone. "I will come visit to help you pick out your dress. Are you wearing a wedding gown or will you disappoint me?"

"You can help me pick out the dress. The wedding is only three months away, Ma. I'm nervous. There is so much to do, even for a relatively small wedding such as ours."

"You know that only virgins should wear white dresses…."

"Enough already. I will hang up, because I don't want to talk anymore."

"Alright. I'll fly to LA this weekend, Liebchen. I can't wait to meet this future son-in-law."

The conversation with her difficult mother totally exhausted Tina. Afterward, she called Helene, who greeted her warmly.

"Mazel Tov on your engagement. I actually spoke to your mother. She wants to be friends again. When is the big day?"

"April 23rd."

Helene paused. "Are you sure that this is what you want to do? You're moving very fast. Give it some time. You've only known each other a few months. I don't think you should rush things."

"We met in October, but I know he's the one. I love him so much. I promise when you meet Artie, you'll love him too."

"I hope so for your sake, maidele. Stevie and I will both be there that is, if you invite us. I got the photo. Well, he's definitely not my style, but if you're happy, I'm happy."

"I'm happy, and I can't wait to see you both at the wedding."

"My dear girl," Helene paused. "Your happiness is what matters. Just be careful. Anyway, I will shut my mouth now."

They laughed together before they hung up.

It was difficult to scale down the guest list because of Artie's numerous acquaintances. Finally, the couple narrowed down the invitees to the 50 closest family members and friends. Artie knew or worked with most of the guests. Tina's guest list only included Helene, Stevie, her parents, Rick, and Sydney, who was her maid of honor, her boss and two coworkers.

★   ★   ★

Soon, the couple had dinner again with Maria and Luisa, who both gave Tina the cold shoulder. Afterward, Tina said, "Cielito, I think your family is mad at me."

Artie hesitated for a moment. "I told them I was converting."

Tina ran her hands nervously through her hair. "They're blaming me. I didn't force you."

Artie turned to her. "Don't worry about it. Ask Mom to teach you Argentine cooking." He thought a second. "Luisa would probably like it, if you ask more about her poetry. Now," he pulled her towards him as his eyelids dropped, his nostrils flared and his lips parted. "There are more important things like fucking." Tina laughed and pulled him by the hand into their bedroom.

★   ★   ★

Cool at first, Maria gradually warmed up enough to Tina to speak about the Argentine war. A good historian, Maria confirmed what Tina had heard about the torture, murders and disappearances of innocent citizens. Nobody was considered immune.

"Juan Peron was our president twice. At first, he was leftist. His wife Eva advocated for the working people. That was good, but she was evil and self-centered, an ex-prostitute just out to promote herself."

"I read about Eva in my high school history class," said Tina. "We didn't learn much about her, but our teacher told us she was an Argentine icon. My mother has the same name."

Maria frowned and shrugged her shoulders. "She died young, and in a few years, Peron was kicked out of office and exiled. He returned in the early 1970s, but this time he was much more right-wing. When he died, his second wife Isabel became president and things got worse. Her evil prime minister Lopez Rega controlled Isabel and ran the government. The military government took over and cracked down on political left-wing supporters. The peso fell, innocent civilians were persecuted and disappeared. The whole country was torn upside down in the Guerra Sucia. My husband Agustin was a reporter, who was not afraid to criticize the government. He disappeared one day, a *desaparecido*."

"Artie told me. I'm sorry."

Maria also told Tina about the family's comfortable life before they fled the government almost penniless. In turn, Tina shared that her parents survived the concentration camps. This connection strengthened the bond between them to some extent.

★　★　★

One evening two weeks before the wedding, Artie sat at Tina's kitchen table and scored some music for a show. He was deeply absorbed in his work as he sipped his mate. Artie always drank mate, so Tina kept supplies at her apartment.

Clad in her robe, she pushed a chair next to Artie to watch him work. Suddenly, a loud noise outside made her jump up. Her elbow accidentally hit Artie's cup and knocked it over. Liquid spilled all over his score. Tina grabbed a rag and wiped up the mess. "I'm so sorry," she said. "Clumsy me."

Artie blew up. "You're dumb and careless," he yelled at her. "Stupid! I can't believe you did this. Do you know how fucking hard I worked on this score?"

"I-I-It will d-d-dry." Her eyes filled with tears. "I'm sorry. I'm so sorry."

He stood up and glared at her. "Thanks to you now, I have to recopy this whole fucking page. Damn it!" He got up, stormed into the living room and sat down on the couch with his arms folded over his chest. His anger hit Tina hard and hurt her as much as if he plunged a sword through her body.

Tina anxiously wrung her hands. Her body shook. Anxiety swept over her. She ran into the living room to appease Artie. She apologized again, as he gazed at her reproachfully. Tina wrung her hands repeatedly, chastised herself for getting him so upset and decided she needed to make him happy. Sex was always the best choice.

She slipped out of her robe and threw her arms around him. However, Artie pushed her away. Rejected, Tina went to the bedroom in tears. Two hours later, he joined her. This time, he pulled her close to him. "I was angry," he said softly. "Don't be so clumsy, mi vida." He kissed her gently, and Tina responded. Sex that night was tender and insistent.

Artie snored loudly in his sleep, while Tina lay wide awake. His angry outburst still devastated her, especially since he had called her names. Tina rationalized that he was stressed about his project and the upcoming wedding, so she excused his behavior.

★   ★   ★

APRIL 1988

A chuppah covered with white flowers stood on the lawn surrounded by the Pacific. A white runner lay in the center aisle between rows of guest chairs covered with pink roses. To Tina, this was the happiest day of her life. Eva and Irving had paid for the wedding to give Tina her dream, which softened her heart toward her mother. Mutton sleeves accented Tina's beautiful white Victorian-style satin and lace dress. A doubled ruffled veil with a floral headband graced her delicately curled hair, and her soft makeup accented her features. She looked exquisite as she carried a large bouquet of calla lilies. Sydney wore a lovely rose lace dress with flowers in her hair. Her bouquet was a smaller version of the bridal flowers.

Artie wore his tuxedo, and Rick was his best man.

The rabbi who converted Artie married the couple. True to Jewish tradition, both Eva and Irving gave Tina away. In the short but beautiful ceremony, the bride and groom faced each other as they pledged their love and exchanged rings. They kissed after the rabbi pronounced them husband and wife. Artie stomped on the cloth-covered lightbulb which symbolized the glass, and everyone shouted Mazel Tov and congratulated Mr. and Mrs. Diaz. Maria, now 'Mama' to Tina, hugged and kissed her son and new daughter-in-law. Luisa stiffly hugged Tina and gave her an awkward peck on the cheek.

The simple, elegant reception featured hors d'oeuvres and a buffet, along with wine, champagne, and wedding cake. The couple spent the night at the inn. Tina's expensive sheer red negligée from a Rodeo Drive shop stayed on for about three minutes. After her new husband fell asleep, Tina glanced at the crumpled garment on the floor and thought to herself that it had been a waste of money. The next morning, the couple drove to Napa Valley and honeymooned in a romantic resort there for five days.

Artie moved into Tina's apartment when they returned home, but their cramped quarters made them realize they definitely needed more room. Thankfully, the larger first floor apartment became vacant a month later, so they moved downstairs. There was enough room for Artie's Steinway and the cats.

People commented how Tina and Artie seemed like the ideal couple, completely in love and both casual with a sense of humor. Unlike her husband, Tina focused on common sense and practicality. Yet, distress signs emerged behind the scenes. Artie's obsessiveness about Tina drove him to demand her complete attention when he was home. After work, it was difficult for her to drop everything to give him attention or the constant sex he wanted. Artie's schedule was irregular, so it was difficult for him to comprehend her 9-5 workday.

Once a week, they dined with Artie's family. In spite of Tina's improved relationship with Maria and Luisa, they both still seemed uncomfortable with the marriage. Luisa rarely interacted with her sister-in-law, while Maria frequently criticized Tina's clothes, cooking, or housework; Artie did not intervene. Tina realized how much Maria influenced her son. Despite the problems, Tina was always pleasant and polite to her new family and remained non-confrontational; she just wanted a good relationship with them.

★ ★ ★

Meanwhile, Tina began to realize she did not know her new spouse as well as she thought. Artie loved to indulge himself with food and sometimes with alcohol. He also loved to gamble when he had the chance. When he wanted something, it mattered little whether they had available funds. He pressured Tina to let him handle the family finances, but she learned quickly she needed to manage the family money and stood firm, until Artie resentfully and reluctantly agreed to contribute a set amount for expenses. He grudgingly handed her money on a regular basis but blamed her for not contributing what he considered to be her "fair share," almost her entire paycheck. Tina already realized her husband never discussed serious issues. If confronted with a problem, he would circumvent the conversation topic, tell jokes, or even disappear for an hour or two. She also noticed that he was not always cheery and charming to everyone. In fact, Artie was at times incredibly arrogant, rude and condescending to people who provided no advantage for him.

At the same time, Artie's name surfaced more frequently in the musical world. He was especially known for Oscar and Broadway work and as a featured accompanist for many classical singers and pop stars; yet, he often complained about lack of appreciation and acknowledgement. Although he steadily made a reputation for himself and was always busy with work, he continued to doubt himself. Surrounded by glamorous celebrities, pop singers, and movie moguls who dripped with money, it was easy to feel out of place.

Artie desired acceptance into glittery social circles but remained an outcast. Tina cared nothing about status.

The new bride also learned soon enough that Artie was not the easygoing person he appeared. On the one hand, he was an extrovert known for his puns and humorous behavior, but his rage in private surfaced whenever he drank too much, became stressed or frustrated, often without much provocation. He would shout, curse, and slam his fist on the table. Sometimes in his anger, he smashed a plate or cup to pieces against the wall. He directed his rage often at his wife, sometimes at others. Tina silently cleaned up after him and said nothing.

Artie often criticized Tina. He told her he did not find her clothes sexy enough, and that she spent too much household money. He said Tina's cooking was too bland or too spicy. Sometimes he criticized the way she cleaned the apartment, but he said he was too busy with his music to help out. He always found fault with her. His behavior distressed Tina, but she looked the other way. Tina attributed his behavior to "idiosyncrasies." He often confused and upset her, but she thought that was due to his gifted artistic personality. She believed artists and musicians were more or less eccentric and moody by nature and blamed herself when he got upset. Besides, she wanted to protect Artie since he had such a troubled life in the past, so he could heal his old wounds. After all, he was such a nice guy, everybody said so, and he told her repeatedly how much he loved her. Yet it hurt; a knife tore through her with every argument, but she told herself that her response was an overreaction. Tina also told herself to block out negative thoughts. She focused instead on her love for her husband and her pride at his musical accomplishments. She thought to herself how fortunate she was to be married to such a talented and popular man.

In spite of their arguments, they experienced a wild sexual attraction for each other and usually ended up in bed together. Sex was quick; they exploded and melted in each other's arms as they became one entity. Sex calmed Artie down and relieved his stress. It put him in a better mood afterward. After Tina was satisfied, she always pushed all unpleasant situations from her mind and forgave him for whatever he said or did.

One day, Artie got a call from *Light Up LA* magazine for a feature article. The young female reporter and the photographer interviewed the couple at home and took photos, while Artie provided a few old photographs of his own.

The August issue featured a photograph of Artie in performance on the front cover. Black-and-white photos of Artie as a chubby baby, and as a suited heavyset smiling teenager posing next to Argentine pianist Martha Argerich surrounded the article. A large color photograph of Tina and Artie topped the headline which shouted, "LA's Big Bear of Broadway Continues to Make a Name for Himself." The reporter praised Artie's career, his talent and superb technique and said Artie was a performer not to be ignored. The story mentioned Artie's 'legendary' sense of humor and also spoke about Artie's new marriage and his lovely, charming bride and snidely remarked how Big Artie got lucky to get such a beautiful 'catch' for a wife. The article also mentioned the couple's Napa honeymoon and how well they had settled into their cozy little nest.

Tina reread the article several times. They were depicted as happy newlyweds. Was this the true reality or depiction of reality? Finally, she decided that she and Artie were as happy as depicted in the article, and she pushed any pessimism aside about the relationship.

★   ★   ★

AUGUST 1988

Tina had lived in California already for a year. Her life had changed 180 degrees, but she still paid her Florida storage locker fees and needed to return to get her stuff.

Artie's schedule was relatively free in August, so they decided to fly that month to West Palm Beach, rent a car, and stay with Eva and Irving in Boynton Beach for a week. Then, they planned to rent a small truck, drive to Orlando to clean out Tina's storage unit, and visit Disney World before they drove back to California. It seemed like a good plan in spite of the predictable Florida late August heat.

One day shortly before their trip, Artie told Tina that Luisa wanted to come along. Tina was not happy, as she found Luisa morose and difficult, but after Artie convinced his wife that Luisa would help with the move, Tina consented after she checked with Eva. Neither Artie nor Luisa had ever visited Florida before.

A few days after their arrival, Eva argued with her daughter about whether she had folded the newspaper correctly after she read it, so Tina and Artie left and drove to Miami and Key West for the weekend. Luisa, however, declined and said she wanted to stay at the condo; she sunbathed daily at the complex pool. When Tina and Artie returned to Boynton Beach however, Eva met them at the door. "Isn't your sister with you?"

Artie shook his head. Eva looked puzzled. "She left early yesterday and took her suitcase. We were still asleep."

"Che," said Artie, startled. "She must have returned home. Why didn't she wait for us?"

"Are you sure?" said Tina. She glanced around and noticed an envelope addressed to Artie on the table.

Artie told Tina to open it. She handed the handwritten Spanish note to her husband.

Artie read aloud as he translated.

My dearest little brother and Mama,

Forgive me for my hasty departure. I met Luis at the pool, and we fell in love. He just got a new job in Miami, and we're moving there together. I quit my job and will send for my things. All my love to Mama and you, my dear Arturito, and I will be in touch very soon.

Your sister Luisa

Speechless, the couple looked at each other. Irving overheard the letter. "Luis is our maintenance man here."

Artie sat down and rested his face in his hands. "How could my sister do this to us?" he said bitterly. "This could kill Mama."

Tina sat next to him and put her arm around his shoulders. "I'm sorry, Cielito. I just hope she'll be happy." Artie said nothing and reached over to pick up the phone, but after a moment, he hung up the receiver.

"I don't want to upset Mama. Maybe Luisa will contact her before we get back. Otherwise, I'll tell Mama myself when we return."

They picked up the truck and left for Orlando early the next morning. Artie drove in silence. He appeared distraught over his sister's departure, and it upset Tina to see her husband suffer over the situation, but she still worried about their own marriage. Another angry outburst had occurred on the way to Key West, because Artie thought Tina had lost his keys and started a fight. Now on the four-hour trip to Orlando, she debated whether she should leave him. Although she loved him, she could not tolerate his moods much longer. His insensitivity to her needs and lack of emotion also frustrated her.

Neither of them was in the mood for theme parks, and both wanted to return home as soon as possible; Maria would not handle the news well about her daughter.

When they arrived in Orlando, they drove to the storage unit and loaded up the truck. Artie cheered up and made puns. He pushed packing cartons around with his feet and announced he was boxing. Tina laughed and softened toward him once more. They stayed in a motel that night and the next morning drove up Interstate 75 to Route 10. During their four-day trip back to LA, they drove fast with few stops, but when they passed through El Paso, they made a side trip to Juarez, Mexico, where the couple enjoyed a Mexican lunch and drove around the old town.

Nauseated, Tina woke early the next day. She sat up in bed, holding her stomach. Artie stirred, opened his eyes and watched her. She turned to him. "I'm feeling sick. There had to be something wrong with those burritos yesterday."

"I feel fine," he said as he sat up. "I had tacos, and they were okay, I guess."

Tina did not answer, jumped up, covered her mouth and ran to the bathroom where she vomited. She returned and sat down on the bed. "Whew. Now, I feel better."

However, she was sick again the next day. Artie thought she might have the flu, but although Tina said nothing, she realized her period was late. She slowly realized she might be pregnant. If so, a separation or divorce was out of the question for her; she did not want to raise a child by herself.

Exhausted, Tina dozed off frequently when Artie drove. Her breasts hurt. She could barely eat, because she either vomited or food tasted strange.

"You'll have to see a doctor when we get home," Artie told her, while she said nothing about her suspicions.

The morning after their return, they visited Maria. Tina sat on the sofa nervously wringing her hands.

Maria greeted them after their trip. "Where is Luisa?"

"Mama, sit down." Artie avoided eye contact with his mother. He pulled out Luisa's letter. "Luisa ran away with a man and left this note."

Maria took the letter from him with trembling hands. Her shriek echoed throughout the house.

"No. How could she. No. This is not possible." Maria cried out in a loud voice. Tina ran to the bedroom and returned with a box of tissues. "How could she do this? How could she leave just like that?" Artie comforted his mother, while Tina sat down next to her and stroked her hand.

A few minutes later, Maria raised her head, her face blotched from her tears but with angry eyes. She took a tissue, wiped her face and turned to Artie.

"My daughter is dead to me," she said slowly. "Muerta." She did not take her eyes away from her son. "I only have one child now."

Her remark stung Tina, as it implied Maria did not see her as part of the family. Tina stayed silent.

Tina still said nothing until her doctor confirmed her pregnancy. When Artie returned home from rehearsal that evening, Tina hugged him and told him the news. He stiffened, his face without expression, but then broke into laughter.

"If it's a boy, it's a *nene*. If a girl, it's a *nena*. Spanish pet names," He added.

Tina said nothing but pressed her head against his chest.

Everyone congratulated the couple. For the first time since Luisa's departure, Joy crossed across Maria's face. "I will be an *abuelita*, a grandmother."

Tina's excitement soon overpowered her initial anxiety, while Artie's obvious ambivalence overshadowed his verbal pride. He never accompanied Tina when she visited children's clothing stores, doctor's appointments or shopped for baby furniture.

★   ★   ★

MARCH 1989

One chilly evening in late March, Tina went into labor. Her contractions grew more intense until her entire insides radiated pain; even a spinal block did not significantly ease her discomfort. Hours later, in the delivery room, the nurses and doctor directed her to push. Artie brought his camera to photograph the baby, but could not watch the actual birth. He closed his eyes and pressed his face against Tina's cheek. Covered with sweat and exhausted after 22 hours of labor, Tina cried out once and after she pushed the baby out, Artie cut the umbilical cord.

Wet with fluid and a shock of black hair plastered on his head, Adam Michael Diaz cried loudly at birth and was deemed healthy and alert. Artie disapproved of his son's eminent circumcision, but let the matter drop, and the family celebrated Adam's bris when he was eight days old with a few guests and a small catered bagel breakfast.

Maria asked Tina whether she and Artie were planning to baptize Adam. When Tina responded that babies are not baptized in the Jewish faith. Maria's mouth twisted in disdain, and she turned toward Artie, who said nothing.

★　★　★

SEPTEMBER 1989

When Tina returned to work in September, she had lunch with Sydney.

"Are you okay?" Sydney noticed Tina's pale and worried face.

Tina forced a smile. "I'm fine but worn out. I miss my baby. Maria now takes care of him during the day."

"That saves you some money. So, are you guys then getting along better?"

Tina shrugged her shoulders. "Not really. She always tries to get her own way, and I can't stand it."

"Have you talked to her about that?"

"I haven't, because I'm scared she'll get mad and stop babysitting."

"Did you ask Artie to talk to her?"

"Not yet. He's so busy with work."

"Does he help you with the baby?" "He doesn't do anything. No feeding or changing diapers. Always too busy."

"You're still breastfeeding the baby, right?" "I'm bottle-feeding him now. I've run out of milk."

"What? You told me a couple of months ago, you had too much."

Tina swallowed, and her face reddened. She did not respond and continued to eat her food.

Puzzled, Sydney was taken aback at Tina's obvious embarrassment.

"How's Artie? I saw him two weeks ago. He looks like he gained weight."

Now, Tina's face turned bright red. She put down her fork and napkin and motioned for her bill. "I got to go. I have to get back to work."

It took a moment before Sydney realized the connection. She had always found Artie weird, but "what kind of wierdo drinks his kid's breast milk?" She said to herself." Not just a wierdo, but a fucking wierdo."

★   ★   ★

Tina returned home to find her living room rearranged. Maria stood in the kitchen, rocking the baby in her arms and cooing to him. She ignored her daughter-in law.

"What happened here?" Tina's jaw dropped as she walked around the room. Maria did not answer and continued to tend to Adam. Angrily, Tina strode into the master bedroom and opened one drawer after another to find them rearranged. Maria had even neatly placed the spermicide next to Tina's hairbrush and book on the nightstand.

Rage spewed over. Tina ran into the kitchen. Maria looked up.

"Why did you rearrange everything?"

"I want to help."

"But it's our home," said Tina. "You should have asked us first."

Maria set Adam down in his crib and when she returned, she put on her jacket, picked up her handbag and said, "I baptized him too under the kitchen faucet, so he'll go to heaven." Before Tina could respond, Maria opened the front door and left without another word.

Tina wrung her hands. Tears of anger spilt from her face. She began to page Artie, but stopped. He was teaching in Chicago and would surely be annoyed that she did not wait until he returned home.

Tina had to speak to somebody. She called Helene.

"Hi, Tina. What a nice surprise. How is everybody?"

"I don't know where to begin," said Tina.

"Well, maidele, why don't you start with 'Hello, Helene'?"

"I'm sorry…" Tina's voice trailed off as she began to cry.

"Maidele, what's wrong? Is your husband acting like a schmuck?"

"It's Maria."

"So, what happened?"

"I came home," said Tina between sobs. "She had rearranged everything and baptized Adam under the kitchen faucet without our permission."

"Oy," said Helene. "You have a problem there. She overstepped her boundaries."

"What should I do?"

"It's your fault in a way," chided Helene. "You must demand respect. Remember I told you once 'nose in the air'? That means you must command respect, not walk around with sloped shoulders and your head down. Didn't I tell you if people don't respect you, you're not going anywhere?"

"How's that important now?" Tina sounded obviously upset. "This is her fault, not mine."

"What I'm saying is that people are less likely to go over your head if they respect you. Your mother-in-law is a difficult person, and she has to learn to respect you. Speak up."

"I'm so pissed off at her. She rearranged drawers and actually moved furniture around. We told her we were raising Adam Jewish and didn't want him baptized. Then she tells me she baptized him under the kitchen faucet. I can't get over this."

"That's bad," said Helene after a pause. "Avoid her."

"I can't. She watches Adam and saves us a lot of money. I don't know what else to do. It'll be tight for us financially if we have to pay someone."

"You do whatever is necessary. In the meantime, your husband needs to talk to his mother, tell her that this was wrong and to stop being a meddlesome *yenta*."

"Artie doesn't stand up to his mother well," sighed Tina. "He avoids arguments with her. She controls him."

"Talk to him right away. He needs to make a concerted effort to support you. He is a married man now."

They sent kisses to each other before they hung up.

Tina hated to confront Artie about anything, because she dreaded his outbursts. Although things were calm at home right at the moment, she never knew what would set Artie off on a tirade.

He returned home late the following evening due to a flight delay, set down his briefcase on the kitchen table and walked to the living room, where he lay back on the recliner and closed his eyes. Then, he sat up and looked around. "Why is the living room different?"

Tina tried to stay calm. "Cielito, I must talk to you."

"Can't it wait? I'm tired."

"Your mother rearranged everything. She even baptized Adam herself."

His eyes widened as he sighed. "Do we have to discuss that now?"

"I'm so upset about this," she continued. "She went over our heads. She rearranged our drawers. She is meddling with everything."

Artie shrugged his shoulders. "The living room looks fine. I'm sure the drawers look okay too. Who cares if Mama baptized Adam or not? He's a baby. It made Mama happy. Let's forget it."

"She needs to stop interfering," Tina said loudly. "She's a busybody, a yenta. I don't know what to do now. We need her help with the baby, but I don't trust her anymore." Tina's voice trailed off.

"Just forget it, mi vida. It's not important. It's just how Mama is. I will speak to her. Don't mention it again." He got up, sat down at the kitchen table and perused a musical score he retrieved from his briefcase. The conversation was over.

★   ★   ★

DECEMBER 1989

One Sunday night, Artie arrived home from Chicago. Sulking in anger, he walked into the kitchen and slammed down his briefcase.

"What's wrong?" asked Tina. She reached out to hug him, but he ignored her as he walked to the cabinet, pulled out a bottle of cognac and poured himself a drink.

"I'm done with that place," said Artie. "The department head criticized me, and you know what? I told him to go to hell and quit right then and there."

"I'm sorry," said Tina. "It's just we need extra money now that we have the baby."

Artie paused to kiss her. "Don't worry. I have a lot of jobs coming up. Besides," he kissed her again, "I don't have to fly to Chicago anymore."

★   ★   ★

A few days later, Sydney stopped by to visit the couple and brought small Hanukkah gifts. Tina invited her into the living room and brought out some cheese, crackers, and wine. Artie lay back in the recliner; the women sat on the couch.

"Hey Artie, I haven't seen you in ages. Are you sure you still live here?" joked Sydney.

He laughed. "I'm home until after the holidays. Just local gigs after that."

"Where?"

"Oh, everywhere. I've got a concert at the Hollywood Bowl. I'm the ballet rehearsal pianist for the West Coast Ballet's *Nutcracker* production. There's a new production of *Grease* and I'm the pianist for a dinner party for –." He named one of the most famous stars in Hollywood.

Sydney laughed. "You're busy, all right, as a musician and new dad to boot. You were also in the movies once, right?"

"The movie *Lansky* was a big hit and got three Oscar nominations. I played a shopkeeper."

"That movie was about Meyer Lansky and Bugsy Siegel, two gangsters. You ran the kosher grocery store."

"That's right. The casting director discovered me walking down the street on my way to rehearsal. She said I was the perfect type for the part."

"Tell me about the movie, Cielito," said Tina.

"It begins in 1911 in New York's Lower East Side. My first scene is where I go to synagogue in a big fur hat, but my big scene is as the clerk in a grocery store. Meyer and Bugsy who are kids, come into the store and try to steal from me. I yell at them and kick them out. After that, I stock some shelves and tell shoppers and my coworker 'Good Shabbos, 'as I prepare to close up the shop to go to synagogue. The goons come in, shoot up the store and kill everyone, including me, because the store's owner had a rival gang."

"Have you seen it yet?" Sydney turned to Tina who shook her head.

"I missed it at the movies, and I didn't have a VCR until we got married."

"Let's watch it now." Artie walked over to the top-loader VCR and inserted the tape.

Sydney got up. "I have to run, sorry." He did not answer. Tina thought he seemed offended by Sydney's departure.

Shortly after the movie began, Tina heard Adam cry. She got up and told Artie to pause the VCR while she took care of the baby.

When she returned after a few minutes, Artie appeared annoyed. "Just once, I would love your damn undivided attention."

"He needed a diaper change. Just play the movie," she said wearily.

In his first brief scene, Artie appeared dressed in a black suit, coat, and a large fur streimel. In the grocery store scene, he looked like a Hasidic shopkeeper with a white shirt, a yarmulke and an apron, but his body language was stiff and awkward. He seemed out of place. Tina thought to herself that Sydney had correctly assessed his acting ability.

After the movie was over, Artie looked disappointed. "Do you know that no critic ever mentioned me in their reviews? I never got any recognition."

"That probably happens to a lot of actors in bit parts," said Tina.

Adam's wail again floated into the living room. Tina excused herself and got up, warmed his bottle and fed him in the bedroom armchair.

Artie scowled and returned to the VHS player to rewind the tape.

★   ★   ★

MARDI GRAS 1990

The couple had never been part of the Hollywood crowd, although Artie had unsuccessfully attempted several times to become part of the inner sanctum; therefore, it surprised them both when they received an invitation to a producer's exclusive Mardi Gras-themed costume party in Hollywood Hills. Together, the couple created a unique costume on a budget. Artie dressed in overalls and held a trowel. Tina painted a large poster board to look like a brick wall. It hung around her neck. A sign over the board said, "Just Laid."

They drove up to the elegant mansion and left their car with the valet. Loud Cajun music greeted them from a live band. The hostess immediately welcomed them and gushed over their costumes before she disappeared.

Elaborate food and liquor floated throughout. Most of the guests arrived dressed in Mardi Gras colors, purple, green, and gold. Tina and Artie received several compliments, but nobody stayed to chat with them.

When they entered the main room decorated in the same colors, Tina immediately recognized some famous actors chatting together. Men in business suits stood in a corner, and Artie pointed out two studio executives to Tina. Several producers and directors gathered together near the front of the room along with some guests dressed in colorful bold costumes. A woman stopped and introduced herself to Tina and Artie as a studio makeup artist. Several young starlets clad in the festive colors, obviously hoping to get noticed, mingled near the studio filmmakers. Liquor took over as the evening wore on; a few young women bared their breasts at the promise of Mardi Gras beads. Voices became louder and guests became rowdier. Tina and Artie stood in the middle of the floor most of the time, while Artie spoke loudly and made jokes so people would notice him.

He took Tina's hand, and they walked out into the garden. A heavy floral odor floated through the air punctuated by voices and the smell of weed. Two guests sat on a bench and snorted white powder. Three other guests laughed and joked as they passed joints around. Artie greeted the group, took a joint and inhaled deeply. Then he took a pinch of cocaine, which he snorted up his nose.

Stunned, Tina had suspected Artie smoked pot, but never suspected he used cocaine.

He rolled up a pot joint and offered it to Tina who hesitated, then put the joint between her lips. She inhaled deeply. It burned her throat, and she began to cough violently. Finally, she threw the joint to the ground and stomped it out with her foot.

"Yuk," she said. "Now, I need a drink of water."

Artie snorted more cocaine, turned to Tina and laughed. "You just don't appreciate the good stuff. You're the only person I've ever seen who had a bad reaction to pot. Now, try some coke."

Tina shook her head. "I can't."

The others chuckled to themselves.

"Hey, Tina, lighten up."

"Yeah. Coke gives you great sex."

"Artie, you better teach your wife right."

He reached out, grabbed Tina and passionately kissed her, but she pushed him away and walked briskly back towards the house.

"I'm leaving now," she said emphatically. Artie hesitated and then quietly followed her.

Shocked beyond belief, Tina stayed silent on the way home. There were so many things she did not know about her husband, and she wondered what else he was hiding from her.

★   ★   ★

FEB 1991

There was no word or sign from Luisa, and Maria took it especially hard in spite of her words of rejection. Every year on Luisa's birthday, on the day of her disappearance, and on her saint's day, Maria lit a candle before her statue of Mary which stood on her dresser. She said the rosary for her lost child and wept. Artie told Tina how much he missed his sister, so together they searched for her without telling Maria. They researched phone books and newspapers at the library but found nothing except Luisa's 1988 Dade County record of marriage to Luis Gonzalez. Finally, they gave up and assumed Luisa had probably died.

★   ★   ★

MARCH 1991

A few days before, Artie had returned home briefly after two weeks away at a San Francisco seminar and packed for an upcoming six-month Broadway tour. Exhausted, he slept most of the time and displayed little interest in his family. His upcoming extended absence distressed Tina, but six months was the minimum contract; it paid well, and they needed the money.

★   ★   ★

Now alone again, she lay naked in bed with her pillow over her head. Her head ached and eyes burned from her deep intense sobs, while her back hurt, and her bruised ankle smarted as a painful reminder of her husband's behavior earlier that evening.

After her earlier shower, she dried herself off with the large blue bath towel on the rack and walked into the bedroom, shivering in her nakedness to get her robe. Artie's suitcase lay on the edge of the bed as he packed for his trip. He stopped and looked at his wife.

"Did you take my black wool slacks to the cleaners?"

"Cielito, I'm so sorry, but I forgot. You should have enough clean clothes."

"Damn it," His deep voice reverberated throughout the apartment. "I don't ask much. You're so incompetent." Tina recoiled and wrung her hands, as Artie pulled her toward him until his face was close to hers. His now red contorted face with its bared teeth and angry eyes shocked her. Tina defensively raised her hand as she feared he was going to hit her. Instead, he roughly pushed her face-down on the bed.

"Cielito, I'm sorry." She tried to get up to calm him down.

Instead, he pushed himself on top of her back with such force that Tina could barely breathe. His weight crushed her, and she could not move. She struggled, and her ankle banged against the bedframe. With her head down and voice muffled by the mattress, she begged him to release her. Instead, he tightened his grip and forced her to assume a doggie-style position before he unzipped and pulled down his pants. He thrust himself into her with brute force as he grabbed her breasts, and Tina cried out in pain. Although the act seemed like an eternity, it only lasted a few minutes; he groaned, and it was over. Afterward, he released her and pulled up his pants. He ran his hands through his hair, walked into the bathroom to wipe his sweaty face and then returned to his suitcase and continued to pack as before, while Tina lay prostate on the bed and sobbed. Artie ignored her.

After he finished packing, he walked over to the bed and looked at her with contempt. "Oh, quit crying," he said. "We just fooled around, that's all. Can't you take a joke? You should have enjoyed it."

Tina looked up, her face wet with tears. "How could I enjoy rape?"

"We're married. There is no rape. Lighten up, mi vida. You're too damn uptight."

She did not answer. He bent over and tried to kiss her, but she turned away and covered her head with her pillow. He slammed the door as he left.

After a few minutes, Tina heard Adam's voice in the other room. Earlier, she had put her son to bed. She threw on her robe and went to check on him. Now wide awake, Adam stood in his crib holding on to the railing. When he saw Tina, he pointed to his bookcase.

"Mommy. Read book."

"Adam, please go back to sleep."

"No. Read book." Stubborn, he could be a handful.

"Okay." Tina pulled *Goodnight Moon* from the bookshelf. She picked up her son, and they sat together on the couch as Tina read to him. *Goodnight Moon* was Adam's favorite book, and he loved to look and point at the pictures. He wanted Tina to read the book to him all the time.

Adam lifted her spirits. Maybe Artie was right, and she had overreacted. Maybe rough sex was normal between couples; still, numbness and shock surrounded her very being. Her mind drew a blank like a chalkboard wiped clean of any comments or thoughts.

Artie called her the next day, and his upbeat happy voice announced he had arrived safely in New York. Tina listened aimlessly as Artie described his hotel room. He sounded elated when he described his dinner at Mama Leone's and added his rehearsals would begin tomorrow.

"I have to go," said Tina. "Adam needs me. Bye." She hung up the phone. His assault flashed again before her. She swallowed hard and closed her eyes, as she found it hard to believe Artie's conversation was without mention or remorse.

Tina thought perhaps she was to blame after all, since she forgot to get his pants cleaned. No wonder he overreacted, she thought, and now, she felt guilty, so she blocked out the incident, and the details disappeared into her subconscious. Yet an uneasy intuitive feeling nagged her and danced in her thoughts. She and Artie had not had sex in months prior to the incident, but her gut instinct made her wonder whether she was pregnant again.

After she missed two missed periods, Tina reluctantly bought a home pregnancy test which confirmed positive results. Stunned with shock, Tina's hands shook and sweat crept over her forehead. Her intrusive flashbacks increased as the memory of the incident infiltrated her brain again. She felt once more his rough hands on her breasts, the pain and his body gyrating against her back.

She dreaded telling Artie the news. Even the thought turned her stomach into knots and made her short of breath. Her deep instinctive sense told her he would not welcome another child and might never come home. Panic and pain set in, as she did not know what she would do if he left her, so she decided to wait until he returned home to tell him about the baby, and even then, her chest filled with dread at the thought.

She called Sydney for advice. "Even if you don't tell him, Maria will," said Sydney. "How are you going to deal with that?"

Tina sighed. "You're right. Although I haven't told her yet, I can't hide it from Mama forever." She paused. "I just got an idea. Let me see how she'll react."

"Good Luck," said Sydney.

Maria arrived the next morning as usual to watch Adam before Tina left for work.

"I have some news," said Tina as she embraced her mother-in-law.

"News? What kind of news?" Maria looked at Tina a bit suspiciously.

"You must promise not to tell Arturito. It's a surprise."

"Che. Of course, I won't say anything if you don't want me to do so."

"Okay." Tina swallowed hard. "I'm pregnant, but I want Artie to be surprised when he comes home. Please don't say anything." Maria's face lit up. "Another baby. How wonderful. *Felicidades*. I'm so happy." She stopped when she saw Tina's anxious gaze. "It's our secret, okay? Please. I don't want to upset Artie if there are problems and want everything okay when he gets home so I can tell him."

"Tina, I told you I would say *nada*. You must trust me for once."

Tina nodded and hugged Maria. "Thank you, Mama," she said. "I trust you."

★　★　★

OCTOBER 1991

When Artie finally returned home, Tina swallowed hard and greeted him holding Adam, who shouted "Daddy" and held out his arms to his father. Artie scooped up his son and embraced him tightly, but as soon as he caught sight of Tina's belly, his eyes widened, and his mouth dropped open. Shocked, Artie stepped back and set Adam down without taking his eyes off her.

"Why didn't you tell me?" he said slowly.

Tina did not answer. She cringed at the thought he was going to lose his temper, but instead, Artie turned around and slowly walked into the second bedroom, which Tina had decorated with pink butterflies. Still in a daze, he returned and stared at his wife.

"It's a girl?"

"My ultrasound said so. No penis sighting."

She noticed the disappointment in her husband's face, but in a split second, his expression turned to anger. "Why didn't you tell me?" He screamed into Tina's ear. She backed off, covered hers and shook when she saw Artie's angry blotched face. He raised his arm as if to hit her, but then dropped it.

"I-I was afraid you would cut your tour short," she said. "We need the money." She trembled and pressed her back against the wall ready to shield herself. However, he backed off and said nothing but shot her a contemptuous look, before he left for the bedroom to unpack his suitcase.

When Maria arrived at the house the following day after Tina got home from work, she embraced her son and whispered to him in Spanish.

"No, I did not know. She just told me," Artie said in a loud voice. He glared at his wife.

"I'm sorry, Cielito," Tina said. "I wanted to surprise you."

Marie turned to her son. "Arturito, you should be happy. Wonderful news."

Artie walked toward Tina, and reluctantly kissed her cheek. Later, he told Tina, "No more children. Tomorrow, I'm going to call and get a vasectomy."

He did not mention the subject further, but Tina assumed he had the procedure.

A week later, he softened toward Tina. They attempted sex, but he stayed limp and stared at her large belly. With a pang, Tina realized that he had never until now drawn a line between wife and mother, object of sexual desire and fertility goddess. He lay down next to her and stroked her arm before he fell asleep.

One afternoon, they sat in the living room as Adam played at their feet. Tina pushed herself up by her arms at her side. "I have been thinking, Cielito, this apartment will be too small for our family." She was surprised that he agreed. "I have been thinking the same thing. We need a larger place." They began their search and soon found a house in Los Feliz, five minutes away from Maria's home. The four-bedroom and two-bath white stucco bungalow was large enough, but the ugly dated brown exterior hinted at the inside, where the orange shag carpet and the garish wallpaper with pink, green, and orange flowers blared 1970s. The couple found the décor atrocious and decided to use part of Artie's recent earnings to improve the eyesore. They got rid of the hideous wallpaper and awful shag rug. New paint, carpet and tile improved the house. They also remodeled the bathroom and kitchen and installed new white appliances. It delighted Tina to see the avocado fixtures and appliances disappear from their lives.

★   ★   ★

THANKSGIVING 1991

Tina toyed with hosting Thanksgiving dinner, but she had difficulties during this pregnancy stage. Whenever she stood for a period of time, her legs swelled and fatigue overwhelmed her. In addition, she had to keep a constant eye on Adam, now an active toddler. Artie refused to consider a holiday restaurant meal; therefore, they would dine at Casita Diaz again.

Thanksgiving morning, Tina lay in bed in her flowered nightgown, her hands on her abdomen. Baby Girl Diaz vigorously kicked inside her mother's womb. Sweat-covered Artie had kept her up during the night when he awoke from one of his nightmares. Tina comforted him, wiped his sweat away and rubbed his back and neck until he relaxed. Tina often wondered about his dreams which seemed to possess him with a fear Tina had not seen anywhere else. She asked him about them several times, but Artie merely shrugged his shoulders and said nothing.

★   ★   ★

Tina got up early and tiptoed into the kitchen. Everyone else was still asleep. She prepared the turkey for dinner, prepped the green beans for the casserole and made mashed sweet potatoes.

The kitchen phone rang. Tina quickly answered in a hushed voice. She did not want to wake up her husband.

"Cuzzie, cuzzie, cuzzie!" Tina immediately recognized the exuberant voice on the other end.

"Stevie!" She was so happy to hear from him, she almost shouted, but she caught herself.

"Are you hatched yet?" Stevie laughed.

"Hey, man, when I hatch, you'll be the first to know. Happy Turkey Day."

"Same to you. What are you doing today?"

"Going to see Mama."

"Are you going to have turkey over there or some kind of weird Argentine bird?"

"Of course, we're having turkey. What kind of Argentine bird?

"A birdnos aires."

"Stevie, get outta here." Tina laughed so hard, the baby, still awake, kicked her mother soundly in the abdomen. "Ouch. She's at it again. She is kicking me. She kept me up all night. What are you doing today?" She knew Steve was back together again with his old partner.

"Mark and I are going to have a quiet dinner at home." Stevie paused. "So do you have a name picked out yet?"

"Not really."

Stevie laughed. "You could name her Balabusta." Both laughed.

"There's Yente," she laughed.

"I was thinking Bubbeleh. She'll be a great housekeeper, busybody, grandmother."

"She is not even born yet," laughed Tina.

"Let's put it together," laughed Steve. "She could be Balabusta Yente Bubbeleh Diaz." He paused. "Seriously, cuzzie," he asked. "Which names do you like?"

"Not sure. We can't decide."

"Oh, I almost forgot. I have news for you."

"You do?"

"Mark got a job in San Francisco. We're moving there next month. I'm so excited. We put my condo up for sale two weeks ago and already found a buyer."

"Oh, how wonderful. You'll only be six hours away instead of sixty million."

"He got a job in finance, and I'm going to pursue work on stage there. I still want an acting career."

"Then you should move here to LA."

"Maybe one day."

"Artie knows some people. He could get you an audition."

"Honey, I wouldn't ask your husband for a favor if my life depended on it. He doesn't like me."

"I'm sure that's not true."

"I don't want to rain on your parade, but Rico, a queer Latino friend who played music with him down at the Schubert last year, told me he thinks Artie hates gay men. I haven't seen your husband roll out the welcome wagon for me."

"Who's this Rico? Freud? Come on. Artie likes everybody."

Just then, Artie entered the kitchen in his robe. Half asleep, he walked slowly toward the coffee maker.

"Stevie, gotta run," said Tina. "Happy Thanksgiving. Love ya. Say hi to Mark."

"Love you too, cuzzie. Kiss Artura for me when she says hi to the world, okay?"

Tina laughed and hung up. Her husband in the meantime fixed himself a cup of coffee.

She walked over to Artie, hugged him and kissed him on his frowning lips. "Cielito, Stevie is moving to San Francisco next month."

"Why?"

"His partner got a job in the Bay Area. I'm thrilled that he'll be closer to us."

Artie frowned, sat down at the kitchen table and sipped his coffee as Adam skipped into the kitchen. "Nene." Artie's eyes lit up as Adam responded to his nickname, ran up to him and jumped in his arms. Artie laughed and hugged him tightly, while Tina popped some bread into the toaster for breakfast. Afterward, when the roasted turkey was ready exuding a rich brown color and juiciness, they headed for Maria's house.

With their toddler in tow, Tina and Artie arrived early in the afternoon. Maria's house, now completely repaired with some government aid, exuded true charm.

Maria regarded Tina's green maternity top and faded jeans with disapproval. "I don't think your clothes suit you, and your hair is a mess." Then, she tasted some of Tina's green bean casserole. "You need more seasoning," she said and added more salt and pepper.

Tina backed away. Demeaned and demoralized, she berated herself for not being a better cook, as she smoothed down her permed hair and straightened her blouse. She turned helplessly to Artie who had just walked into the kitchen behind her, but he said nothing, which did not surprise her. Their marriage was the only instance she could recall where he had ever contradicted his mother.

Tina, with Adam by her side, helped Maria prepare and carry out her side dishes to the dining room. It was then Tina noticed Adam was no longer in the kitchen. She poked her head into the living room.

"Cielito, is Adam with you?"

Artie shook his head. "He can't be far."

"Then, where is he?" Tina's eyes widened.

She did not wait for an answer. Panic shot through her as she ran to the best of her ability through the house calling her son's name. Maria joined the search, while Artie got up and called after Adam. Tina's heart jumped with shock and fear as she saw the front door wedged open. A small tipped-over stool stood near the doorway.

"Cielito, Adam is gone. He climbed up on the stool and unlocked the door." She burst into tears.

Artie said nothing but ran outside. Tina followed him filled with dread. They walked up and down the street and called their son.

"Mommy." Tina turned to see Adam standing on the sidewalk across the street with Lucy the Chihuahua. A puzzled look crossed his face as he held on to Lucy's leash.

Tina ran up and took him in her arms. "My baby." She hugged him tightly. "Oh, my baby. What are you doing here?"

"Mommy, Lucy had to go bafroom."

Tina grabbed ahold of Lucy's leash. "We were so scared something happened to you. Never run off like this again. You always need to stay with Mommy, Daddy, or Abuelita."

"Nene, good to see ya," Artie joked as he took Adam from Tina's arms and carried him back to the house. As they entered through the front door, Artie turned around and made sure the door was properly locked. He took Adam to the living room, where they watched cartoons together on TV.

Tina breathed a sigh of relief, as she returned to the kitchen to help reheat the food. Maria frowned and stood by the counter, arms folded across her chest. Her eyebrows furrowed together in an angry expression.

"Why can't you watch your child?"

Tina looked up. "I watch him every second. I only turned my back for a few minutes."

"You know, he could have died."

Tina stopped. "Don't you think I was worried sick?"

At that point, Artie stepped into the kitchen. He had obviously heard the conversation, did not speak but looked reproachfully at Tina. Finally, he said, "Mama is right. You should have kept a better eye on him."

"How about you?" said Tina. "I can barely get around. Why didn't you watch him? You were doing nothing but sitting in the living room watching TV. Adam walked by you to get to the front door."

Artie's face turned red. Maria turned to him. "See? I told you not to marry her."

Dead silence fell like a thud. Tina just wanted to go home, but she quietly set the table, propped Adam into his booster chair and cut up his food, avoiding eye contact with the others. Nobody spoke during the meal. Afterward, Maria prepared mate in the kitchen, which she brought out with her homemade prize-winning apple cake made with filo, walnuts and honey. Tina cut herself a small piece but declined the mate, as she had never acquired a taste for the tea. Relieved when it was time to leave; she could hardly wait to return home.

Her ambivalence about Maria now turned to utter dislike, although she knew how badly they needed her help with childcare. She and her mother-in-law had always been cool but cordial to each other. Now, Tina wanted Maria to apologize for her comment, but she knew that would not happen, because Maria never saw wrong in what she did or said. Fiercely protective of her own children, Maria meant well within her own family, and others admired her for her kindness and charming personality. When Maria babysat Adam, the family always came home to a clean house with supper ready and the cats fed. It confused Tina that Maria was meddlesome and controlling, yet helpful and caring in other ways, and their strained relationship made Tina fear Maria's disappointment at their marriage would never go away.

The following Monday, Tina's legs and back hurt, but she reluctantly got ready for work. Maria arrived early as usual and greeted Tina with a smile. Adam ran up to his grandmother, and Maria scooped him up in her arms. Tina could see their tight bond and decided she would try harder to get along with her and avoid family conflict.

Two weeks later, with a much easier labor, Tina gave birth to a daughter, who bore a striking resemblance to Artie's infant photos with her large round head, small eyes, flat mouth and dark hair. Most babies are cute, Tina thought, but her husband and daughter were definitely ugly babies. There was no other way to describe them. Guilt swept over her, and she chided herself for considering her infant unattractive.

They brought Leah Mara home two days later wrapped in a pink blanket and hat. Tina sat down on the sofa with her daughter, and Adam ran toward her excitedly to see the baby.

"This is your baby sister," said Tina. "You're a big brother now."

He paused and looked intently at the new baby. "What's baby sister's name?" he asked.

"Leah," said Tina.

"Leli," said Adam.

"No, Nene, Leah." said Artie

Adam bent over and kissed his sister's cheek. Then he turned, looked at his parents and smiled. "I love baby Leli."

Both parents laughed. Tina said, "Sweet boy, say 'Le-ah.'"

"No." Adam looked down and stuck out his lower lip as his lips curled into a stubborn frown. "Baby Leli."

"That's actually a cute nickname," laughed Tina. "'Leli. I like it."

The name stuck.

When Maria saw Leli for the first time, she said she thought she was looking at Artie as an infant.

★   ★   ★

FEBRUARY 1992

With two months of maternity leave left, Tina often called others to alleviate her loneliness. Artie was rarely home, and Sydney had little time to visit.

One evening, Artie asked Tina why the phone bill was higher than usual. She responded she called to speak to her family and friends.

"Why are you calling all these people?"

"I miss them."

"The bill is too high. You don't need to call them." His voice sounded agitated.

"I only call once every two weeks. Besides, it's my money too."

"Let them call you."

"They do, and sometimes I can't make it to the phone, so I return their calls."

"And," he continued, "You call Sydney all the time. Why? What are you telling her?"

"We don't see each other often. She's too busy." Tears sprang to Tina's eyes. "We catch up." Artie's agitation bewildered her.

"Your responsibility is to me as your husband and to your children. Do you understand? You don't need anyone except us."

"Are you telling me I can't even call Helene? She's like a mother to me."

"Helene meddles. I bet you tell her everything about us. You probably even tell her about our sex life."

"Where did you get that idea? I don't talk about us."

"And furthermore," he walked up to her, stared her in the eye and pointed his index finger in her face. "You better stop flirting with other men. I know you talk to guys. Who knows if you slept with them? Maybe these aren't even my kids."

"I can't believe you said that."

"Don't bullshit me, Tina. I heard you tell your little Stevie on the phone how much you love him."

"He's my childhood friend. He's also gay. I think of him and his mom as family. Knock it off, Artie."

"You don't need him as a friend," he intoned as he continued to stare at her. His voice dropped to a whisper. "You have me."

"Artie!" Tina was totally indignant. "What's the matter with you?"

"I love you, mi vida. I can't bear hearing you say 'I love you' to any other man."

"What's the matter?" Maria popped her head through the door.

"Mama, Tina spends too much time on the phone with other people," said Artie. "It needs to stop."

Maria gave Tina a stern look. "Listen to your husband," she said.

Tina stopped calling family and friends from home and began using a payphone with rolls of quarters stashed away in her drawer for this purpose.

★　★　★

APRIL 1993

One early Saturday morning, everyone except Tina was still fast asleep. She arose early and went into her little office, opened her desk drawer, reached under a sheaf of papers and pulled out a library book about troubled marriages. She read it when Artie was not around and hid the book from him when he was home.

She opened the book turned to the last chapter she read. It was about communication. She sighed, because she had reached an impasse with her husband in this area.

Artie now tried to control every aspect of her life. He opened her mail, still closely monitored the phone bill and questioned almost every call she made. He discouraged her from spending time with her friends. If she came home late from work, he reprimanded her. He also continued to accuse her of looking at other men and having affairs at work. Whenever Tina went anywhere without him, Artie raged she neglected her responsibilities at home.

Anger brewed in Tina that the household chores and childcare lay on her and Maria, and Artie's causeless accusations put her in a bind, but she did not want conflict around the children, so she stopped almost all social activities. Tina's social life whittled down to meeting Sydney occasionally for lunch.

The phone rang. She quickly picked up the receiver and answered the call. It was Stevie. He sounded more somber than usual.

"Cuzzie," he began.

"Hi, Stevie." Tina spoke in a low tone. "How are things?" She had not heard from him in a while and guilt poked its head, because she had never visited him in San Francisco.

"You first," said Stevie.

"Same old shit. Nothing exciting," she responded. "When are you coming down to LA again? The kids love their Uncle Stevie, you know."

"I'm sorry, but I'm not feeling well."

"What's wrong?"

"I don't know. Maybe I'm just stressed and tired of this audition shit getting nowhere. I can't even find a regular job right now. Please don't say anything to Mom, or she'll worry herself sick, okay?"

"Sure," said Tina. "I wish I could come see you, but it's tough with both the kids."

"You mean your three kids including Artie. Don't worry. I understand. Love you, cuzzie."

"Same here." Tina heard the children. "I have to go. The kids are up and making noise. If they wake Artie up, it will piss him off."

"Don't piss on him no matter how much you would like to do so," Stevie joked. "I will do the honors next time I get to LA." They laughed before they hung up.

The conversation worried Tina, who hoped Stevie had nothing serious, and when she saw Artie was still asleep after she hung up, she sighed with relief.

★ ★ ★

145

MARCH 1994

The Buenos Aires Philharmonic booked their native son for a series of three concerts at the Teatro Colón. Artie accepted the offer with mixed emotions; this was his first trip back to Argentina since he left at age 19.

The trip excited Tina. She had heard so much about Argentina, that she could not wait to visit in person. However, it saddened her they would not be back in time for Adam's fifth birthday, so they promised him a special treat when they returned.

After a long flight, Tina and Artie arrived at Ezeiza International Airport. A blast of hot humid air hit Tina in the face when she stepped outside; it was now the end of summer and the heat reminded her of Florida. They took a taxi to their hotel, an elegant former historical palatial mansion. A large crystal chandelier crowned the ceiling in their elegant air-conditioned room.

In the following days, they met and spoke with many people and heard repeatedly how it was a national shame that Argentina lost the Falkland Islands in 1982. Carlos Gardel, considered the father of the tango, was often a conversational topic. Eva Perón was described as a sinner or a saint, which reminded Tina how much her mother-inlaw disliked this cultural icon. Tina also noticed wistful melancholy around many of the people they met and wondered if that was due to Argentina's bloody history.

New smells, sounds, and sights bombarded Tina's senses. The city's beautiful architecture and boulevards had a distinctive Parisian flair. The smell of fresh coffee wafted from sidewalk cafés. Grilled roast meat from open grills scented the air.

The couple visited the San Telmo district where tango bars lined the cobbled streets. Couples embracing in sensuous dance moved like shadows in the open doorways or in the street. They also visited Artie's old family home in the Palermo Viejo district. One afternoon, they ended up at the city's oldest café, the Café Tortoni. Artie remembered visits with his mother and grandmother. The café's lofty ornate interior had both fascinated and swallowed him up as a little boy.

As he and Tina now stepped inside, an elegant hostess showed them to a table. They looked around. Tango music played in the background, while male guests in suits and exquisitely dressed and coiffed stick-thin women sat at the other tables as impeccably groomed waiters served them coffee and delicate cakes. Several patrons shot looks of disdain at Artie with his bushy black hair and beard, casual jeans, and LA City Symphony T-shirt. A few women also glared at Tina's casual clothes. Two women chortled something about low-class Americans, but Artie turned and stared at them, and they realized he understood every word they said. Embarrassed, they turned away.

The waiter took their order of coffee and cake, as Artie eavesdropped on other table conversations. With his index finger to his mouth, he chuckled as he relayed how the women around them spoke about their stingy lovers or their plastic surgeries. He almost roared out loud with laughter, as he translated one woman's dramatic conversation about her husband's mistress, and she told her friend the mistress wore fancier clothing, but she as the wife gave better blow jobs. The woman made a theatrical gesture as she flicked her long red nails and said theatrically, "*Soy devastada.*" Artie whispered in his wife's ear, "She is devastated. It's the end of the world." They both broke into laughter.

One morning before rehearsal, they walked past the theaters and nightclubs on the Avenida Corrientes. They visited the artistic Boca district. From the steps of the Teatro Colon, they saw the Plaza de Mayo, home of demonstrations surrounded by despair in Argentina's chaotic political past. Nearby stood the Casa Rosada, the dark pink official building where Evita Perón gave her famous speeches.

When Artie was busy with rehearsals, Tina visited the Museum of Decorative Arts, and toured the Once district to visit the old Jewish synagogues and the Jewish museum. The city's elegance tinged with decay both dazzled and shocked her. Crumbled facades overshadowed once elegant buildings. Broken or chipped monuments and statues stood throughout the city. The train stations lay in disrepair. She saw many poor people who squatted in doorways or tried to sell cheap items, and families crammed into formerly opulent buildings, now with boarded broken windows and clotheslines on the balconies, which marked the presence of poverty. Souvenir shops everywhere displayed pictures of Evita on mugs, magnets, keychains, and T-shirts.

In spite of Artie's hectic schedule, the couple reconnected with each other. Their sex life resurfaced once more as strong as ever, aided by the sensuality which surrounded them everywhere. The steamy heat and smells permeated their senses. Tango dancers clung erotically to each other as they performed in the streets. Artie's musical passion radiated throughout his performances to rave reviews.

On their last day in Buenos Aires, their suitcase lay open on the bed. Tina folded and neatly packed their clothes. Artie had left for a while, so she handled the packing herself.

Suddenly, he ran into the room, slammed and locked the door behind him. He gasped with loud audible breaths without taking his eye off the door. Copious sweat stained the back of his shirt, his armpits and ran down his forehead. "Don't open the door. Leave it locked."

"What's wrong?"

He didn't answer but moved from the door to the window where he anxiously watched the street through the curtain.

A white packet dropped on the floor. Horrified, Tina bent down to pick it up.

"Artie, what the hell is wrong with you?"

He tried to snatch the packet away from her. "Please, bombónita. Please give it back to me. I need it."

Tina stepped back, the packet clutched in her hand. "You told me no more drugs."

"Bombónita, I need this. It enhances our sex life."

"We're not talking about sex here. You know I vehemently hate drugs of any kind. You promised me to stop."

He did not reply but turned back toward the window.

"Do you have any more of this shit on you?" Tina banged her fist on the table. "Empty your pockets out now."

He ignored her.

Tina walked over to him, threw her hand down his pants pockets and grabbed several packets and his billfold. He mildly resisted but remained too focused on his vigilance to stop her. Tina riffled through his wallet. It had been filled with pesos the previous evening; now it was empty.

Tina held up the packets. "We're going home tomorrow. If Customs finds these, what do you think will happen? Do you want both of us to go to jail?"

He did not answer and continued to watch the street through the window. Suddenly he spoke in a low-throated whisper. "He's here."

"Who's here?'

"Pablo."

"Who's Pablo?"

"You don't want to know."

"I certainly do. Who's this Pablo?"

"Quiet." Artie clasped his hand over her mouth. He pushed her on the floor under the window behind the bed and lay on top of her, his sweaty body pressed against her back filling the air with the strong scent of perspiration. His weight almost choked the air out of her lungs. Tina's heart pounded inside her chest as she heard quick heavy footsteps, which got louder as they neared their door. Her face pressed against the carpet; she heard her husband's hoarse breath as he lay his head on hers. Her body went cold with fear and terror as loud knocks pounded on their door; Tina froze. An angry man's voice shouted something in Spanish, and then to her relief, his footsteps suddenly disappeared down the hall.

Tina knew enough Argentine Spanish to understand Pablo's words, which left her cold as ice. "You owe me money, you son of a bitch. The whore that birthed you won't protect you now. If you don't have my money by tomorrow afternoon, I will blow your head off. Then I will tear you from limb to limb and feed you to the sharks, you bastard."

The couple's plane left early the next morning. Terrified, Tina lay awake all night while Artie slept peacefully beside her. They left for the airport in early morning darkness. Tina sat frozen and shook with fear, but Artie seemed nonplussed. After they checked their luggage, they sat in the furthest corner in the airport waiting area with their backs to the wall and vigilantly watched everyone around them. Tina breathed another deep sigh of relief when they finally boarded the aircraft for home.

★   ★   ★

MARCH 1995

The children loved Purim, celebrated on the 14th day of the Hebrew month of Adar. On Saturday before the holiday, Tina stopped at a nearby bakery which sold different varieties of hamantaschen. These triangle-shaped cookies symbolized the villain Haman's hat. Everyone at home loved the sweet treats and made them disappear in no time.

Adam and Leli loved to hear the story of Purim again and again. how Queen Esther, the wife of King Ahasuerus, and her cousin Mordecai outsmarted the wicked grand vizier Haman and saved the Jewish people. They looked forward to the annual Purim party at the Jewish Community Center and loved that they got to dress up as one of the characters. Adam usually wanted to be Haman, and Leli loved dressing as Queen Esther. They also made a donation to charity each year. Tina helped Leli retrieve coins from her piggy bank, and Adam contributed two dollars he saved for this event.

A food basket for friends and relatives was another holiday tradition; instead, Tina and the kids donated a box of groceries to the local food share, which fed the homeless poor of Los Angeles.

This year, Helene, arrived for a visit, first to see Stevie and then Tina and her family for the first time. The house was cramped, so Helene stayed in Adam's room while he slept on the living room sofa.

The Jewish Community Center Purim Party took place on a Sunday. Tina and Maria made Leli a new Queen Esther costume. Tina found Leli's glitzy pink blouse, two strands of purple and gold Mardi Gras beads and a small plastic tiara at a local thrift shop, while Maria sewed a long pink skirt for her granddaughter and a black robe for Adam, Tina made him a large cardboard and fabric triangular black hat and hoped Adam would be the best-dressed Haman at the party.

Pink outfits highlighted Leli's dark curls and fair skin. She still resembled her father, but had become a pretty child. Dressed as Haman the year before, Artie attended the party and clowned around, delighting the children. This year, he had a previous engagement, and Maria felt too ill with a cold to attend.

When they arrived at the festivities, abundant snacks including kreplach and hamantaschen greeted them. Hebrew Purim music played in the background. The party featured games and a costume contest. Everyone gathered in a circle and sang:

Oh, once there was a wicked, wicked man
And Haman was his name, sir.
He would have murdered all the Jews
Though they were not to blame, sir.
Oh today, we'll merry, merry be
And nosh some hamantaschen.

Leli won first prize for her costume and received chocolate and a grogger. Tina and Helene sat and watched the activities.

"Aren't all these kids here amazing?" said Tina. Helene did not respond.

Tina continued to watch the children. "What a great party the JCC put together. Don't you think so?"

Helene still did not respond. Tina turned around and, to her horror, saw Helene slumped over the table.

"Helene, Helene, wake up!" Tina shook her by her shoulders, but could not arouse her friend. Tina blanked out with anxiety and shock. Someone brought a blanket, and several people helped Tina lay Helene gently on the floor.

The ambulance arrived. In the meantime, Leli and Adam ran over to their mother. "Why is Aunt Helene on the floor? Is she sick?" Tina turned to her children and put her fingers to her lips. "Aunt Helene isn't feeling well and has to go to the hospital." Although sickened, Tina forced a smile.

The paramedics tried to revive Helene and then took her away to the hospital. The rest of the party was cancelled, and the families went home.

Tina frantically called Stevie, who immediately drove to the airport to get on the next flight to LA. Tina dropped the children at Maria's house, before she returned home to change clothes and go to the hospital. However, the phone rang as soon as she walked in the door. Steve phoned her from the airport, sobbing. He could barely speak. "Mom is dead." He wept audibly. "She suffered a massive stroke." He paused sobbing. "She was only 74. That's not so old."

"Oh no." Tina's legs felt as if they would collapse from under her. Devastated, she burst into tears.

"I-I have to make funeral arrangements and fly her home to Fort Lauderdale."

"Can I help you?"

"No, I will be fine. Then, I will sit Shiva and fly home afterward."

"I want to come to the funeral and sit Shiva with you. I can take off work and catch a plane even if I have to bring the kids."

"Like hell you will." She turned around to see her enraged husband, who had just returned home. "Where do you think you're going?" Tina noticed his bright red face and angry dark narrowed eyes, which looked like black volcanic pools ready to erupt.

"Helene died," Tina wept again and could barely speak. "I want to go to her funeral and sit Shiva."

"Over my dead body. Your place is here at home with me and your children."

"I will take them with me. They loved Helene."

He punched the living room wall, leaving cracks in the paint and turned again to Tina.

"You would pull them out of school? What a bad mother you're." He walked up to his wife and grasped her shoulders with his hands. His face was close enough to her to feel his breath. "If you dare, and I mean dare, to leave, we'll be gone. I will divorce you, and you'll never see the kids again, rest assured."

Tina slowly backed away from him and retreated to the bedroom, shattered and heartbroken. She tried but could not sleep as thoughts raced through her head. He controlled almost everything except the joint account. He had stopped bullying her to gain full control, but he rarely contributed money in time to pay the bills. He rarely cut his hair, his ill-fitting pants, which were often too long, his old t-shirts and worn sneakers did not accentuate his appearance. He only cleaned up for rehearsals, events and concerts. She could not reconcile how bafflingly different he was in public. Still known as a charming eccentric and brilliant pianist, Artie made people laugh with his piano props, hilarious hats and costumes. His antics and jokes earned him increased popularity, but behind the curtain, nobody except his family knew the real man.

When Tina awoke the next morning after a restless night, she found Artie asleep on the couch. When he heard her, he opened his eyes, stretched and got up but coldly ignored her and retired to his music room.

The following day, Tina sent her regrets to Stevie along with a fruit basket. In Helene's honor, Tina and the children donated to the Jewish National Fund to plant a tree in Israel.

★   ★   ★

AUGUST 1995

Before the summer ended and the new concert season began, the family flew to Florida for two weeks. To Tina's surprise, Eva showed the nicest behavior she had shown in years. There was no sign of alcoholism, and she and Irving seemed happy together. They welcomed the family warmly and treated them well. Capped with a gentle breeze, the intense August heat made days at the beach ideal. The Gumbo Limbo Park sea turtles delighted Adam and Leli. Miami and South Beach beckoned. After a week, the family said goodbye and drove to Orlando, where the children delighted in going to Disney World, Universal and Sea World.

Mysteriously, Artie disappeared for a few hours one evening, leaving Tina and the children at the hotel to entertain themselves, so they ate at a local Italian restaurant and walked around International Drive. The children were already in bed when Artie returned. He blew his nose repeatedly and followed Tina into the bathroom.

She tried to brush her teeth and change into her nightgown, but Artie put his arm around her while he caressed her breasts, stopping only to blow his nose. Suddenly suspicious, Tina turned around and saw some faint white dust under Artie's nostrils. She pulled away and confronted her husband.

"You swore you were not using coke anymore. What's that white dust?"

"Nothing. I swear."

"I don't believe you."

"Are you calling me a liar?"

"I just asked you a question, that's all," responded Tina.

"Damn it, Tina. You're just a bitch."

"Artie, please. Stop trying to fit in with your celebrity friends and their drug parties. Stop kissing the assholes of the rich and famous. You're hurting us."

He glared at her. "You're nothing without me. Don't forget that."

She glared back. "You know what, Artie? Sos un schmuck."

His eyes blazed with angry fire. "I'm not a schmuck. Your Argentine Spanish sucks. I'm going down to the bar," he said. "I'm done."

The door slammed behind him as he left.

★   ★   ★

DECEMBER 1995

The contrast between their lives was clear. Artie's work revolved around the famous and glamorous, while Tina held a conventional job and led an ordinary life with her family. She often sought joy in her children's antics, a good distractible in hard times.

A precocious raconteur, Adam repeated the same joke to any willing audience.

"What did one pencil say to the other pencil? You're looking sharp.'"

Every time he had a chance, he told this joke. People laughed, although they had heard it before.

One Saturday, both children received an invitation to a neighborhood child's birthday party. Tina accompanied them and chatted with the child's mother, when Adam loudly announced he wanted to tell a joke. Tina smiled to herself and assumed he would tell his pencil joke again. Adam spoke in a loud authoritative voice to command everyone's attention.

"What starts with F and ends in uck?"

Tina turned white.

"Firetruck."

Tina sighed with relief. All the kids laughed.

Leli also chimed in. "I have a joke, too." Adam turned around and sighed in disgust as he did not like his little sister to upstage him.

She ignored him as she continued, "What starts with G and ends in uck?"

Silence.

"Garbage truck," she said brightly.

Tina smiled. The children were always up to something. One day after work, Tina came home to black curls scattered on the floor and Maria asleep on the living room couch. Leli, her now-short hair in uneven clumps, sat on the floor and played with her dolls while Adam played with Legos. A pair of scissors lay on the floor nearby.

"What happened here?" Tina tried to sound stern, although she almost burst out with laughter. Maria stirred and sat up. She rubbed her eyes, and walked up to Leli aghast.

"What did you do to your sister? Turn around and look at me," said Tina firmly.

Adam put the Legos down and looked up shyly at his mother.

"Mommy, we played beauty shop," he said.

"Adam cut my hair," said Leli with a serious look in her eyes.

"Che, I took a nap. I did not see them doing this," said Maria softly. It was almost an apology.

Tina stifled a laugh and put on a serious face. "Her hair is a mess. Now, she has to go to a real beauty shop to get her hair fixed."

Adam hung his head. "I'm sorry, Mommy."

She hurried into the kitchen, where she burst out laughing to herself so hard, she cried. As she grabbed a paper towel and dabbed her eyes, she thought of Leli's thick black curly hair, now gone, but hair could be fixed. In the meantime, her children's antics gave her joy and provided a good distraction with their innocence.

★   ★   ★

FEBRUARY 1996

Tension wrought with anxiety continued around the house when Artie was home. He frequently lost his temper over minute issues. His seething boundless unpredictable rages and ambivalence toward his children kept the family on edge and surrounded by constant fear of tripping his anger.

Intermittently, he showered Adam and Leli with affection, played with them and showed them off in public, but without warning, he would rage and then ignore them. He also relentlessly criticized Leli but showed Adam leniency.

Likewise, Tina hovered between passion and pain around him, as she tried to tolerate his moods, but helpless anger arose in her when he directed his rage at the children.

One routine Saturday afternoon, a burst of piano music floated through the house as Adam played Beethoven's *Für Elise*. As Tina listened to her talented son play, she felt a tug at her shirt, turned around to see Leli and smiled. "Wow. Isn't that beautiful? Adam's so talented." She stopped when she saw Leli's distressed face.

"What's wrong honey?" Tina bent down and took Leli in her arms.

"How come Daddy likes Adam better than me?"

Tina paused. "That's not true. Daddy just wants to make sure your brother learns how to play the piano."

"But he won't teach me, and Daddy spends more time with Adam even when he doesn't play piano."

"I thought he gave you some lessons."

"Daddy told me he wasn't going to teach me anymore, because I wasn't learning good."

"Daddy still loves you even if you can't play piano. Just hang in there, okay? You're talented in other ways, darling." Leli nodded and walked away to play with the cat.

Tina sighed. Artie clearly favored his son over Leli in every way. Without a doubt, Leli was a cute child but bore a strong resemblance to her father. She had his dark hair, his fair skin, the shape of his eyes and mouth. Tina thought it might not be inconceivable, that he projected his self-loathing onto his daughter amidst the irony of her conception.

Later, Tina tidied up the children's room. One of Leli's crayon drawings lay on a table. It made Tina stop cold in her tracks. The red triangle roof topped the square house. The doors and windows looked like a face in agony. Next to the house stood a huge purple monster with jagged teeth, dark curly hair and a beard, a tiny stick figure boy, girl and woman next to two cats. Heartbroken, Tina immediately knew how Leli perceived the family.

★   ★   ★

APRIL 1996

It was the first night of Passover, and Tina prepared a small Seder for the family to remember the flight of the Jews from Egypt. Maria, Sydney and Rick also attended. Tina prepared brisket and salmon. Sydney made a dessert.

The family considered themselves Jewish but did not keep kosher or get rid of the leavened foods, the chometz, before Passover. Although Tina did not buy leavened goods during Passover week, she made sure that the children understood the traditions, and that the family made at least one Seder. The previous week, the children had begged for marshmallow peeps, so Tina had picked some up at the supermarket.

She prepared the salmon for the oven; and brisket in the slow cooker. The Seder plate preparation followed as she set down the charoset, horseradish, an egg, a chicken bone instead of a shank bone, and parsley. Tina had made the charoset the day before with chopped apples, sweet wine, honey, and cinnamon. It symbolized the mortar of the Egyptian slaves. She also set aside a plate of matzo, covered with a white cloth.

Tina stopped to take a break, lay down on the couch and watched some TV as Artie rehearsed for an upcoming recital. Suddenly, Tina heard the children's raucous laughter in the kitchen; she immediately suspected mischief. Besides, Artie hated it when they made a lot of noise, especially during his practice sessions.

"Kids," said Tina and stopped as soon as she entered the kitchen. They stared at the microwave as they whooped and howled with laughter.

"Kids, what is going on?"

"Uh, nothing," said Adam sheepishly.

"I don't believe that," said Tina. She turned to Leli who averted her eyes.

Tina opened the microwave door and gasped. The whole interior was covered in pink and purple mush. Two empty packages of Peeps sat on the counter. Tina turned around and glared sternly at her children.

"What happened here?"

Leli spoke up. "We wanted to see the chickens fight."

"Yeah," Adam chimed in. "When you put them in the microwave, they get real big and attack each other."

"We made a big army," said Leli. "There was a pink army and a purple army."

"Oh, good grief," said Tina. "You're now going to clean up the mess. Here." She pushed out the stepstool while she gave them some paper towels and water mixed with vinegar. "I want to see that microwave clean as a whistle, do you hear me?" Adam stood on the stepstool and wiped out the microwave, while Leli dipped paper towels into the bowl of water before she gave them to her brother.

Artie entered the kitchen to make himself some mate and walked over to the microwave to heat some water, but stopped in his tracks when he saw the children busy at work. He turned to look at Tina.

"They played with the microwave and made a big mess," she said. She turned to the kids. "Hurry up. I have to start preparing dinner for tonight."

When they finished, Artie patted them both on the back. "Come on, kids. Let's go watch some TV." They followed him to the living room.

Tina set the large dining table for dinner. She added the extra leaf and topped the table with a Passover tablecloth. She set out the Seder plate, the cup of salt water, and a glass of wine for Elijah. After she set the table for eight, she lay a Haggadah at each place setting.

As she finished preparations, Tina chuckled to herself. The kids' mess the previous year was worse. The day before Passover, she had come home to a strong scent of burnt meat in the house. Maria stood in the kitchen agitated, and all the kitchen windows were open to air out the place. "I took a nap and then woke up to something burning," she told Tina.

"What happened?"

"I woke up to the smoke alarm. I ran into the kitchen. It was full of smoke. Then, I opened the oven to burned meat. When I asked Adamito, he said they wanted to help, so he and Lelita put the brisket in the oven. No pan."

"Oh no, Mama. There could have been a fire."

"The oven's a mess."

Tina went into the kitchen and opened the oven to find a charred, smelly fiasco. After the women and the children cleaned up, Tina went out and bought another brisket.

This year, Maria, Sydney, and Rick came for dinner. The Seder was short instead of the traditional lengthy Passover ritual. Everyone read the prayers and story of Exodus from the Haggadah text. Leli, the youngest present, asked the first question: "Why is this night different from any other night?" She stumbled over the words, so Adam read the remaining three questions. Everyone around the table read passages and followed the traditional rituals. They dipped their parsley into salt water to remember how the Jews suffered under Egyptian bondage, and guests spread charoset on their matzo to symbolize the brick mortar. Everyone sang *Dayenu*, the ancient Passover song which gives thanks for the gifts to the Jewish people. They opened the door momentarily as a symbolic gesture for Elijah.

Finally, it was time for dinner. Tina passed around the plates of brisket and salmon along with the side dishes. Kosher for Passover chocolate cake followed. Afterward, Artie hid a piece of matzo. The children searched to win a prize. Tina gave the $5.00 prize to Leli, the lucky winner.

Tina treasured those memories.

★   ★   ★

JUNE 1996

Tina's boss Bob called her into his office and smiled at her.

"Hi. Have a seat and close the door. I registered you for a week-long management course in Sacramento," he said. "It's in two weeks. Please go to the front office, which will take care of your per diem, plane ticket, and accommodations."

"Thanks Bob," said Tina. "I will be there." Stevie flashed into her mind as she returned to her office and knew she had to visit him. Although they often spoke by phone during Tina's lunch break at work, they had not seen each other for eight years. At that time, Stevie had been in LA for an audition, and since Artie was out of town, Tina and the children met him for lunch. Her gut feeling had told her he was ill at although he always insisted, he was fine. She had to see him face-to-face and confirmed he would be home that Sunday.

With a frown, Artie watched her pack. "When are you coming home?"

"Friday night."

"Who else will be there?"

"Managers statewide, I guess."

"How many of them are men?"

"Oh, good grief. What is this about?"

"You know how I feel."

"Do I ever give you a hard time when you go out of town for work? I don't ask how many women you work with." She turned around to see he had already left the room.

She flew into Sacramento early Sunday morning. Upon arrival, she picked up her rental car and headed toward San Francisco.

Stevie and Mark lived in the Castro district. Tina followed her map, found their house and parked the car. She walked up the steps to the front door and rang the bell; Stevie opened the door, Tina nearly gasped in horror, as he was almost unrecognizable. Emaciated and fragile, he resembled a walking skeleton. His once handsome and lively face was now a skull with hollow eye sockets. Purple blotches covered his skin, and oxygen tank tubes hung from his nose. In shock, Tina gave him a gentle hug. He smiled, offered her a chair, after which he slowly walked to the couch, pulling the tank behind him.

Tina looked around the elegant home furnished with antiques, gold-leafed walls and a large crystal chandelier in the dining room. Helene's "Everyone is Entitled to my Opinion" pillow sat on the couch. Mark walked into the room, greeted Tina with a hug, sat down nest to his partner and put his arm around him. Mark had not changed.

"You look good, cuzzie," Stevie said in a barely audible voice. "I wish I could have gotten back to LA to visit you..." he paused to catch his breath.

"It's okay," said Tina in a soft tone. "I'm glad we can visit today."

Stevie took a long breath. "This is probably our last visit together," he whispered. "I have AIDS and Kaposi's Sarcoma." He held out his arms covered with purple blotches. "Easy to get if you have AIDS. I've reached the end of the road." Then, he smiled. "I'm so happy to see you again. I missed you." He stopped to catch his breath. "How is everything?"

"The same," she smiled and hastily wiped away the now approaching tears. "Why didn't you tell me you were so sick? I would have come sooner."

"I didn't want to worry you."

"I wish I could help you in some way."

Stevie paused. "After I go, I'll be cremated, but no funeral. Mark will scatter my ashes in the ocean."

Sadness strained the conversation and soon, Stevie could barely stay awake. Tina realized it was time to go and stood up. Goodbye, cuzzie," he said in a faint voice. "Please don't worry about me. I'm okay with death. It will give me peace."

Tina said nothing but simply took him into her arms for a last hug. She kissed Mark and left before the tears flowed freely.

She wept all the way to Sacramento.

★ ★ ★

Two weeks later, Mark called Tina and told her Stevie had passed away that morning. Overwhelmed with sorrow, Tina blamed herself for not insisting on a visit sooner. Numb with grief, she floated robotically through house daily life.

"Quit moping already." A frown crossed Artie's face as he stopped his wife in the hall, his arms folded across his chest. "He's dead."

It was as if a dam blew and all her emotions burst forward. "Go to hell." Artie backed up at the scream. "You don't understand me. You don't understand anything."

"What I do understand is that you're neglecting your household duties. Mama is doing everything, watching the kids, laundry and shopping. Snap out of it."

"Artie, you make me want to leave you when you act this way. Why are you so mean?"

He glared at her, walked into the music room and slammed the door in her face.

Later, he walked into the living room where Tina sat staring at the television.

"Don't leave me, please. I love you, bombónita."

Tina startled. He had not used that term in years.

"I didn't mean it, Cielito. Besides, if I left, our moms would hate me, and the kids would think I was a bad mom. I don't want to break up our family."

Artie sat down next to her and took her hand which he pressed between his.

Almost overnight it seemed, Artie became kinder and more attentive. He no longer smelled of alcohol or pot and again displayed a strong sexual interest in her. Their mutual intimacy together made Tina feel loved once more. He changed. He really changed, she thought.

★   ★   ★

AUGUST 1996

One day, Sydney called Tina and dropped a bombshell. "I'm breaking up with Rick."

"Really? Wow. That's a shock. You've been together so long."

"Well, to be honest, I've met someone else. Don't be shocked now."

"Shocked?"

"My new love is LaRhea Jackson."

"The LaRhea Jackson? She's a famous star."

"That's her. She was here for a show, and we met at a party."

"So, you're a couple? I didn't know you were bi."

"Yes and no. It's a long story. This is so exciting, but I'm moving in with her next month. She lives in Manhattan, in a Penthouse. Can you imagine?"

"So, you're leaving?" Crestfallen, Tina turned to her friend. "I'm happy for you, but I'm crushed."

"I'm moving back to New York, but of course we will stay in touch. Now, there's email, so we can write each other every day, and I'll put in a good word about Artie, so she'll hire him to play for her, okay?"

Tina swallowed hard. Another loss.

Later, she told Artie what happened. He laughed and shook his head. "I know LaRhea. I've played piano for her in the past, but she was a he once. He had a sex change."

Tina had never met a transgender person, and wondered if this information was true, so she did a bit of research online on the family's new desktop computer, a novelty for her. When she typed in LaRhea's name, she found her biography. Indeed, she had once been Charles Jackson Jr from Pittsburgh, but after her transformation, changed her name to LaRhea Jackson. When Tina saw LaRhea's photo, she was stunned by her beauty. LaRhea had the perfect figure, a flawless complexion and exuded elegance.

She hoped things would work out for Sydney.

★   ★   ★

HALLOWEEN 1996

The cool wind rustled through the trees, as the faded blue sky displayed a partially waning moon. No stars were visible, as the air was heavy with smoke from the recent wildfires, and the wind did nothing to stop them. The fires glowed in the distance and lit up the dark sky, but neither Tina nor Artie worried about any immediate danger. They did not want to disappoint Adam and Leli who had looked forward to this night for weeks.

Tina and Maria sewed a gold sash, red pants and a pirate scarf for Adam, who wore the ensemble with a white t-shirt, an eyepatch, a large plastic gold earring and the scarf around his head as he waved a plastic sword. Leli wore the gray one-piece hooded pajamas, gray gloves with pink paw pads and a matching hood sewn by Maria. Tina drew black whiskers on Leli's cheeks and a beard and mustache on Adam's face

Artie decided he would dress up and accompany the kids. He kept his costume a secret until he appeared as a woman, complete with makeup, a wig, and a green sleeveless scoop-neck dress. He carried Tina's large empty black handbag and wore Mardi Gras beads around his neck. When they saw him, Tina and the kids laughed so hard that their sides hurt.

"Oh no!" Tina laughed. "You look like a drag queen."

"Mommy, a queen is a girl," corrected Leli. "Daddy is a boy."

Tina clapped her hand over her mouth. "Oops."

"Nena, it's all about the candy," said Artie. "Come on, kids."

Tina stayed behind. A few trick-or-treaters came to the door, and she passed out candy.

After a while, Tina lay down to doze off before the next group of children arrived. The house was eerily quiet. Miles, their gray cat, jumped up and kneaded her stomach. His purrs made Tina doze off.

Loud knocks awakened her. She jumped off the couch and peeked through the front door peephole; two firefighters and a police officer stood outside her house. When she opened the door, the smoke burned her eyes, as the fiery stench flew up her nostrils. Tina covered her mouth and coughed. Her eyes widened. "Is anything wrong?"

One firefighter greeted her. "Hello, ma'am. The fire is closing in and may strike here any time. Right now, it can't be contained. You and your family will need to evacuate immediately."

Tina's palms flew up to cover her cheeks. She was numb with shock. "My husband and children are out trick-or-treating, and he didn't bring his phone. I don't know where they are." She began to breathe rapidly.

"Please describe them for me." Tina provided the information. One firefighter took notes.

"Ma'am, we'll find them, but you must pack up what you need and leave right now."

A frenzied Tina grabbed the cat carriers out of the closet, ran through the house and rounded up their three cats. They did not like being confined and meowed loudly. She frantically packed a suitcase with clothes for everyone and grabbed photo albums, pictures and mementos, along with Artie's Startac phone, throwing everything into a box. Tina almost hyperventilated, as she rushed everything out to the car. She loaded the trunk and set the cat carriers in the back seat.

One of the officers returned. "Ma'am, you need to leave right now."

Tina became hysterical. Tears ran down her now-red face. "I can't leave without my family," she sobbed. "My kids. My husband. They're lost."

"Ma'am, I said we'll find them. You need to leave now. Immediately."

Tina grabbed her cellphone and called Sydney, who lived in the San Fernando Valley. When she answered, Tina burst into tears. "I have to evacuate. I don't know where Artie and the kids are. The fires...."

"Well, come on over. There are no fires in our neighborhood."

"I have to check on Maria first in case she has to leave."

"You're welcome here, darling, and bring the old hag with you if you must."

"How will my family find us?"

"Call the police and tell them you're here. I'm sure Artie and the kids will be okay. The cops will find them."

Tina got into the car. Tears flowed from her eyes so rapidly, it was difficult for her to see the road. The smell of smoke seared her nostrils and made her gag. The cats meowed loudly in their carriers. Tina backed out of the driveway with the thought that she might never see her home or even her family again.

She drove to Maria's house as the fires spread a red glow with an eerie brightness from the sky. She wiped her eyes as she parked the car in the driveway. Maria immediately answered the door. "The police just came here and told me I have to leave. Che, where is everyone?"

Tina took Maria's arm. "Artie took the kids trick-or-treating; the police will find them. We must leave now. We'll go to my friend Sydney's house. It's safe there. Artie will find us." Tina tried to sound reassuring. Maria's hands trembled as she looked with large frightened eyes at her daughter-in-law. The older woman disappeared into her bedroom, and shortly afterward, reappeared carrying a small valise and Pepito, her old Chihuahua.

Tina put the suitcase in the trunk, as Maria climbed into the front seat with the dog on her lap, and pulled a wooden rosary out of her handbag.

The freeway traffic was worse than ever, stop-and-go all the way. The darkening sky highlighted the black hills dotted with glowing smoky fires. In deep thought, both women said little to one another; the silence was broken only by Maria's whispered Hail Marys and Our Fathers, as she fingered her rosary.

The 15-mile drive took three hours in the bumper-to-bumper traffic; the red tail lights before them stayed woven into one continuous chain.

They finally arrived at about 11:00 P.M. Sydney showed them to her guest room and made coffee. Tina took care of the cats. Maria walked outside on the balcony and stood expressionless, holding Pepito in her arms.

The other two women joined her as they watched the red orange glow in the distance. At one point, Maria reached over to Tina and drew her close. Neither spoke, but both knew shock and devastation bound them together at this significant moment. There was nothing left to do at this point except wait.

A short time later, Tina climbed into bed with her cellphone nearby, lay in the dark and prayed for her family. She had just drifted to sleep when her phone rang; Tina sat up and grabbed it off the table so quickly, that it almost tumbled onto the floor.

"Mi vida, where are you?"

"Cielito! Where are you? Are you and the kids okay?" Tina practically shouted into the phone. Maria opened her eyes and sat up in bed.

"We're fine," he answered. "Have you heard from Mama? I can't reach her."

"She's here with me and the cats at Sydney's house. Where are you?"

Artie said, "The police found us and ordered us to evacuate then and there. We're staying with a colleague. Oh, imagine when I showed up in my dress," he laughed. "Everything is fine. Let me talk to Mama."

Tina handed the phone to Maria, who spoke joyfully to her son.

The next morning, as they awaited Artie and the children, Maria took Tina's hand and looked her in the eyes. "I just want to say that I'm happy you married Arturito. I know it was hard for me at first, but you're a wonderful person. I want you to know that."

Sydney's mouth dropped open. Astonished at Maria's honesty, Tina squeezed her hand, but before she could respond, the doorbell rang.

Tina rushed into Artie's arms, hugged and kissed the children. Maria followed. Leli and Adam still wore their costumes, but Artie wore slacks and a T-shirt. That struck Tina as strange, why only Artie had changed his clothes, but then told herself the most important thing was that everyone was safe. Her joy at reuniting with her family pushed any doubts aside.

"Mama and I were worried sick about you." Tina turned to her children. "I'm glad everyone is okay."

"We drove by both houses," said Artie. "Good news. No fire damages."

Tina breathed a sigh of relief. "All this had to happen on Halloween."

Artie laughed. "Adam complained yesterday he didn't get enough candy."

Tina giggled. "That's our boy. I'm so happy everybody got through this and our homes survived, so let's go home as soon as possible."

Maria rode with Artie and her grandchildren. Tina followed behind with the cats. They drove first to Maria's house, past smoldering embers and burnt structures. Maria's street was untouched. Both cars pulled into her driveway and Artie dropped Maria off and brought her to her front door.

"Gracias, Jesús," shouted Maria, her hands clasped in prayer.

Both cars drove back home. The surrounding blocks were damage-free.

After dinner, her heart still filled with joy, Tina inspected the candy in the trick-or-treat bags.

Leli tapped her on the shoulder. "Mommy, can I have some candy now?"

"I have to check everything first," said Tina, as she threw away a homemade brownie in a plastic bag and smiled at her daughter. "I'm so happy we're back home," she continued. "Did you have fun at your sleepover?"

"Miss Donna is a nice lady. We had dinner and watched TV. It was fun. She gave us ice cream."

"I'm glad you had a good time."

"Me and Adam slept in the same room. He moved around all night."

"Yesterday was tough for everyone, Leli. I was so worried about you."

"We were sad, but Daddy seemed happy as soon as he saw Miss Donna."

Tina vaguely remembered some months back that Artie had introduced her to the first violinist Donna of the Los Angeles City Symphony; Tina remembered her first name but little else.

"So, Daddy and Miss Donna talked a lot?"

"Yeah. He stayed in her room. And we even saw him kiss her." An electrical shock flew through Tina and almost knocked her over.

She got up and found Artie in his studio playing his Steinway.

Tina glared at him, shaking with shock and rage. "Arturo!"

"What? I'm busy." He took his hands off the keyboard and looked up at her. Tina never called him by his formal name.

"Guess what the kids told me." Tina walked up to him and stared at him coldly. "Did you and that woman sleep together last night?"

Artie turned his head away and did not respond.

"The kids said you slept with Mistress Donna." Tina emphasized the 'Mistress'. "You cheated on me. How dare you? And with the kids there, too." Her voice got louder.

Artie turned to look at his wife. "We have to talk."

"I'm waiting for a fucking explanation."

"Tina," he paused. "I don't know what I want right now. I really don't."

She froze, as nausea overwhelmed her. "Do you love her?"

"I don't know."

"How long has this been going on?"

"A while."

Tina paused, took a deep breath to calm down. "And I thought you were making an effort to improve our relationship. Instead, you were trying to cover up the truth. Get out." She stared at him with an icy glance. "Leave."

He looked aghast with disbelief. "You mean move out?"

"Immediately. How dare you bring our children to visit your whore, you schmuck. Fuck you. Get out."

"Fine." He paused and stared at the floor, got up, closed the piano lid and walked to the bedroom.

"Also, you better send me money for those kids," shouted Tina after him. She walked into the bedroom to see him packing his suitcase.

"I will send you her address. You can reach me there. I'll pick up the rest of my stuff soon."

Tina now realized where he got his change of clothing that morning.

He left without a word to the children. Tina heard him drive off.

After his departure, Tina locked herself in the bathroom and wept. When she composed herself, she looked in the mirror and washed her face and red puffy eyes. Then, she walked out to the living room. Leli and Adam lay on their stomachs propped up on their elbows as they watched a TV cartoon. They shrieked with laughter every few seconds.

Tina walked into the bedroom, closed the door and called Sydney.

Tina sobbed as she told her about Artie's girlfriend. "I don't know what to think. He takes the kids to his mistress Donna. Leli told me they slept together. He admitted it, and said he doesn't know what he wants. I kicked him out."

"And good riddance," said Sydney. "He's an ugly piece of shit. No great loss."

Tina wept again so hard that she was difficult to understand. "I don't know what I did wrong. All I did was love that man and be good to him."

"He's an abusive jerk. I've heard the way he talks to you at times. Did you want to spend the rest of your life with that drama king?"

"I tried so hard to hold our family together. All I wanted for us was to be a real family."

"It's not your fault. He's crazy and not good looking either. I'm glad your kids didn't turn out with three heads. Let him go." Tina did not answer. Sydney continued. "He was always nasty and I know you hurt now, but in time, you'll heal. Take it one day at a time."

Tina sighed. "I don't understand him. I thought we were getting along better. In fact, he was always scared I'd run off with another guy. Now this. I don't know how I'll sleep tonight. I'm so drained right now."

"Get some rest. Take it one day at a time."

"Hey, Sydney, should I file for divorce?"

"Don't do anything until you figure out what you want to do," cautioned her friend. "Go slowly. Just be there for your kids. This will be hard on them."

After Tina hung up, she washed her face before she walked out of the bedroom. Both children stood near the bedroom door and obviously had overheard part of the conversation.

"Mommy, where's Daddy?" Adam looked up and worry spread across his face. Leli reiterated the question.

After a pause searching for an answer. Tina knelt down and hugged them. "Daddy is going away for a while."

"Did he go to work?" Adam's chin quivered.

"He wants to live in a new place for right now."

Leli began to cry. "We'll never see Daddy again."

"No, no, you will. Now, let's get ready for bed."

The weekend passed without a word from Artie.

Through silent days and nights, Tina left his belongings as they were. He could pack up his own stuff, she thought.

★   ★   ★

On Wednesday, a postcard arrived in the mail with only Donna Overton's address and phone number. Now that Tina knew Donna's last name, her curiosity got the better of her. She could not picture Donna and wanted to see a photo of the woman; there would probably be one in a file somewhere at the public library.

Tina called in sick on Monday. She was too stressed out to focus on work anyway, so that morning after she got the children off to school, she drove to the library.

When she arrived, she stopped at the reference desk. The librarian provided her with a folder about the orchestra. Tina stumbled across Artie's concert program the year before and quickly put it away. A brochure about the symphony featured the musicians and a photo of Donna Overton, first violinist with a brief bio. Tina noticed Donna's shoulder-length wavy blonde hair and the resemblance to herself.

Witch.

Tina slammed the folder shut and returned it to the reference desk.

During the ride home, as she thought about Artie and Donna, Tina's anger turned into tears once more.

After she took a nap, Tina watched TV, her mind still numb with shock. She had just washed her face again to hide her tears. The children would be home soon. Maria arrived first with Leli, whom she picked up every day from nursery school. Leli ran to her mother and hugged her with obvious insecurity. With a somber look across her face and a jar of homemade lentil soup, Maria greeted Tina and put the soup in the refrigerator. Tina noticed her troubled expression; she obviously knew something.

"Mama, I am sorry. Artie moved out."

"Yes, I know."

Tina did not elaborate further. Not only did she avoid discussing the situation around her children, but she suspected Maria would support her son, matter what the circumstances were.

Two weeks later, the phone rang while Tina and the two children watched TV. She answered, her mind still focused on the screen.

"How are you and the kids?" Artie sounded cheery and upbeat.

Taken aback, she uttered, "Fine."

"I need to get my stuff, and I'd like to come over Saturday with my friend."

"Mistress Donna is not welcome here."

"I mean my friend Joe who has a pickup truck. I will be there around 10."

"Fine."

When Saturday arrived, Tina sent the children to a friend's house, so their father's presence would not upset them.

After Tina greeted Artie and Joe coolly when they arrived, she ignored them. Within a few hours, the two men had packed up Artie's belongings as they laughed and joked together. Tina tried to block them out, as their cheerfulness increased the sorrowful pain within her.

When they finally finished carrying the boxes to the truck, Artie found Tina in the kitchen, her back turned to him, busily wiping down the refrigerator. "I'll arrange to pick up my piano as soon as I can."

"Fine." She did not turn around.

"I'll call you."

"Whatever."

"Can't you at least say goodbye?"

Tina turned to face him. "Why should I say anything? Go back home to your mistress."

He quickly walked towards the door and left. Tina noticed his studio was completely empty except for the Steinway B, an empty desk and bare bookcases. He had taken his electronic keyboards, notebooks, and music scores.

When she walked to the bedroom, Tina noticed a check folded on her nightstand. She picked it up and saw Artie had written her a $100.00 check. *Big whoop.* She put it in her purse to take to the bank.

Over the following weeks, Tina slowly adjusted to the thought of being single again. Part of her ached over the rejection, yet she also was relieved that she would no longer have to face Artie's explosive moods. She told herself to stop thinking about him and to stay strong.

Nights were the worst. He forcefully invaded her thoughts, her dreams. He floated into her mind before she fell asleep and into her first thoughts when she awoke. While she remembered how badly he treated her, she nevertheless could not forget him. There was an obsessive drive within her that longed for him, that remembered only the tender moments. Often, she cried herself to sleep in despair.

There was little word from him. Checks arrived sporadically and in varying amounts. He sent Tina $100.00 to buy the kids Hanukkah gifts and $50.00 for Leli's birthday. The holidays this year would be difficult. The children continued to be upset, and they missed their father.

★　★　★

DECEMBER 1996

It was the day before Hanukkah. Tina herself did not feel up to any celebration but planned a small low-key party for Leli and Adam. When Tina stopped at the local supermarket to pick up potatoes for latkes, she noticed on the community bulletin board that a divorce support group met on Wednesday nights at a local church. She wanted to go; a neighbor with young children agreed to watch Leli and Adam the following Wednesday.

The group met in the church basement. Tina walked into the room and immediately saw about 20 people, mostly women. The group leader welcomed Tina and introduced herself, as she handed her a business card which said 'Tamara Stone, LCSW, Licensed Clinical Social Worker.'

Tina smiled as Tamara asked her to take a seat and welcomed the group, which sat in a circle on folding metal chairs. "Thanks, everyone, for coming this evening. We have a few guests here tonight. Feel free to share when you feel comfortable to do so. We go by first names only. Who would like to begin?"

A young woman named Stacey spoke about her abusive marriage. Her husband beat her to the point that she was hospitalized. He was in jail. She had two young children. Terrified that he would return to kill her when he was released, she began to cry. Tamara handed her a tissue box.

Another woman introduced herself as Hasmik. She spoke about how her husband had returned to Armenia and cleaned out the bank account. She did not know his whereabouts. Unemployed, Hasmik had lost everything and was living in a woman's shelter.

A third woman, Anita, had a comfortable life, but when she discovered her husband was a chronic cheater, she threw him out.

Lisette spoke up. She wanted to separate from her husband, but she could not afford childcare, so they continued to live together. He often hit her in anger.

Dave, the lone man in the group said his alcoholic wife abused him for years, and he finally divorced her. His story reminded Tina of her parents' relationship years ago.

Others also spoke about their troubled relationships.

As Tina listened to the other victims' stories that evening, she wondered where her story fit in with the others. She thought afterward that her problems could have been worse. Did she really need this support group? She could handle these things herself. She did not need to go to a meeting again. After all, most of those women had wife beaters for husbands. Not her.

Yet something stirred inside her and jabbed uncomfortably at her insides. After she arranged with her neighbor to watch the children again, Tina returned to the group the following week. That evening, the group served coffee and homemade brownies. Tamara greeted everyone and announced she would make a presentation. The room became quiet.

"Everyone usually thinks of abuse in physical terms. Tonight, there will be a brief presentation on emotional abuse, which can be just as bad and often, worse. It can cause lifelong emotional scars." She opened her laptop and clicked on her PowerPoint presentation.

"Emotional abuse," continued Tamara, "can take many forms. Let's go over some of the techniques abusers often use to intimidate their victims." Tamara clicked on the first slide which showed a mirror and a question mark. "Projection," Tamara explained, "is when someone won't admit his or her thoughts and actions but instead accuses or blames others for these issues. People who project can also attribute their own feelings to others." Tamara had the entire group's full attention. "For example, some guy is obsessed with a woman who doesn't reciprocate. He won't acknowledge that, though, and believes that she is obsessed with him. Does anyone want to share an example of their own?"

Stacey spoke up. "My husband always accused me of stealing money and hiding it from him when in fact he hid it from me." Then Anita spoke. "My husband always told me I cheated, when it was really him who fooled around." Nobody said anything else, but Tina remembered how Artie often had accused her of things that were actually true of him.

The next slide showed an antique gas lamp with a flame inside. "Gaslighting is one of the worst things for the victim," said Tamara. "The abuser provides false information to make the victim doubt their own sanity and perceptions. For example, the victim knows something is true, but the abuser denies it ever happened."

Artie had often tried to gaslight Tina and the children. Tina said nothing.

The next slide showed a cartoon of a man asleep at his desk. "Passive-aggressive behavior can be one of the most frustrating behaviors around," said Tamara. "These people indirectly resist and avoid direct confrontation. They can sulk, procrastinate or sabotage a situation."

"That's exactly what happened to me all the time," said Diane, another participant. "When I asked my partner to clean up after herself, she would drag it out, and when she finally did clean, she left a big mess instead." The next slide showed a cartoon of a man and woman battling with swords. "Now let's discuss defensiveness," said Tamara. "When they perceive criticism, Abusers often hurl back retorts and accusations. Sometimes they also use projection."

"Oh, you could never discuss anything with my husband without it becoming a big argument," said Hasmik. "He would hurl all kinds of insults at you."

The next slide showed a cartoon of a woman with a sousaphone head blaring at her cowering husband. Several participants laughed. "This woman is obviously intimidating her partner," said Tamara. "I don't think there is beautiful music here. She is yelling loudly, and the man is obviously afraid of her. You know what intimidators also do? They threaten divorce or worse to frighten the victim into compliance. Often, they call the victim derogatory names such as bitch or something else. They criticize the victim's looks, behavior, and everything the victim enjoys, the abuser tries to destroy. The victim becomes trapped in fear. I want to make you aware of these abuse techniques and not blame yourselves. Nobody should have to tolerate these behaviors."

★   ★   ★

Later, Tina thought about the presentation, as she drove home after the meeting. Confusion reigned with a heavy heart and chest pain. Why did she love Artie so much if he treated her so badly? She continued to attend the weekly meetings but was reticent in sharing her story, so she just listened.

One day, Anita no longer came to the meetings, and Tina heard she had reconciled with her husband. Tina could not believe Anita took him back; she had sounded so resolute in moving forward. Tamara replied that victims return to their abusers most of the time.

★   ★   ★

FEBRUARY 1997

As Tina settled into her routine, her mood improved, and she enjoyed time with the children. She debated whether she should file for divorce and resolved to find a good attorney for advice.

Artie called her two days before Valentine's Day.

He sounded upbeat. "How's everybody?"

"What do you want now?"

"How are the kids?"

"Do you really care? You haven't seen them since you left."

Artie ignored the comment. "You know, it isn't the same without you."

Tina was silent.

He continued in his soft sing-song voice. "I'd like to come home."

"Forget it," Tina said quickly.

"Mi vida, please listen to me. I broke up with Donna and am living with my mom. I realized how much I love you." He spoke rapidly. "I love you too much to lose you. I adore you. I will kill myself without you. Please, bombónita. I miss you. You're my Valentine."

"Cut the shit. Adios, Arturo." Tina hung up the phone. She could not believe he actually called her and asked her to take him back. Maria had never mentioned that Artie moved back to her house.

Later, Tina telephoned Sydney. "He wants to come home."

"Oh, no. He has nowhere to go now that he broke up with his girlfriend. I wouldn't take him back," her friend replied.

"Don't worry," laughed Tina.

"Wow. Do you know this is the first time I've heard you laugh in months?"

"I guess I'm feeling a bit better."

"Great. What made you turn around?"

"I found a divorce support group and go once a week."

"Great," said Sydney. "Keep it up, Girl. Is it helpful?"

"Every week, we discuss a new topic. A therapist runs it. We share our stories too. Do you know what I learned? I learned about body language and family dynamics. I never understood that before. I still don't understand all of it, but it opened my eyes.

★   ★   ★

On Valentine's Day, a large pink rose bouquet in a crystal vase arrived for Tina at her office. The card simply said, 'I love you'.

The flowers were too beautiful to trash. Tina gave them to a delighted co-worker.

The next day, another bouquet arrived at work. The card said he missed his bombónita.

The following day, a belated Valentine's Day card arrived in the mail, where Artie wrote how much he adored Tina and the children and begged Tina to take him back.

After counting ten phrases adorned with exclamation marks, Tina threw the card into the trash.

He called that evening. "How did you like the flowers?"

"Artie, please. It's over."

"It will never be over for us, my love. Nobody will ever love you as much as I do. I want to see you and the kids this weekend."

"Adam is sick. He can't," she said with fingers crossed behind her back. "I can't. I'm busy."

"Okay, I'll check back." The charm had disappeared from his voice as he quickly hung up. Tina sighed with relief; she did not want to see him.

The following evening the phone rang.

"How's Adam doing?"

Tina had almost forgotten her fib." Still not feeling well."

"I want to see you and the kids. When can I come over?"

"Artie, please don't start."

"Mi vida, I miss you and the kids so much."

Tina's head began to hurt. She paused. "Good night, Artie."

Flowers and chocolates showed up almost daily at her workplace. Resigned, Tina put them into vases or gave them away. One weekend, a large bouquet of roses showed up with a large pink teddy bear, which Tina gave to Leli. Afraid to confront Artie, Tina just wanted him to leave her alone. She had stopped answering her phone, and her answering machine was inundated with his romantic messages.

Sydney called her friend and asked her, "How many bouquets today?"

"Just one. A big one, of white and yellow lilies.

"He's sending you every flower in LA. This is ridiculous."

"He wants me to take him back. He leaves me messages saying how he loves and misses me."

"He won't give up, will he? He is really harassing you. Maybe you should go to court, file a restraining order or something."

"I don't know. He confuses me. I wish Mama Helene were still alive. I need her so much now."

"Don't give in. You're doing so much better."

"I didn't say I'd take him back. Did you get the photo of all the flowers in my office? I emailed it to you a few days ago."

"I did, and your office looks like a funeral parlor."

"Thanks a lot."

"A pretty funeral parlor. I didn't say an ugly one."

Tina sighed.

"Don't weaken," said Sydney. "You don't need him. Stay strong. If you miss sex, use a vibrator, a cucumber, a banana, anything besides him."

"It's been ages since we had sex, and it became so mechanical. He'd hump me just to get his rocks off, and I'd think about the grocery list."

Sydney laughed out loud. "Tina, you crack me up."

Tina broke into a smile. "Sometimes, I'd think also about stuff to do around the house."

"Stop it, girl. Shut up. Gotta go." Sydney hung up the phone.

The following Thursday, the washer broke down. Tina expected a service call for her washer and answered the phone when it rang.

"How are you, my love? Let me see you and the kids this weekend."

Tina sighed. "I'm busy. When do you want to pick them up?"

"Saturday at 11."

Tina agreed. She had run out of excuses.

Artie showed up in jeans and a black long-sleeved T-shirt, which minimized his heavy mid-section. He smiled and greeted Tina as if everything were normal. He appeared unchanged.

When they heard his voice, Leli and Adam ran from their rooms screaming to greet their father, who bent down and hugged each child tightly. "We're going to lunch and a movie," he said. "See you later," he said to Tina as they left.

The stress of seeing Artie made Tina eat a pint of rocky road ice cream from the freezer. Her emotions flew about like turbulent ravens amidst a dark sky. He dropped the happy children off in the late afternoon but did not stay.

During the week, Tina received orchids and yellow roses accompanied by passionate love declarations punctuated by capitals and exclamation marks. It puzzled yet relieved her, that Artie had not become romantic at his visit.

He called a few days later. "Mama wants the kids to stay the weekend."

She sighed. "I guess." The conversation was short and brief.

He showed up Saturday morning and left with the children. Early that evening, Tina clad in her robe, was engrossed in a new science fiction novel. When the doorbell rang, Tina sighed, put down her book and got up to answer the door.

Artie stood alone, dressed in a black t-shirt and jeans. Emanating strong cologne, He smiled and stepped inside.

"Where are the kids?" asked Tina.

"With Mama," he answered. "I'd like to take you out to dinner and chat."

"Well, I guess we need to work things out."

"That's not what I want to talk about. I have a surprise for you and the kids."

Tina shrugged her shoulders. "I have to change clothes. Excuse me." She disappeared into the bedroom for a few minutes, puzzled at the intended "surprise." What was it? A greenhouse to grow her own flowers? Her lips curved into a smile as she chuckled to herself.

They dined at a casual but expensive restaurant. Artie waved to the famous singer at the table nearby, as he smiled at his wife. "We recently did a show together in Vegas," he added as he ordered a bottle of expensive pinot noir.

"I guess we need to sort things out," Tina said. "So, what's the surprise? Let's discuss the children and our separation instead."

The wine arrived, and he clinked her glass.

"I guess we'll have to work out visitation," said Tina. "I want full custody of the kids." She took a sip of wine. "I can't stand your episodic rages, Artie. You're not nice to the children. You blame me for anything that goes wrong. You drink too much, and you cheated on me."

"Hey, I've changed. I won't do any of that anymore. You'll see a different guy, bombónita. Now, when did we last take a vacation?"

"Ages ago. I don't remember."

"I think we need a wonderful vacation, you, me, the kids and Mama. I'm going to treat all of us to a Caribbean cruise next month. We'll leave from Miami, and you can visit your parents."

"Really?" Tina crossed her arms and looked at him with suspicion. "So, what's in it for you?"

"I want all of us to have fun. When I told the kids, they were so excited. We'll get our passports, and everyone will have a good time. I'm booking a suite for everyone, and you don't have to spend a cent."

Still puzzled, Tina took a moment to catch her breath. He did not take his eyes off hers as he reached his arm over the table and touched her cheek. An electric shock flew through her, because he had touched her the way he often did when they were dating. She took a breath and closed her eyes.

"Okay," she said. "It will be a good experience for the children to see us get along." Artie held his thumb up on his right hand and laughed.

A month later, they flew to Boca Raton. The family visit with Eva and Irving in their pink and gold condo went surprisingly smoothly. Eva did not argue and doted on the family during the visit.

After three days, they boarded the cruise ship. Artie had booked a deluxe suite, which had two bedrooms and a grand piano in the living room. Artie and Adam slept in one bedroom, while Maria, Leli and Tina slept in the other. Tina realized she enjoyed this experience more than she had anticipated. She inhaled deeply the fresh salt air, and as she walked through the ship, she marveled at the elegance, the beautifully laid-out spaces, the baroque duets emulating from the atrium during the day and the upbeat rock music from the theater at night. She marveled as the skies turned from blue to bright orange and red at sunset before fading into dark obscurity. The clear turquoise water of the Caribbean Sea circled the ship like a halo and gave way to pristine sugar-white beaches.

Over the next few days, magical life never seemed to end. Everyone loved the activities, the pool and the food on the ship. Several cruise ships docked at each port, but in spite of the many tourists, the family still enjoyed the islands as an exotic attraction. Tina played with the children, and they swam in the ocean together while Maria waded in the shallow shore. Artie joined them, and he and the children splashed each other. They looked like the ideal family, Tina thought to herself.

One afternoon during the day at sea, Tina enjoyed a relaxing morning with a massage and facial in the spa, as the rest of the family had several activities scheduled for the day Afterward, she decided to go to the pool and made her way back to the suite to change into her swimsuit. She startled when she saw Artie seated at the desk with music scores.

Tina stopped. "I thought you were all going with Mama to the cooking class."

Artie looked up. "Changed my mind." He took off his reading glasses and put the scores away. "Let's sit on the balcony." Tina didn't mind; she was in an exceptional mood. As they watched the ocean waves roll by, a cigar-sized ship was seen on the horizon, floating on top of the waves. Tina's eyelids became heavier and she felt herself nodding off.

"We have a couple of hours to ourselves," whispered Artie. He reached over, embraced and kissed her. Seduced by the waves, the sea, the joy of the trip and Artie's whispers of love, Tina succumbed to him, and they ended up making passionate love. Tina's head swum with lightheadedness.

They hurriedly dressed before the others returned. Exhausted, Tina remained in a daze for the rest of the evening.

The next three days flew by in a whirl. Tina and Artie had sex once again before the ship returned to port. Tina knew she still loved him and told herself she forgave him for the children's sake.

A week later, Artie moved back home. The children were overjoyed to have their father return to them.

Embarrassed, Tina downplayed the reunion to Sydney who said, "It's your decision to take him back and mine not to interfere anymore."

Soon enough, Tina found herself back in the old pattern. Artie had not changed, but Tina did not regret her decision to take him back. Putting her misery aside, she told herself she was holding the marriage together for their children. She convinced herself that in spite of everything else, Artie's passionate interest meant he loved her.

Tina never returned to the divorce support group.

★   ★   ★

JUNE 1997

Sydney called Tina. "Can I come and visit you for a few days?

"Sure. Do you mind an airbed?"

"No problem. I can sleep anywhere."

The following Friday, Tina picked up Sydney at the airport. She wore a loose top and jeans and had gained some weight. Tina helped her with her suitcase. "You'll sleep in Leli's room."

"Oh that's unnecessary."

"She's fine with it. We don't get guests very often. How is LaRhea?"

"Oh my gawd, she is so busy with work. She's in the new Broadway hit *Brick Roof Queen* and she's been reviewed so often by the *New York Times* and other papers, that if she set the articles end to end, they'd reach from New York to California."

"She's amazing. I know Artie misses working with her. She hasn't been out to California in a long time, probably because of all her New York Broadway work, right?" "Correct, but she hasn't forgotten Artie. She brings him up from time to time and says she's never worked with a pianist as fantastic as him."

"That's good news." "I have better news. Ready? I'm four months pregnant."

"What? Congratulations. Who's the father?"

Sydney smiled. "You know LaRhea was born a man, right? Well, she underwent hormone treatments and all her surgeries except the last one. She chickened out and didn't want her family jewels cut off."

"Wow. He still has his prick and balls."

"She," Sydney corrected her. "We decided we wanted a kid and tried for some time. Now, voila."

"When's the baby due?"

"November. It's a boy. You'll meet the future Nathan Dimante Jackson soon.

Tina smiled and shook her head in amazement. "Let's celebrate." The family and Sydney had a pleasant four-day weekend together. Before Sydney flew home on Monday, Tina told her to let her know when the baby arrived. They had a tearful farewell together, and pledged a lifelong friendship.

★   ★   ★

AUGUST 31, 1997

On a busy Saturday, Artie accompanied a singer at a recital. Tina, who most of the time bought clothes for the children at thrift stores, now took Leah and Adam to back-to-school sales. Leli could not contain her excitement and anticipation over kindergarten. Adam, however, especially hated these sales, since they signaled that the end of summer vacation was near, and told his mother he'd rather stay home and play on his Nintendo. Tina ignored him. Afterward, armed with two large shopping bags, Tina and the children ate a late lunch at a family restaurant. Later, Tina phoned Sydney and joked, "I used to think my favorite three words were 'I love you.' Now they're 'Kids Eat Free.'"

★ ★ ★

After dinner that evening, Artie played with the kids before bedtime. They whooped and laughed as they played Twister, while Tina decided to make toll house cookies from the chocolate-chip bag recipe. She pulled out a wooden spoon and listened absentmindedly to television news, as she stirred the dough in the ceramic bowl. It was almost 9:00 P.M, and she had to get ready for work the following day, but she decided to finish the cookies first. That's when she heard the breaking news that Princess Diana had been in a serious car accident. Tina froze; she admired Princess Diana and had followed her life since her 1981 marriage to Prince Charles. At the time, Tina was a recent college graduate and spellbound, had watched the entire royal wedding with Helene and Stevie.

Now, Tina hurried into the living room to see the latest news about Diana. She sank into the recliner and with tightly closed eyes, prayed for Diana's recovery. The others stopped their game to watch her. When the oven beeped to signal the preheat cycle was complete, Tina returned to the kitchen to spoon the dough on the cookie sheet and put the cookies in the oven to bake but with her eyes focused on the television screen the entire time. In the meantime, Artie walked into the kitchen and picked up the almost empty bowl, as he gleefully dug with a spoon into the leftover raw cookie dough. Tina walked over to him, smiled, and lightly slapped his hand. "Don't eat raw dough. You can get sick." Too late. Artie put the now-empty bowl in the sink, smiled and kissed her on the lips. As she got Leli and Adam ready for bed, she was still worried about Diana and told herself that the princess would surely be okay by morning. Afterward, Tina bathed and dressed the children in their pajamas, tucked them into bed and read them *Where the Wild Things Are.* Artie dropped by, and both parents kissed the children goodnight before Tina turned off the lights.

At 10:00 PM, she heard the newscaster announce Princess Diana's death and turned to Artie. "Cielito, I can't believe it. I'm devastated."

"Who cares?"

"I admired her so much. She was a wonderful, inspirational person."

"People admired Evita."

"What the hell does Diana have to do with Evita?"

"Both whores married powerful men for money."

"Diana wasn't a whore."

Artie's sunny disposition suddenly disappeared. It was as if a dark raincloud blew in, turning the blue-sky gray, and covered him with gloom. He walked over to the kitchen cabinet, pulled out his favorite bottle of whiskey and poured himself a shot which he quickly downed. He tried to pour himself another shot, but nothing happened. Artie looked inside the neck of the bottle, saw it was empty and tossed it into the recycle bin.

"Cielito," said Tina slowly. "Didn't you just buy that last week?"

"And what if I did? What's it to you?"

"Cielito," Tina hesitated. "I worry because you still drink a lot."

"Goddammit!" He threw the shot glass in the sink. It shattered. "Why does it bother you? Am I lying around drunk all day? Mind your own business!"

Tina quickly put her finger to her lips, as he began to swear rapidly in Spanish. "Artie, the kids."

"Fuck the kids." He walked up to her and grabbed her shoulders. "You better listen to me. You're a bitch, do you hear me? A fucking bitch. Apologize."

Tina began to cry. "Cielito, I'm so sorry. I didn't mean to upset you."

"You better be. You owe me. It's your fault I got mad," Anger contorted his face. He whirled Tina around with an embrace and kiss and stared at her. "You know what I like."

Without a word, Tina followed into the bedroom, stepped out of her clothes, unzipped his pants and knelt before him.

Afterward, they lay in bed as Artie fell asleep. The pleasure had been his alone. Humiliated and saddened at his lack of interest, Tina felt her eyes burn, but she wiped her face and tried to sleep. She knew it was going to be a long night.

The next morning, he was as kind as he could be with no mention of the previous evening.

★　★　★

DECEMBER 1998

The year passed surprisingly without incident. The previous November, Sydney delivered a healthy baby boy and emailed Tina regularly with photos. Artie displayed attentive and loving behavior at home to both his wife and children and showed no signs of drugs or alcohol. Tina and Maria got along well. It seemed a happy time, and Tina hoped things had finally improved.

★   ★   ★

An invitation arrived via mail in a gold envelope from a famous Hollywood producer for an exclusive black-and-white film noir themed holiday party at his Bel Air mansion, black and white attire required. It surprised Tina as they were not part of the Hollywood crowd, and it delighted Artie who, on the night of the party, wore his tuxedo while Tina wore a black dress, simple jewelry and black high-heeled sandals. Her husband drove, and the car sped into the night as the lights of LA flashed by.

Artie named a big Hollywood director. "I hear he'll be there tonight. I'd like to meet him. You know, I wouldn't mind being in a movie again."

"But you're such a wonderful musician, Cielito. Do you really still want to be an actor?"

"I always dreamed of an acting career," said Artie. "Did I tell you what a great experience it was to act in *Lansky*?"

Tina laughed. "Many times. I wish you luck, darling, but you're first and foremost a wonderful pianist."

Artie reached over and touched her left hand. "I know if the director sees and talks to me, he'll give me a part. I just know it."

Tina smiled and nodded as she gazed through the car window into the night.

They arrived and entered through the mansion's grand foyer; everything was draped in black and white. A huge Christmas tree stood in the grand entranceway bedecked in black ornaments and white lights. A waiter walked up to them with a tray of black and white hors d'oeuvres. The maids and serving staff wore 1940s garb. Vintage movie props strategically stood around the entertainment areas. Black and white Christmas trees decorated almost every room.

Artie's eyes searched the party guests until he found the man he sought. The director was deep in conversation with a woman, a known studio powerhouse. Artie greeted them, and they smiled and shook his hand. Tina stood next to her husband, smiling politely but silent.

"I remember you, Artie," the director said after a pause. "Didn't you wear a T-shirt to rehearsal?" He paused and laughed. "Something about a penis and a piano?"

Artie laughed. "Pianist, Penist, Organ."

"Yes, that's it." Everyone laughed. The director pulled a cigar out of his pocket and thrust it in his mouth. He offered one to Artie, pulled out a lighter and lit both cigars. Artie inhaled and blew out smoke rings.

"Do you like this cigar? It's Cuban. Handmade. You know, I'd like to talk to you about my newest movie and the score." The director motioned Artie over to a room. "Let's go chat in the study."

Artie turned to Tina, as his eyes gleamed with excitement. "This may take a while. Please amuse yourself." Tina nodded. She stood alone right in the middle of the room, surrounded by cliques of successful well-dressed moguls and stars. She searched for someone to converse with, but everyone was too engrossed in their own little world, so Tina decided to look around.

Each room had unique decorations. White carpet and furniture covered the living room like a snow blanket, accented by black drapes and pillows. The theme continued to the minimalist kitchen, which held the latest expensive stainless appliances. Tina sighed with a bit of envy.

She sought a restroom but there was nobody around to ask except guests, so she tried a closed door in the nearby hallway, but when she opened it, she froze in shock. Devoid of furniture, the black painted room had mirrors on the ceiling, large black floor pillows and black carpet. Several naked couples were scattered in the room engaged in sexual acts. When one man and his partner saw Tina, they invited her to join them for a threesome. Tina shook her head, and quickly shut the door again.

She finally found a bathroom, ran in and locked the door. As she sat on the toilet, she buried her face in her hands, shocked at what she had seen. Afterward, she returned to the main room to find Artie, but he was nowhere in sight.

She stood by herself in the main room, sipping a glass of wine and smiling at other guests who passed by, but nobody stopped to chat with her. Tina told herself not to be such a shy chicken and walked over to a group of four smartly dressed women. Tina greeted them and introduced herself. The women nodded as their artificial smiles turned upward with lips parted to show perfect white teeth.

"You must be an actress." One woman said.

Tina shook her head and smiled. "I'm a case manager."

"Oh?" said another woman in a black dress adorned with silver beads. "I never heard of that job." She seemed at a loss for words. Finally, she asked, "So who invited you here?"

Tina named the producer. "My husband is a pianist and plays scores for his movies." Tina named a recent film.

"That's nice," said another woman in a chic long black-and-white sheath. "Say, you look familiar. Didn't I see you at a store on Rodeo Drive the other day?"

Tina smiled. "I don't think so."

"Are you sure? I swore I've seen you in Beverly Hills. Don't you live there?"

Tina shook her head. "We live in Los Feliz."

"Oh." The third woman in a black strapless dress walked up to Tina and admired her silver Y necklace. "You got this at Tiffany's, right? I saw a similar one there."

"I got it at an art fair in Sausalito a few years ago. It's real silver."

The woman said nothing, backed off and looked at Tina disdainfully.

The fourth woman in a black bustier and short skirt spoke up.

"Where did you get your dress? It's so black."

"Yeah. I think I saw a dress like that at K-Mart." The other woman shrieked with laughter.

"What?" laughed the third woman. "I never shop at that place. Wouldn't be caught dead there."

All four women laughed loudly and reminded Tina of mean junior high school girls. Her brow furrowed and her lips curled into a frown; she hated bullies. "You know what, ladies?" Tina smiled her sweetest smile. "Go fuck yourselves."

She turned on her heel and quickly walked away. Still angry, she walked to another room and opened the door where strong scents of incense and pot hit her nostrils. People sat or lay around the room as they inhaled, snorted, or smoked assorted substances. A few had rubber hoses around their arms as they injected themselves. Colorful pills sat in a candy dish by the door's entrance. Tina recognized them as ecstasy. She quickly left the room and turned around to face Artie, who scowled at her.

"What are you doing?" he asked angrily.

"I walked in by accident. They're all high in there."

"Don't bullshit me. You were flirting with the guys there."

"What are you talking about? I never even spoke to them."

"You're lying."

"You're out of your mind. I don't do that."

"Let's go." Angrily, Artie yanked Tina by the arm and walked toward the exit.

"Artie, let go of me." He ignored her and pulled her outside. "You're hurting my arm. Quit it." He did not answer in spite of her protests. When they arrived home, the children were already asleep. After the couple returned, Maria left for home.

"Come with me," said Artie. His hostile eyes framed his angry face, as he pulled Tina into the bedroom. Tina stared at her now-bruised arm.

He made her undress and lay down on the bed, while he bent over and examined her closely for sexual evidence. "I don't fool around," she kept repeating, but he ignored her. Finally, after he failed to find anything, he straightened up and left the room without a word.

The next morning in bed, Tina awoke as Artie slept. Still fraught with anxiety from the night before, she looked at the ugly bruise again but told herself it was surely an accident; he hadn't meant to hurt her.

Artie stirred, got up and went to the bathroom. When he returned, Tina was still in bed, although she was awake.

His lips pursed together in a frown, Artie sat down on the bed and stared at the wall with a dark angry expression across his face. "He told me there was no part for me in the movie, because I'm not the right type, but he still wants me to play the score."

Tina paused a moment. "I'm sorry, Cielito, but he knows what a great pianist you are. You'll rock the music."

He did not respond. She got up and hugged him, then held out her arm.

"Cielito, this was an accident, right?"

"What?"

"I mean, you didn't bruise my arm on purpose?"

"I didn't bruise your arm. I had nothing to do with it."

"But you grabbed my arm and pulled me," she responded.

"I don't know what you're talking about," he said now angrily. "All I did was touch your arm so we could leave. You know what? You're so clumsy. You probably banged your arm somewhere last night and are blaming it on me."

"I'm not blaming you …," Tina tried to explain, but he cut her off.

"You always blame me," he continued. "You imagine things. Go do what you have to do," he said dismissively. "Go look after the kids." He walked into the closet and pulled some socks and underwear out of the bureau drawer, totally ignoring his bewildered wife.

At that moment, Adam popped his head through the door with an anxious look on his face. He had obviously heard the fight and then smiled. "You wanna hear my funny joke?" The boy often tried to ease the tension at home to some extent with humor.

"Ok, let's have it," said Artie gently.

"What do you call an alligator in a vest?"

"I don't know, Nene," said his father. "What do you call an alligator in a vest?"

"An investigator."

Both parents laughed.

"What do you call someone who stole the octopus at the aquarium?"

His parents shook their heads.

"A squidnapper."

Everyone laughed. Tina smiled, and Artie bent down and kissed her bruised arm.

The children always brightened their lives and brought Tina joy. She loved to remember their past antics such as when Adam was in first grade, and he brought a spider he had found and named Brandon to school. As a result, his teacher, who had serious arachnophobia, had such a panic attack, she had to be hospitalized. Tina still remembered being called to the principal's office to take him home.

Twice, the children brought home wildlife as pets, one time a coyote pup and once a raccoon. The animals were freed, but Tina was touched by the kind intentions and the funny incidents.

After breakfast, Artie practiced in his studio; Tina sat in the living room armchair listening to his fingers flying over the keys for the next two hours, as she realized he had not changed after all.

★   ★   ★

Artie had become his old self, and life with him had continued to grow increasingly difficult again for Tina, as he argued about everything. When Tina mentioned her favorite male singer, Artie accused her of being in love with the man. Sex, the glue that once bonded the couple together, had turned into a weapon which Artie now used against his wife. His once-addictive sex drive and deep sexual interest in his wife had waned. Tina had given up attempted hobbies, because Artie mocked her efforts. He invalidated her clothes, her weight, cooking, or any attempted venture. Confrontations made him defensive or change topic. A great deflector, he wanted to win every argument. He made Tina out to be a total failure, but what hurt even more was his unpredictable behavior toward his children. Hindered by an inability to read body language or decipher verbal cues well, Artie saw his children simply in black and white, as he seesawed from a loving and caring parent to total detachment. He often got angry at Leli and Adam for perceived misdeeds, although he readily forgave Adam sooner than his sister. Still, both children had to be careful and stay especially quiet during his practice sessions, or he would fly into a rage.

He continuously favored Adam, and as a result, Leli became jealous of her brother. Artie fueled the fire and told Leli that Adam did not like her that much, so an angry Leli hit Adam on more than one occasion. Tina intervened as best she could. Every day brought one more thing she dealt with in the course of life. She wore blinders to survive, but now slowly remembered Tamara's words about abusers, so she resolved to prove Artie wrong and make him desire her again, which she hoped would cause his negative behavior to stop.

The only family member Artie treated consistently well was Maria. Around her, he acted charming, attentive, the best child she could have. He loved to hear people compliment him for being a good son.

★   ★   ★

JANUARY 1999

Artie's performances amazed critics and audiences and put him in high demand. Since he had recently become the LA City Symphony's official pianist, he cut back on his tours and focused on local work. He continued to be popular for his eccentric and outrageous behaviors, which always brought him attention. At a July 4th concert, where he performed *Rhapsody in Blue* at the Hollywood Bowl, he wore an Uncle Sam hat and for his encore pecked out Yankee Doodle on the piano with his nose to orchestral accompaniment. A laughing, cheering crowd rewarded him for his efforts.

Artie remained a master of unexpected exaggeration with props or hats. Ever a popular oddball known for his humor, he once faced the audience while performing with his hands behind his back. Another time, he played blindfolded at rehearsal. He always had something up his sleeve. At a concert, Artie delighted the audience by playing *Chopsticks* with actual chopsticks between his teeth. He often placed an Argentine flag, flowers, lollipops or other items in or around the piano. Yet, his perceived unexpected repetitiveness became the expected in his quest for attention.

When he played onstage for musicals, he wore a fedora perched jauntily on his head making him unmistakably noticeable. He continued to manipulate, charm and make others laugh, He even inspired a cartoon character named Arthur Ibis, a piano-playing birdlike creature, in a popular children's show. Artie no longer told anyone that he was a finalist at the piano competition in his 20s. Instead, he said he won first prize. He also made sure everyone knew he had acted in a movie. Few people realized his behavior drastically differed at home.

After Artie's blood pressure shot up dangerously high, he reluctantly went to the family doctor, who convinced him to lose weight, but after 40 pounds, Artie resorted back to his old eating habits. Tina said nothing, because confrontation made him defensive, but she begged him to stop giving junk food and snacks to the children.

Suddenly, the snacks disappeared, and Tina wondered if he had really listened to her, but soon, she found bags of potato chips in the linen closet, chocolate doughnuts under the sink, and a stash of candy bars in the back of the cupboard. He wanted his snacks to himself.

★　★　★

APRIL 1999

Tina still excused much of Artie's behavior to work-related stress and hoped to improve their relationship again. She remembered their blissful reunion on their Caribbean cruise, so when their 11th anniversary drew close, she knew she wanted to take advantage of that opportunity and suggested a resort vacation to Artie. He was amenable, and they booked a week in Maui together at a luxurious resort. However, Tina had some guilt, because she did not include the children, but she told herself they would have a family vacation in the future.

They arrived in the afternoon at the beautiful oceanfront resort and were shown to their luxurious room with its view out to the sea. One day melted into another. After breakfast, they swam mornings in the large tropical pool before they spent the day sightseeing. They took a bus to Hana, and after the heart stopping ride up the mountain road, they saw the magnificent vista. They also enjoyed a whale watch and often meandered around Lahaina before dinner. At night, they wandered out among the stars, which reflected in the dancing sea. Tina became confident that things were now finally okay once and for all. Their freedom on the island along with their renewed passion filled Tina with joy. It was with a tinge of sadness they both returned back home.

Four weeks later, after a late period, Tina tested positive on a pregnancy test. That puzzled her, because Artie supposedly had a vasectomy years ago. When he returned home from rehearsal that evening, she greeted him and told him to be seated.

"I'm tired. It's been a long day. I just want to relax and have a beer."

"I'm pregnant."

"What?"

"I don't understand. You had a vasectomy years ago."

"Nope. Never did. I changed my mind, because. I didn't want anyone cutting me there." He glared at her, his voice tinged with anger. "Bitch, this is your fault."

Tina's mouth twisted into a grimace of tears. "Please calm down."

His voice in response became even louder. His face turned red and his eyes, black as flaming coal, bored into Tina's demeanor. "Take care of it." He said. "No more kids." He went out into the night and slammed the door. Tina heard him start his car and drive off.

She curled up in bed, and sobbed softly. When the soft touch of a hand grazed her neck, she turned around to see Adam, who gazed at her with childhood confusion in his grey eyes. Then, Leli climbed up on the bed and embraced her mother. Immediately, Tina wiped her face, to hide her tears, got up and hugged them tightly to reassure them. She forced a smile, as she put them to bed.

After Tina washed her face and changed into her nightgown, she picked up the phone and called Sydney.

"Oh Tina, how wonderful. Mazel Tov. How far are you along?"

"About a month."

"Are you excited?"

"Artie isn't. In fact, he's really pissed off. He wants me to get an a–b–o–r."

"What?"

"He told me to 'take care of it'."

"Fuckin' asshole. What will you do?"

"I don't know." Tina choked through her tears. "I was thrilled when I found out about the baby, but he doesn't want any more children."

"He lied to you about the vasectomy. Do you want the baby?"

"I love him or her already."

"You know, it's your body and your choice alone whether you want to keep the baby. Do you understand that?"

"I don't want him to stay angry."

"Whatever happens, you need to make the choice. You make good money, right?"

"Decent. We're not rich."

"If he left you, could you support the baby and your other kids?"

"By hell or high water. My kids come first. I would manage somehow."

"Okay. There's your answer. Your kids come first. What do you want to do?"

"I'm going to have this baby."

"If that's what you really want, tell him to go to hell if he objects."

When Artie got home that evening, he got ready for bed. When Tina told him her decision straight to his face, and he gave her the silent treatment for two days. Devastated, she hoped he would change his mind. He ignored her, and their sex life came to an abrupt halt.

Over the next few months, as Tina's pregnancy advanced, Artie poked fun at her, insulted her, then laughed and told her it was just a joke. He called her a *vaquita*, little cow, and joked that her large belly could carry an entire herd. He patted Tina's stomach and proudly told others he was a good shot. Tina tried to laugh; after all, the whole world was a joke to him, yet she hurt inside. Still, she told herself she was too sensitive. After all, he was such a likeable, popular guy.

Maria welcomed the news; she adored her grandchildren, and when Tina's ultrasound showed a daughter, Maria spoke excitedly about new outfits she would sew for her new little *nieta*.

★   ★   ★

JANUARY 2000

One late afternoon in mid-January, Tina's water broke, and she went into labor. She called and left messages for Artie on his cellphone and at the rehearsal hall. Almost in panic mode, Tina made some additional phone calls. Maria came over within a few minutes to watch the children, and Tina took a taxi to the hospital, where her contractions become closer and more intense, but she sensed something was wrong. The doctors confirmed the baby's position and heartbeat as abnormal, so Tina underwent an emergency C-section and also had her tubes tied.

She awoke but faded in and out with grogginess as the nurse positioned her pillows.

"Congratulations Mrs. Diaz. How are you doing?"

"Did anyone stop by?"

"I'm sorry. No."

Gradually, Tina became more awake. Another nurse stopped by to check her vital signs.

"How are you feeling?"

"I'm awake, sort of. How is my baby? Is she okay?"

"She's fine," said the nurse. "She's beautiful and healthy. Are you ready to meet her?"

Tina smiled weakly and nodded.

The nurse returned with Sarah Rachel Diaz and handed her to Tina, who gingerly sat up in bed and winced. The baby resembled a tiny china doll with her large round alert eyes, a delicate nose, rosy lips, and a full head of dark curls. Tina held her close and delighted in her soft sweetness. Little Sarah looked up and suddenly clasped her tiny hand around Tina's index finger.

Tina heard Artie's loud laugh as he approached the room and joked with the nurses. With an obvious strong scent of alcohol, he walked over to the bed, bent down and kissed his wife. As they posed for photos, Artie awkwardly held his new daughter like a parcel, after which he diverted his attention to the pretty nurse who took the photos.

Still in recovery, Tina returned home a few days later. Weak, fatigued and exhausted, she just wanted to sleep; Maria almost lived at the house now, absorbed with childcare and chores while Artie was often out evenings, rehearsing. He now had also begun playing poker with his friends.

When Sarah was three months old, Artie told Tina there would be no sex until she was a better wife and focused on his needs. She thought to herself that he was angry, because she spent so much time with the baby, his unwanted child, so one night, she waited naked in bed and seduced him. To her unexpected horror, Artie renewed his breast milk obsession along with sexual interest in her, but now, afterward, all energy and life seemed to leave her body. Sleep, just sleep, she thought, covering her embarrassment and shame.

Artie demanded that Tina continue to nurse Sarah, until he decided she needed to stop. As she withered under his obsessive control and bad temper, she often wondered if their current postpartum sex life was even normal and whether adult men routinely got their rocks off by sucking women's lactating tits. However, she found the topic too embarrassing to discuss with anyone.

One day, she visited Artie at rehearsal to bring him lunch and noticed him speaking Spanish with another man. She smiled and caught his attention, but he continued his conversation. While she waited for him, Tina began to chat with a Chilean French horn player, who introduced herself as Dolores.

After Tina told Dolores she was Artie's wife, Dolores turned towards him with a frown. She listened to his conversation and then turned back to Tina.

"I worked with your husband for many years. You seem like a nice woman."

Tina thanked her.

Dolores continued. "I regret to tell you, but he is speaking disrespectfully about you to that Argentinean violinist."

Tina nodded slowly with apparent apprehension. "Would you mind translating?" Artie's Spanish slang was often too difficult for her to understand.

Dolores hesitated before she slowly spoke. "He is describing your body and sex life and says women are only good for sex. Now..." Dolores paused again. "He is talking about you nursing your baby and bragging..." She stopped.

"Thanks. I don't need to hear anymore."

Hurt and ashamed, Tina took action and immediately switched Sarah to bottled formula and until her milk dried up, she put cold cabbage leaves in her bra to sooth her aching breasts. Artie in turn acted offended that Tina had ignored his instructions and found excuses again not to be home.

★   ★   ★

SEPTEMBER 11, 2001

When Eva called Tina in late August to tell her she and Irving were coming to California to visit the family, Tina dreaded hearing the news. She remembered the family's last visit with the children in Florida, a few years before, which had been relatively pleasant, but critical Eva still criticized Tina at times about raising and disciplining her children. This would be Eva and Irving's first California visit since the 1988 wedding, so Tina hoped to welcome them, stay positive and let children enjoy their grandparents' first visit.

"I just found out this afternoon my parents will be coming mid-September to visit us for a week," Tina told Artie. "They're going on a cruise and then want to visit us, but they'll have to stay with Mama. There's no room here."

He frowned but said nothing. Tina continued, "I know you don't like them, Cielito, but I can't say no. They want to visit us, so please, It's only a week."

He shrugged his shoulders. "Your mom better be nice to me, because otherwise, you won't see me for the rest of their visit."

★　★　★

September 11 started off as a beautiful warm day with blue skies, but when Tina arrived at work, the day's disastrous events greeted her. She watched the breakroom television with her coworkers in horror, as the news recapped video of the plane crashes into the Twin Towers. Audible gasps echoed through the room. The cameras turned to the people jumping out of the top windows onto the ground below. Tina could not watch anymore.

Shaken, she returned to her desk. Tina remembered her many trips to the World Trade Center years ago. She loved the elevator ride to the 107th floor observation deck, where she captured city views with her Canon rangefinder. She remembered an old friend Jane from her college days. They had gone to different schools, but they had gotten together occasionally while Tina still lived in New York. Jane worked at Cantor Fitzgerald, and Tina met her for dinner on one occasion at the Windows on the World restaurant; soon after Tina moved away, they had lost touch. Now, Tina wondered if her friend had perished or survived. After a moment, Tina bowed her head and said a silent prayer for the victims and their families. She wiped her wet eyes and blew her nose as she touched her family photos on her desk.

Children were on the hijacked planes. What if they had been her children? The horrible thought sent a shockwave through her. Tina closed her computer documents; she could not focus on this terrible day.

Shortly after lunch, the receptionist called Tina downstairs to the reception area. Two police officers and another man in a dark suit awaited her.

"Are you Ms. Diaz?"

"That's me."

"May we talk, please?"

"Is my husband in trouble?"

"Let's go to the conference room." Tina walked ahead, and the men followed behind. She opened the door to the room, and everyone took a seat.

The man in the dark suit identified himself as an airline representative. "Ms. Diaz, I regret to inform you that Eva and Irving Weinstein were on United Flight 175, which crashed this morning into the World Trade Center. You were listed as an emergency contact. I'm sorry." Then he requested she come to the airport office for further instruction.

Stunned, she did not respond. "Let us take you home, Ms. Diaz." A pale Tina let the officers lead her out of the building and drive her home in a squad car.

Numb, she barely made it through the next days. She would not eat or sleep. She cried off and on. Tina's devastation was not so much because she missed her mother and stepfather, but because she envisioned their last experiences. Between floods of tears, Tina wondered what Eva and Irving experienced in their last moments with the hijackers. Were they terrified? Did they realize what was happening? Did the hijackers injure them beforehand or single them out because they were Jewish? These questions haunted Tina, and the more she thought about them, the harder she wept.

Yet, she felt both guilt and relief that her mother would no longer be around to create drama. Tina also wondered at one point whether Eva had provided for her grandchildren in her will but quickly admonished herself for these thoughts; she should not think in monetary terms about the dead.

The search for victims turned from rescue to recovery. Finally, Tina and Artie were flown to New York where they received a hotel room and meal vouchers. The brightest part of the visit for Tina was seeing Sydney again and meeting Nathan, a charming little boy who resembled his mother. Artie was also delighted to reconnect with LaRhea, and they both had a private jam session together at her home.

Tina provided a DNA sample as did one of Irving's sons. During the following two weeks, everyone sat on edge and hoped that once fragments and body parts underwent DNA tests, one or the other parent's remains could be identified. Sadly, no matches were found, so Tina and Artie finally returned home.

During those days, Artie showed his wife unprecedented tenderness. He brought home takeout for the family and flowers for Tina. He massaged his wife's back as he kissed and comforted her. He cancelled some upcoming concerts and helped soothe her emotional pain.

Irving's oldest son Michael, who lived in Fort Lauderdale, was the executor of the couple's will. He arranged a memorial service in Florida for mid-October. Tina and Artie flew with their three children to Florida to attend the service.

They stayed at the Eva and Irving's condo a week beforehand; everything looked untouched. The place was eerily quiet, but Tina could feel her mother's presence, her perfume, the way she wore her elegant clothes. She heard her mother's voice in her head. At night, she dreamed Eva stood near her, held and kissed her. Nothing changed though in reality, except that her mother was gone.

Tina went through her mother's jewelry box, but only found costume jewelry. Then, she remembered whenever Eva left town, she always buried her best jewelry at the bottom of the laundry basket. Tina reached under the dirty towels and other items where she found a box full of fine jewelry. Eva owned a heavy gold bracelet with her engraved name, gold necklaces and earrings along with several rings and a diamond tennis bracelet. Tina found her parents' gold wedding band engraved with MAX on the inside. At the bottom of the box lay another heavy gold bracelet with an inscription: *Dear Eva, Thank you. With Best Wishes for the Future, John Farswell, Farswell & Pryne.* Tina thought to herself this was an unusually generous farewell gift for someone who worked at the company for only three years. She had never seen her mother wear it.

Tina lifted a shoebox off a closet shelf. When she opened the lid, she saw old family photos taken in Europe before the War. Tina sat down and put the box on her lap; she had never seen these photos before. A photo of Eva as a teenager indicated to Tina the pictures belonged to her mother. One photo showed Eva dressed in an 18th century costume obviously singing opera. On the back, the photo just said "Susannah." Tina assumed Eva was in a performance of Mozart's opera *The Marriage of Figaro.* Indeed, fragile German program notes from a 1949 *Figaro production* lay at the bottom of the box. Tina saw two 1946 wedding photos of Max and Eva at the refugee camp. Eva wore a white dress and a veil, while Max wore a somber suit. They would have been 26 and 36 years old. *Eva und Max Perlstein* was written on the back of the photo;

Several photos showed unknown individuals including three photos of a little boy with the name *Jakob* written on the back. He appeared about two years of age in one picture and a year or two older in the other photos. Tina assumed these were her photos of her uncle, as she vaguely remembered her mother once mentioned a much younger brother, who died in Auschwitz as a child without ever mentioning his name.

Another photo shocked Tina and made no sense to her. Dated *February 21, 1937* on the back, Eva wore a bridal gown with a long train and veil, held a bouquet and stood next to a tall well-dressed man, who appeared slightly older. Eva had never mentioned being married before; now, Tina wondered what other secrets her mother had.

She packed the jewelry and photo boxes along with her baby album in her luggage.

★ ★ ★

A few days later, the family attorney read the shocking will, signed by both husband and wife. Irving's sons inherited the entire estate worth several million dollars, while Tina and her family received nothing. Stunned and devastated, she reeled not only at the straightforward rejection, but she had been totally ignorant her parents had possessed such wealth. Although most of the money had belonged to Irving, Tina was sure Eva intentionally encouraged disinheriting her daughter, and this wounded Tina to her innermost core. Selfish and narcissistic, Eva had no problem with revenge. As a final insult to their strained relationship and her dislike for her son-in-law, Eva had turned her back to Tina and her family with a slash of her pen when she signed the will.

The couple's remains were never found, buried in the abyss of debris that was once the World Trade Center.

★ ★ ★

FEBRUARY 2003

Thanks to Sydney, Artie had received a call last October from LaRhea's agent, who booked him to accompany the famous singer at her Manhattan concert. Artie immediately agreed, especially because they had always worked well together in the past, the keyboard solos highlighted the music and the salary was excellent.

LaRhea was now a superstar, in high demand for her dazzling performances. She had achieved national fame not only for her magnificent voice, her beauty and stage presence, but also because she was transgender and an object of fascination for others. One of LaRhea's signature songs in concert was her version of Billie Holliday's "God Bless the Child," and her shows sold out every time.

Sydney lived in LaRhea's shadow and worked at the Metropolitan Museum of Art as an administrator. They lived in an elegant midtown Manhattan condominium with every luxury available and a governess for Nathan.

On the night of the concert, Tina huddled in her heavy coat to ward off the cold, which covered her gold cocktail dress. She thought Artie looked handsome in his tuxedo. A limo brought them to the packed sold-out theater. LaRhea wore a stunning low-cut long red dress which hugged her body. Her outfit and her elaborate beehive hairdo reminded Tina of old Diana Ross photographs. Dressed head to toe in silver, Sydney sat with Tina in the audience.

Artie performed keyboard on stage as lead musician along with a bass player, two guitarists, and a drummer. When LaRhea burst into "God Bless the Child," the audience went wild, cheering and clapping for several minutes.

After the successful concert, Tina was very proud of her husband.

The next morning, the *New York Times* posted a glowing concert review, which raved over LaRhea, her musicians and. mentioned Arturo Diaz's spectacular piano performance. Tina and Artie read the review at breakfast, whooped and cheered, embraced and kissed. That day was also Artie's birthday, so after breakfast, they explored Manhattan together and visited the Brooklyn Botanical Gardens. In the evening, they had dinner at a famous Argentine restaurant in the theater district, the Chimichurri Grill and celebrated with champagne. In addition, Artie downed two whiskey shots.

Tina's cell phone rang. Sydney sounded somber.

"Can we meet for lunch tomorrow? We need to chat."

"I'll ask what Artie's plans are." He overheard the conversation through the phone. "No, you go ahead," he said. "I have some business to take care of."

Dressed in an elegant suit, Sydney's perfectly styled dark straightened hair flowed around her shoulders. She looked a world apart from her casual self in the past. They met at a delicatessen near the Museum.

Tina ordered cheese blintzes and latkes while Sydney ordered a pastrami sandwich.

"How do you like your job? You look so elegant."

"It's great. I have always loved art, so this job was really a great opportunity. I mostly manage fundraising, a talent I never knew I had, but I'm pretty good at it." She laughed.

"You're so bright, you can do anything, you know," said Tina.

"How is everything your way?"

Tina nodded. "Okay."

"That's good," continued Sydney. "I'm glad someone is happy."

Tina shook her head. "I didn't say I'm happy. Right now, things are okay. What's going on with you?"

"LaRhea and I are having major problems. She's as mean to me as Artie has been to you. Sorry to bring that up, but I'm breaking up with her. We fight all the time. She uses drugs and surrounds herself with phonies. I've had enough. I miss LA and am looking for a job there."

"What about Nathan? I hope you don't have an ugly custody battle."

"She doesn't care about me or him. She'll probably fight with me over child support, so I'm not going to ask for any. I've been squirreling money away for some time, and I just want a clean break. I'm going to tell her that I'm staying with my parents in Brooklyn for a few days, but in reality, I need to fly to LA as soon as possible to find an apartment. Can I stay with you?"

"Of course." In spite of sad feelings over Sydney's plight, Tina knew she would be thrilled to have her friend living in LA again, so they could see each other often.

After lunch, Sydney had to return to work. Tina gave her a hug. "Call me once you have your plans."

"Thanks." Sydney hurried out the door so she would not be reprimanded for being late as Tina hurried back to the hotel. Artie was in the room taking notes and scoring music. Tina felt relieved at seeing him after she remembered the Buenos Aires incident.

They attended a symphony concert that evening at Avery Fisher Hall, and two days later, they flew back home to Los Angeles. Tina said nothing about Sydney and LaRhea's breakup to Artie, because she knew he would immediately notify the star of her partner's intentions.

★　★　★

APRIL 2005

Sydney worked as a fundraiser for a major nonprofit arts organization and lived in Orange County in a beautiful condo. Although they spoke often by phone, Sydney was too busy most of the time for in-person meetings. She traveled extensively, and on weekends, stayed busy with Nathan, now almost eight. When they did have time, the two women visited, and Sarah and Nathan played together. The friendship stayed firmly cemented.

The 9-11 investigation lasted for years. Human remains were discovered, but Eva and Irving's remains were never identified. Tina continuously thought about life. She no longer believed in a deity, although she took her children to temple on a regular basis, sent them to after-school Hebrew classes, and celebrated the Jewish holidays. She did everything except keep kosher and believed at least, she was doing her part as a Jewish mother.

The children were growing up, but dealing with Adam became increasingly difficult for Tina. He was 16 and defiant toward his mother; often, he refused to listen, rolled his eyes or got into a shouting match with her. He played Tina against Artie, who usually acquiesced to his son. Adam had become a proficient pianist, and Artie always doted on him and praised him.

Leli at age 13 also had her difficult moments and defiantly shouted, went to her room and slammed the door when faced with discipline or refusal. Still, she was not as difficult to deal with as Adam, plus she avoided her father, who continued to be cool and indifferent to her.

Thankfully, both children had good grades.

Pretty Sarah at five charmed everyone with her outgoing personality and appearance. Set apart from her siblings by age, she had her own life, playing with her friends. Artie was also pleased that she showed musical talent at the piano, and Sarah clearly adored her father, who loved to show her off in public but often ignored her at home.

Overwhelmed at times with her full-time job and the household, Tina continued to cope with Artie's controlling behaviors. When he became angry, he now always threatened divorce, so she dared not oppose him. Withdrawn and depressed, she lacked confidence, gained weight and except for an occasional outing with Sydney who was now living back in LA with Nathan, socialized little outside of the children's activities. Sometimes, it seemed to her nothing mattered anymore.

★   ★   ★

MAY 2006

Diligent about obtaining the freshest, healthiest food for her family, Tina especially loved neighborhood ethnic groceries. Gino's Italian deli near her office featured incredible Italian specialties; the store sold the finest olive oil and balsamic vinegars, along with the best pasta sauce in town. The main showcase displayed a large selection of Italian cheeses, meats, and antipasto, while Italian desserts behind a glass display greeted visitors. In fact, celebrities often shopped there.

Tina especially loved the deli's special provolone cheese. Sometimes she also brought home cannoli for dessert or mortadella sausage, pancetta, or fresh pasta as a rare treat for the family. Gino, the owner, always greeted Tina, knew her by name, and welcomed her every time she shopped there.

One day after another marital argument, she stopped at Gino's after work. She thought that a nice Italian dinner would put everyone in a better mood. A tall man smiled at her from behind the counter. She returned the smile.

"Hi, there," said the man. "How may I help you?"

"Hi," said Tina. "Are you new here?"

"I'm Gino's nephew Nick Romano. I'm filling in for him, since he's on vacation in Italy for a few weeks." Nick reached out and shook her hand.

"Nice to meet you."

"I just moved here from Brooklyn to further my acting career."

"Well, I hope you're successful. Maybe I'll see you in the movies."

He laughed. "I hope so too. That's my goal."

"Well then, Hollywood is the place for you," said Tina.

Tina thought he'd make the perfect movie star by appearance alone. Mesmerized, she thought to herself she had never seen such a handsome man in person before. Nick appeared in his mid-thirties, with a chiseled physique, short curly black hair, and deep piercing green eyes. His dark olive skin showed off his well-defined features. Tattoos covered his arms. He flashed perfect teeth and a gorgeous smile as he pulled a packet of salami from the back fridge.

"I would think that with your looks and charisma, you'll be a star," said Tina.

Nick paused as he tied his red apron tighter around his waist. "You're not so bad yourself." Tina blushed.

"So, are you married?" he asked.

She nodded. Nick continued, "I hope your husband appreciates you. You're one sexy woman. I hope you don't mind I said that," said Nick. "I can't stop looking at you."

Flustered, Tina did not respond. She turned toward the showcase and forgot what she wanted; Nick took her focus away. As she spoke to him, she could feel her heart pound in her chest.

Their eyes locked together. "I want to fuck you," he said. Tina stood and said nothing, so Nick calmly locked the front door as he put up a sign, 'Back in an Hour'. He took Tina's hand as he led her through the back of the store directly into a house.

"Where are we?" she asked.

"Gino's house. I'm staying here until he gets back."

"That's really conve…." Tina could not finish the sentence as. Nick kissed her with an intensity she had not experienced in a long time. As ardor arose in her, her whole body ached. She wanted Nick more than ever.

As their kisses heated up, Nick took her hand again as he gently led her to the bedroom. In the darkened room, Nick swiftly unbuttoned Tina's blouse. He unhooked and pulled off her bra, hungrily taking her nipple in his mouth. Her lace panties flew off into the corner when he pulled down her pants. She unbuckled his belt and reached down into his pants. She put her hand around his rather large penis. He slipped off his clothing, and they lay down together naked on the bed. Nick pressed his hard muscles against her. Almost immediately, his hands and tongue traveled over her body, which intensely aroused her. As Tina writhed in pleasure, Nick mounted and entered her. He controlled himself well although inside her. He continued to thrust back and forth and kept caressing her with his fingers until she reached a powerful orgasm. Tina writhed and screamed as she let herself go with abandon. Nick held her firmly against him. Meanwhile, his penis stayed hard inside her. As soon as she was calm, Nick began to stimulate her again. All the while, Nick controlled himself as Tina's cries and moans increased until she reached a second orgasm. Finally, Nick let himself go with passionate thrusts inside her until he himself reached an intense climax.

They lay next to each other breathless. Tina could barely drag herself out of bed; her limbs were weak, yet she was delirious and happy. Nick rose and sauntered into the bathroom where he ran the shower. Tina could not help but stare at his buttocks.

He walked back into the bedroom and held out his hand to Tina. He led her to the bathroom and continued holding her hand as she stepped into the shower.

The water cooled her bare skin. Tina and Nick washed each other in between gentle kisses. He asked when he could see her again; he hoped soon.

Tina took off work early the next day to return to the deli. Nick again put the sign on the door before they left for the house. Sex between them intensified. Nick threw Tina again into an orgasmic frenzy with his intense sexual technique. There was little actual conversation between them. They never spoke about their personal lives, and Tina never asked Nick any questions.

One day, he told her he was obsessed with snuff films and watched them constantly online. Tina had never heard of them, and Nick casually mentioned they depicted actual deaths. That shocked her, so she asked him why he liked those films so much. He responded with a laugh they were entertaining. Puzzled, Tina dropped the subject.

After their encounters and a shower, Tina had to leave, always with reluctance. Happiness overflowed within her as she thought constantly about Nick. She slipped away with him as often as she could. Their steamy erotic affair offered powerful satisfaction.

In comparison, Artie's lack of pride in his appearance and his behavior disgusted her. He only became neat for an event. Usually his unkempt hair, worn T-shirts, pants with torn hems dragging scraggly hanging threads and cheap sandals or sneakers never bothered him. Tina began to fix his pants, but he became angry, so she left him alone. Leli called his look "Early American Thrift Store". When she now compared Artie to her immaculately groomed handsome lover, she visualized herself falling in love with Nick and out of love with Artie.

That changed when one afternoon a few weeks later, as she lay blissfully in Nick's arms after sex, they chatted with each other.

"Tina, did I tell you Gino is coming home next Tuesday?"

"So soon already?" she asked. "What will you do?"

"I rented an apartment. You see, my wife and two kids will soon be moving here from New York to join me."

The news punched Tina in the chest. He ignored her and continued.

"Theresa is such a gorgeous redhead, a real knockout. She's also a great mom. My two boys are six and eight. They play baseball and love cartoons, trucks, and trains. Did your kids like those things too at that age?"

Tina stayed silent. She got up and quickly dressed. "I have to go." She turned to him. "Thanks for everything. See ya." She hurried out the door.

Wife and two kids? Tina somehow always assumed Nick was single. Devastated and mortified, the truth hurt her deeply. Her eyes burned with tears. Behind the steering wheel in her parked car, Tina began to sob hysterically. What did she expect after all? To Nick, she was nothing more than a horny cougar.

Yet after a while, Tina realized the affair had taught her what she missed in her life. She was no longer self-conscious about her body. Nick had made her feel sexy and in control.

Her powerful sex drive had awakened once again with its former intensity, yet, as she experienced all these things again for a brief period, they disappeared as quickly as they had appeared in her life.

★　★　★

SEPTEMBER 2006

Artie hired photographers and artists to draw and photograph him. His symphony office was devoid of family pictures but filled with photos of himself with celebrities including Hollywood and Broadway stars and sport figures including Argentine soccer stars.

Adam continued to emulate his father. A handsome young man about Artie's height with short brown hair, a well-trimmed beard and striking gray eyes, he used his looks and charm to his advantage. He was more reserved than his father, but at times, Adam was arrogant and self-centered. He argued often with Tina and his sisters and rebuffed his mother's attempts to convince him to continue his education. Yet under his bravura, Tina sensed an inner strength and hoped her son would change his attitude as he got older.

Strong-willed and determined, Adam remained vague about his future plans, and avoided being home whenever possible. He hung out regularly with his best friend Mike on his family's farm. Together, they fixed cars and shot piled-up cans in the woods for target practice. They secretly smoked pot in the shed and drove around in Mike's F150 pickup. Tina worried about Adam to no end, but the more she expressed her concern, the more defiant he became, so she shrugged her hands in despair, because by complacence, Artie supported his son's actions, because Adam was still a proficient pianist who practiced regularly in his father's studio.

Leli, in contrast, was pleasant, social and highly intelligent. Attractive, Slim with an athletic build, her wavy dark hair contrasted with her fair skin. She had a small oval face with a gently sloping Roman nose, deep-set slanted brown eyes, and her thin upper lip and fuller lower lip accented her small teeth when she smiled. There was no question though, she strongly resembled Artie.

Leli was of average height, but something about her appeared much taller, as she was exceptionally mature for her age. Determined to be a nurse, she excelled in math and science and as an avid swimmer, participated in the school swim team. Notably, she read constantly, watched the news and had strong opinions ranging from politics to health. An excellent debater at her age, she always won arguments. Yet, she had a kind and compassionate heart.

Sarah was beautiful, gentle and focused on music. At age five, she began piano lessons with Maria, developed a good sense of rhythm and became an excellent sight-reader. Music surrounded her with fire and with passages so beautiful, it made her heart ache and moved her to tears of joy. Since she especially loved to sing and was always learning new songs which she sang to herself all day, Tina enrolled her in the Los Angeles children's chorus and made sure she attended rehearsals. Soon, Sarah became infatuated with opera, which opened another world for her. She loved romantic plots and frequently fantasized that she was the heroine. Sarah begged Tina to take her frequently to the library and to live opera performances at the LA Opera. Afterward, she always wanted to wait by the stage door to meet the singers.

One day after school, Leli sat at the kitchen table with her laptop. Tina had taken the afternoon off and relaxed with a book. The school bus's brakes squealed at the usual time near the house. Sarah walked into the house but with loud sobs.

"Baby, what's wrong?" Tina got up and quickly walked over to her youngest daughter.

The child could barely speak. "Today, I told my class about opera. Nobody knew about *Tosca* or *Madame Butterfly*. Nobody ever heard of Maria Callas, that famous singer."

"Is that why you're crying?" Leli looked puzzled.

Sarah nodded. Tina smiled. "Most kids don't know as much about as you do about stuff like that, so you taught them a bit today about something new. You did a good deed." Tina opened the refrigerator, pulled out some fruit and set it on the table. Sarah calmly bit into an apple. Leli reached over and took a pear.

Tina sighed. She knew Sarah's musical taste was quite sophisticated, especially for an almost-seven-year-old child. Her three very different children posed a unique challenge.

★ ★ ★

OCTOBER 2006

After dinner one evening, Tina checked the family bank account and reviewed their bills. She saw Artie again had not deposited his share of the household expenses. Recently, she had shielded him from some bill collectors who called and had simply paid the bills herself. Tina closed her eyes; she dreaded having to deal with him constantly about financial issues.

Tina walked into his studio where he was busy scoring a piano part for an upcoming show.

"Cielito, you forgot again to put money into the checking account."

"I haven't thought about it. I'm too busy." He did not look up.

"Please take care of it. I need to pay bills."

"When I get time," he snapped. "Now leave me alone. I said I'm busy."

Two days later, he still had not added funds to the account. Tina was not surprised, because this occurred on a regular basis. Sometimes when he added funds, he put in less than the agreed-upon amount.

After dinner, Tina confronted him again. "Artie, I need money now, please."

"I told you I would get to it when I get a chance."

"Now is your chance," said Tina. "Three bills are due."

Artie frowned at her, got up and wrote her a check from his account for the difference. Tina took the check and took his hand; he pulled it away. Her eyes burned with pain. She knew she would cry any second. "Please, Cielito. Don't give me a hard time over money and bills. I manage the best I can, but it's hard for me to handle everything alone."

He looked away. "Spend less."

The next afternoon, when Tina answered the phone, a businesslike female voice asked to speak to Arturo Diaz.

"This is his wife. He's not here."

"This is the First National Bank credit department. Your husband's bill is two months overdue."

"No kidding. Thanks. He'll take care of it today."

Ten minutes after she hung up, the phone rang again. This time an angry male asked for Artie.

Tina repeated that he was out.

"I'm calling about your husband's debt. Your husband is three months behind on his personal loan payment."

"I know nothing about this."

"Well, you better tell him that if he doesn't pay up, we'll take him to court, and soon," the man shouted at her in an angry tone.

"We'll take care of it," Tina reassured the debt collector.

Artie had never told her about these debts. He fell behind on bills she never even knew existed. When she confronted him that evening, Artie became angry. "It's my business," he replied.

"It's mine too. Why have you been hiding this stuff from me? As your wife, I want to see the bills."

"You don't need to see them." He glared at her.

Tina frowned. "Any significant money matters concern both of us. I don't like it when you keep secrets from me. What did you need this money for? Your poker games?"

He went to his desk, pulled out several paper bills and threw them into Tina's face. "Here," he replied. "You take care of them." He went into his studio and shut the door.

She called Sydney who listened and said, "I'm not surprised he sneaks around with money. Is he still drinking?"

"I see empty liquor bottles in the trash. He comes home sometimes with alcohol on his breath. He is never drunk though. He loses his temper if I say anything, so I don't."

"I remember you told me one time about that Princess Diana incident."

"That was bad. He's not easy to live with. We're now in serious debt. He took out some secret loans, possibly for poker, booze and other shit. $11,000, Sydney."

"Holy shit."

"I will pay it off somehow. Otherwise, it will ruin our credit."

"If you need money, I'll lend it to you." "Thanks but I'll manage."

"He's such an ass. Why do you protect him so much?"

"He's my husband." She paused. "Forget what I said about him needing money for shit. I'm probably overreacting."

"I doubt it. Why second-guess yourself? Is he treating the kids any better?"

"The same. Hot and cold. He still likes Adam best."

"Call me if you need me."

After the call, Tina stared for a long time at her wedding and engagement rings which caressed her left ring finger. She pulled them off and threw them into her nightstand drawer.

★   ★   ★

DECEMBER 2006

December was a busy month. On the 14th, Leli celebrated her 15th birthday with friends at Disneyland. The December 16th Hanukkah celebration marked a festive time for the family. Tina brought out the gilt menorah and set it on the side table. At sundown, Artie lit the Shamash. Afterward, he lit the first candle while Leli and Adam recited the blessings in Hebrew and in English.

We kindle these lights for the miracles and the wonders, for the redemption and battles you made for our forefathers, in those days at this season, through your holy priests. During all eight days of Hanukkah, these lights are sacred. We're not permitted to make ordinary use of them except for to look at them in order to express thanks and praise to Your great Name for Your miracles, your wonders and Your salvations.

Sarah with her melodic voice sang the Hanukkah song by herself. The others joined in after the first verse.

Hanukkah o Hanukkah
Come light the menorah
Let's have a party
We'll all dance the hora.
Gather 'round the table
We'll give you a treat
Sevivonim to play with and latkes to eat.

The family members went through the holiday gestures, ate food, and Sarah played with the dreidel on the floor, but the tension was there like a stretched rubber band ready to break.

The family visited Maria on Christmas Eve, and the next day, Artie had a gig at a celebrity's glamorous private party. Tina decided the rest of the family should volunteer at a homeless shelter to serve Christmas dinner to the poor. Although Sarah was too young to serve food, she came along. Tina wanted to make her children aware of others less fortunate than themselves.

Even Adam cooperated. Tina drove them downtown and found a serendipitous parking spot nearby on the empty streets. At the mission, they walked into the kitchen and Amy, the supervisor, greeted them. A pleasant woman, she wore a large blue apron over her jeans.

"Thanks for helping out," she said cheerily, as she led the family to the kitchen counter. She gave them plastic gloves, and everyone a task. Sarah counted out apples and bananas. Leli laid out silverware Adam mashed potatoes, and Tina cut up carrots. Other volunteers cooked, baked, and cut up vegetables and fruits.

Volunteers cut up and sliced the donated roast turkeys and hams on the food line. Pans of mashed potatoes, yams, cranberry sauce, stuffing, carrots, and green bean casserole accompanied the meats. Dozens of apple and pumpkin pies stood on the dessert table along with bowls of fruit.

The homeless formed a line which wound around the block. They knew the mission treated everyone with respect and waited patiently until doors opened for a good meal and some social interaction. At noon, the volunteers welcomed the guests, as the volunteers stood behind the counter at their stations. Tina dished out the green bean casserole to guests while Leli handled the yams. Adam stood at the dessert table with Sarah and handed out slices of pie with whipped topping.

Afterward, the family stopped at each table to chat with the guests. It saddened Tina to see many families there with young children.

An older homeless woman sat alone as she ate her meal, clad in old worn clothes, her gray cornrows stuck out haphazardly under her purple headscarf. Yet, she held her shoulders back and her head high with dignity in her eyes. She showed exquisite table manners and took dainty bites of her food, after which she delicately wiped her small mouth with the paper napkin. This person had obviously seen better times.

Tina and the children walked up and greeted her.

"Hi, and Merry Christmas to you. I hope you're enjoying your meal today."

The woman turned to Tina with a gap-filled smile.

"Thanks, honey. It's delicious. I'm enjoying it, all right. Do you work here?"

"I'm Tina, a volunteer. My family and I are helping out today."

"Well, nice to meet you. I'm Adella."

"That's a pretty name."

"You sound like you're from New York."

"Queens. How about you?"

"Newark," said Adella. "Home of my alma mater, Rutgers University." She noticed the surprised look on Tina's face. "I have a doctorate in psychology. Surprised that I'm homeless?"

Tina paused. "I have seen people from every background go through rough times. Adella, I work at the State Community Assistance Center. If you need me, I'll be glad to help you get extra services. Perhaps I can help you with senior housing and benefits."

Adella elegantly cut her meat and placed a forkful in her mouth. "Oh, that's really nice of you," she said. "I could use some help. Things have been rough for me the past few years."

Tina gave Adella her business card. "Come see me, and I'll make sure that you get assistance." She hoped Adella would follow up.

After the meal, the family helped the other volunteers with clean-up, before everyone left for home.

★   ★   ★

One day in early January, the receptionist notified Tina that she had a visitor. Puzzled, she walked out to the reception area, where Adella sat on the worn waiting room couch.

"Hi, Tina," she said. "I took you up on your offer to come see you for help."

Tina smiled. She genuinely liked this woman and greeted her. "It's so nice to see you again. Please come with me." Adella followed Tina to her desk.

"How may I help?" asked Tina.

"Please," Adella began to sob. "I need help so bad. I'm an addict. I've been arrested twice. I just got released from jail last week, and I'm scared."

"What's going on? Tell me more," Tina said as she handed Adella a tissue, but the woman had already wiped her eyes with her sleeve.

"All I think about is crystal meth and heroin. I'm clean right now, but I want my fix. I want it so badly, but I want to quit for good."

"Did the jail refer you anywhere?"

Adella shook her head.

Tina sat down and pulled up a list of rehabilitation treatment programs. "Let me see what's available." After she made a few calls, she hung up the phone, turned to Adella and smiled. "I found a place which will help you. Heaven House has a great rehab program. Does that sound good to you?"

Adella smiled. "I will do anything to get clean."

"Great," said Tina. "I'll help you."

"Thank you. Did I ever tell you about my life?" Tina shook her head.

"I grew up in a family of junkies, and I was raped when I was nine. As a clinical psychologist with a doctorate from Rutgers, I thought I escaped that path. One day, though, my boyfriend introduced me to drugs. I got hooked," Adella added.

"I'm so sorry," said Tina.

"It's a miracle I've survived all these years. I shot up every day." Adella stopped and held out her needle-pocked arms to Tina. "I'm 51, but I know I look 80. Drugs fried my brain; I can't work anymore," She paused and continued. "I came out here to stay with a relative. She did drugs too and died of an overdose. I lost my home and lived on the streets. I prostituted myself for drug money. The Lord has blessed me today."

She gave Tina a hug.

"I'm glad this is a fresh start for you," said Tina.

Tina logged off her computer and signed out. She drove Adella with her few belongings to Heaven House. Before they said goodbye, Tina told Adella she would stay in touch to check on her.

★   ★   ★

JUNE 2007

"I'm not ready for college yet," Adam told his mother right after his high school graduation. "I'm gonna get a job in tech support."

Tina dreaded hearing those words. She had suspected as such, because Adam had not applied to college in spite of her periodic reminders. "I don't know what to say. We planned all your life for you to go to college." She paused. "Does Jessie have anything to do with this?"

Jessie was Adam's girlfriend he had met during his senior year.

"Are you blaming Jessie? I thought you like her, because she's Jewish."

"That's not the point. You told me she's not going to college, and now you're doing the same thing. I told you before I don't think she's a good influence. She's too eccentric with that nose ring, pierced eyebrow and all those ear piercings. Also, I think her dark hair with all those blonde highlights looks awful."

"Stop. When you married Dad, you didn't care about his looks or how crazy he was. Jessie is great. You don't know her. Did I tell you she's from Orlando? You worked there."

Tina shrugged her shoulders. "Did you tell your father about your plans? He won't be happy. He wants you to study music and be a concert pianist."

"I haven't said nothing, because he'll get pissed off, but I don't give a shit. I can make more money and work from home."

When Artie heard the news that evening, he frowned but did not criticize his son. Instead, he kept encouraging Adam to keep playing piano.

Soon, Adam landed a part-time tech support job for a computer company and told Tina that Jessie had gotten a job as a Disneyland restaurant hostess but had to remove her piercings. He also joined the musician's union and played a few gigs.

One day, Tina heard a loud engine noise outside the house and looked out of the window to see Adam getting off a motorcycle. He held a helmet in his arm as he entered the house.

"Hi Mom," he greeted her. "Did you see my new wheels outside?"

"Where's your car?"

"Oh, I sold that old piece of junk."

"Who taught you how to ride a motorcycle? They're dangerous."

"Mike showed me, and I just got my license."

"Why didn't you say something?"

"It's none of your fuckin' business."

"Adam, I resent it when you're rude. I thought we went over that before."

He ignored the comment. "I've to tell you something. Jessie's homesick, so she got a job at Disneyworld and is moving back to Orlando in two weeks."

"You'll miss her, I'm sure."

"Um-that's the next thing I was going to tell you. I'm moving to Orlando with her."

"You're what?"

"We're getting an apartment together. When we get there, I'll find a job."

Tina backed away from him with her hand on her forehead, aghast at what she had heard. Adam broke into a smile. "I will get a computer job there. Did you know I'm an awesome hacker?"

"Isn't that illegal?"

"Not if you use it for good."

"Your father won't be happy about this for sure."

"Too bad. I gotta get away, Mom. Please take care of our Abuelita."

"You know I will."

"Gotta get over to check on Abuelita and then call Dad." Adam put on his helmet and left. Tina heard the motorcycle roar off into the distance.

Artie flew into a tirade when he heard Adam's news, blamed Tina and drove her to tears.

The following week, with most of their possessions shipped to Florida, Jessie and Adam left for Orlando on his motorcycle.

★   ★   ★

MARCH 2009

Time passed with much of life unchanged. Adella appeared to be on the path to recovery at the Heaven House rehabilitation program, and Tina respected her for her courage and intelligence.

One afternoon, Adella called Tina at the office.

"I don't want to bother you, but I have good news," she said. "I'm in touch again with my son. It has been years. He's a physician in Palisades, New Jersey and wants me to move back home with him, now that I'm clean."

"Is that something you want to do?" asked Tina.

"Oh, absolutely. I'm leaving next Friday."

"Oh, so soon, but I'm happy for you," said Tina. "We hope we stay in touch."

"You know it," said Adella.

On impulse, Tina said, "Would you like to come over for dinner Saturday night? You can meet my family."

"Are you sure?"

"Why not? We don't have a client relationship anymore. Now we can be friends."

"That would be lovely," said Adella.

Saturday afternoon, Tina picked Adella up at Heaven House. The older woman looked good with neatly styled hair, a green print dress and makeup. She carried a small black bag and wore matching shoes.

Tina complimented her. "You look well."

Adella smiled. "Life is changing for me."

At home, when Tina introduced Adella, Artie turned on his full charm. He took Adella into his studio, showed her his awards and concert scrapbook. He described the photos of himself, which hung on his studio wall and bragged about his achievements. When everyone sat down to a dinner of chicken and shrimp stir-fry, vegetables, rice, and salad, Artie fawned over Adella like a VIP guest.

"I read about your career. You're amazing. All those movies you made should have earned you an Oscar." He reached over and patted Adella's shoulder.

"What? I'm sorry, Artie, but I was never an actress."

"But I know I saw you perform."

"It wasn't me. Sorry. Once I was a psychologist and then was homeless with an addiction problem. Thanks to Tina who found me housing and help, I was able to get back on my feet."

Annoyed, he frowned as he stirred the food with his fork and looked up at his wife.

"You know I hate carrots."

"Sorry, I forgot to take them out of the recipe."

He set down his fork. "I'm not going to eat this *mierda,* this shit."

"I'm sorry, Cielito. Let me fix you something else."

Everyone else at the table fell into the deep silence due to discomfort faced from the confrontation.

Tina hurried into the kitchen, pulled a small pizza out of the freezer and put it in the microwave.

She returned to her seat. "Your dinner will be ready in a few minutes." Artie said nothing but scowled and gave her a reproachful look. In the meantime, Tina heard the microwave bell and returned with the pizza on a plate, which she set before him.

Artie looked at Tina. "I also told you I hate that dress. You told me you wouldn't wear it again."

"I'm sorry, dearest Cielito," said Tina. "I forgot." Her voice reflected a touch of irony. She piled food on her plate and began to eat.

"That dress is too low-cut," he continued. "Every man will look at you when you wear that."

"Oh, for goodness sake," Anger showed in Tina's face. "Stop it already."

"Mommy, can I have pizza too?" Sarah asked.

"Eat what is on your plate, please," snapped Tina.

The stressful silence continued throughout the meal.

Before Tina brought Adella home, they stopped at a diner, ordered coffee, and shared a piece of apple pie. "I apologize about Artie's behavior at dinner," Tina said.

Adella turned to her. "How often does he act this way?"

"It depends. At least he didn't yell and shout tonight."

"Let's talk a minute." Adella sat down next to her. "Your husband treated you badly this evening."

"He gets like that sometimes," said Tina "Stuff sets him off, and I just tune it out. He has always been like this."

"Does he treat the kids the same way?"

"He runs hot or cold with them, back and forth."

"Yet you're not that way," said Adella. "You're the rock that holds everything together."

Tina sighed. "I have thought many times about divorce. I keep hoping that things will improve, because I don't want to deprive the kids of their dad."

Adella thought for a moment. "He needs professional help. Tina, you're a strong woman. Please put yourself and the kids first. He has no right to treat you the way he does."

"I tried counseling, but he won't go," said Tina. "He tells me I'm the sick one, not him."

"What do you know about his childhood?" Adella's eyes stayed focused on Tina.

Tina told Adella what she knew about Artie's past.

"What is your relationship like with his mother?"

"We didn't get along well at first, but it's better now. I think she was overprotective of him, but I don't know why."

"Well something may have happened to him when he was a kid," said Adella, "but right now, I'm more worried about your situation. Abuse only gets worse." She continued, "Artie has obvious mental problems, and I want you to stay safe."

"But he is so intelligent and gifted, "said Tina. "Besides, everyone loves him and thinks he's great. How can he be that ill and such a successful musician?"

"That happens often. Those two things are completely separate. By the way. I didn't want to upset you, but one reason I'm going home to live with my son is because I was recently diagnosed with a glioblastoma brain tumor. The prognosis is not good. We may never see each other again, but I'll always remember what you did for me. Please take care of yourself and your children. I love you." She hugged Tina, went inside and closed the door.

Tina's eyes burned with shocked tears, but they stayed in touch by email, because Adella did not feel well enough to chat by phone.

Three months after her move, Adella passed away. Tina grieved and one night, as she got ready for bed, she thought about their conversation before Adella moved away. On the outside, Artie appeared outgoing, but he was really a loner in a way without close friends. He had neither insight nor awareness of when his behavior made him look like a buffoon. He also never seemed to understand or care how to interact with his wife and children, nor did he understand emotional intimacy, only sex. That was his expression of love, and Tina had accepted that.

Tina slowly began to see her husband in a different light, but she still profoundly loved him. Adella was right, but there was nothing Tina was ready to do about it.

★　★　★

SEPTEMBER 2009

Tina celebrated her 50th birthday quietly at a restaurant with Artie and her daughters. Earlier that day, she had received flowers from Jessie and Adam. Recently Tina had a lengthy and surprising conversation with her son. He told her that Jessie's family communicated and treated each other so well, that he realized he should have treated Tina and his sisters better. He actually apologized and then said he was going back to school while working in tech support. He planned to get a degree in cybersecurity, while Jessie focused on business and marketing.

That fall, Leli began nursing school at UCLA. Still living at home to save money, she moved into Adam's former larger bedroom. After she painted the walls a soft blue, she rearranged the furniture and added her own minimalistic touches.

Tina stopped by the open doorway and saw Leli working on her laptop at her small white desk. "Looks nice," Tina said.

"Thanks. I think it works for me," said Leli. She stopped and looked up. "Mom, I worry about you, because of your weight. Watch your diet and start exercising. Just go walking every day and join a gym. You can go there after work."

Tina shook her head as she looked at her daughter. "I know I need to do something, but you're always giving advice to everyone, and you need to stop. If people ask you, that's different, but don't unless asked, okay?"

"But I know what I'm talking about," said Leli "I'm telling you for your own good."

"Leli, please…" Tina stopped as Artie came down the hallway.

"Do we have any pizza left from last night?"

"Artie, you shouldn't eat pizza. It's bad for you. You need to lose weight and should watch your diet," Leli's voice was loud and clear. She never called him anything but Artie.

He walked into Leli's room and towered over her at her desk, glared at her with narrowed eyebrows and waved his index finger in her face and shouted, "Basta, Leli, basta." His face was red. "Leave me and my pizza the fuck alone. Do you hear me?" Leli cringed and turned pale. She thought Artie was going to hit her. Instead, he turned and went into his studio and slammed the door.

"Why are you bossing him around? It only aggravates him."

"I can't stand to see him like this. He's got to listen to me. I know all about health and nutrition."

"Maybe you do, and I'm sure you have good intentions, but please stop lecturing him," Tina sighed. "He'll never change, no matter what you say. He's hardly home anyway, and your nagging makes worse. We have enough problems with his bad temper already. All these fights are stressful to everyone. Just stop, okay?"

"He's always criticized me, Nena, this, Nena, that. Nena, you're not musical, so I'm not bothering with you. Fuck him, I'm not walking on eggshells anymore."

"So, is this revenge like in turn the tables?"

Leli did not answer the question but turned to her mother. "You guys fight a lot, and he picks on you all the time. I don't know why you're living with this asshole. If you see me in my room a lot, you'll know why. I have books to read. If you hear the TV on full blast, it's to drown out your arguments."

Tina's face darkened with sadness. "You triggered a memory," she told her daughter. "I always hid in my room to avoid my argumentative parents."

★   ★   ★

APRIL 2011

Two years later, little had changed overall, but Sarah's musical talents blossomed. Her piano technique improved, but she still loved singing most of all and with her exceptional bell-like voice for a young girl, she participated in the opera children's choir, the school choir and other musical activities. Tina took her everywhere, and Artie was usually busy and rarely present at her performances or recitals.

Artie had an upcoming concert in San Francisco, so he and Tina decided to take a short vacation there to celebrate his 52nd birthday.

His performance of the Rachmaninoff Piano Concerto no. 3 brought an excellent review in the *San Francisco Chronicle* the following morning. The couple celebrated and spent the day visiting the city.

"Cielito, I want to get you a gift, and you still haven't told me what you want for your birthday," said Tina at dinner. "I've asked you all week."

He shot her a mischievous look. Tina laughed. "Oh, I will fuck you anytime you want. Anything else?"

He laughed as he winked at her. "Bombónita, would you really give me anything I want?"

"Cielito, name your gift."

"Do you love me as much as I love you, mi vida?"

"Of course, and I'm so proud of you."

"Tell me more."

"I admire you and love you so much."

"You would give me anything, right? You would do anything for me?"

"Of course. Anything you want."

After dinner when Adam texted a birthday wish to his father, and Maria and the girls phoned him, the couple found themselves back at their hotel room, Artie found sensuous jazz on a cable television station. He took Tina in his arms, and they slowly awkwardly danced to the music, until he almost stepped on her foot.

"Cielito," she laughed. "You're no dancer."

He held her tightly. "Neither are you." They both laughed. He awkwardly bumped against her and hoarsely whispered in her ear. "Mi vida, remember you promised me anything for my birthday, right?"

She laughed. "I'll even serve it on a silver platter for you."

They collapsed on the bed while they continued to laugh. Artie sat up as he looked at her.

"I want a threesome. There is a beautiful girl someone recommended, who will provide services for us. I will pay her."

Tina pulled away from him. She shuddered and sat up with a horrified look in her eyes as she shook her head. "No. Not that. The thought makes me very uncomfortable. Please, anything else but that."

"You promised me anything for my birthday. Anything!" He pleaded with her. "Please, mi vida, I promise you'll enjoy my fantasy very much." His face was up against hers. She felt his beard scratch her cheek.

"Artie, I'm straight, plus I could not bear to see my husband make love with another woman. Please."

"How about if I let her give me head?"

Tina turned her face away.

He sounded impatient. "You always said you'd also be there for me if I needed you. I need this for my birthday."

Anxiously, Tina sank back down on the bed, her chest heaving with anxiety. Finally, she said, "You won't have sex with her?"

"Not if you don't want me to."

Tina did not respond.

Artie disappeared for a moment, then returned with a drink for her. "Here, my love. Drink this. You'll relax."

She sipped the strong drink. It took the edge off her anxiety. Her mind went blank.

"So, yes? I will call her right now."

Slowly Tina unzipped her dress and pulled it over her head. She continued to take off her clothes and when she was naked, she shivered and crawled under the sheets.

Artie made a quick call on his cell phone.

About 15 minutes later, there was a knock on the door. Artie answered, and a young blonde woman entered the room. She was tall and slim, and wore a short miniskirt and a low-cut top without a bra. Her white boots went up to her knees. Tina thought to herself that the woman looked like the stereotype of a prostitute. The hooker greeted them cheerfully with a British accent and introduced herself as Chanelle. Tina clutched her sheet around herself. Artie hugged Chanelle as he kissed her on the mouth. Tina quickly looked away. Lightheadedness overcame her. The room began to sway, and Tina realized the drink was spiked; everything around her seemed vague, distant and unreal.

Her mind spun and whirled. Through her dizziness, Tina saw the woman undress until she revealed her nude body with small uplifted breasts and a shaved pubic area, tattooed with a blue butterfly. It would have startled Tina if she had been less dizzy.

Artie excitedly hurried over to the bed and pulled Tina's sheet away. Exposed and vulnerable, Tina lay there as her head spun like a runaway merry-go-round; unreal dreams and distortions revolved around her. She heard Artie's voice in the far distance as he gently pushed her down on her back. Almost immediately, Chanelle got on top of Tina, kissed her body and tried to arouse her. Tina noticed Artie lay nude on his side propped up on one elbow; he grinned as he watched the women. Tina's dizziness and lethargy prevented her protests; nothing mattered anymore except the spinning motion in her head.

Chanelle touched and caressed Tina's body; she flinched. She heard Artie say something unintelligible to the hooker, who rubbed and sucked Tina's nipples. In between, Chanelle tried to put her tongue in Tina's mouth, but she resisted and turned her head away in disgust. Still extremely dizzy, she lay back in a daze as the Chanelle woman slid her tongue between Tina's legs, as Artie pinned back his wife's wrists. Tina was too dizzy to protest. She closed her eyes and rode it out on the tide rushing through her brain. Chanelle tickled and teased her. She finally brought Tina to orgasm, much to Artie's delight, but Tina did not feel pleasure. She only wanted her head to stop spinning, and this woman to get away from her.

Chanelle then climbed on top of Artie, who responded with a steamy kiss. Tina, through her now-hazy roller coaster agony, saw fellatio, then Artie slipped on a condom. Chanelle mounted him. After a few thrusts, moans, and thrashes, it was over.

Nauseous; Tina's stomach hurt worse than ever. Her mouth filled with saliva. She got up as fast as she could with her world spinning around her, staggered to the bathroom, and vomited into the toilet. A wave of nausea engulfed her again almost immediately as she collapsed on the tile floor and vomited again.

Artie walked into the bathroom. He threw the used condom in the wastebasket and pulled his robe off the back of the door. "Come say goodbye to Chanelle. She is ready to leave."

Tina shook her head. "I'm sick. Leave me alone."

He said nothing and shut the bathroom door. After a moment, Tina got up and ran the shower. She turned on the water as hot as she could tolerate, soaped up and scrubbed every inch of her skin until she was raw to wash away any trace of that encounter. After she finished, she slipped on her robe, walked and sat down in the large blue corner chair. Drained, Tina closed her eyes to calm herself and visualized a peaceful seashore where water splashed upon the rocks.

Artie's hands strayed inside her robe and interrupted her thoughts. He kissed her cheek.

"Thank you," he whispered. "You were wonderful. See. I knew you would enjoy it."

"I hated it!" Tina burst into tears. "It was awful." She pulled away from him, got up and threw herself on the bed with loud sobs. "I can't believe you put me through that I just can't. You promised me you wouldn't have sex with her. How do you think I felt?"

Artie sat next to Tina and kissed her lips.

"My love, you must understand; I couldn't help myself. It was the most exciting thing to watch both of you. When you came...." He paused. "I found it absolutely sensational. I used a condom with her, but I like your pussy better. Now, it's your turn."

"I'm not in the mood."

"Mi vida, it's my birthday. You said you would do anything for me plus give me all the sex I want."

"No more."

"Did you like the drink?"

"It made me sick. What was it?"

"I mixed some happy pills with bourbon and soda."

He kissed her mouth again as he played with her breasts. "No woman has as sexy a body as you, my bombónita." She stopped protesting as she knew it was useless to resist, as he pulled off her robe and slipped off his robe as well. Exhausted and distraught, Tina had no energy to fight him off. Ashamed about her own past affair, she rationalized to herself now she could not blame Artie for anything, since she also once cheated on him. Meanwhile, her husband made love to her as Tina's mind wandered away, back to the peaceful seashore.

★   ★   ★

The next day Tina could barely tolerate Artie. Her anger about this nightmarish incident mounted and burned inside her, and she wanted to distance herself from him in the worst way. On the way home, Artie was back to his old high-spirited self, while Tina barely tolerated sitting next to him on the plane. She pulled out her headset, closed her eyes and listened to music. When they arrived in Los Angeles, they picked up their car and headed home. Finally, Tina spoke.

"Artie, don't ever ask me again to do what we did yesterday evening. Ever."

He slammed on the brake so hard that Tina almost fell forward in spite of her seat belt and pulled the car over to the side.

"Selfish!" He shouted at her. "*Egoista!* All you think about is yourself. How about me? Che, you don't care what I need." Artie glared at her with open hostility as if he wanted to kill her.

Stunned, Tina responded. "You cheated right in front of me. It was humiliating."

"I never heard you complain about our sex life or a lack of it. I give you all you want. If I fuck other women in front of you, I'm not a cheat. I don't care what you think, Bitch. You should appreciate me. I'm a healthy man with a healthy sex drive. There is nothing wrong here, just because I wanted some variety, especially on my birthday."

His remarks knocked the wind out of her, and she did not respond. She only wanted to get home and stay far away from hm.

★　★　★

MAY 2011

Tina avoided Artie whenever possible and was thankful his many jobs kept him away. When he was home, Tina pretended she was busy and often left the house. When he came to bed, she pretended to be asleep and scrunched herself over to one side of the bed to avoid any contact with his body.

Most nights, she could not sleep, ate more than usual from stress and gained another ten pounds. Her doctor prescribed pills for anxiety and depression, but Tina continued to put up a good front for the children.

One evening when Artie was away, Tina lay in bed in the dark. Her thoughts turned to the divorce group she attended so many years ago. The therapist Tamara had mentioned ways spouses could manipulate each other, but Tina could remember little else. It was so long ago now.

Tina began to search for a therapist, as she wished she had done this years ago, but she had consciously or subconsciously never found time to deal with her abusive reality. It thrilled her to see Tamara Stone, Ph.D., the therapist who ran the divorce group years ago, on her insurance provider list. Tamara Stone the social worker was now Tamara Stone, Ph.D. Tina set up an appointment after work.

★   ★   ★

Tamara recognized Tina as soon as she saw her seated in the large office armchair. Tina grabbed a handful of chocolates on the table next to her and began to peel off the foil from one chocolate. She suddenly caught herself and stopped.

"I'm sorry. I didn't ask you whether it was okay for me to take some."

"Of course," smiled Tamara. "How have you been?"

Tina began to speak, but immediately choked up and burst into tears. Tamara said nothing, but held out a tissue box. Tina wiped her eyes, blew her nose and grabbed a few more chocolates from the candy dish.

"I would like to know how to handle my husband. I still love him, but I don't think I want to stay married. He tries to control us and humiliates me and always puts me down. Sex was always great, but after he made me join in a threesome, he spoiled intimacy for me too. He doesn't get along well with the kids either. I don't know what to do. I'm scared." Tina spent the hour describing her life with Artie.

"Let's work on your home situation," said Tamara after the session. "Our time is up. In the meantime, don't put yourself in any danger." She handed Tina a card for the local women's shelter. Tina thanked her. "I don't think I'll need this though. I just need to work out my life. I will see you next week."

Tamara smiled and nodded. "You're on my calendar. See you then."

Tina mentioned to Artie that she started seeing a therapist. He smiled. "Well, you're the crazy one, not me."

"I'm not crazy," she almost shouted at him. "I'm stressed out because of our home life."

Artie shrugged his shoulders. "Che, I really can't understand you. I help provide for us. I work hard. We have everything we need. I fuck you when you want it, but you don't want it anymore."

Tina did not respond. He stopped and looked at her blankly. His lack of insight and empathy drove her into despair.

A few sessions later after Tina mentioned repeatedly her troubled marriage, Tamara looked at her sympathetically.

"Tina, you really should bring your husband in for a session. It would be helpful."

Tina shook her head. "I doubt he'll come, but I'll ask."

Afterward, she pondered how to get Artie to accompany her. She decided she would need to make him feel as if he had made the decision himself.

★　★　★

JUNE 2011

One evening after dinner, Tina said to Artie, "You know I'm in therapy. I think it would help if both of us go to a session together."

"I don't need an asshole telling me what to do."

"Then why don't you come and let Tamara know how you feel? She has only heard my point of view about things."

"Che, I'm too busy."

"Please. Just once."

"Oh dammit, Tina." He paused. "Bueno. Just once, but you're the one that needs therapy, not me. Now, leave me alone."

After the session the following week, Tamara dictated her observations.

Mr. and Mrs. Diaz arrived on time for the appointment. Mrs. Diaz was tearful when she discussed the couple's marital problems in front of her husband. Alert and fully oriented, Mrs. Diaz had a depressed mood and appeared worried and distraught. She had normal thought processes, good insight into her condition plus excellent judgment.

Mr. Diaz was an obese male, dressed and groomed in a casual manner. He was pleasant but appeared nonplussed by his wife's concerns and responded with jokes and attempts to divert the conversation's focus. When asked what he would do if he found a letter on the ground, he said he would open it and if there was a check, he'd cash it; however, he didn't hope for money. He *really wanted sexy pictures. When asked to spell 'world' backwards, he spelled 'f*ck' instead. He became visibly agitated when his wife shared personal information. He admitted to a troubled past in part due to the Argentine war but would not go into detail. I don't believe he has a good prognosis.*

Tamara stopped dictating her report. She definitely could identify his narcissistic traits but his other behaviors posed a challenge. After some thought, Tamara wrote "Rule Out Asperger's Syndrome" on the report. She added Borderline Personality Disorder and Alcohol Abuse.

When they left the office, Artie stayed silent until they got into the car.

"Why did you tell her all our private stuff?" he said in an angry tone.

"Tamara is a trained therapist. She has to know what's going on if she is going to help us."

"There is nothing going on. We can work out our own stuff. I don't need to discuss our personal problems with a stranger."

"Artie, she is a professional counselor with a doctorate in psychology."

He glared at his wife. "You embarrassed me, Tina. I'm fucking unhappy about this, so don't even think I'm going back there. You talk about us, so you're not going back there either or I'll divorce you."

Tina's mouth opened as if to say something, but she knew arguing with him would do no good, as she realized she had to arrange her sessions from now on in private.

★   ★   ★

JANUARY 2012

Sydney now had less time than ever. A year before, she had met Bill, a corporate executive, online, and although he was 15 years older than she, Sydney considered themselves a perfect match.

Tina joined Facebook to find friends. Intrigued, Artie followed and was instantly hooked. Social media wooed him, as he posted on both his professional and personal pages about his concerts or bragged about his accomplishments. He now had a venue for increased antics in his quest for attention and resorted to hats, helmets, props or outfits he felt would bring him the most recognition. Sometimes he wore a hardhat which said, "Always Hard." His theatrics during his performances caused a stir, and he clearly chose many scores for their prop potential. However, he also used props during concerts for no particular reason. People asked to befriend him by the score, many obviously out of curiosity to see what he would do next.

His many Facebook friends and followers always responded to his posts. The more they laughed and joked with him, the more excited and hyperverbal he became, until he spewed out endless bantering back and forth with his friends. He never mentioned his family in his posts except Maria on occasion.

At an Orange County college recital, Artie surprised his audience when he appeared in a clown outfit to perform his opening piece

"Send in the Clowns." He then wore a wizard's hat and robe to play an electrifying piano version of *The Sorcerer's Apprentice*. At another concert, Artie propped up large lollipops under the piano lid. He resorted to lick all of them before he sat down to play. He also played "Chopsticks" with real chopsticks. Once he performed his arrangement of "Puff the Magic Dragon," dressed as a green draconian creature with a toy beast propped up under the piano lid. Another favorite gag was to play a Chopin waltz facing an audience with his hands behind his back on the keyboard.

One evening, he accompanied the famous Argentine sibling violin duo Dos Argentis. Instead of a tuxedo, Artie showed up dressed as a gaucho in baggy blue pants, a leather belt around his waist a loose white shirt with a scarf around his neck and his fedora perched on his head. The performance itself went well, although his choice of outfit had several audience members comment that his apparel distracted from the concert.

The following morning, Artie posted photos of himself with the siblings Pilar and Paolo. A short video clip showed Artie carrying the beautiful petite Pilar in his arms and when he set her down, he kissed her on the cheek, as his hand swept across her breasts. People liked and commented on the post, but Tina felt slapped in the face, as if he had thrown a brick at her.

★   ★   ★

A week later, Artie returned home in the afternoon and sat down at the kitchen table. He opened a bottle of expensive cognac, poured the liquor into a large glass and soon finished the contents. As he drank, he repeatedly banged his fist on the table. Hearing the racket, Tina hurried into the kitchen, as he glared into space with bleary bloodshot eyes. His eyebrows furrowed together and he tightened his lips. "They fired me."

"Who did?"

"The fucking symphony, that's who."

"Why?"

"Pilar complained about me touching her boobs and said Dos Argentis never wanted to perform with me again. My boss told me I was too offensive and an embarrassment to the orchestra."

"I'm sorry. What are we going to do about money now?"

"I have plenty of gigs. The fucking orchestra didn't appreciate me anyway." He tried to get up but staggered. Tina ran over to him and supported him to the bedroom. He lay down and soon snored in deep slumber.

"Now he has another excuse not to provide enough money for us," she thought.

OCTOBER 2012

In her senior year at UCLA, Leli did her practicum in the Magnusson Hospital emergency room. Calm, collected and in control, she enjoyed the challenges that emergency work provided and handled crises well. Hospital staff and patients praised her for her exceptional abilities and competence.

One morning after her shift, she returned home with bandages on her face and her previously shoulder-length hair now cut short below her ears. She walked in the door, shot a quick glance at herself in the hallway mirror and dropped her books off in her room.

She passed Artie talking to Tina in the hallway. They stopped and stared at her. "What happened to you, Nena?"

"I got attacked last night in the ER," she said breathlessly. "This guy was out of his mind, high as a kite. Crystal meth. He got combative and when we tried to restrain him, he grabbed my ponytail and wouldn't let go. It took two aides and a security guard to get him off me."

A horrified look crossed Tina's face. "You could have been killed. Maybe you shouldn't work in the ER anymore. It's too dangerous."

"Mom, it was scary but part of my job. I'll be okay. Just scratches, but my hair will stay short forever."

"Don't give up, Nena. You're smart, just like me."

Leli smiled. "Thanks, Artie. That's the nicest thing you've ever said."

★   ★   ★

MAY 2013

Now that Artie was no longer employed with the symphony, he took out-of-town jobs and often flew back and forth between Los Angeles and New York to play for Broadway shows and concerts. He still was difficult about money, and Tina's anger and ambivalence simmered, but she resisted divorce. Yet, she sighed with relief when he was away.

One day, when Artie worked in New York, Tina sat at the computer to review their joint account and noticed something odd, a withdrawal two days earlier for $3,000. He had never withdrawn such a large amount, so Tina thought that maybe he had an unforeseen large expense and ignored it. The following week he was still out of town but Tina saw he withdrew $5,000. She called and left him two messages, but he did not call back. She could not clarify the withdrawals with him, and the rapidly depleting funds frightened her, so she went to the bank, where she froze the account.

Two nights later, Artie called with an anxious tone. "My ATM card was denied."

"I've been trying to reach you for two days. Why did you take out $8,000 in two weeks? Why haven't you returned my calls? What's going on here?"

"Oh, bombónita, I love you so much." His voice charmed, but with a sense of urgency. "Mi vida, I need more money to pay some bills. It's very important."

Tina's heart dropped into her stomach. She almost reeled in panic, as her sixth sense warned her. "What kind of bills? Please explain to me the urgency. This money is our household mainstay. Are you using drugs again?"

"Tina, I... I'll call the bank to unfreeze the account myself."

"Please answer the question."

"Ciao." He ended the conversation.

Two minutes later, her phone rang again. The man had a thick traditional New York accent, and Tina could hear Artie shouting at him in the background.

"Is this Tina?"

"Who're you and why are you calling from my husband's cellphone?"

"Let's say, hmmm, I'm his financial – em ... advisor. Let me give it to you straight. Mr. Piano Man here owes big bucks for his poker debts."

Tina's heart dropped further in her stomach.

"Tina, he needs to pay up. Do you understand? You don't want me to – eh – rough him up a bit, do you? After all, what a shame if he couldn't use those pretty hands to play piano anymore."

"Thank you. Yes. Let me take care of it." Tina slammed down the phone and wrung her hands, because she had not realized the extent of Artie's gambling problem. Her eyebrows slanted upward, her lips parted slightly and her eyes opened wide with fear. She knew she could not let anything happen to him, but she had to protect the family money, so with her new plan, Tina hurried to the bank to unfreeze the funds but transferred most of it to her own account.

Artie arrived home the next day. His lips tightly shut, his large eyes expressed concern. He pulled a handful of peanuts from the pantry, which he piled on a plate and without a hint of his cocky attitude, sat at the kitchen table with his face buried in his hands. The smell of body odor, mingled with cigar smoke and stale alcohol hit Tina's nostrils as she sat down across from him.

"Artie, how much do you still owe that man?"

He hesitated before he spoke. "About ten grand."

Tina's mouth dropped open in horror and her voice reverberated through the house. "How could you do this to us, your family?"

"Oh che, I play poker games when I'm out on the road. I never thought it would get this bad. I bet a little here, bet a little there. Sometimes, I win; sometimes, I lose. You know, mi vida, it's just a matter of time before I win back the money."

"You're bankrupting us, plus this is the second time you've jeopardized our safety with your recklessness. In Argentina, that drug dealer almost killed us, because you owed him money and now, there's a mob guy involved." She paused and glared at him, but her voice softened. "I'll bail you out this once, which means, I'll take money out of my retirement account, but I'll never do this again. I'm sick of the way you fuck with our family."

"Che," he smiled at her. "But I enjoy a poker game now and then. A man needs some entertainment on the road."

"Artie," she did not break her eye contact as she took a breath. "I don't trust you anymore, so I've transferred most of the funds to my account. Things have to change."

He jumped up, his face red with anger. "Damn it, bitch!" he shouted. "I'm not five years old."

Tina forced herself to stay calm. "Don't act like it. You'll continue to contribute your usual share to our joint account. Do you understand?" He stood like a statue and clenched his fists as he glared at Tina, picked up his plate and hurled it to the floor, where it shattered to pieces. "Fuck you. I'm outta here. Gone this weekend." His mouth twisted in anger. "I have a gig in Vegas. I may be home Sunday night, maybe not. In fact, I might be gone every weekend."

She closed her eyes and took a deep breath. "Breaking things doesn't accomplish anything. Please don't forget Leli's college graduation next Saturday."

He stopped and paused for a second.

"Please don't disappoint your daughter on her big day. She's graduating *summa cum laude* and is giving a speech too."

He pulled up his phone and shrugged his shoulders. "It's on my calendar."

Tina followed him into their bedroom. She watched him sit down on the bed, and kick off his sneakers. He lay down and dozed off, ignoring her. Filled with sadness, Tina returned to the kitchen, where she cleaned up the broken pieces and finished making a chicken pot pie.

Tina believed Artie was stressed in part due to Maria, who had been diagnosed with Alzheimer's disease the year before. Now 81, Maria's dementia had significantly advanced. Often confused, her clouded mind no longer recognized her family or friends. She required total care at this point for all her needs and lived in a memory care facility.

After his nap, Artie took a shower and repacked his suitcase with a white dinner jacket, slacks, good shoes, socks, and underwear. He ignored the others and did not join his family for dinner; instead, he left the house and after he returned late, he crawled into bed beside Tina. He fell asleep, and his loud snores permeated the room. When he got up, dressed and departed quietly the next morning. Tina pretended to be asleep.

That weekend, Tina repeatedly checked the family's accounts online and saw no ATM withdrawals. Artie returned home in a better mood Sunday night and gave his wife a quick peck on the lips, before he unpacked and threw his laundry into the hamper.

Adam and Jessie flew in for the graduation, and their upbeat presence lifted everyone's mood, while Artie was as warm, personable, and upbeat as ever. Only Maria's absence cast a shadow over the festivities.

On Saturday morning, the family arrived early at the auditorium and obtained prime seats close to the stage.

After the graduates marched in procession, Leli sat in the front row, her robe decorated with ribbons and honors. On the back of her mortarboard, Leli had drawn a white boulder with the inscription 'Nurses Rock!' and before the diplomas were handed out, she gave an eloquent speech about the future of nursing. The family wildly applauded when they called Leli, and she walked on stage to receive her degree.

After the ceremony, everyone celebrated at a popular restaurant. The next day, Adam and Jessie flew home. Artie drank continuously during the weekend and by Sunday evening was obviously intoxicated.

Leli retired to her bedroom to focus on her licensure exam.

Tina had taken Monday off to recoup. She began the day by tending to the long-neglected laundry. As usual, Tina started to sort white and colored items and always checked pockets before she put the items in the washer. As she picked up Artie's slacks, she wrinkled her nose and put her hand in the back pocket. At first, she thought she had pulled out trash, but when she looked down, she saw a crumpled receipt along with a wrapped foil condom package. Tina stared in horror at the credit card receipt for several hundred dollars from Miss Pussycat's Ranch, Pahrump, Nevada.

A bolt of fire shot through Tina's body. Her legs weakened and she steadied herself as she held on to the laundry room door. Her face crumpled followed by deep loud sobs. She now had to face in her heart what she denied to herself for a long time: the marriage was over.

As she wept, her anger rose like a roaring forest, as she stormed into the bedroom where Artie lay asleep under the sheet, his puffy face on the pillow, eyes closed and lips parted.

"Wake up, asshole!" She shook his shoulders. Artie sat up somewhat dazed and stared at her.

"Asshole motherfucker. How dare you?" Tina screamed at the top of her lungs. She threw the receipt along with the condom package in his face.

"Shit," He rubbed his eyes. "I don't want to discuss this now. I have a fucking headache." He was obviously hung over.

"Yes, we have to discuss it now. Did you think I would never find out? How dare you go whoring, drinking, and gambling, while I do my best to hold this family together. How dare you do this to us."

"Can I explain?"

"Forget it. You hear me, schmuck? Nada. We're through."

Artie did not respond, but shut his eyes again as he got up and brushed back his disheveled curls. As he walked gingerly to the bathroom, objects repeatedly hit his face, and he stopped. Tina first threw a pair of sneakers at him, one shoe at a time, followed by a pair of heels; one hit him on his cheek. Artie touched his finger to the wound, then went into the bathroom and quickly shut the door. Tina continued to shout at him at the top of her lungs from outside the door.

"Get out of here, you fucking hungover asshole! You can go fuck yourself and afterwards, you can fucking drop dead, you disgusting bastard prick!"

Artie came out of the bathroom with a puzzled look on his flushed sweaty face and shrugged his shoulders. His calm attitude angered Tina even more. "You can drop dead, you lying, cheating cockroach. We're through. You'll hear from my lawyer."

Artie looked down and pressed his hand to his forehead. "Tina, let's talk about this. Please."

"It's over. Life is hell with you. Just send your fucking child support payments. Otherwise, I don't care if you live or die." Tina burst anew into tears.

He said nothing, walked into the closet and pulled out his suitcase. Without a word, he packed as quickly as he could, while Tina stood nearby and shook from head to toe. He turned to see his two horrified daughters as they stared at him from the hallway. Leli held her arms tightly around her younger sister who wept bitterly.

Artie stopped and turned to Tina as he left. "My sister lives there," he said. "I visited her."

"Yeah, right. My aunt is the Queen of England! Nobody's heard from Luisa in years, so don't involve her in your dirty lies and imply she's a whore."

Leli let go of her sister and walked up to her father. Her angry eyes pierced into his own. "Artie, you've destroyed this family," she said. "Look what you've done to Mom and to us. You never cared."

Without another word, Artie opened the door, picked up his suitcase, and left.

Tina walked to the living room and lay down on the couch. Sarah continued sobbing uncontrollably, and Leli hugged her tightly, before she sat down next to Tina and gently stroked her mother's hair.

"Mom, Sarah and I heard the whole conversation. We're glad he's gone."

Tina slowly sat up and rubbed her eyes. "I'm so sorry. That was between your father and me. I feel so bad about everything right now."

"It's okay," said Leli softly and handed Tina a tissue. "He's always been a jerk. Look how he treated you and us kids."

"I'm so sorry about this, but I can't stand him anymore. I'm filing for divorce."

Leli touched her mother's shoulder. "Please don't apologize. You're doing the right thing." Sarah came over and the three family members embraced. "Group hugs are the best," said Sarah, through her tears.

Drained, Tina walked into the bedroom and drifted into an exhausted sleep. Leli remained calm and turned to Sarah. "Please do the laundry since Mom can't now. Throw Artie's clothes in a separate pile and leave them." Sarah nodded.

Leli left and drove to Ralph's supermarket to get empty boxes. When she returned home, she methodically packed her father's clothes, music, possessions and dirty laundry into separate boxes, which she neatly labeled with large neat letters: "Music," "Clothes." "Papers," plus one big box marked "Etc."

The following day, Tina called in sick. However by Wednesday, she pulled herself together and went to work.

Leli did not feel well that morning. She had planned to study for her boards, but the day before, a wasp stung her arm, which still burned and seared from the pain. She also woke up that morning with a severe headache. Ibuprofen did not help, so she put a cold compress on her forehead and lay on the couch as the family's large orange cat Punkin jumped up on her stomach with a loud purr.

"Hey, Punkin Man," she whispered to him before she closed her eyes and dozed off.

Soon, she floated down into the sea among the fishes. She saw a chest underwater with a key, swam towards it and heard the key turn. With a start, Leli sat up and rubbed her eyes, as Punkin jumped to the floor. Artie stopped, obviously surprised to see his daughter at home. Leli took a deep breath before she rose and calmly gestured toward the boxes.

"All your stuff is packed," she said.

"Thanks."

He began to lift the boxes to put them in his car, while Leli stood in the room, arms folded across her chest and watched him.

Artie picked up the cat, grinned and made funny faces at Leli. "Hey, Nena," he said. "Punkin is telling me Monday was an absolute CATastrophe, right?" He emphasized the first part of the word.

Leli was not amused.

"Oh c'mon, Nena. You should laugh."

"Not much to laugh about. Put Punkin down, please. He's not part of your separation package."

Artie did not answer but set the large ginger cat back on the floor, before he returned to the boxes. Leli stood motionless and expressionless as she watched him, her arms still crossed over her chest.

He walked towards Leli, put his arm around her shoulder and pressed her face against his chest. Leli stayed stiff and motionless, so Artie pulled his arms away.

"I'll get my piano soon."

"Whatever." She remained stone-faced.

Artie bent down again and kissed her cheek. "Bye, Nena."

Leli did not respond and quickly backed away from him.

He said nothing but turned around, opened the door and walked out. As he got into his car, his daughter stood in the doorway and shouted after him, "Bye, Felicia."

As soon as he left, Leli slammed the door shut, glad that he didn't touch her stung arm.

★   ★   ★

Sydney comforted Tina. "You're almost through the shit storm," she said. "There is light at the end of the tunnel."

"Thanks. I feel better already," said Tina. "Much better. There are still bad days, but it was over a long time ago. Do you know how I knew for sure he no longer wanted to be married?"

"How?"

"He used to wear a shirt which said, 'I'll always be there when I need you.' He thought it was funny, but when he stayed away all the time, I knew he really didn't need us anymore."

★   ★   ★

JUNE 2013

Tina realized she had underestimated Artie's resistance to their pending divorce. He hid assets, argued with Tina about visitation for Sarah and was especially slow to respond to any demands. He made no effort to see his children except for a few emails to Adam, where he bemoaned the divorce and spoke about how difficult it was for him. Adam stayed neutral.

In the meantime, a coworker's mother could no longer care for her dog, so Andrea gifted Tina with the tan rescue dachshund puppy. The family named him Hans, and his playful personality lifted everyone's mood.

Tina realized she had endured years of abuse and made excuses for Artie to save the marriage. The strange feeling of soon being divorced lingered around her. Soon she would be free of Artie, but some nights, she expected him to walk in the door, as if he had never left. She knew she faced a rocky road ahead, but at the same time, firmly set her mind against any reconciliation with him. Tamara's supportive sessions made life somewhat easier.

One day, Tina displayed motivational signs around the house for moral support. She hung in the kitchen a large yellow sign with a smiley face surrounded by the words, "You Can Do It." A poster of a mountaintop which read: "Insurmountable Obstacles are Surmountable" hung in the hallway.

Tina's favorite sign, though, she had made herself. One night, she printed out a small professional headshot of Artie which he used for his program bios. She wrote herself a whimsical poem underneath the photo:

"Insurmountable
Attainable
DisARTIEculate
Disharmonize
Theorize AND
Survivorize.
You Can Do It!"

With a big red marker, she drew a circle around his photo, then drew a diagonal line through it.

★　★　★

JANUARY 2014

Tina suspected hidden funds, so she hired a forensic accountant, who discovered Artie had more money than expected. In the end, they each got half their community property, but Tina also got the house. Artie agreed to 'reasonable visitation' with Sarah and a set amount for child support. The divorce was finalized by October, 2013, and Tina legally changed her surname back to Perry, while Artie bought himself a large early 20th century house near downtown LA.

★   ★   ★

One January day, Tina dusted the dark antique wood dresser in the hallway, and something prompted her to open the bottom drawer. There lay the box with forgotten photographs Eva had left behind. Tina remembered them and carefully lifted up the box, as Sarah appeared in the doorway.

"I just found your Oma's old family photos. I had forgotten all about them."

"I wanna see them."

Tina motioned Sarah into the living room. They both sat on the couch and perused the photos.

"Who's Jakob?" Sarah held up a photo of the child.

"That had to be your uncle, who was killed by the Nazis," said Tina. "I don't know any of these people in the photos except your Oma."

"You should do a family tree, Mom."

"Good idea." Soon Tina hired a Jewish genealogist and researched records from the Holocaust Museum in Washington.

★   ★   ★

Meanwhile, Leli passed her nursing boards, she found work in Davis as an emergency room nurse with lucrative pay and benefits. She shared an Ikea-furnished apartment with Shaina, another Jewish nurse. Soon afterward, Leli told Tina she had started dating a medical resident, but it wasn't serious. She stated her work was her primary focus, and Tina was not surprised, as Leli had always put school or work first. Sometimes, Tina wondered whether Leli's poor relationship with Artie had affected her ability to sustain relationships.

Adam and Jessie seemed happy in Orlando. They also acquired a new family addition, a boxer rescue puppy they named Daisy. Since their relationship had mended, Adam texted or phoned Tina regularly.

Sarah began voice lessons with a private teacher and although her grades were good, she mainly remained focused on her musical studies with little interest in other subjects.

A few months after the divorce finalized, Artie surfaced again to visit Sarah. Tina inwardly dreaded seeing him but hid her feelings, as she did not want to damage Sarah's relationship with her father.

Artie acted charming and had changed since Tina last saw him. He had lost weight and looked toned with muscles defined in his chest and arms. He still wore black t-shirts, jeans, high-top sneakers and now spoke with a slight lisp displaying a mouth devoid of teeth. Sarah commented on the lisp.

Artie laughed. "I'm a Catalan now." He saw the puzzled look on Sarah's face.

Tina laughed. "I get it. Catalans from Barcelona speak Spanish with a lisp."

★   ★   ★

Tina always made dinner at 5:30 PM, and when Artie visited around that time, Tina always set out an extra plate for him. Over the next few weeks, his visits increased, while he demanded Tina's and Sarah's full attention as all conversation focused on himself. He bragged endlessly and spoke about his workouts and weight loss. Sarah adored anything he said, but he expressed little interest in her life.

Artie's ongoing friendly manner and sense of humor made the visits unexpectedly pleasant. Soon, he dropped by almost daily, right at dinnertime.

One evening, Tina went to the movies with Bill, a coworker. They had just returned to her home when the doorbell rang. Artie stood in the doorway.

Tina stepped back. "Yes?"

"Did I forget my sunglasses here yesterday?"

"I haven't seen them." Tina looked awkwardly at Bill.

"Aren't you going to introduce me?"

"Artie, meet Bill. Bill, this is Artie. Goodnight."

"'Ciao." He walked towards his car and drove off.

The next day, Artie showed up for dinner again. "So, who's Bill?"

"A friend and coworker."

"Where'd you go?"

"We saw a movie, *The Grand Budapest Hotel*, okay?"

Artie pressed his lips firmly together with an expression of disdain. Tina ignored him, walked into the kitchen and pulled the roast chicken from the oven. The delicious aroma filled the kitchen. Uneasy about Artie, Tina stayed silent during the meal as he and Sarah chatted back and forth.

One evening, he left, but an hour after his departure, Tina heard an engine start up outside. She looked out the front window to see his car slowly drive away.

The next day, when he arrived as usual, Tina confronted him, her brows furrowed and eyes brimming with suspicion. "Why were you still outside for an hour after you left?"

"My car wouldn't start. I waited awhile to start it again."

Tina did not take her eyes off him. "I didn't hear anything until you finally left. If there was a problem, why didn't you let us know?"

"I didn't want to disturb you." His eyes flashed and locked into hers.

Tina shuddered as chills went down her spine.

Worried that Artie was stalking her, Tina blocked him on Facebook. He still came over, and although his visits gave her the creeps, Tina did not want to damage his and Sarah's relationship. However, he told silly jokes and his pleasant demeanor at every visit put Tina somewhat at ease in spite of her apprehension. She eventually thought she had overreacted and had too vivid an imagination.

In the meantime, she slowly began to toy with the idea of a new life away from LA. After so many years in government work, she had enough. Tina knew with her experience, she could find another job somewhere else, but she hesitated, because she worried how Sarah would adjust to a new environment. However, she slowly moved forward with plans, and after a home inspection, fixed whatever was necessary, had the whole house painted and replaced the carpet with tile and wood flooring.

Cautiously, Tina sent out feelers about relocation. An Internet job search in other states yielded some possible leads, so a priority was to sell the house. Los Feliz was a popular neighborhood, and Tina hoped things would move quickly. She also asked at work about realtors, potential buyers and spoke to a former coworker who had just moved back to LA from the Orlando area. Edna recommended some excellent schools near and around Winter Park near Orlando. It seemed like a good place to raise children, but Tina's gut told her to keep her plans secret. When she saw a caseworker position vacancy online at her old place of employment, she applied immediately.

One warm June night, Artie showed up promptly at 5:30 with a bottle of good Malbec. His smoky gray curls crowned the top of his head and curled over his ears. His almost-white neatly-trimmed beard framed his face. He wore a dark grey jacket and indigo jeans.

He smiled, kissed Tina's cheek and set the wine on the table. "Sarah told me she wouldn't be home tonight."

"She's staying at a friend's house," said Tina as she set out a place setting for Artie. She had fixed a large dinner salad, and piled some on his plate.

He scowled. "Don't you have anything else?"

"Hey, this is not the Ritz." She pulled out a leftover pork chop from the refrigerator and placed it in the microwave. "There. That's it. Take it or leave it."

They made light conversation during dinner, almost like old times, chatted and drank wine.

Tina looked up at the clock. It was time for her favorite TV show, and she had not set the DVD player. She really wanted to be alone, but when Artie asked if he could also watch the show, she politely agreed.

They brought their wineglasses to the couch, and Tina clicked the remote and turned on the TV. Artie sat down next to her, his side pressed into hers. Tina instantly stiffened and became uncomfortable.

His hand touched her wrist and his fingers slowly traveled up her right hand. Tina startled and turned to see Artie's intense stare.

"What?"

He inched up so close to her, that she could smell the wine on his breath, put his left arm around her neck and pressed her against him. "Bombónita, I still love you, and how I miss you."

Before she could respond, he threw both arms around her, began to kiss her lips and neck and forced his tongue into her mouth. He pressed his face against hers so hard that his rough beard irritated her skin. At first in total shock, she quickly pulled away from him.

Artie looked at her with pleading eyes. "Please let me stay over tonight. Look." He pulled a Viagra packet from his pocket, grinned and winked at her. "I already took one."

Tina uttered a nervous laugh, shook her head and then became serious. "No, Artie. That's not going to happen," she said as she got up and clicked the remote power button to turn off the television.

Without a word, he reached out, put his hands around her waist and pulled her down on the couch against him. "Oh, how I miss what we used to have." Then he rolled on top of her and positioned himself between her legs. Tina began to panic and gasp under his weight.

"Get off me."

He ignored her and continued to kiss her. Tina struggled to get away, but he firmly pinned her down, his arms locked around her like an iron vice.

"Artie, Please. Enough already."

"Just relax, bombónita. You want me as much as I want you. Let me make you happy."

"Asshole, you'll make me happy when you let me go."

He ignored her and tried to unbutton her blue shirt with one hand without success. Frustrated, he lost patience, ripped her shirt open and tore the buttons off. Tina struggled, but Artie unhooked her bra and began to grope her breasts. He relaxed for a second, and Tina wrestled free.

She ran to the door, but Artie jumped up, blocked her, and pinned her up against the living room wall. Tina realized she had underestimated how strong and agile he was now. His tousled hair, rumpled shirt, and wild eyes frightened her, and she recognized his determined look, as she had often seen the same expression when he played technically difficult piano pieces.

He embraced her again tightly, pinning her arms against her sides. Tina could barely breathe.

"You know you need it as much as I do," he whispered in her ear. "I know what turns you on. I want to renew our love. Let me take care of you."

"Artie, you're fucking crazy. Let go."

He kept his arms locked around her and began to kiss her again. "I think about our passionate nights all the time. How can I ever forget them?"

"Let me go. Stop it, schmuck." Tina's voice got louder. Artie now terrified her. She began to cry. He continued to ignore her protests as he groped and kissed her. His voice was eerily calm. "You know you want it, and it will be ecstasy for you. You're mine." As he kept his arms locked firmly around her so as not to release his prize. his eyelids drooped, his nostrils flared, and his lips parted slightly. Tina recognized that expression signaled his sexual arousal. He grabbed her hand and pressed it against his crotch as he tried to slip his other hand through her waistband.

Suddenly the earth shook and growled; the house rattled loudly and distracted Artie for a single moment. He loosened his grip and Tina got away. She stared at him in horror.

"Get out," she sobbed as Hans barked loudly and lunged at Artie's leg. Tina shook from head to toe. "Get out of here, you fucking asshole. I never want to see you again. Ever. If you show up again, I will call the cops."

He stopped at the front door, turned around and stared at his ex-wife in utter disbelief. His eyes narrowed. "Sempre sos mi esposa." He paused. "You are my señora forever." He stormed out the front door, slamming it loudly, got into his car and drove off so quickly that his tires squealed.

Tina shook and barely held on to the wall, until she collapsed on the floor with loud sobs. She trembled as the animals all ran toward her. A moment later, Leli called and Tina's loud sobs and inaudible words greeted her.

"Mom. I'm leaving right now and coming home. Please call the police right now and tell them what happened." After they hung up, Tina called Sydney, who said she would be over right away and also told her to call the police.

"Is that necessary? I told him that if he ever showed up again, I would call the cops."

"Bullshit. He tried to rape you. You need to file a report, so the cops can arrest him. I mean it."

Tina called to report the attempted rape.

She walked into the bathroom, washed her face with cold water, and noticed an ugly bruise on her left arm. She threw on a t-shirt and tossed her torn shirt in the trash. It had been one of her favorites; now she could no longer stand the sight of it. A thought then came to her that she might need the shirt as evidence, so she retrieved it.

The young officer arrived about ten minutes later. He sat at the kitchen table and wrote the report as Tina sat down and recounted her story between sobs.

"My ex came over for the evening. He knew our daughter was away at a sleepover. We had dinner. Afterward, I wanted him to leave, so I could watch TV. He asked if he could stay and watch TV with me, and I said okay. Then he tried to rape me. He told me I needed it, and he knew I would love it. I got away because of the earthquake tremors, He left, but I'm scared."

When Sydney arrived, she sat down next to Tina at the kitchen table.

"So your ex didn't actually rape you," said the officer. It was more a statement than a question.

"He tried."

"Is there any physical evidence? Any bruises or body fluids?"

Tina showed the officer her arm. "He also tore off my shirt."

"Describe him please."

"He was wearing a black shirt, dark slacks and a jacket. He's about 5'10" with dark gray curly hair and a beard. He has a hawk nose, and pig-like brown eyes with bags under them. He is also missing teeth."

The officer smiled. "Quite a description. Do you have a photo?"

"Check his website or Facebook page."

"Do you have his address?"

Tina provided the information.

"Thanks, Ms. Perry. We'll go and get a warrant for his arrest."

"Great," said Sydney.

Tina thanked the officer. "I need a restraining order too."

"We'll get an emergency order, Ma'am." Said the officer. He photographed Tina's bruise, put on gloves and took the shirt for evidence before he said goodbye and left in his patrol car.

Sydney noticed Tina's puffy face and swollen red eyes. "Your lovable funny ex-husband tried to rape you." Her voice rang with sarcasm. "You know what? I'm not surprised."

"If it hadn't been for that tremor, I don't know what would have happened."

"Yeah, it really hit here too. My house shook."

"Thankfully, he's gone. I'm scared though he'll come back. He's so impulsive and won't let go." Tina wrapped her robe tightly around her and sat sat down wearily on the couch, as she wrung her hands. Her eyes betrayed her extreme anxiety. "I was shocked. I have never seen him this bad. I mean he was determined, come hell or high water, to have sex. All the time, he was saying how much he loved me. Isn't that ironic?"

"Well, that shows you don't know what he is capable of. Look at all those news stories about guys who kill their wives, ex-wives, kids, you know, homicide-suicides. Everyone says what a great guy he was, and they never thought he would kill someone." Sydney put her hand on Tina's shoulder. "You know what? You've got to get away from here. Don't let him find you."

Tina leaned back and closed her eyes. "I don't know if he has any weapons, but I'm scared what he'll do next. Do you know what he said when he left? 'You are my wife forever'. He said it in Spanish and in English for emphasis. That really scared me. I'm going to get a restraining order."

"He'll ignore it. He doesn't want to let go. He's shown tonight he's dangerous and wants total control."

Tina paused a moment. "I keep thinking, what if I had given in and screwed him so he'd go away? Just the thought alone scares me."

"Tina, he tried to rape you. Don't forget that. Coercion either way," said Sydney. "You're a very strong resilient person and probably would have said no regardless. Don't speculate."

Tina pulled out a tissue and wiped her eyes, as Sydney hugged her again. "He forced you, and that's rape regardless. You told him to stop. As we know, your ex is a master bullshit manipulator. He turns on the wit and charm to get whatever he wants. Often, I wish I had never introduced you both. You and Sarah need a new life with a fresh start away from this mess. I'm staying here tonight until Leli gets here."

"How about Nathan?"

"He's home watching TV."

"I can't believe he's 16. He's so cool." Tina thought of the boy's friendly demeanor and social nature and smiled through her tears. "Thanks, Sydney, for being here for me. You're right. We must get away from here. Far away." She sighed. "Poor Leli has to drive all the way from Davis."

"She obviously wants to be here for you."

Tina lay on the couch as Sydney reclined in the chair. They chatted until they dozed off.

Leli arrived at 4 AM still in her scrubs, embraced her mother and as she heard Tina's story, Leli's eyes flashed with anger. "Damn him. Fucking nasty jerk. How could he do that to you?"

"I'll be okay, Leli. Don't worry."

"I hope so. He was never nice to me and always put me down, no matter how much I tried to be a good kid," said Leli.

"You make him uncomfortable, because you're outspoken and look like him," said Tina.

"Oh, please don't tell me I look that bad. I don't act like an idiot either."

"You're very pretty and smart," said Sydney. "And you don't have his schnozz."

"He thinks he's so hilarious," said Leli. With that, she crossed her eyes, held her nose and stuck out her tongue. "That's what I think."

Now, Tina and Sydney both laughed.

"Do you feel a bit better, Mom?"

"You're a goofball, kiddo."

"Anything to cheer you up. Now, let's get serious."

A sad look clouded Tina's face. "I've been thinking for a while it would be a good idea to move away."

"Great idea, Mom."

Tina shuddered. "He was a regular Jekyll and Hyde last night. I'm terrified he'll show up again as if nothing happened. The cop said he was going to arrest him, but I'm sure Artie has enough bail money to bond out. He might even return tonight. I'm getting a restraining order regardless whether he goes to jail or not."

"The police will take care of him," said Sydney.

Tina pulled her knees up to her chest and closed her eyes. "What about Sarah? She is stubborn and won't understand. She adores Artie and will keep texting him. He'll find us."

"Let me handle her, Mom, and get that restraining order."

Sarah returned home later that morning. It surprised her to see Leli standing in the living room.

"Wow! Whatcha doing here?"

Leli gave her a hug. "I missed my little sister."

"Hi, sweetheart," Tina smiled and acted upbeat. "Did you eat breakfast yet?"

Sarah shook her head and turned to Leli. "You're really here. Great!" She kissed Leli's cheek, laid her cellphone on the table and walked into the kitchen. Tina grabbed the phone to check for texts from Artie. Nothing.

Leli took the phone and quickly deleted and blocked Artie's number before Sarah saw her. She paused. "It's Friday. Tonight Shabbat begins. Let's make a proper dinner. Sydney, please join us."

Tina smiled and thought that if anyone remembered Shabbat, it would be Leli. While Tina's interest in religion had waned, Leli had become an observant Jew, who kept kosher at home.

The smell of toast wafted through the house. "First, though," continued Leli, "I must speak with my little sister."

Sarah returned to the living room, munching a piece of toast with peanut butter.

Leli motioned her over toward the couch. "Come sit down, Sarita."

Sarah smiled and sat down next to Leli, who put her arm around her younger sister's shoulder. "I don't want to scare you, but this is serious. Artie came over last night, got violent and threatened Mom." Sarah's eyes widened and her lips parted slightly, her partially eaten toast visible in her mouth, and her upbeat mood disappeared.

Leli continued in her matter-of-fact way. "Sarah, this is a very critical situation right now. Our lives may be in danger. You have to listen to me. He's being arrested and mom's getting a protective order. Don't contact or talk to him. Stay away from him."

"But why?" Sarah's eyes widened and her voice shook with anxiety. "What did he do?"

"He tried to rape Mom. She's getting a restraining order, which means he must stay away. You've got to go no contact. That means do not email him, text him, or talk to him. Do not visit him. Don't tell him anything. Please unfriend and block him on Facebook and keep your phone GPS turned off at all times so he can't track you. This affects every one of us. You understand?"

Sarah stuffed the last piece of toast in her mouth and began to cry. "I can't. This is totally wack. I can't." She sank to the floor.

Sydney got up, sat on the floor next to her and reiterated what she told Tina about family homicides and suicides. Leli handed Sarah a tissue box. "Please. You must be strong now."

Sarah finally took a tissue, sat up, wiped her eyes and blew her nose.

"You must cooperate with us," said Tina "I know you love your dad, but that's not the issue here. We all have to stay safe."

Sarah stood up, ran into her room and left her phone behind, which Leli checked again for signs from Artie, but she saw nothing.

"Mom, I don't think she's going to be happy about moving." "I'm glad we didn't bring it up. She's already upset. She would have really had a fit."

Tina told Leli to rest. Sydney left to give the family time alone and promised to return later for dinner.

The phone rang. It was the police officer who had interviewed Tina the night before.

"Ms. Perry, we arrested Mr. Diaz early this morning, and he went before the judge."

"He probably denied everything, right?"

"He pled not guilty and was released on his own recognizance. We also obtained an emergency protective order for you, but you'll need to complete forms and petition in court to get a domestic violence restraining order."

She shuddered. "He must have charmed his way out. He thinks he's always right and so important, but he is a minnow in the sea of big fish," she added. "As an LAPD cop, I'm sure you're used to real celebrities. I'll do what's necessary."

Immediately afterward, she called her divorce attorney to help obtain the restraining order and then turned her attention to the Shabbat dinner preparations. Leli enjoyed cooking, a skill and talent passed down from Maria, and offered to prepare most of the meal.

With Leli's grocery list, Tina and Sarah drove to a large kosher market known for freshly butchered meats, fish and delicious non-dairy side dishes. A bakery two doors down was famous for its challah. Across the street, another kosher restaurant sold prepared dairy products.

By the time they returned with armfuls of groceries, Leli had showered and changed into jeans and a UCLA t-shirt. Tina watched her daughter put the groceries away and skillfully set up the ingredients for the meal. Artie had frequently picked on Leli as a child, lashed out at her and showed minimal affection. Yet in Tina's opinion, Leli had become the most resilient and strongest of the children.

Baked salmon, and Leli's homemade matzo ball soup filled the house with heavenly aromas. Leli knew how to make featherlight matzo balls and used premade organic chicken broth. Sarah set the table. which glowed with Tina's best white tablecloth, her gold-rimmed bone china dishes and ornate silverware, all wedding presents. Leli placed two candleholders with Shabbat candles in the center of the table. In the meantime, Tina set the challah bread on a plate, before she covered it with a white cloth. Leli brought the silver Kiddush cup that stood in the glass cabinet and filled it with wine. Sydney arrived, and everyone took a seat around the pristine table.

The sisters stood in front of the candles to light them. They waved the traditional gestures with their arms and hands as they welcomed the Shabbat light. Leli covered her eyes while she prayed.

Blessed are You, Lord our G-d, King of the universe, who has sanctified us with His commandments and commanded us to light Shabbat candles.

She took the Kiddush cup and prayed over the wine, followed by a Hebrew prayer over the challah. She then broke off a piece of bread and ate it per tradition, paused and closed her eyes as she prayed for peace and protection for the family. "Bless all of us with your kindness and protection. Shabbat shalom."

"Leli, I bet you'd make a good rabbi's wife," said Sydney.

"Or an even better rabbi," laughed Leli. "Remember, I aim high."

Along with the challah, matzo ball soup and baked salmon, the dinner included vegetables, noodles, carrot-raisin salad, and a tasty apple crumb cake from Sol's bakery.

Everyone's spirits improved during the meal, which upheld the highest tradition as it welcomed Shabbat. Tina meanwhile kept glancing anxiously through the front window, but 5:30 passed without a sign of Artie.

Afterward, Sarah returned to her room.

Leli looked at her mother. "School just let out last week for the summer, right?"

Tina nodded as she finished wiping off the kitchen counter with a rag.

"Shaina, my roommate, is working at a medical clinic in Ecuador this summer. She won't be back until late August. Before she left, she was worried about her share of the bills, I just texted her to see if it's okay to let Sarah stay a few weeks if I pay all the expenses."

"I'll help you with that," said Tina.

"No problem. In the meantime, you can pack, sell the house, and make plans to get out of here. I know my sister. The less she knows about your plans until the last minute, the better. She might end up spilling the beans somehow."

Tina nodded. "You're so right."

A beep resonated from Leli's phone, and she checked the screen. "Shaina said Sarah is welcome. Good." She got up and walked to Sarah's room. The door was ajar, and Sarah looked up from her book.

"Sarita, how'd you like to visit me for the next few weeks? I've got some awesome fun plans, so we can spend time together."

Sarah nodded with excitement. "Really? Wow."

"We'll drive up and since Shaina is away, it'll be just you and me.

"I'm lit! Can we go to San Francisco and see the seals?"

"Anything you want."

Sarah loved and admired Leli. To spend a few weeks with her was thrilling.

A few days later, the sisters left for Davis, and Tina was alone for the first time since the incident. The house seemed unnaturally quiet. Her attorney notified her the protective order was in place, but Tina remained terrified that Artie would refuse to stay away. A horrific nightmare kept her awake at night. In the recurrent dream, Artie appeared at the house in disheveled clothing and with bared teeth and angry narrowed eyes, raped and choked her. Tina usually woke up screaming and crying, as her heart pounded loudly against her chest and sweat covered her face. Afterward, she could barely catch her breath as she lay in the cool dark stillness of her bedroom. Hans often jumped on the bed to lick her face. The cats cuddled with her, and she buried her face in their fur for comfort.

She continued therapy with Tamara to help through her trauma. Tina discussed her plan to move away.

I think that's wise," Tamara told her. "I'd move somewhere hard for him to find you."

"I've been thinking of moving back to Florida. Do you think that's too drastic? It would be a big adjustment for Sarah and me."

"Check it out and see what you find," said Tamara. "When you move though, do it quietly, and make sure he doesn't find out."

"I worry he could fight me for visitation with Sarah, mainly to see me. He really doesn't care that much about being a dad."

"You have a protective order. That's usually good for no contact for three years," said Tamara "Keep me posted. See you next week."

Tina searched Florida jobs online with a preference for the Orlando area, where she would be near Jessie and Adam. The cheaper cost of living delighted her.

One day, the district attorney's office called. "Good Morning, Ms. Perry. We have a court date scheduled for April 2015 to prosecute Mr. Diaz for assault and attempted rape. We'll send you the paperwork."

"April 2015? That's almost a year away," said Tina.

"The courts are backed up, and that is the earliest available date."

Tina hesitated. "Let me call you back."

"Thank you."

After she hung up, fear crawled up her spine. She knew her divorce lawyer did not do criminal cases and would not be of assistance; she would have to testify on her own. The thought of being in court in front of Artie even a year away filled her with dread. Like a furious hornet, Artie would take any opportunity to hurt her without remorse. If he went to jail, she also worried he would no longer be employable, and all child support would cease. Besides, she knew their children would suffer if their father were a convicted felon.

At first, she wanted to discuss the problem with Leli or Sydney but decided against it. The decision to press charges had to be hers alone.

After several sleepless nights, she finally decided not to pursue the criminal charges. She still feared Artie but just wanted to move away at that point, so she called the district attorney's office and requested that the charges be dropped.

★   ★   ★

JULY 2014

Tina's main objective was to start a new life as soon as possible, and things went into motion quicker than expected. After a phone interview, she received a job offer for a case manager position with her old employer in Orlando. The job did not pay well but had decent benefits. With her California pension, she knew everything would be fine.

One of Tina's coworkers Dave was also a part-time realtor, so when she saw him at work the following day in the breakroom, she spoke to him about her house. He smiled. "You shouldn't have a problem. Los Feliz is a popular neighborhood. He made arrangements with her to list the house, and they set up an appointment for the following week.

A few days afterward, Dave stopped her in the hall and greeted her warmly. "I mentioned your home the other day to a potential buyer, and he's really interested. He'd like to see the house and is willing to pay cash. When is it okay to come by?"

She laughed. "How'd you find a buyer so fast?"

"Actually it's my uncle Oliver. He's an attorney and loves Los Feliz. Wants to move there."

Dave's uncle bought the house as quietly as a mouse walks in the snow with the closing date a few weeks away.

Overjoyed, Tina packed up during Sarah's absence, and Sydney took time off to help her friend. One morning, Tina climbed into the attic and pulled down several boxes, including a large box marked "Toys," filled with Legos, toy cars and trucks, Leli's Tickle Me Elmo Doll and her Furby. She unwrapped Sarah's Barbies who lay at the bottom of the box with their outfits. Another carton contained the children's well-loved books, including *Goodnight Moon*, the *Eloise* and *Madeleine* series and *Charlotte's Web*. To her delight, Tina also found her own old nursery rhyme book and her German *Grimm's Fairy Tales*.

Tina opened another box of children's clothes. She unwrapped tissue paper to reveal Sarah's pink ruffled infant dress with booties, Adam's tiny blue and white suit, and Leli's green toddler dress, handmade gifts from Maria. Three handsewn baby blankets by Tina completed the contents.

Another box marked "Albums" contained the scrapbooks Tina had made for each child. Tina set them on the floor next to Sydney, who thumbed through them with delight.

At the box's bottom lay Tina and Artie's wedding album with its black cover and "Our Wedding" printed in script letters. Tina handed it to Sydney.

"I don't know what to do with this."

"Maybe your kids want it."

Tina shrugged her shoulders. "Not sure. I know I don't want it anymore."

In the meantime, Sydney opened the album to look at the photos.

"Oh, Tina. How young we all were. Look at this."

In a portrait, Tina looked down at her bouquet, the Pacific Ocean behind, her white train fanned out around her.

"What a gorgeous photo," said Sydney. She continued to look at the pictures. "Hey, even Arturito looked handsome. Oops. Sorry. I won't mention him anymore."

"Thanks."

"Hey, Tina, I have an idea. Let's burn the album in a ritual bonfire."

"What? You're crazy, girl."

"I mean it. Let's put your patio fire pit to good use."

The sky flamed as the sun dropped toward the horizon. Sydney and Tina carried the album to the metal fire pit. After they piled wood and newspaper into the opening, Tina struck a match. Soon there was a roaring fire.

"Ready, girl?"

She nodded with a big smile.

"One-two-three!"

Tina threw the book on the fire. It went up in flames.

"C'mon, Tina. Selfie with the fire." Sydney aimed her phone. The friends posed together in front of the flames.

Suddenly a firetruck roared down the street as its loud siren resonated through the neighborhood. It stopped at Tina's house.

The two women looked at each other; then they burst out into laughter. "Oh shit," said Tina.

Two handsome, muscular firefighters ran into the backyard. The taller, older man spoke. "A concerned person called us about a fire in your yard."

"Oh, it's okay," said Tina. She pointed toward the flaming fire-pit.

"We'll put it out. You're not allowed to burn anything at the present time due to hazardous fire conditions." He returned with a fire extinguisher and doused the fire until it extinguished itself.

"Oh sorry, we didn't know," said Tina.

"We burned her wedding album to officially celebrate her divorce," laughed Sydney.

"Don't do it again or you'll get fined, okay?" said the firefighter.

The women nodded. The men got into the firetruck and drove off.

"Oh, holy fuck," laughed Tina. "Let's go inside."

"We'll toast to your new start in life. Got any wine?" laughed Sydney.

Tina pulled a bottle out of the refrigerator and poured the wine into two glasses. "Girlfriend, you'll stay in touch and visit us in Florida, won't you? I'll miss you so very much."

"Don't worry," laughed Sydney. "We'll be down for sure; Nathan loves Disney. Just move the hell away from here, so that maniac doesn't harm you. I'll be there for you guys forever."

★   ★   ★

FEBRUARY 2015

Six months after the move, Sarah seemed settled. She got good grades, but most of all, she loved taking music classes, singing in the local choir and her private voice lessons with Arielle, her new teacher. As well as she appeared to be doing, she still had occasional tantrums and meltdowns, but Tina considered her a typical teenager.

They planned weekend activities to the parks and beaches. Often, Cheryl and her daughter Maggie came along.

Adam and Jessie both kept busy with work, school and their new puppy in their Waterford Lakes apartment. They often rode their motorcycle to the Daytona Beach Bikefest and similar events.

Adam had matured and his former frequent anger diffused from a large fire to a small candlestick. While he could still be as stubborn as a nail in a rock, he became kinder toward his mother and sisters after the assault. Artie once texted Adam, but then Adam had never heard from him again. That disturbed Tina, although when Adam denied disclosing her whereabouts, she felt somewhat relieved. A few months prior, Tina's child support from Artie suddenly ceased, but a call to Child Support Enforcement in Los Angeles remedied the situation. It seemed apparent the family was now out of Artie's sight and mind as well, but Tina's sixth sense told her he could and would surface again.

★   ★   ★

MARCH 2015

"No, you can't stay out until midnight on a school night." Tina remained firm, and Sarah had a meltdown. Often argumentative, she easily burst into tears without much provocation, but that evening, she walked into her room and slammed the door loudly without a word.

Tina's cellphone rang. She picked up the phone and spoke to Cheryl. "Sarah's upset, because I won't let her hang out late tonight with her friend."

"She sounds stressed."

"I think she's homesick and still adjusting to life here. She's in a kid's choir here in school, but it's not like in LA. She's on the Internet a lot, and I have to monitor her computer time. I'm always scared she might run off with some predator. I heard about how these guys con girls into being sex slaves."

"Keep checking on her. Make sure she's safe."

Tina walked into the den and turned on the desktop computer to monitor Sarah's activity but noticed nothing suspicious besides Sarah's regular searches for Artie. Tina noticed a folder named Sperm Donor in Sarah's account. Puzzled, Tina clicked on it and saw numerous photos of Artie in concert performances and lectures, apparently saved off the Internet. It stunned Tina for a moment to see Artie's imagery before her, but then, she chuckled at the folder name.

Sarah and Artie always had a complex relationship, compounded by love and hate, acceptance and rejection, adoration and verbal abuse. Out of the three children, Sarah had tried the hardest to please him, but it was a double-edged sword. Although Artie liked that Sarah had musical talent, and he also showed her off at times, he could change to coldness and rejection with one quick misstep on Sarah's part. Sarah adored him, which was verified by the folder photographs.

One Monday morning, Sarah told her mother she did not feel well, so she stayed home from school while Tina went to work. Sarah remained in bed until 10 A.M, got up, went to the bathroom and then walked out to the kitchen, still in her pink and blue cat nightshirt. She pulled out a cereal bowl from the cupboard and fixed herself a bowl of raisin bran with plenty of milk. Afterward, she let Hans out in the backyard and sprawled in the new living room recliner, while she surfed the Internet on her phone. She played a few games, lost interest, yawned, returned to bed and slept until 2:00 PM, before, she finally got up for the day.

She threw on a Yosemite Park T-shirt, her favorite jeans, and her pink slippers, walked Hans and fed the cats, then sat down at the desk and switched on the computer. A YouTube notification about two new videos of Artie appeared on the screen, so she clicked on the page. In one video, he performed a recital at a small LA theater. In the other, he gave a piano performance master class peppered with his typical humor. Sarah burst into tears. She shook with despair and anguish, while a giant weight crushed her heart.

Tina returned home at 4:30 to see Sarah in the kitchen holding her arm, blood dripping on the floor and spattered against the white cabinets. A kitchen knife lay on nearby.

"Oh my God." Tina screamed and grabbed a towel which she wrapped around Sarah's wrist. It failed to stop the bleeding.

"I hate it here," Sarah sobbed. "I wanna die. I don't wanna live anymore."

Tina called 911 and watched with horror as her daughter clutched her wrist, as the blood soaked through the towel and flowed through her fingers. The paramedics and police arrived within three minutes, rushed over to Sarah and applied a tourniquet to her wrist along with gauze and pressure. After they got the bleeding under control, they placed her on a stretcher, and the ambulance sped off to the nearby hospital. Tina followed anxiously behind in her car.

The nurse triaged the dazed young girl in the emergency room, the physician on call examined Sarah's injury, and the nurse bandaged the girl's wrist and gave her a tetanus shot. Sarah was told to change into a hospital gown, and provide a urine sample. Afterward, the nurse placed Sarah in a private curtained partition with a hospital bed, a chair, several machines, and an IV pole. Sarah sat on the bed as her lower lip quivered and she covered her eyes with her hands. She looked like she would burst into tears again, but instead she lay down, turned toward the wall and closed her eyes.

A few minutes later, a cheery lab technician who carried a small plastic tray of different colored vials arrived, greeted Sarah and smiled. "I need to take a blood sample."

Sarah opened her eyes and sat up again, supported by her palms, which straddled the bed. Her eyes grew large. "Why?"

"Doctor's orders, honey. Please hold out your arm." After she felt for a vein, the lab technician tied a rubber tube around Sarah's upper arm and gently inserted a needle.

Sarah winced and closed her eyes again as the technician drew blood. In the meantime, the emergency physician consulted with the psychiatrist on call. The ER doctor, the nurse, and the social worker on duty stopped and spoke separately with both mother and daughter. Tina mentioned the family was in-hiding.

A short time later, Sarah's lab results came back negative for alcohol or drugs. After additional tests, the ER physician told Tina that Sarah's wound appeared more superficial than originally thought, so she would not need stitches or surgery. However, she needed to be Baker Acted to the adolescent psychiatric unit for a three-day observation at the downtown hospital After Tina signed papers, staff members escorted Sarah downtown to a unit behind a locked door which clicked loudly when shut.

At midnight. Tina was still at the hospital and called Cheryl.

"Honey, I'm so sorry to wake you up."

"No, you're fine. I'm just watching some TV in bed," said Cheryl. "What's going on?"

"Sarah tried to kill herself," said Tina.

"Good lord, I'm so sorry," said Cheryl. She thought of her own daughter.

"I knew you'd understand. Would you mind doing me a big favor? I'm so sorry to call you this late."

"Anything, Girlfriend. Just name it."

"Hans needs to go out. I can't leave the hospital. A spare key is taped under the green lawn chair out back. The cats should have enough food and water. Oh, and stay out of the kitchen. There is blood all over the floor."

"Don't you worry about a thing," said Cheryl. "You just get some sleep, y'hear? Your baby girl will be fine. I know that in my heart."

"I don't know how to thank you."

"Never you mind. Just go and get some sleep."

"I can't think straight. I'm exhausted. Should I call Artie and let him know?"

"What? Are you bananas? Absolutely not. Do you want to get killed?"

"She's crying over him. Maybe if he called her…."

"Don't. Just don't. Okay? Leave him alone. Please."

"I'll call the others in the morning. I don't want to disturb them now."

"Good night, darlin'. I'm heading over to your house now and will check on the pets again in the morning. Sleep tight."

Cheryl got dressed, got into her car and drove to Tina's house, found the key and let herself in. After she walked Hans, she entered the kitchen. Then, Cheryl donned rubber gloves, pulled bleach out of the cupboard and cleaned Sarah's dried blood off the floor and countertop. All the while, she said to herself that Tina and her daughter did not need to come home to this mess. They were already in a world of hurt.

When Tina awoke from the uncomfortable waiting room couch, it was already daylight. Her joints ached as she slowly sat up. After she called Leli and Adam, she took the elevator to the locked adolescent unit, and once she was buzzed in, the door clicked behind her. She found Sarah sitting upright in bed, dressed in a hospital gown and eating breakfast.

"Hi, sweetheart. Did you sleep well?" Tina hugged her daughter, but Sarah pulled away from her and did not speak.

"What do you care?"

"Why do you say that?"

"If you cared, you wouldn't leave me here."

"The police had to Baker Act you because of your suicide attempt."

"Well, I'm okay now, and I wanna get outta here. It be like I don't need a hospital."

"You'll get out as soon as you get better. I love you."

Sarah did not respond. She continued to eat her scrambled eggs.

"Sarah, do you want me to stay for a while?"

The girl frowned at her mother and shrugged her shoulders.

"Okay. I'm leaving and will be back in a bit."

"Whatever." Sarah gave Tina a dismissive stare.

Tina returned home to walk the dog and saw that Cheryl had cleaned up the kitchen. When she tried to call her friend to thank her, Tina only reached her voicemail and left a message of gratitude.

She returned to Sarah's room a short time later to see her daughter asleep and gently bent down and kissed her daughter's forehead before she left.

Three days later, Sarah came home, and Adam invited her and their mother to dinner at his favorite steak restaurant. Sarah's eyes squinted as she viewed the menu choices. "I want the onion blossom and a salad." She turned to her brother. "I don't eat meat, bro."

"Sarah, your brother knows you're a vegetarian," said Tina. "Don't be rude."

"That's okay, Mom," he said. "I'm the opposite. I want meat and lots of it."

Tina laughed. "Between both of your food preferences and Leli's insistence on organic food, I used to feel as if I was running a restaurant at home."

The server took their orders and returned with their drinks, During the meal, Jessie watched Sarah idly twirl her fork in her food before every bite.

"Are you feeling better?" said Jessie. "We really worried about you over the past few days."

Sarah nodded as she stared at her onion and dipped pieces into the accompanying sauce.

"How was the food at the hospital?" asked Adam.

"Okay."

"What did you do all day?" asked Jessie.

"Therapy and stuff."

"That's all?" said Adam.

"I started reading *The Hunger Games*. It's pretty good. I listened to some music and watched TV. I stayed to myself."

"You're more talkative. I can tell you're feeling better," said Tina. "We all love you so much. If you had died, it would have devastated our lives. If you feel suicidal again, please let me know right away, so we can get you help."

"I'm okay, Mom. Don't worry." Sarah smiled as she ate the last piece of onion. "In fact, I had time to really think about the future and now I have plans, so I don't wanna die."

"What plans?" asked her brother.

"Stuff. I wanna sing opera and go to college, maybe abroad. My dad said I couldn't do a thing with music, because I didn't play the piano as good as he wanted. Fuck him. I'll sing better than he ever played anything."

Tina's lips tightened and she shot Sarah a look. "Cool it with the language please."

"I'm serious. I'm going to bust my butt to do this."

The others smiled. "Keep up your dreams," said Tina.

★ ★ ★

JUNE 2015

Slowly but steadily, life returned to normal. Sarah's psychiatrist prescribed antidepressants for her, and she attended weekly counseling sessions. She told Tina everything helped and she hoped to wean off her medications soon.

Adam graduated with a degree in computer science and found a government position in cybersecurity. Jessie took a job with a business conglomerate downtown.

One day after work, Tina stopped for groceries at Publix supermarket. After she picked up a chocolate cake at the bakery, she added a bunch of flowers to her cart. Her next stop was the produce department. She reached over to grab a melon which slipped and fell to the floor. Before she could reach down, a man retrieved it and placed it in her cart.

"It looks unbruised, so I hope it's okay." He smiled at her.

"Thanks." Tina returned his smile. He was about her age, tall, rather thin, with gray hair and a mustache. He held out his hand. "Hi. Nice to meet you. My name's Ben."

Tina introduced herself, and they held a discussion about organic produce.

"I have a hunch you're a New Yorker." said Ben.

"Originally, but I haven't lived there in years."

"You never lose that accent." He smiled and stole a quick look at her hands. "You're not wearing a ring?"

"Divorced."

"Me too. Do you have any plans for Saturday?"

"Why, uh, no."

"I have an extra ticket for the big Musicale show at the Amway. Would you like to go?"

"Uh, sure." Tina smiled. "Why not?"

"Ok. I'll pick you up, we'll eat dinner first, and then see the show."

They exchanged phone numbers and emails. Tina gave him her address.

Back home, her stomach began to hurt. She broke into a sweat and shook like a leaf. This was her first date since her divorce. Plus, she had given a strange man her address and phone number. Although she chided herself for her stupidity, the idea of a pleasant date excited her.

Both Jewish and ex New Yorkers, Tina and Ben discovered a lot in common. A divorced podiatrist with two grown sons, Ben also lived in Winter Park. The relationship was upbeat and fun. They joked and laughed. He teased her about her gentile name, and she responded, "Yeah. I'm Jewish incognito."

As they dated and embarked on their relationship. Tina found it exhilarating but also proceeded with caution. She was not quite ready to get emotionally involved again.

★   ★   ★

AUGUST 2015

One evening Tina and Ben went to a dinner at a club where a dance band played afterward. Ben asked Tina to dance, but she hesitated.

She looked at him sheepishly. "I never learned how."

"How about I teach you? When I was young, I took professional lessons, and my ex and I loved to dance. Did you know there is a German club here in town? I heard they have nice dances and you might like to go there since you're German."

"The German club? I didn't know there was a German Club here. Where?"

"Casselberry. Not far. Let me show you some dance steps." The band struck up a Fox Trot. Ben took Tina's right hand and placed his right hand on her back. "Now place your left hand on my shoulder."

He held her close. "I lead and you follow. Put your right foot back first as I put my left foot forward. Let's do the Fox Trot. We go slow, slow quick, quick." Tina let him lead her as they danced in place. "Hey Tina, you're doing pretty well. You know, I'm a member of the Moose and Elk too, so we can go to their dances. There's even a great dinner dance at the Senior Center ballroom in south Orlando."

"Sounds like fun, especially the German Club." "Great, and we'll practice our dancing, the fox trot and rhumba and wait. I will teach you the waltz too."

"Oh goody. I just hope I don't step on your feet." Ben laughed. "I'll wear steel-toed shoes. Just kidding."

Tina thought to herself how different Ben was from Artie, calm, normal and pleasant. They saw each other two or three times a week for dinner and sometimes a movie, concert or play. Sometimes, they went to theme parks. Overall, they enjoyed each other's company, casual sex and nice activities.

In early September however, Ben had to take a leave of absence from his job and go to New York to take care of his ailing parents' business affairs. Meanwhile, Tina decided the family needed a vacation and found a good deal at an all-inclusive resort in the Bahamas late that month. Cheryl and Maggie also planned to go and split expenses.

To Tina's disappointment, Adam couldn't get off work, and Jessie would not go without him. However, Leli was able to get time off and flew in from Davis. Tina pulled Sarah out of school for the week.

The all-inclusive Four Winds resort with private cottages awaited them in Georgetown on Great Exuma Island. Tina and her daughters packed everything including new swimsuits and breezy tropical clothing they had bought in New Smyrna Beach.

Everyone excitedly planned events. As expected, Leli and Sarah expressed completely different interests. Shopping and the scheduled excursions to the marine iguanas on Allen Cay and Pig Beach on Big Major Cay especially delighted Sarah. She loved pigs and wanted to see the wild hogs swim in the ocean. Now a recently certified scuba diver, Leli mainly focused on undersea adventures in the clear waters among the coral reefs.

After their pleasant flight to Nassau, they took a city taxi tour during their layover. It surprised the girls to see cars drive on the left side of the road. Their first stop was the famous straw market. Vendor stalls, which sold straw baskets, wallets, hats, and other items, filled the aisles. Sarah watched, fascinated, as the basket makers wove their straw together into a piece of useable merchandise, but became consumed with the large collection of counterfeit handbags, which hung displayed against one wall. Sarah finally bought a pink wallet and a small blue and gold shoulder bag before she and the others strolled through the rest of the market.

Afterward, they headed back to the airport to catch their next flight, a small prop plane for the short ride to Georgetown, and after they landed, they took a taxi to the Four Winds resort.

A large fountain graced the lovely central building, which led to several restaurants. All meals were included in the travel package. The blue, green and pink colorful beachfront cottages looked out towards the sea, and the families' charming three-bedroom two-bath cottage perched on a slight hill facing the ocean. The windows framed a magnificent view of the turquoise water surrounded by the white beach and swaying palms against the deep blue sky floating with clouds. The whitewashed walls set off the coastal-style furniture, the white kitchenette and clean white beds. A blue and white striped rug graced the living room floor. A DVD player stood next to the satellite television on a shelf filled with movies. Outside, the sound of the surf intermingled with crowing roosters.

Sarah and Leli shared one room; Cheryl and Tina shared the second, while Maggie had the third room to herself.

The sisters giggled as they entered the cottage. "Oh, this place is lit," said Sarah.

Maggie smiled. She looked better than usual in a blue and green tropical sundress. Her pale face now had some color, while her chic haircut highlighted her red hair and blue eyes. "Wow," she said.

"How beautiful. I feel at peace." Then, she excused herself to retreat to her chosen bedroom to rest; the trip had already exhausted her.

Cheryl's brow furrowed. "I'm worried about her fibromyalgia," she whispered to Tina. "Maggie is always tired and in pain." Tina nodded her head in sympathy and turned around to look outside.

"Why don't we check out the beach, everyone?" said Tina.

The two sisters tossed their suitcases in their room, threw off their shoes and ran out the door to the ocean while they pressed their toes into the sand. Tina followed soon behind. As it was only mid-afternoon, the beach beckoned, so everyone returned to the cottage, slipped on swimsuits and slathered on sunscreen before heading back to the beach. Maggie surprised everyone as she ran into the water with a burst of energy, her hair glowing like gold fire in the sun. Afterward, they dried themselves in their thick hotel towels, spread them on the sand, and lay on the beach.

Tina regarded her daughters with concern. "You better reapply sunscreen, girls. The sun is strong here."

"I'm the one who usually gives instructions like that," laughed Leli. They all reapplied more lotion and lay back on their beach towels.

"I'm hungry," said Sarah.

"The restaurants open at 5," said Tina. "We have 30 minutes."

"I can't wait."

"Good grief, Sarah," said Leli. "You're always hungry. I'm surprised you're not fat as a house."

Sarah ignored Leli, picked up her towel, got up and went over to the fresh water beach shower. She washed off the sand before she dried herself and slipped on her flip-flops; the others followed before they returned to the cottage.

They changed clothing and everyone hung their wet swimsuits on the patio to dry. When they entered the main restaurant, a huge

Caribbean buffet, which included conch salad and chowder, rice and peas, and fresh Bahamian lobster surrounded by tropical fruit, greeted them. Two large bowls of rum and virgin punch stood on the adjacent table. Sarah poured herself a glass of the alcoholic punch.

Tina admonished her. "Sarah, give it to me. You're too young to drink."

"Oh, ma'am, we're not strict here," said one of the servers. "Your daughter can have a drink if she wants."

The remark annoyed Tina, because it sabotaged her own instructions. Sarah paused.

"You heard me."

The girl reluctantly handed the drink over.

"Watch your alcohol," said Tina. "You've got drunks on both sides of your family."

"Shit. The struggle is real. I have ugly DNA. I can't drink because I'll become an alcoholic. I can't eat because I'll get fat. I'm wack." Sarah pouted, poured herself a glass of the virgin punch and plopped herself down on her chair with an annoyed look.

Cheryl chuckled. "Sarah, I'm sorry you're upset, but your mom's right."

Leli sipped her rum punch slowly. "Don't pout, sis. This is minor. You're hundred and the GOAT. One amazing talented kid.".

"What?" asked Tina, puzzled.

"Oh, Mom, that means she rocks. Greatest Of All Time. 100 means she's the best."

"Thank you. I thought you called your little sister a barnyard animal."

Leli paused for a moment with a mouthful and swallowed, as she motioned over toward a couple at a nearby table.

"Did you hear those people over there? They're talking about a possible hurricane coming here in the next few days."

"Oh, I'm not worried," smiled Tina. "I doubt we'll get a real storm here. Hurricanes are rare."

"I won't worry about it either, then," laughed Leli. "I hope the only hurricane we'll encounter is in my book I'm reading on Kindle, *Their Eyes Were Watching God.*"

"Zora Neale Hurston was a fabulous writer," said Maggie. "I've read all our books."

"Let's concentrate about our boat excursion tomorrow to Pig Island, and whether Sarah will see her swimming pigs. Otherwise, she'll be bummed." said Tina.

"Yeah, I can't wait," said Sarah.

"I signed up online for a dive trip the day after tomorrow," said Leli. "What will you and Cheryl do, Mom?"

"We'll probably just end up on the beach with piña coladas. Right, Girlfriend?"

"You betcha," said Cheryl.

Tina pulled a book out of her purse. "Oh, I forgot to leave this back in the room."

"What are you reading?" asked Maggie. *"Harry Potter and the Sorcerer's Stone."*

"You never read that before?" said Sarah.

"Hey, I'm a little behind, okay? I only saw the movies with you kids. With everything on my shoulders 24/7, when did I have time to read?"

The sisters looked at their mother and nodded in sympathy.

Back in the room, Sarah pulled out two dozen chocolate nut bars from her bag and put them away in the kitchen cabinet.

Leli began to laugh. "That was Artie's favorite candy."

"I don't wanna talk about him."

"Good idea. At least not on this trip," said Tina. "We don't need him vacationing rent-free in our heads."

"Maybe we'll see him tomorrow on Pig Island with his little porcine eyes," said Leli. "Seriously, what's the story with the pigs?"

"Nobody knows how they got there", said Tina. "Some say sailors left them behind."

When the excursion boat arrived at the island. Everyone saw several pink and multicolored swine in the ocean near the small sandy cay, as stingrays swam between them. Sarah excitedly waded into the water as she shouted, "Piggies! Piggies!" The others followed her, and soon everyone splashed around and petted the pigs. They also touched a few stingrays. After their adventure, they returned to the hotel, and Sarah promptly posted her photos to Instagram.

Later Adam called Tina. "I'm worried. I heard on the morning news that there's a hurricane possibly heading your way. Maybe you should cut your trip short."

"Thanks, but we'll be okay," said Tina. "You know how hurricanes turn to go off in different directions. We're having such a good time that I don't want to disappoint the girls and leave early Don't worry about us. However, we miss you."

"Okay, Mom. Whatever. I don't know why you booked this vacation during the height of hurricane season." She heard him audibly sigh over the phone.

"It was such a great deal, I couldn't resist."

"No wonder. Who wants vacation with hurricanes?"

"We'll be fine." She reassured him again. "Remember, we had earthquakes, mudslides and fires back in California. I'm not worried."

The next day, Leli met the dive team. Dressed in her blue one-piece swimsuit, she brought along her rented equipment. The group boarded a large fishing boat, and when they reached their mid-ocean destination, they dropped anchor. Each group member teamed up with a dive buddy. Leli partnered with Jack, an older man from North Carolina. After she put on her mask and equipment and made sure her diver's knife was readily available, she slid into the water along with the others and slowly descended to the bottom.

The sight took her breath away. The coral reefs sparkled like rich jewels, underground weeds waved gently in the water and colorful exotic fish circled around her. She saw several sharks overhead, which ignored the divers. Two sea turtles floated past her. Jack photographed her with his underwater camera as she pointed upwards to the sharks. Afterward, she drifted over to a broken shipwreck, sunk halfway in the sand. She explored the wreckage for a few minutes until it was time to ascend. Then, she rejoined Jack, rising slowly to avoid decompression sickness.

Meanwhile, the others visited a local crafts market in Georgetown. Sarah again watched straw artisans weave personalized designs on straw items and chose a bag embroidered with red and pink flowers; the stall vendor deftly stitched SARAH between the blooms. Afterward, the two families stopped at a small beachside restaurant for lunch.

"What are we doing tomorrow?" Cheryl took a sip of her Bahama Mama, her long pink manicured nails encircling the glass.

"Allen Cay, remember? We're going to see the marine iguanas," said Maggie.

"I read the iguanas enjoy being hand-fed," said Tina. "We can pick up some lettuce here at the market for them." Tina stopped and looked closely at Sarah as she sat in her white shorts and t-shirt, her dark curly hair tumbling out of her baseball cap. "You're already too tanned. Easy does it."

"I use sunscreen." Sarah adjusted her sunglasses and glanced at her left hand with its pink acrylic nails with rhinestones in the center.

"Could have fooled me. Stay in the shade."

The next day, they walked around the small rocky island where large brownish iguanas roamed the white beach, again surrounded by the turquoise water. The families hand-fed the docile creatures lettuce and took selfies.

When they returned to the hotel, they walked into the lobby to see anxious staff standing around the television, as a hurricane warning flashed on the screen.

"Do you think it will come here?" Tina asked the desk clerk.

"They say it may," said the woman. "It's not certain yet."

The next day after breakfast, the families relaxed again on the beach. Tina and Leli read, as Sarah lay in the sun listening to music on her earbuds. Cheryl and Maggie took a walk along the shore.

Leli looked up. "Listen to this quote," she said. "Zora Neale Hurston says it all."

They are waiting for a hurricane. They sat in company with the others in other shanties, their eyes straining against crude walls and their souls asking if He meant to measure their puny might against His. They seemed to be staring at the dark, But their eyes were watching God.

"Don't jinx this trip," laughed Tina.

"Hurricane, go away," said Sarah. "I'm so lit here; I feel like I never wanna leave."

Maggie and Cheryl returned from their walk, just as a steward ran toward the beach. He stopped when he saw the women.

"Excuse me, ladies. There is a hurricane warning for the island. We'll know shortly when we have to evacuate."

"Oh, no," whined Sarah. "I don't wanna go back yet."

Tina ignored her daughter and turned to the steward. "What should we do now?" she asked.

"Management will be glad to help you change your plane reservations if it comes to that, ma'am. The airlines are quite responsive here."

Tina stood up. "Girls, we better pack up, so we'll be ready if we have to leave."

"Absolutely," said Cheryl. Sarah and Leli reluctantly rose and walked to the room behind the others to the cottage.

That evening at dinner, the hotel manager Mr. Preston announced that Hurricane Joaquin was bearing down on the Bahamas, and mandatory evacuation was in effect for the following morning. He told the worried guests that the hotel would assist with flight changes. The two families listened as they ate dinner in anxious silence. Immediately afterward, they stopped at the front desk and provided their flight information to the clerk Anita before they returned to their cabin. She called an hour later.

"You're in luck. We had difficulty rebooking your flight, as the airlines stopped taking reservations. However, we were able to reserve seats for you on the last flight that leaves the island tomorrow."

Tina and Cheryl returned to the front desk, tipped and thanked Anita. Tina texted Adam, who replied that he was glad to hear the family was coming home.

The next day, everyone reluctantly headed home with their suitcases in a taxi toward town. When they neared the straw market, Sarah turned toward her mother. "Hey Mom, let's stop at the straw market one last time. Please."

"Oh, for heaven's sake, what for?"

"I want to get one of those cute purses for my friend Megan."

"Why didn't you think of this before?" asked Tina.

"I forgot it's her birthday," said Sarah.

Tina sighed. "Okay. Make it quick though."

Many vendors crowded the open market and hoped to make a quick sale to the tourists still in town.

Sarah walked around and could not decide what to buy.

"Okay. Enough. We have to leave," said Leli.

"Come on, Sarah. It's time to go," Tina said in an impatient tone.

They turned around. She had disappeared.

Everyone hastened through the aisles calling Sarah's name. Nothing. Tina almost hailed a Royal Bahamas Police Force officer for assistance, when Sarah showed up 30 minutes later holding a bag.

"It's about time," said Leli in a loud tone. "Let's get out of here."

They frantically hailed a cab, but crowded roads to the airport brought the traffic to a halt. Sadly, by the time they reached the Exuma International Airport in Moss Town, they missed their plane. Tina checked with all the airlines and verified there were no more flights. Devastated, everyone panicked.

Leli's cool manner tumbled, as she burst into rare tears, which flowed like a river down her flaming cheeks and nose. "Fuck you, Sarah. I could kill you right now. This is all your fault, and now we have to ride out the storm. You're wack."

Sarah began to sob loudly. "I didn't mean to."

Leli stopped crying after a moment, composed herself and blew her nose as she pulled a tissue from her purse. She took a breath but still glanced angrily at her sister. "Quit your boohooing and face the music!"

Sarah sobbed louder. "Shut up. I hate you."

Leli finally looked away, her arms folded her arms across her chest. "Thanks. Now we're stuck here."

Cheryl spoke. "Y'all are being ugly, girls, so quit. What's done is done. You know what I'm sayin'? Tears won't help us get home."

"Cheryl's right. There's nothing we can do now except to go back and ride out the storm," said Tina.

When they arrived at the Four Winds, Anita came out to greet them.

"I'm sorry you missed your flight," she said nodding her head in sympathy. "The storm is supposed to make landfall late tonight. You can sleep in the lounge if you want, or return to your cabin. We put hurricane shutters in place earlier today."

Cheryl and Tina shot glances at each other. "We'll go back to the house," said Leli.

"Let me get you enough food," said Anita. She hastily packed bread, peanut butter, a few bananas, apples and bottled water in two bags and also handed Tina two flashlights and candles with a book of matches. "You may need these."

They thanked her, and returned to their cottage. The closed shutters created a gloomy darkness inside. Tina put the food provisions away, set one flashlight near her bed and another on the kitchen table.

"There's still some leftover candy," said Sarah and pointed out the packages that remained in the cupboard.

"We may need all of it. Thanks hon," said Cheryl.

The women stepped outside, as the sea churned before them. Foamy whitecaps formed, as the waves rolled forward on the beach and back to the sea. The rain began falling relentlessly and pounded the cottage roof with a deafening sound.

The wind picked up that evening with a low howl. The whole cottage shook with each powerful gust, as if the earth at the end of its rope wreaked one final turmoil upon the world. Then the lights went out.

Fear had returned this time with a menacing vengeance.

The wind continued to howl and roar nonstop in the darkness. The cottage trembled as the shutters rattled back and forth. Cheryl lit a candle, set it on the kitchen table and sat down with her laptop.

"Girls, it's not so bad," she said and waved her hand toward the table. "Come on over."

The candle illuminated their faces with a soft glow, as it sent huge flickering shadows across the walls. The only sound they heard was the house, which convulsed and swayed in the wind.

Leli sat down and laughed nervously. "It looks like a séance here."

"I'm so scared. It's wack," said Sarah.

"Let's keep our cool," said Tina.

"Do you want to play a board game?" said Cheryl.

Leli shook her head. "I'm too nervous."

"Me too," said Sarah.

"Well, let's tell jokes," said Cheryl cheerily. "Do you know what redneck couples say when they break up? 'Let's just be cousins.'"

Everyone laughed. "I'm glad you're here, Cheryl. You're so upbeat," said Tina.

"I got a joke too," said Sarah. "This isn't a hurricane. It's a himicane. If a himicane and a hurricane had a baby, its name would be Stormy." She smiled. "I, Sarah, made up that one myself. Can I have an amen?"

"Funny," said Cheryl.

"Rather juvenile," said Leli.

"Well then, make a better joke," said Sarah haughtily.

"I'll make a poem instead."

"English was always one of your favorite subjects," laughed Tina. "Take it away, Emily Dickinson."

Leli turned to Cheryl and Maggie. "I used to write a little bit of poetry, when I was in high school. Let me see what I can come up with." She thought for a moment. "Okay. Joaquin, you're a fuck. Go away. You suck."

Maggie chimed in. "I have got one too. 'Joaquin, you won't ever win. We'll bust your big fat ass through thick and thin.'" She stopped. "Oh, what the hell. I'm a pianist, not a poet."

"Oh, you're fine, honey," said Cheryl. "Everything you do is gold."

"Well, you girls are clever for sure," said Tina. "Go ahead and make jokes. Hey Mon, no problem."

Everyone laughed again. Maggie stood up and rubbed her eyes. "Goodnight, y'all. Let's get some rest."

"I hope we get some sleep, in spite of the storm. Come on, Sarah," said Leli. They left the kitchen and headed for their rooms.

Tina lit a second candle and set it on the kitchen table.

"That gives us a bit more light. I think one candle is too eerie."

"Want some wine?"

"Sure. Why not?"

Cheryl retrieved two glasses from the cupboard and poured some chardonnay. "Cheers."

"A cloud crossed over Tina's face, as she clinked glasses with Cheryl. She quickly drank her wine and poured herself another glass. "I don't normally drink this much, but I'm freaked out."

"This is the worst thing I've ever been through," said Cheryl. "A total nightmare."

"It's probably peach pie though compared to the hell I went through with Artie." Tina lowered her voice. "He was so abusive, that I was a shell of myself while married to him." Tina turned her head toward the bedroom doors. "I hope they can't hear me."

"You've told me before how bad he treated you and the kids, how he raped you and forced you to do all kinds of nasty, embarrassing stuff. Horrible."

"I used to hide everything, because he made me feel so ashamed."

"But none of it was your fault, honey. I don't know how or why you put up with him for so long, but you did a great job of raising your kids, that's for sure."

"Thanks. They were all difficult as teens, especially Adam, but I think he's turned around. He actually apologized to me. Told me after he saw his girlfriend's nice family interact with each other, he realized he was being a jerk."

Cheryl smiled and poured herself a second glass as Tina paused a moment.

"I think I told you that before our divorce, we had a session with my therapist. I got a copy of the evaluation. Do you know what she said about Artie? She said she thought he had Asperger's."

"Not surprising. He sounds weird. That makes sense."

"She wrote a bunch of other stuff, but that's in the past. Now, Sarah worries me the most," said Tina. "I knew it would be hard for her to adjust, because she grew up in LA and sang in a lot of big events and operas. She's in much smaller groups now, but she has a great voice teacher and is making real improvement."

"When we went to her school concert last spring, I was amazed by her voice," said Cheryl. "She sang her solo so beautifully and with so much expression." She paused and bit into a chocolate bar. "I never told you much about me. I met Joey doing a commercial photoshoot downtown. He had quite a photography business, weddings, portraits, commercial stuff. He shot photos for the ballet and opera as a volunteer and also acted in several plays at a local amateur theater. Joey was single, funny as all get out and looked a little like Gene Wilder with reddish curly hair. We fell in love, but he was 22 years older than me and when we got married, people told me I was nuts, because of the age difference. Actually, I was already pregnant, and Maggie was born, right after Joey's 51st birthday. She was his only kid. When she was about four, we saw her playing around on her aunt's piano, so we bought her one and got her lessons. By the time she was seven, an obvious child prodigy, she played Mozart and Chopin and Beethoven unbelievably well, but at that time, it was hard to find a teacher who knew how to work with her. We always encouraged Maggie and found her a great teacher.

"Joey was kind, energetic and funny, but he tried to hide from me that he was gay, and I resented him for a long time after our divorce, until he became horribly ill and died." She took a sip of wine and continued. "His death devastated Maggie. She was only 11, and they had a very close relationship." Cheryl paused. "In spite of our differences, Joey was a kind person and a good father. I think I understand him better now."

"I guess we've both moved on," said Tina thoughtfully. "You know, how I survived? Every time he hurt me, I turned away, and my turns became increasingly distant. I disassociated myself from his abuse. You know, I was so naïve when I met him. Today I'd never even talk two seconds to a guy like him." She got up and poured them both another glass of wine. "He was nothing to look at, but I was so impressed by his talent and attention he gave me. He showered me with love, made me laugh and wanted to marry me. I was a different person then."

"The other night, Maggie told me they're Facebook friends."

Tina wrung her hands. "Oh no. Please tell her not to mention us."

"Don't worry," said Cheryl. "They only worked together professionally. Maggie finds him friendly and funny, but odd and rather gross."

339

Tina sighed. "I'm glad I met Ben. He's so refreshing, such a nice Jewish guy. We're different though. His family has been here for generations and didn't go through what my parents went through. Sometimes, it's hard for him to understand me." She startled as a gust of wind blew around the house.

Cheryl tried unsuccessfully to get a weather update on her laptop and sighed. "Shit. No signal."

CRASH. A thunderbolt boomed over the cottage, which shook violently in the darkness. Sarah screamed and ran into the kitchen. Something splashed against the wall accompanied by the sound of trickling water. Leli appeared, pulled out the flashlight, and shone it on the door.

"Oh no. We're flooded!" screamed Tina. "Quick! Get to higher ground!"

"Grab your stuff off the floor and put it as high as you can," said Cheryl. Everyone moved their belongings to the dresser tops.

"Let's at least try to get some rest," said Tina. "I think everybody should stay on their beds, since the house is flooded."

Cheryl nodded in agreement, go up and went to the bathroom.

"No running water. Can't flush the toilet. I'm glad we saved water in the tub."

"We can throw it in the toilet tank to flush the commode."

"That only works for pee," said Sarah. "How about if we have to poop?"

Maggie laughed. "Sarah, only you would think of something like that at a time like this. Just fill up several buckets."

Tina turned to her daughter. "As they say in Yiddish, *geh kacken im yam.* Go shit in the sea."

Leli laughed. "Didn't Tante Helene say that?"

Tina sighed. "That was one of her good Yiddish sayings. Gosh, how I miss her and Stevie. Let's get to our rooms. The carpet is already soaked."

Leli pulled off her shoes and sloshed over the wet carpet with her bare feet. "Watch out everybody!" she shouted. "Don't get electrocuted. Watch out for snakes." The others also pulled off their shoes and walked barefoot into their rooms.

Sarah and Leli sat on their beds. Maggie came to the doorway with her flashlight.

"Can I hang out with you?"

Leli moved over to make room, and when Maggie reached Leli's bed, she sat down, pulled out a towel and dried off her feet. "I come prepared," she laughed.

"Good idea," said Leli.

"Hey Sarah, how are your voice lessons going?"

"Awesome. Music in my blood, and I want to keep on singing," said Sarah.

"You're talented that's for sure," said Leli.

"You need to be dedicated, work like a dog, take master classes and do well in competitions," said Maggie. "Even then, there are no guarantees."

"I'll give it a good shot," laughed Sarah.

"You're an ambitious kid. I'd like to hear you sing someday," said Maggie. "Maybe I can even accompany you on the piano." She stopped and sighed. "That is, if my left hand ever recovers."

"I'm sorry," said Leli. "What happened?"

"My little sports car skidded out of control, and I injured my left hand. Nerve damage."

"That's so tragic."

"After the accident, I tried to drown myself. That's how despondent I was, because my career was over. I walked into the surf in New Smyrna Beach, swam until I encountered a riptide and let the water rush over me. I was ready to die. Suddenly, a lifeguard's strong arms pulled me to shore, and I just collapsed on the sand. The next thing I knew I was in the hospital psych unit."

Sarah spoke slowly. "Same here. I tried to kill myself last March, because I missed LA, missed...," she hesitated, "my dad. One day, I just slashed my wrist before Mom got home. I'm glad she found me in time." Sarah held up her arm with the still-obvious pink scar.

"I hope you got counseling afterwards," said Maggie. "I've been seeing a therapist."

"I see Bonnie every week and take depression meds," said Sarah. "I feel better, and now, I want to live."

"I can see definite improvement," said Leli. "You still have your moments, but you're definitely more upbeat."

"How's work, Leli?" asked Maggie.

"The ER has always a challenge, but I feel so needed there. I've thinking about grad school, because I want to be a nurse practitioner."

"Where is grad school?"

Leli shook her head. "Not sure yet. We'll see. Right now, I'm glad to be away from home. I recently broke up with my boyfriend, and my grandmother is in a nursing home with dementia and doesn't know me."

"Sorry about that," said Maggie. "I guess you're not in touch with your dad, huh?"

"We haven't had contact since he hurt Mom. I'm done."

"You know," said Maggie slowly. "I performed together with your dad in LA a few years ago." She stopped and looked closely at Leli. "You kinda resemble him."

"Now, you're not my friend anymore."

"Sorry. No offense meant. You're much better looking."

"Don't worry," laughed Leli. "You're forgiven as long you guys aren't friends."

"Just on Facebook, but no contact, girlfriend. No worries."

"Thankfully nobody's heard from him in ages. He's even ghosted Adam. He must be respecting our restraining order."

"Hashtag rude crude dude," said Sarah. "My therapist Bonnie helps me understand it wasn't my fault that he dissed me, and that he has mental problems." She turned toward her older sister. "Mom said once someone told her dad was Ass pear something."

"You mean Asperger's?" said Leli. "Possibly. He has other mental issues too. It's not us."

"That's what Bonnie said. Hey, I feel better now."

The sisters laughed. "Good," said Leli. "When I was in college, I went into therapy to deal with my anger, frustration and relationship problems, all mostly because of him. I struggled, but I'm better now as well."

"How strange to feel suddenly at peace during a hurricane," said Maggie as she leaned back against the headboard.

At that moment, the powerful wind died with a final roar and whimpered mild gusts, as the patter of rain danced around outside. Shutters and loose boards banged outside. About five inches of water now flooded the cottage.

Leli looked up. "I think this is the eye. This isn't over yet."

Shortly afterwards, the storm began again, and the wind continued to howl around the cottage while the rain pounded the roof. Then, all was quiet.

Tina lay on her bed wide awake for what seemed forever, as the hot humid air inside the cottage stifled her, and the wind howled outside. Finally, the wind lapsed into stillness, so she slipped on her flip flops and tried to open the window, but she had forgotten about the shutters. Luckily, they were loose, so she was able to push them out, and a cool breeze blew into the bedroom. Tina walked back out to the main area. Cheryl still sat in the dark without looking up, her face illuminated by her laptop. "I had a signal for a few minutes. They say this is the worst storm to hit the Bahamas in the last century."

"I wouldn't doubt it," said Tina. "It was pretty scary for a while." She sat down next to Cheryl. "I wonder if there is any wine left."

"Check the cupboards. I'm game."

Tina returned with a bottle of red wine and two of Sarah's nutty double chocolate candy bars.

"When in crisis," laughed Cheryl. "Morning is here already."

Leli appeared in the doorway. She gingerly sloshed through the water to the kitchen.

"Chocolate," she whispered as she also helped herself to a candy bar, took a wine glass out of the cupboard, sat down next to the women and poured wine into the three glasses. "Chocolate wine would be even better."

Cheryl paused to wipe her face. "Boy, it's really muggy in here."

"Let's open more doors and windows," Leli said. "It's already light outside," as she peeked through the window and saw that the early sunrise had left the sky a pale peach-gray. Leli carefully opened the door, but as water flowed inside between her feet, she stepped back and quickly shut the door. After a moment, she said, "I guess I'll step outside and check out what's happening right now."

"Be careful, okay? Oh, what the hell, I'll go with you." Tina slipped on her flip-flops.

"I'm going too. Give me a moment." Cheryl slipped into her room to return shortly wearing shorts and a T-shirt.

The three women stepped outside and quickly shut the door behind them to keep out the several inches of water outside the door. Thankfully, their little cottage had survived and was more or less intact. The same thing sadly did not apply to the other cabins. Roof pieces and shattered glass panes lay on the ground. Blown-off doors floated along with broken furniture in the ocean. Large gaping holes took the place of windows and doors. The storm had reduced several cottages and nearby homes to matchsticks. The main building had lost most of its roof. Torn curtains flapped through broken windows and swayed to the breeze.

Debris lay everywhere. The women waded carefully in the ankle-high stagnant water to move around as a strong fishy scent wafted in the air and floated into their nostrils. Tina tried unsuccessfully to text Adam without a signal.

Carefully, the women made their way to the clubhouse and there, terrible damage awaited them. Broken patio furniture lay throughout the property. The hole-covered walls still stood, but shattered glass lay everywhere. The restaurant where they dined the night before was unrecognizable. Turned-over tables and chairs scattered around the room. Nobody else seemed to be around.

Cheryl turned to Tina. "Let's hope we don't run into looters."

Just then, they heard voices in the kitchen and saw three staff members briskly sweeping up debris.

"Hi, honey," said Cheryl brightly as she spotted one of the dining room servers. "Do y'all have any food for us?"

"I'm sorry, but most of the food spoiled in the storm."

"Oh dear," said Tina. "What do you suggest?"

"I don't know what to tell you. All the roads are blocked and there's no power. Our manager Mr. Preston is not around right now but knows you're still here."

"Thanks. I guess we'll have to figure something out," said Tina.

"Wait." Another woman in the kitchen called out, "Ma'am, please wait a moment. I'm one of the cooks here." She quickly walked into the pantry and the freezer before she returned with bread, butter, and cheese. "That's all that's left," she said. "The cheese is still cold, so it's good." She laid the food on the counter. "And how many guests, please?"

"Five," said Leli.

The cook smiled and made five sandwiches as Tina spotted an intact table with several chairs in the corner.

"May we leave these sandwiches here while we get our daughters?" asked Tina.

"Of course," smiled the cook.

"I'll watch them for you. Maybe there won't be five," joked the man in the kitchen.

"Are you a cook too?" asked Tina.

"Oh no, madam," laughed the man. "I'm only one of the houseboys."

As the women thanked them and left, Tina turned to Cheryl. "I haven't heard the term 'houseboy' in years."

"It's a British term," said Cheryl. "I read it somewhere in an article."

They returned to the cottage.

"Ok. Let's get dressed so we can leave after we eat." Tina made sure she spoke in a loud voice.

Maggie stood in the kitchen, already dressed, her suitcase on a chair. "I'm ready," she said softly.

"Where's Sarah?" asked Leli.

"Still asleep," said Maggie.

"She's got to get up," said Tina, who walked carefully through the water into the girls' bedroom. Leli followed gingerly behind her.

When Sarah slept, it sometimes took a miracle to awaken her. Tina nudged her several times, until the girl finally awoke and rubbed her eyes.

"Let's get outta here and up to the hotel. Get dressed," ordered Leli. She picked up Sarah's suitcase and took it to the kitchen table. Sarah retreated to the bathroom and let out a shriek.

"What's wrong?" asked Tina,

"I hate my hair. It's frizzy and gross," said Sarah as she pulled her curls back, frowned and looked in the mirror.

"Are you kidding me?" said Leli. "We've got a crisis here, and you're worried about your hair?"

"The struggle is real," said Sarah.

"Struggle, schmuggle, let's get out of here," said Tina.

Everyone grabbed their suitcases and handbags, which they held as high as they could as they waded through the murky water and walked up the hill into the main building, where they sat at a table alone and ate their sandwiches amidst the debris. Afterward, they walked towards the lobby, which appeared surprisingly intact, while the outside looked like a disaster movie with crushed flooded cars, boats turned upside down on shore, rubble everywhere, and downed telephone poles and wires.

"What a great way to get electrocuted," said Leli. "How shocking. Bad pun intended."

"Oh Lord," Anita appeared. "I thought I heard voices. Are you okay?"

"We're fine, but the cottage has severe damage," answered Cheryl. "Now I reckon we need to get home as soon as we can."

"My apologies," said Anita. "The electricity is out, and we don't have cellphone service. Cars cannot navigate the roads, which are all washed out."

"No cellphone service? Excuse me. I have to go die now," cried Sarah. Leli shot her a dirty look.

"Well," said Anita slowly, "There is a ham radio on the premises. Mr. Preston, our manager, knows how to operate it."

"Is he around?" asked Tina

"He went home last night before the storm," Anita replied.

"Oh no," said Tina. "Is there any way to reach him?"

"He lives nearby," said Anita. "I'll go get him. It's a short walk to his home."

"Thanks, but please be careful," said Tina. "I need to let my son know we're okay."

The women sat back on the sofa, closed their eyes and waited. Almost two hours passed before Anita and Mr. Preston arrived back at the hotel.

"Thank goodness you're here," said Cheryl.

"How will you work the radio without electricity?" asked Maggie.

"We have generator backup in case of emergency," said Mr. Preston. "Come with me."

The two families followed him to a back room, which had a large ham radio with a receiver and microphone on a table. Besides a desk chair, the room was otherwise empty.

"Excuse me a moment."

The women heard a distant noise outside and suddenly the room lit up.

"Isn't that dangerous with the downed power lines?" asked Leli when Mr. Preston returned.

"Our generator only powers this small area," he said. "The breakers are off everywhere else."

He sat down and turned on the radio, began moving dials and before long, reached a ham radio operator in Miami. Tina asked him to contact Adam to let him know everyone was safe and provided her son's phone number and email. Mr. Preston also asked the operator to contact the Royal Bahamas Defence Force to help evacuate the resort.

When they returned to the lobby, Sarah stretched out on the chair, pulled up her phone and set it down again in frustration. Her mouth twisted to one side, and her eyebrows narrowed. "I'm so wack. No signal. I can't check my phone. Can't play games, nothing."

"Please get off your high horse," said Tina. "This is a tough enough situation as it is."

Sarah got up and walked to the window, where she looked out onto the ocean. Suddenly she shouted excitedly, "Someone's here. I see a ship ready to dock."

Outside, a ship anchored in the water, and several small motorboats headed toward land.

Everyone grabbed their things belongings and ran down toward the shore.

One man steered his boat right up to the beach. One by one, everyone climbed into the boat and when they arrived at the ship, they saw several other stranded individuals.

"We're taking you to Nassau," said one of the RBDF officers. "From there, a special plane will take U.S. citizens to Miami. Make sure you have your passports ready for customs once you arrive. An American embassy representative will be there to assist as well."

Three hours later, the ship docked in Nassau. Maggie noticed the scores of cameras and reporters.

"This must be big news," she said as she turned to her mother.

"Oh, good gracious," said Cheryl. "I hope I look presentable."

After the main doors opened, passengers proceeded down the gangway to an explosion of camera shutters. Sarah followed behind the others but tripped at the bottom of the gangway; an officer lifted her up and set her down on land, as camera shutters whirred.

At the airport, the two families received reissued airline tickets. Tina now had a phone signal for the first time and saw three frantic texts from Ben and two from Adam.

The phone rang with a call from Adam. "A ham operator you contacted let me know you guys were okay. Then, I saw you on CNN."

"What? We're famous?"

"You were on the news."

"Amazing. We're leaving soon for Miami, and as soon as I have our flight plans to Orlando, I'll text you."

"Safe travels. See you soon. Bye."

When they finally arrived that evening, Adam greeted them, and they all hugged each other with relief.

"I'm so glad we're home," said Tina. "That was not a fun experience."

"I bet," laughed Adam. "Let me help with the luggage." He picked up the suitcases and bags which he piled into the back of his new silver Jeep, and with an upbeat mood, they headed down Semoran Boulevard toward Winter Park.

"So, what's new?" asked Tina. "Is everything okay?"

"Well...." Adam stopped. "I got a text."

Tina shivered. The air around her turned to ice.

"A text from...?" Tina asked. "Your father?"

Adam nodded. "It's the first time I've heard from him since you moved here."

A horrific shock flew through Tina's body like electricity as her stomach dropped like an anchor to her knees. "Did he ask where we are? I hope you didn't say anything."

"Mom, really," said Adam in a somewhat indignant tone. "Actually, it was a kind of bizarre. I'll read it to you when we get home."

When they arrived at the house, Cheryl and Maggie put their suitcases in their car, said goodbye and left for home. Adam pulled out a beer from the refrigerator.

"Okay," said Tina anxiously. "What did he say?"

Adam matter-of-factly pulled out his phone from his pocket.

"It was crazy ass as usual. He also sent a photo." Adam showed Tina the message.

Dear Adam, I hope this is still your number. Damn headache here.!! Bad bourbon after concert. I LOST $$$ at poker last night!!! I saw mom and sisters ON THE NEWS!! Are they with you?

Tina turned pale and handed the phone back to Adam who continued, "I texted him back and told him everyone was fine and to leave you alone. I reminded him about the court order. Haven't heard back since."

"Oh Yuck." She stared at the photo with a look of horror and disgust, but could not tear her eyes away. "He looks drunk and hungover. I bet he shot this selfie purely for attention."

Artie's distraught contorted moon-like face was framed in semi-darkness, and his head rested wearily in his left hand. His tuxedo was clearly visible.

Tina handed the phone back to her son. "I'm freaked out, because I'm still afraid he'll find us."

"He has no idea where you are. I'm sure of that." Adam finished his beer and threw the bottle into the recycle bin. "I'll keep you safe and monitor him on Facebook. He blabbers about everything."

★   ★   ★

OCTOBER 2015

Tina and Sarah followed the realtor through the mid-century Winter Park three-bedroom, two-bath modern bungalow, upgraded with restored wooden floors, a contemporary remodeled kitchen with the latest stainless-steel appliances and newly outfitted bathrooms. As Tina and Sarah gazed at the white stucco house with the palm tree in front, they knew it would be their perfect new home.

Sarah chose her bedroom, and it delighted her to finally have her own bathroom.

★   ★   ★

NOVEMBER 2015

Tina sat at the computer, her head spinning so fast, she could not think straight on that quiet Saturday morning. She was alone, since Sarah had stayed overnight at a friend's house. Adam and Jessie had gifted Tina a DNA test for her September birthday and now, she shook her head in disbelief at the results and aghast, stared at the emails sent her by the genealogist she had hired.

It was too much. She had to speak to someone in person, so she called Cheryl.

"Can you come over?" asked Tina. "I'm really freaked out right now."

"Sure, honey." Cheryl sounded alarmed. "What's going on? Is it your ex again?"

"It's something else." Tina could barely get the words out.

"Give me an hour."

When Cheryl arrived, Tina answered the door, pale with uncombed hair and a faraway look in her eyes, as she wrung her hands.

Cheryl gave her a quick hug. "Oh my God. What's wrong?"

"I had news today about my family. Come in." She motioned Cheryl to sit down. "My DNA came back." She caught her breath. "I'm 50 percent Jewish and 50 percent English and Irish."

"What? Maybe there's a mistake."

"That's what I thought at first. Then, the DNA test matched me up with my relatives. I have a half-brother, Michael Farswell. Farswell was my mother's boss when she worked on Wall Street. Max was not my biological dad. I'm shocked." Cheryl became wide-eyed. Tina walked into the kitchen. "I just made coffee. You want some?"

Cheryl nodded, and Tina returned with two steaming mugs. She disappeared into her bedroom and returned carrying a box before sitting down next to Cheryl. "There's more. I got my genealogy report back today. I knew about Dad's past and being sent to Auschwitz, but nothing about my mother except she came from Berlin and had a younger brother who died in the camps. After the War, she and my dad married at a refugee camp and when they arrived here, they changed their last name from Perlstein to Perry. Today, I found out about Mom's past, and I had to talk to someone."

Cheryl took a sip of coffee. "Tell me about it."

Tina blew on the coffee cup to cool the hot liquid. "In 1940 when she was 20, Mom married a Jewish lawyer named Felix Regenbaum." Tina opened the box and pulled out the photograph of Eva's first wedding.

"They were a beautiful couple," said Cheryl. Tina nodded and then showed her friend the photos of the little boy.

"When I first found these photos after Mom died, I thought it was her brother, but Jakob was my half-brother."

"I see a faint resemblance," said Cheryl. "So sorry about this."

Tina took the photos and returned them to the box. "There's more. The Nazis arrested Felix in 1942 and sent him to the Sobibor camp. I also learned Mom and Jakob went into hiding, but the Nazis found them and sent them to Auschwitz in late 1944. Jakob died of typhoid a few months later just after his fourth birthday. Mom was transferred to Buchenwald during the last months of the war and lived to see the American soldiers liberate the camp." Tina took a breath as she closed her eyes. "She never told me any of this."

"How'd you find all this out?"

"A genealogist and the Holocaust Museum in Washington helped me research my family tree."

"Wow," said Cheryl. "Your mom was probably too traumatized to mention her past."

Tina toyed with her coffee mug. "I'm in total shock."

"Give yourself some time to absorb this, sweetie." Cheryl got up. "I have to run. Maggie has a doctor's appointment. Call me if you need anything."

After Cheryl left, Tina emailed a brief note to Michael Farswell and introduced herself. However, when she checked her email later, there was no response. Tina sighed; she had expected too much.

★   ★   ★

One Sunday, Tina drove to the airport to pick up both daughters. who arrived at different times. Leli worked for six months as a cruise ship nurse and after endless Caribbean and one British Isle trip, she decided not to renew her contract. She was flying in from Miami and would stay the weekend before heading home to Davis. Sarah, on the other hand, was on her way home from Frankfurt, where she had lived several months as a foreign exchange student. She spoke fluent German along with Spanish, so her decision to spend a semester in Germany was no surprise to Tina. Although Artie had protested against Leli and Adam learning German since he did not speak the language, by the time Sarah was born, he no longer cared, so Tina taught Sarah German.

Leli arrived first in the late afternoon and greeted her mother warmly. "I have some news," she said. "But first, let's get a bite to eat. I'm starved."

"Great. Let's have an early dinner. Sarah won't be arriving until eight. I don't feel like driving back to Winter Park, so we'll hang out here if that's okay." They headed toward a country western steakhouse, perused the menu and ordered small filets and sides. Leli ordered a margarita for each of them. When the drinks arrived, both women clinked their glasses.

"Cheers. Welcome home, Leli. Are you going to stay a few days before heading home?"

"Here's my news. I got accepted into the University of Florida's graduate nursing program, and I just got my Florida nursing license and a new job. I'm moving to Orlando."

Tina's jaw dropped. "Wow. Congratulations on getting into UF. Tough school. Where will you be working?"

"Our Lady of Mercy Medical Center. I start the last week of May."

"That new hospital that just opened?" said Tina.

"They hired me as an ER nurse for their trauma center."

"You didn't like cruise ship work?"

"I loved it, and I even helped save a couple of lives. I saw the eastern and western Caribbean, Great Britain and Ireland. My joke is that I've been to Hell and back, Hell in the Cayman Islands." She laughed and brushed her hair away from her face. "I miss ER work, and being out to sea for so long was hard."

"I enjoyed that video you sent of you dancing with those guys in the Irish pub."

Leli laughed. "Speaking of guys, I met a nice Jewish dude. Danny lives in Orlando and is getting his master's online in engineering. His parents are Israeli."

"Great. How'd you meet?"

"At the infirmary last month. Staff isn't supposed to socialize with passengers, but when he asked, I gave him my information, because I was leaving anyway."

"I hope everything works out, but I have some concerns." Tina stopped. "This is a big move for you, and Florida is so different than California. I'm sure you're taking a pay cut moving here. Is this what you really want? You're not just moving because of that guy, are you?"

"Mom, I've been wanting to go back to school for some time. This has nothing to do with Danny, because as I've told you before, I want to become a nurse practitioner." Leli sighed and a sad look swept across her face. "I'm ready to move on. There's nothing left for me back home. My friends and me, we're so busy we don't even see each other except on Facebook. Abuelita doesn't know me. Forget Artie; my family is here. I'm excited about UF. I want to wear blue and orange. Go Gators. I'm psyched."

They chatted as they ate dinner and walked around afterward until it was time for Sarah's flight to arrive.

Tina and Leli were struck by Sarah's appearance as soon as they saw her. She had matured and lost weight. Sarah wore chic blue pants, heels and a stylish blouse. Her dark curls tumbled over her shoulders and accented her soft makeup and dangling earrings. She carried an expensive purse.

"You look amazing," said Tina after everyone exchanged hugs. You're prettier than ever, Sarita. Did you have an awesome time?" asked Leli.

"It was great."

"You've changed your style and you look simply gorgeous," said Tina. "This is a surprise."

"The family I stayed with was great. The mom is a fashion blogger and had lots of clothing samples. She completely changed my style, hence my new look."

On the way home, she chatted with Leli as Tina drove, beaming with shock and glee at all the news. When they got home, Sarah took her suitcase to her room and unpacked as her mother and sister stood in the doorway.

"Are you excited to be home?" asked Tina.

"For now."

"What does 'for now' mean?" said Leli.

"I decided I want to study music over in Germany. I loved it there so much." "But you said you wanted to go back to LA." "Changed my mind."

"You have a gorgeous voice and talent. Think it over though. It's a tough field," said Tina.

"I did, and if it doesn't work out, I have a backup plan. I'll study psychology."

Leli burst out laughing. "With our family background, you should ace that. In fact, you could write a dissertation on Artie." Tina quickly interrupted her. "Sarah needs to rest after her long trip." She motioned her youngest daughter toward her bedroom.

Leli found a furnished apartment, and two weeks later, she moved to Florida with only a few things and her clothes, leaving everything else behind.

★   ★   ★

JUNE 2016

To Leli, the Our Lady of Mercy emergency room presented the ultimate challenge, where the unexpected was expected. She loved her new job and proudly wore her blue ER scrubs, but one Saturday night, she faced the ultimate challenge.

Leli's last patient had left, and she sighed with relief; after a heated argument with his wife who shoved her wedding ring up his rectum and told him "Up your ass," he had shown up at the ER, and his wife was arrested.

Things were quiet momentarily, so Leli relaxed on the breakroom couch, pulled out her craft tote and began working on her latest knitting project, a blue baby blanket with little yellow ducklings for a coworker's shower. A nurse in Davis had taught her how to knit, and Leli enjoyed her new hobby.

Suddenly, the hospital received one emergency call after another; there had been a nightclub shooting. Leli jumped up, quickly returned the tote to her locker, and along with the hospital response team, stood immediately on standby, ready to receive numerous victims. Stretcher after stretcher of the severely injured and dying made their way into the emergency room. Victims ranged from only needing outpatient treatment to being deceased, but most had severe injuries.

Leli immediately realized the numerous gaping wounds indicated semi-automatic weapon injuries and because of her prior ER experience with gunshot victims, she knew the horrific bodily damage these guns inflicted.

Almost robotic, Leli stayed focused to the point of exhaustion as the staff struggled to save victim after victim. At one point, she saw a father throw himself prostrate over his dead son. Family members hugged each other with loud sobs. One victim on a gurney grabbed Leli's arm and said weakly, "Nurse, please tell my mom…." Then, he lost consciousness.

Leli saw a young woman lying dead on a table, stopped and gazed at her young face, which had experienced such terror, but now seemed at peace.

At dawn, she noticed how much blood covered her own clothing and shoes. At 9:00 AM, she finished her shift, showered, rinsed the blood off her shoes the best she could, and changed into her street clothing. Her mind was numb; she had witnessed severe trauma many times before, but neither she nor the other staff members had ever dealt with an emergency on this scale before nor were they emotionally prepared for such an event.

Sunday morning, Tina opened her eyes as she lay in bed next to Ben. Light streamed through the window, and she gazed peacefully at her garden, until the moment her cellphone rang shortly after 9:00 AM. When she answered, Leli spoke in a whisper.

"I…need to come over right now. I can't go home."

"What is wrong?"

"Didn't you hear about the shooting?"

"I just woke up. What shooting?"

"At the nightclub."

"I didn't, but I'll get up. Please come on over." She hung up, as Ben awoke and opened his eyes. They shared a long kiss.

"Hon, you're finally going to meet Leli, but not under the best circumstances. She just got off work and is on her way here."

"What happened?"

"A nightclub shooting. That's all she said."

Ben sat up in bed and put his right hand on his forehead as he shook his head. They both got up and turned on the local news which spoke about the Pulse nightclub shooting and the numerous casualties and injured victims. Ben paused and looked at Tina. "When is all this violence going to stop?"

Soon, Leli arrived, her puffy face showed deep circles under her red teary eyes. She wore jeans and a sleeveless shirt with brand new white sneakers. Tina hugged her daughter tightly, as Leli wiped her eyes.

"Mom, it was horrible. I thought I could handle anything before this happened." Leli pointed to her shoes. "I stopped on the way home and bought these. My old ones were covered in blood. I threw them away."

Leli plopped into the kitchen chair without a word and just buried her face in her hands. Tina brewed coffee and handed Leli a cup. As she sipped her coffee, she noticed Ben, and Tina briefly introduced them to each other.

"I thought I'd seen everything," Leli's eyes filled with tears. "I have seen bad things, but never on this scale. I can't even talk about it."

Tina nodded in sympathy. "What a terrible experience. I'm sorry."

Leli stared into the distance. "I think over and over if there was something more I could have done for these victims. I rack my brain.

I've seen bad injuries before, but nothing like this. Young people's lives were snuffed out on some shooter's whim."

"Go rest," said Tina gently. "It's been a long night."

Slowly, Leli got up, walked to the spare bedroom and shut the door. Tina's eyes followed her as she wrung her hands with worry.

Two hours later, Leli returned to the kitchen and made herself more coffee. She wearily sat down in the recliner and tried to read a book, but after a few minutes, she set it down, got up and returned to the bedroom.

Tina ordered Chinese takeout, and when it arrived, she knocked on Leli's door and told her dinner was ready. Leli refused food and asked to be left alone.

That night, Tina heard noise, groggily stirred awake and saw light through her bedroom door from the kitchen. She got up and saw Leli dressed in her nightgown at the table drinking water and eating chocolate. Tina sat down and took her daughter's hand.

"Honey, are you okay?"

Leli looked up and shook her head. "I can't sleep. Another nightmare about the shooting. It was awful, as if I were back at the hospital with the victims all around me, surrounded by the glassy eyes of blood-smeared faces. I've asked for two weeks leave, just to recover."

"You might have some PTSD."

"Probably. I have to focus on other things." She threw herself into the Hillary Clinton campaign as a volunteer, addressed envelopes and called potential voters.

Tina remained worried about her daughter and called Tamara, who advised Leli get trauma therapy.

★   ★   ★

AUGUST 2016

It was a typical August hot muggy day. Tina sat at her desk at work and reviewed documents on her computer. A small table fan blew air into her face due to the broken office air conditioning. Her eyes grew heavy with fatigue. Although she wore a sleeveless white blouse with a cotton skirt and sandals, her clothing provided little relief from the heat.

Her cellphone rang near lunchtime.

"Tina," Sydney said in an anxious voice. "Can you talk?" She paused.

"What's wrong?"

"You know, I know Oliver, who owns your old house. Well, guess who showed up last week? Artie arrived with flowers, because he thought you guys still lived there, but when he saw a strange man towering over him in the doorway instead of his sweet ex-wife, he lost it. He swore in Spanish, and Oliver-get this-took the flowers for his wife, ordered Artie off the property and threatened to call the cops."

"What? That restraining order means no contact and hasn't expired."

"I know, but when has Artie ever followed rules? There's more. He called me late last night for the first time ever. I knew he was trying to get more information about your guys. At first, he was friendly and asked me how we were and then repeatedly asked me in the nicest way where you were. I acted vague, and he became increasingly upset. Finally, I lied and told him I thought you were somewhere in northern Oregon, and we were out of touch. He went completely berserk and said he wants to see Sarah, and you can't keep him away from his daughter. Then he got on the bullshit train, where he told me how much he misses you and loves you both. I think you need to get a new restraining order."

Tina's sweaty hands almost made her drop the phone. "He's batshit crazy. I knew he'd show up again, I just knew it."

"Are you still friends with anyone who knows him?"

"Just you. I stay in touch with friends on Facebook, but I hide our location."

"We both know he's not playing with a full deck, and he's clearly fixated on you, probably for control, so I'd be very careful."

Tina sighed. "Can't he find somebody else? He knows so many people. Why me? Why is he stalking me?"

"You gave him power. He controlled you."

"Looking back, I can't believe how much I loved him and thought he was so handsome and talented. I overlooked everything about him." She paused. "I think I tried too hard." She paused again. "I just hope he doesn't find us."

Sydney laughed. "Handsome? They say love is blind. Seriously, stay cool girlfriend. Be safe and don't worry. It's not like he's across the street."

After they hung up, Tina's hands shook so hard the phone almost slipped out of her hand. To her horror, she saw an email from him in her inbox.

His eccentric writing style was unchanged.

365

*Hello bombónita ...and what happened to you????**★★
You moved away and you never told me!!!... You didn't
even say goodbye!!... Is this city still Los Angeles because
my angels are here or... is it now just LOS... because
you've flown away???...You know, I had a great steak in
your cooking!!! AMAZING!! I remember when I played
duets with Adam. But when you and I performed together,
we were so ATTUNED to each other!!!..Didn't we play
beautiful music together???......*

*WOW!!!!!***★★★*

*Mi vida, I long for you!! It has been so long since I
covered you with kisses!!!! I would give MY LIFE TO
HAVE YOU BACK!!!... You and the kids are ALL
THAT MATTERS TO ME!! I want you back with
me!!! I love you FOREVER!!!!!*

Your Funny Punny CIELITO

Tina's heart dropped into her stomach, so in despair, she
forwarded it to Leli, who called. "Don't respond, Mom. Save it,
though, in case he turns into a stalker. Don't let him know where
you are." Afterward, Tina called Adam and read the email to him.
"I'm surprised he hasn't called you to find us," responded Tina.

"If he does, I'll handle him. I'm going to check out his Facebook
pages to see if you're mentioned at all. Don't worry. I've got your
back."

After the conversation, Adam logged into Facebook under his
confidential pseudo-account and found his father's personal and
professional pages. Given the circumstances, Adam wanted to keep
track of Artie's whereabouts. Both pages were public and easily
monitored.

When Adam mentioned to Tina that Artie's posts were some of the most bizarre he had ever seen, she drove one evening to Adam's apartment to see for herself. They sat at his computer as Adam clicked first on Artie's Facebook business page titled "Arturo Diaz Hernandez Renowned Concert Pianist and Musical Artist. Renombrado Pianista de Concierto y Artista Musical." A collage of the Argentine flag, the American flag, and a piano keyboard was Artie's featured cover photo. His business profile photograph showed him in performance. The page had 20,000 likes. "This is him at his most normal," said Adam, who then clicked on Artie's personal page and saw 5000 friends plus thousands of followers. Artie's profile picture showed him in front of a white wall. He held a mate cup in his left hand and gave a thumbs-up with his right. His black T-shirt said in Spanish, "Calm yourself, Boludo. Have a mate."

Tina noticed that Artie's smile had changed, and he appeared to have lost even more teeth.

He posted crude jokes, photos and puns all hours of the day and night. One photo showed him playing his keyboard on the beach, wearing only white briefs. His feet, clad in cheap sandals, rested in the water. Other photographs showed him posing with different celebrities including movie and Broadway stars. In each photo post, Artie called the photo subject, "my best friend" or "my dear friend" or "the best musician, (star, actor, director, singer) anywhere."

"I remember Sydney calling him the best 15-minute friend anyone could ever have," said Tina. "He's such a phony." Disgust crossed her face.

"Hey Mom. We can stop."

Tina shook her head. "I'm fine. Keep going."

A photo on his timeline showed a black bra flying from a flagpole in Artie's backyard.

Tina laughed. "Some condemned therapist in hell will have to treat Artie for the rest of eternity." Adam smiled.

They noted that Artie had posted several disturbing self-derogatory comments and photos, which magnified his low self-esteem. He called himself names such as "a fat ugly porteño", a "fat Argentinian" or an "ugly monkey's asshole" in Spanish with English translations to make sure none of his followers missed out.

Adam stopped. "Oh! Check out these pictures," as photos of Artie with beautiful young women appeared on his page. The pictures reeked of misogynism. Artie depicted himself as macho and filled with lust, surrounded by adoring women. Most of the women wore scanty midriff tops, tight hot pants or thigh-high skirts with tall boots. They posed to look sexy. One photo showed him at the piano, while a skimpily dressed woman lay on the floor with her legs wrapped around his.

"I bet most of these chicks are hookers," said Adam.

Tina nodded. "Probably."

They noticed then that one young woman appeared in several photographs, and the newest pictures showed only her and Artie together. Slim, she appeared in her twenties, about Artie's height, and her tight clothing hugged her body. Her short almost bright orange hair surrounded her pale face, which with her prominent nose strongly reminded Tina of John Singer Sargent's painting *Madame X*. The young woman was tagged as Ashley White. Artie posted photos of them at the beach, at an art fair, and in San Diego. Adam turned to his mother.

"Well, Mom, it looks like he has a girlfriend. Let's check her out." Adam clicked on her timeline.

Ashley White

Entertainer at the Hotkitten Night Club, Los Angeles

Hometown: Normal, Illinois

Occupation: Entertainer, Dancer, Model, and Actress.

There was a link to her website.

Adam clicked on the link which led to Ashley's website and "personal photos," which required him to check a box saying he was 18 or over. The site wanted a credit card payment, but Adam hacked the link only to see nude photos of Ashley in suggestive poses. Her large breasts seemed out of proportion to her slight build, adorned with piercings and tattoos.

"Implants for sure," commented Tina.

Adam typed "Hotkitten Club Los Angeles" into a search and saw Ashley on the website as a dancer and stripper.

Tina had seen enough. "You know, I didn't see one thing about you and your sisters. Nothing. He wants everyone to think he's a carefree happy bachelor. Now, I'm mad." She looked at her phone. "I need to leave. It's almost ten, and I have to work tomorrow."

"Okay, fine." Adam bent down and kissed her cheek. After they said their goodbyes, Tina got into her car and headed home.

As she lay in bed, she thought about her ex-husband's Facebook timeline. Artie obviously acted out of desperation for attention and did not realize or care that he presented as a bullied buffoon. He posted the same things or jokes repeatedly, which reminded Tina of racecars going around a track, and she almost smiled. Yet, his self-directed barbs, his misogynistic behavior and juvenile attempts at humor failed miserably in Tina's eyes. However that night, she smiled as she fell asleep and reminded herself to tell Adam about the racecar comparison; he would find that funny.

★   ★   ★

2500 miles away, it still was light outside. At 7:00 PM that evening, Ashley performed oral sex on Artie in her bed When she finished, she rolled off him and pulled out a cigarette from her nightstand, lit up, as she lay next to him and blew smoke rings up to the ceiling.

"Baby, you're so fabulous," she cooed. "I love to suck your hot dick."

He turned to smile at her as he snuggled his face into her neck. "I love to fuck you."

"Oh yeah?" said Ashley. She suddenly sat up in bed and glared at him. "When you banged me last night, you suddenly yelled out 'Tina'! Shut up already about that bitch!"

"Oh," Artie said sheepishly. "Sorry."

Ashley scowled for a minute, then turned to him with a smile. "That's okay, baby." She paused. "You're going to give me rent money for this month, right?"

"Sure," he said. "I'd do anything for you."

Ashley laughed. Then she lay down again next to him and stared at the ceiling. "You know, you complain about your ex and kids a lot, and then you say you miss them. Shit. Make up your mind already."

Artie said nothing and wrapped his arms around her as she squirmed to assume a comfortable position under his body. He kissed her on the lips and reached between her legs to arouse her. "There's only you," he whispered hoarsely. "I hate Tina. I wish she were dead after the way she treated me." After he left, Ashley made a call on her cellphone as she stretched out sensuously on her bed.

Ten minutes later, her doorbell rang, and she ushered a young bearded man into the room. They embraced with ardent kisses. Breathlessly they undressed each other, which led to steamy sex on the bed.

Afterward, they both shared a cigarette, and the man laughed.

"How's your sugar daddy?"

"I spent all afternoon with him. Made him happy, you know. Stupid old fool. He promised me rent money, Kyle. Isn't that great?"

"Oh yeah, baby," Kyle laughed. "Keep it up. We need all the money we can get. Look what I brought."

Ashley sat up. Kyle pulled out a packet of white powder, poured it on a table and made a line with his razor blade, snorting the drug through rolled-up bills into his nose.

Ashley laughed with delight as they shared the cocaine and opened two beers. Sex followed one more time.

"Hope your sugar daddy keeps on giving," laughed Kyle before he left.

★   ★   ★

The alley lay barely visible in the moonless darkness near the Los Angeles abandoned warehouse. Only a street lamp illuminated two profiles in a car's back seat, as a man looked at a photo. He turned it more toward the light and paused.

"It's blurry. I can't see her well, but I'll find her."

"Mike, that guy I work with, recommended you. He should know, because you're his buddy. You better find her soon and get rid of her."

"That's why you're paying me. This should be easy."

"Rough her up, stab her, shoot her."

"I only use my hands, no other weapons. Too messy and traceable."

"You mean you'll choke her?"

"I'll choke her with such force, I will break her neck. She'll die instantly."

"Good. Are you sure?"

"When I've got a job to do, I make sure it gets done."

"As long as you get rid of her."

"She is cute. Can I fuck her first?"

"If you want. Sure. Torture her. Rape her. Just make sure she's dead."

"I like to fuck pretty girls before I kill them. What's her name again?"

"Tina."

"Where can I find her?"

"Not sure, but I'll find out. Did you say you charge $2,000?"

"Half down and half when I finish the job."

"Okay. I'll get you the money."

★ ★ ★

When Tina logged on to her computer the next morning, she saw another email from Artie, who wrote he wanted to see Sarah. After all, it was his right to see his daughter. Tina sighed. She closed the message without a reply and wondered how she should get her restraining order enforced.

The next morning, Sarah got ready for school. She walked into the kitchen to fix herself breakfast as usual, her dark unruly curls pulled back into a ponytail. Dressed in three-inch high heels and flowered sleepy bear pajamas, she opened the refrigerator, pulled out a carton of soymilk and fixed herself a bowl of cereal.

Tina turned to look at her and shook her head. Average height was not enough for Sarah who once read that height meant power and since then, tried to appear taller.

"Mom," said Sarah quietly as she ate her breakfast, "Why does my dad act like such a jerk on Facebook?"

Tina startled. "What brought that up?"

"We're Facebook friends now. Man, what is wrong with him?"

"I thought you blocked him."

"I did, but I missed him so much, I changed my mind."

"I hope you didn't tell him where we are."

She lowered her eyes with a sheepish look. "Well, um, he doesn't exactly know."

"What's that mean?"

"My Facebook profile says Winter Park High. He asked me about school, and I told him about my singing lessons and stuff, but I didn't tell him where we lived or nothing."

"No, but he saw where you go to school. He knows we live in Winter Park. Now, I'm scared."

"Oh Mom, He won't do anything. Besides, we have an unlisted number and a P.O. box."

"It doesn't matter," Tina almost shouted. "He can find us if he tries hard enough. He's dangerous, and I have told you that many times. Why did you friend him, and why did you list your school on your profile? Now, he knows where we are." Tina's eyes widened, and her lips parted as she wrung her hands. "Sarah, how could you? Please unfriend and block him now."

"Mom, you sound real paranoid. He hasn't bothered us in a year except for sending me a Facebook request, right?"

"He's been emailing me, and I'm ignoring him. I'm scared. Excuse me. I've got a headache and have to go lie down." Tina got up and went to the bedroom. She knew Sarah missed her father, but the fact that she friended him on Facebook was too much.

★　★　★

Ashley stood behind Artie and massaged his neck, as he perused his laptop.

"Hey, stud muffin. Whatcha doing?"

"Looking for Sarah's address."

"There are lots of search companies on the Internet that can help you."

Artie nodded, clicked on a search service, and when he typed Tina's name, the site only hinted she lived in Florida and requested payment for more information. After he paid $20.00, Tina's full profile appeared, complete with her new address at 201 Worthington Road, Winter Park, Florida. When, he opened Google Maps to locate the address, a photo showed the pretty white stucco ranch house with the palm tree in front.

Another nightly meeting took place in the same car parked again near the warehouses. The man read the address scribbled on a piece of paper before he put it in his pocket.

"This is where she lives?"

"Yeah."

"She is living all the way in fucking Florida. How am I supposed to get there and do this job?"

"I'll get money for your trip plus all the expenses and a little extra. Anything you need."

"Get me a plane ticket."

"Too traceable. You have to drive."

"Drive? Are you nuts?"

"Shut up. Besides, you can bring along guns, knives, whatever you need."

"I told you I work with my hands. I'm a martial arts master and don't need weapons to take her out."

"Do whatever you want with that bitch. You're welcome. We'll make it look like a robbery by a local street guy. I'll be there, of course. Afterward, return home as quickly as possible."

"You will be in Orlando?"

"Yup. Concert time in December, two months away."

The man grinned. "Looking forward to it. I have time. No work except for special assignments like this." He winked and laughed.

"Fine. You'll meet me in Orlando, but otherwise, you don't know me. I will pay half down as you want and half when the job is completed, okay?"

"Fine. We're good."

★   ★   ★

OCTOBER 2016

Sarah sparkled as she began her junior year with good grades, private voice lessons and parts in various choirs. Gifted with an exceptionally beautiful mature soprano voice, she often sang solos at the reform synagogue, which she and Tina now attended and hoped for an music career. Her timbre and range made high notes float easy like a bell with a touch of smoke. She reminded Tina of Eva's one recording after the War; their voices sounded so alike. Meanwhile, Tina and Ben spent time together several times a week and attended community events and concerts, something Tina had rarely done on her own since her move to Florida; she looked forward to their dates which revolved around concerts, dances and Sarah's performances.

One afternoon Tina received in the mail a flyer for a classical concert series, but to her horror, her veins turned to ice, and her heart pounded in her chest as soon as she opened the brochure and Artie's face stared back, clad in a tuxedo, lips pressed together in a smile, his salt and pepper beard and curls, highlighted by a touch of brown tint. The brochure announced the December 17 concert and described him as the renowned pianist Arturo Diaz. The concert featured pop and Broadway tunes and Beethoven.

Before she called Adam through her panic, Tina thought Artie looked almost handsome in the photo.

"I just got a brochure which shows your father is giving a concert here in December. I'm freaking out right now, because I'm scared. Because of Sarah, he knows where we are, and I'm sure he can find our address."

"Mom, why don't you and Sarah go stay with Ben during Dad's visit?"

"Thanks, but I'd rather stay home. I don't want Ben involved."

Adam paused. "Okay. I'll stay with you if you want while Dad's in town. I'll sleep on the airbed in your room."

"Oh, sweet Adam. You're such a good son."

"If he puts any one of us in danger, I'll do what I have to do."

"You wouldn't regret it?"

"Maybe later. Not at the moment."

"Good night, son. Love you." "Love you too."

★　★　★

"Hon, are you okay?" Ben looked concerned as he took Tina's hand at the Italian restaurant where they were having dinner.

"Oh, I probably have that faraway look in my eyes again," said Tina.

"What's wrong?"

"I got a concert brochure in the mail. My ex is performing here in December." "You don't miss him, do you? You've never mentioned him before," said Ben.

Tina shrugged her shoulders. "Never mind." She had never spoken to Ben about Artie and was not going to start now.

★　★　★

377

Another email from <u>Arturopianista@xdomain.net</u> appeared in Tina's inbox. Again, she froze and took a long deep breath before she opened it.

> *Tina,*
>
> *I'm coming to Orlando in December for a concert...... I really want to SEE YOU AND THE KIDS!!!PLEASE ANSWER ME!!!! Come to my concert!! There will be four tickets waiting for you at the theater WILL CALL window under your name.... Please make sure you bring ****SARAH****.*
>
> *Artie*

Icy fear choked her, so she could barely breathe. As her sweaty hands danced quickly on the keyboard, she feared Sarah might want to move back to California to live with her father and suffer under his narcissism.

> *"I got your email about the concert, so I will let the kids decide whether they want to attend. Please remember the restraining order is still in effect until next year and enforceable. Even if there were no order, I won't be there. Since you attacked me that night, I will never feel safe around you again. I'll also never forget how you put me and the kids through hell with your anger and selfishness. We all became excellent eggshell walkers around you. Over the years, I had to help the kids understand why they shouldn't blame themselves. I'm done. Please don't contact me again."*

She took a deep breath as she sent the email off with a click. Thirty minutes later, a reply landed in her inbox.

IT WAS YOUR FAULT!!!!!!

"Asshole," Tina thought as she deleted his message.

★   ★   ★

NOVEMBER 2016

The family reeled from Trump's election.

"I can't believe this," said Tina as Ben put his arm around her.

Leli shook her head in disbelief. "There goes our democracy, women's rights, civil rights, healthcare," she said. "I'll volunteer and do what I can, because I won't sit still and tolerate this pussy grabber. Mom and Sarita, will you also help?" They nodded.

Two weeks later, Tina and her daughters decided to participate at the women's march at Lake Eola on January 21. Leli pulled several balls of pink yarn out of her tote. "Time to knit pink pussy hats," she said. "I'm already convinced Trump will go down as the worst president in history."

★　★　★

DECEMBER 2016

Only Tina's anxiety about Artie's visit marred her joy about the upcoming holidays. However, she had not heard from him since their last email exchange, much to her relief. Adam, Leli and even Sarah also expressed their ambivalence about acknowledging Artie on his visit or attending his concert.

Yet, Adam noticed his father had recently posted selfies with Ashley at Orlando theme parks on Facebook and was definitely in town, so the next day, after Adam took a short leave from work, he visited his sister and mother, who had the airbed ready for him. Adam insisted on sleeping in Tina's bedroom for safety reasons.

Early Thursday before dawn, Tina rose to walk Hans, who announced with a loud whimper that he needed to go outside. Adam stirred and rose to accompany his mother, but Tina told him to go back to sleep. She pulled her robe around her before she walked the dog outside into the dark street. Suddenly, Hans barked. Tina thought for a second, she saw a shadow move, but blinked and then saw a cat slink down the dark street. Tina could almost hear herself breathe in the still deathly quiet air. She shushed the dog before she quickly returned inside. Her mind played tricks on her sometimes.

As Artie's Saturday concert neared, Tina figured he was busy with rehearsals, so she focused instead on her office's annual holiday party at a downtown Chinese restaurant the following day. Unfortunately, she had to go alone, as she and Ben had a mild disagreement two days before when he kept questioning her about Artie and she had been reticent to answer. Consequently, Ben became angry, told her she was being deceptive and refused to go to the party. Adam suddenly had an emergency work assignment, Leli had no time off, and Sarah had plans with a friend's family.

When Tina walked Hans in the cool dark evening light prior to her departure for the party, something again sent chills up her spine, but she turned and saw nothing. As she drove to the restaurant, she noticed in her rearview mirror a car driving closely behind her. She scolded herself for her paranoia; only Artie would deliberately follow her, and she was sure he was at rehearsal.

She found the restaurant parking lot full with no spaces nearby, so she parked a block away on a side street. She got out of the car, ready to walk to the restaurant on Mills Avenue.

"Hi, Tina."

She stopped and turned to see a man dressed in dark clothing, who walked up to her. She could barely make him out in the darkness.

"Are you heading to the party?" she asked. The man did not answer; chills went up Tina's spine. To her horror, she saw another distant figure move toward her. Now scared, Tina hurried away.

How did that man know her name?

"Hey, what's your hurry?" The man ran in front of her and grabbed her arm. Tina shrieked at the top of her lungs, but the strong muscular assailant clapped his hand over her mouth. Tina tried unsuccessfully to fight him off, as he pulled her into a nearby alley and pinned her down on the ground, so she could not move. "If you say a word, I will kill you, and then go to your house and kill your children." He tore off her underwear, groped her roughly and pushed his fingers inside her. Tina squirmed. The man stopped to undo his trousers, providing a momentary distraction. Tina jumped up, screamed for help and tried again to run away, tripped over her long skirt and fell on the sidewalk. The man tackled her as he pushed her face to the ground. He now lay down on top of her. Despite her terror, she thought she recognized his voice somehow, but it wasn't Artie.

"Oh no you don't," he whispered. "You're not going anywhere." He tried to cover her mouth again, but Tina chomped down and bit his hand. He shouted out and pulled his hand away, as she kicked for dear life and tried to escape in spite of her now severe knee pain.

"I have had it with you, bitch," he snarled and grabbed her throat. In a split second, a huge weight hit them both, and the assailant let go and fell over backwards as a large figure jumped on him and pinned him down. Tina gingerly sat up, unable to move due to her knee pain. She could not see much but through the struggle, she recognized the other man.

Artie.

In the meantime, a woman nearby called 9-11; two Orlando Police Department cars arrived minutes later and the officers quickly handcuffed Tina's assailant as one shown a flashlight in the man's face.

Tina gasped. She had not seen Nick Romano in years, yet she recognized him instantly, as he had not changed. Horrified, she saw him stare at her, his eyes cold as ice.

"Fuck you, bitch," Nick yelled at the female officer, who pushed him into the squad car's back seat before it drove off.

Artie still stood on the sidewalk as he and Tina locked eyes. Neither said a word.

Bewildered, she tried in vain to sort out the situation. It was still difficult to see Artie in the darkness due to his black clothing, but Tina was certain since he had followed her, he had meant harm but saved her life instead. Nothing made sense anymore.

One of the officers walked over to Tina and introduced herself as Sergeant Worthington.

"Are you okay?"

Tina looked up at the officer and shook her head.

"What's your name?"

"Tina Perry" She barely could mouth the words.

"Are you hurt?"

"My knees. I can't...."

Sgt. Worthington made a call through the two-way radio on her shoulder and soon, an ambulance and firetruck arrived, sirens blaring through the night. By now, several onlookers gawked from the sidewalk across the street.

Sgt. Worthington glanced suspiciously at Artie. "Who're you?"

"Her ex-husband," he replied.

"Where were you when this happened?"

"Back there," he gestured toward a group of trees. "I saw everything."

"Let me see your ID, please."

Artie pulled his driver's license out of his wallet.

"Is this your correct address?"

Artie nodded.

"What are you doing here in Orlando?"

"I'm playing a concert tomorrow."

"Why were you following her?"

Artie looked at Tina, then looked at the officer but did not answer. Sgt. Worthington became impatient.

"Please answer or I'll take you in for questioning. Your choice, Mr. Diaz."

Artie slowly followed Sgt. Worthington to her police car, and they spoke a while before Artie drove off.

In the meantime, the EMTs treated Tina. Dazed and in shock, she shrieked when she tried to stand, and was placed on a stretcher and rushed away in the ambulance.

★   ★   ★

"Ow!" Tina flinched as the Stonecrest Medical Center ER nurse pulled specks of gravel out of her knees and thighs, raw with road rash.

"Sorry, but I'm almost done," she said.

The doctor on call had given Tina good news earlier, that no broken bones were noted on her x-rays. However, he told her she needed to stay overnight for observation and see a psychiatrist the following morning for any emotional trauma.

Eyes closed, Tina lay sedated under a blanket, hooked up to an IV in an ER partition. Her bandaged arms and legs covered her dark bruises and road rash. Her face thankfully had only one bruise where Nick had pushed her face into the dirt. Earlier, the medical team had gathered rape evidence since Nick had manually penetrated her. Groggily, Tina roused when she heard Sarah's and Adam's voices as if from a distance.

"Hi, Mom."

She startled and opened her eyes to see her three children. "Hey, guys," she said softly.

"We came as soon as the police called," said Adam.

"I'll be fine," whispered Tina after a moment. "Nothing broken, I'm just banged up." She paused and struggled to become more alert. "I think your father tried to have me killed, but then he showed up and saved me. It makes no sense. Confusing."

Adam touched her shoulder. "The cops will figure it out."

Tina closed her eyes again and began to drift off as the voices disappeared into an auditory blur.

Leli turned to her siblings. "Let's go. Mom needs rest, I have to change and go to work." They said goodbye as they followed Leli to the elevator.

★　★　★

"Ms. Perry?"

She awoke with a start and saw two women next to her bed, one dressed in a dark suit and a police officer.

The police officer greeted Tina. "I'm Lieutenant Johnston, homicide detective with the Orlando Police Department. I need to ask you a few questions. First, please tell me what happened."

"I parked my car and got ready to walk to the How Chee restaurant on Mills. Suddenly, Nick Romano attacked me and said he was going to rape and kill me. I couldn't get away, and he tried to grab my throat. Then my ex-husband showed up out of nowhere and somehow jumped him. He got Nick off me somehow. It was dark, and I couldn't see. There was a struggle...."

"It sounds like Mr. Diaz knocked your assailant off balance," said Lt. Johnston. "Have you ever met Nick Romano?"

Tina hesitated. "Years ago, we had an affair." Tina paused. "I haven't seen him since, but I recognized him immediately."

"Do you think your ex was somehow involved in the attack?"

"Possibly. I was always scared he'd find and harm us."

"Did you see him nearby before Romano attacked you?"

"I saw a figure in the dark but couldn't tell who it was."

"Tell me more about Mr. Diaz."

"A few months after our divorce, he tried to rape me but I got away."

"Did you file a police report?"

"I did and got a restraining order but then dropped the charges. I just wanted to get away. That's why we moved here."

"Has he been stalking you?"

"Recently, my close friend Sydney called, because she heard he went to our old house looking for me. Then, he called her to find our whereabouts. Sydney lied to protect us. He also friended our youngest daughter on Facebook a while back. She has Winter Park High on her profile, so he knew we lived here. He's been emailing me to come to his concert tomorrow and said he wants to reconcile, but I've been ignoring him."

"Do you think that's why he's here?"

"Probably, and he's a pretty popular pianist, so it would have been easy for him to get a gig here."

"Do you know if he is here by himself?"

"I heard his girlfriend is with him."

"Thanks for the information. We'll be in touch." Lt. Johnston said goodbye and left with the other woman who said nothing during the interview.

"We have a bed for you, Ms. Perry." An aide wheeled her to her room. At dawn, a nurse awoke Tina to give her medication, and a lab technician arrived to take blood. When her breakfast tray arrived. Tina sat up in bed, dulled with medication and slowly ate the eggs, sausage, and toast. She turned on the news and watched as Obama promised retaliation for Russian election meddling and Trump announced his daughter would work in the White House in spite of nepotism regulations.

★ ★ ★

After the incident, Artie drove down Orange Blossom Trail in his rental car, until he spotted an adult entertainment club and pulled into the parking lot. He watched the topless dancers as he sat at the bar, ate his sandwich and ordered a second double scotch.

"Are you visiting?" chatted the bartender as he prepared the drink.

"I'm here from LA and playing a concert tomorrow downtown."

"Awesome. What do you play?"

"Piano. Guess what happened today? I saved my ex-wife's life."

"Wow. You're a real hero."

"Thanks. I'm going to post it to Facebook right away, so everyone knows about it. I have 5,000 friends and lots of followers."

"You'll get the word out for sure that way."

"Say," Artie paused. "Are there any-eh sexier bars around with nude dancers? Topless is okay, but..."

"Try the Hot Babes bar right across the street. Totally nude." He turned to Artie and whispered in a low voice, "The girls do lap dances and might even agree to more if you're discreet."

Artie thanked him and after he finished his drink, he crossed Orange Blossom Trail to walk to the bar. As he stepped off the curb to cross the broad street, a sports car suddenly swerved around the corner at top speed and struck him, as it quickly sped into the darkness.

Artie flew up and over the car before he hit the pavement hard, and everything went for him black.

A passerby called 911. The ambulance arrived within a few minutes, but the EMTs could barely see the barely breathing dark-clothed victim who lay crumpled on the street face down and unconscious in a pool of blood. The first responders checked Artie for a neck injury and obvious fractures or wounds, before they stabilized his neck in a cervical collar, tied him to a board to prevent further injury, and placed him on a gurney before they loaded him into the ambulance. A responder tried unsuccessfully to start a saline drip in Artie's arm; but finally found a vein, as the ambulance raced through the streets to Our Lady of Mercy. Artie suddenly stopped breathing en route, and the EMTs quickly intubated him.

That Friday night was quieter than usual in the ER, so Leli seized the chance to knit more pink hats. She breathed deeply to quiet her churning stomach and pounding heart as she thought about Artie's concert, drained even at the thought of him.; they had not been in contact for almost two years. Leli turned back to her knitting and as she worked another row of stitches, she was called to the ER for another patient.

In the meantime, the ambulance arrived with Artie. Other staff members stood by the ER entrance, as the EMTs quickly unloaded Artie from the ambulance and rushed him into the hospital.

The trauma response team worked on Artie, now comatose. He remained unresponsive, but responded with a moan when poked. His sunken eyes stayed closed in his badly swollen bruised face. His body and limbs began to jerk, indicative of a seizure. He also had an obvious broken femur and a comminuted humeral head fracture, the bones penetrating through his skin on his shoulder. Blood covered his body and clothing. Obvious road rash covered his arms, chest, head, and legs. CT scans also indicated a fractured skull and facial fractures, a torn spleen and rip fractures, which had punctured and collapsed his left lung.

After immediate stat bloodwork, the ER staff started IVs in both of Artie's arms. After a quick type and crossmatch, Artie received a transfusion of six units of blood. Staff balloon-tubed his stomach to prevent aspiration. Artie's lacerated liver had caused blood to spill into his abdomen, and he required emergency surgery.

A nurse inserted a Foley catheter in him to monitor his fluid output and sought Leli's help as she had just finished with the previous patient. Two surgeons stood ready to perform neurological and orthopedic simultaneous surgeries.

In her usual calm and focused manner, Leli bent over to monitor the IV but jumped back when she recognized Artie. Shocked beyond belief, Leli's legs buckled, as she became lightheaded and the room whirled around her. Quickly, she asked another nurse to take over and ran to the breakroom. Overwhelmed and shaken, she sank on the couch.

A few moments later, the head ER physician Dr. Donovan appeared and peered at Leli over her glasses. Her brow furrowed, her face reflecting her concern.

"Leah, are you okay?"

Leli shook her head. She could barely speak. "That man in the ER is my father."

"What a terrible shock this must be for you," said the doctor. "You're off duty now. Please go ahead and take care of your dad."

Without further thought, Leli threw her scrubs into the laundry, dressed, and returned to the ER. She immediately met with the neurosurgeon on call and identified herself as Artie's daughter. Her heart dropped in her stomach when she saw for herself her father's severe brain trauma on his CT scans. Artie's prognosis was poor; he might not survive the night. She signed the necessary paperwork and consent forms.

As she walked alongside his gurney on his way to surgery, she touched his face and softly called his name; he remained unresponsive.

Numb and drained, Leli stayed in the surgery waiting room and glanced at the clock on the wall; it was 2:00 AM.

She called Adam who groggily answered the phone.

"It's about Artie."

"Shit. What's going on?"

"He was in a bad accident, and I saw him in the ER. He's very critical. Right now, he's in surgery and may not survive the night. This is just so wack."

Adam paused before he quickly spoke. "I'll come join you at the hospital. Let me stop at the house and get Sarah."

"That's fine. Eighth-floor surgery waiting room."

The siblings arrived at 4 AM. Artie was still in surgery. It was going to be a long night.

★   ★   ★

Leli then called Tina. "Brace yourself. Artie was critically injured in an accident last night. He had to have immediate surgery and it's touch and go."

"What happened?" said Tina, horrified.

"The police said he was coming out of a bar on the OBT, crossed the street, and a hit-and-run driver mowed him down. It's bad, Mom. How are you?"

"Feeling better. After you left, a detective came and asked me questions about Artie and the attack."

"He had to be involved."

"I still can't believe he tried to have me killed," said Tina. "I never did anything to him and have been no contact. Why?"

"Who knows? With him, anything's possible. Maybe it was a staged stunt for attention that got out of hand."

"No, it wasn't. That killer was real. I know he would have raped and murdered me right there."

A young Indian woman in a white lab coat carrying a clipboard stopped at Tina's door.

"Someone is here to see me. Gotta go. Stay strong."

"Ms. Perry? I'm Dr. Krishna, the on-call psychiatrist. May I come in?"

Tina smiled and nodded. She pulled her hospital gown closer around herself.

"Tell me about your traumatic attack."

Tina repeated the story and answered several questions. Dr. Krishna thanked Tina for the information and left, as Tina wondered whether a mental diagnosis would delay her discharge home. Her fears were allayed however, when a staff member notified her, that she was ready for discharge and to wait for instructions.

After she dressed, she looked up to see Ben waiting for her. He acted kind as if nothing had happened between them and said he would drive her home. However, after they stopped at a pharmacy to get her prescriptions, she turned to him.

"Let's go to the hospital and check on Artie and the kids."

"Are you sure?" He frowned.

"Please."

They drove there silently and took the elevator to the 11th floor neurological intensive care unit.

The sign outside the ICU limited visitors to two family members at a time. When Ben and Tina pressed the buzzer, Leli stepped out to greet them.

"I got an okay from the staff nurse here to let all you guys visit at the same time. There are only two chairs though in the room, so some of you'll have to sit on the window seat." She stopped.

Tina touched Leli's arm. "Is he conscious?"

Leli shook her head. "He's out. Medical coma. I just checked on him, but I have to get back to work. My break's over."

Artie lay in a hospital bed surrounded by Adam, Sarah and Jessie, who waved a greeting, then returned to their phones. The windows looked out over the trees to the clear blue lake surrounding the hospital. On the wall, a white board said," Your nurse today is Shelly," written in blue marker.

Tina caught her breath when she saw him motionless with a bandaged head and closed eyes, hooked to several machines. His swollen distorted face made him almost unrecognizable. Mesmerized yet horrified at what she saw, Tina backed off and sat down next to Ben.

The machines' rhythmic steady beeps broke the room's silence. Tina turned to Adam and Sarah. "Has anyone called his manager about tonight's concert?"

"I took care of everything," said Adam. "The show's been cancelled."

"Good." Tina looked at Sarah. "Didn't you tell me your father has pets?"

"I think he still has his two dogs and his cat."

"We have to make sure they're okay."

"Don't worry about that either," said Adam. "I found a number on Dad's phone for a pet sitter. When I called, she told me she'll take care of them as long as necessary, and I'll pay her."

Before Tina could respond, an older thin woman with short dark grey hair stopped at the doorway. Gentle distraught dark eyes peered from behind her glasses. She wore simple navy slacks, a threadbare denim jacket and pulled a small rolling suitcase.

Without a word, she walked to the bed, and when she saw Artie, she burst into tears. "Arturito! O Dios Mio." She sobbed bitterly and covered her face with her hands before she wiped her eyes and blew her nose with a wrinkled tissue she pulled from her pocket.

Tina suddenly recognized her. "You're…"

"Luisa. Hello, Tina." She gave a faint smile. "You haven't changed."

"We thought you were dead. What happened to you all these years?"

"It's a long story." She turned to the kids. "You're my niece and my nephew, yes? Let me see," she turned to Sarah, who appeared totally bewildered. "You're Sarita or Leli?"

"Sarah," said Tina.

Luisa smiled weakly and turned to Adam. "We spoke on the phone."

Adam nodded. "I found a number in Dad's phone this morning for a Luisa, and I called to see if it was his sister. I told her about the accident and got her a plane ticket here on the first flight out."

"Adam is so sweet," said Luisa. "I'm so grateful to him." She embraced him and before she turned to hug a stunned Tina.

"It's great to see you, but I'm in shock. Where are you staying?" asked Tina.

"The Three Points Motel around the corner. That's all I can afford."

Adam and Jessie whispered to each other for a moment.

"That dump? Druggies live there," said Adam. "I told you that you can stay with us if you don't mind dogs or sleeping on a futon."

"I don't want to impose."

"We insist," said Adam.

Jessie nodded in agreement. "Yes, come stay with us. Please."

"Thanks. Che, money is tight for me right now. I can help you around the house and watch the dog when you're at work."

"I took leave, so I'll be home," said Adam. Luisa followed Adam and Jessie when they left. They took her back to the motel, checked her out and drove home to their apartment.

Ben dropped Tina off at home but excused himself, and said he couldn't stay due to his work. Tina was still too much in shock to respond.

Leli called a short time later. "I just wanted to be sure you got home okay. Ben's with you, right?"

"He didn't stay. Said something came up, so he went home."

"What? I thought he'd be more supportive than that."

"I don't care. I'm just too wigged out by everything else right now."

"Is Adam still staying over?"

"He went home today, since Artie's not a danger anymore'"

"I'll come over then tonight, okay? You shouldn't be alone now."

"Sure," said Tina. "I'll have everything ready."

"Don't do anything. You both relax. I'll handle everything."

Tina took her prescribed sleeping medication and drifted off into a deep slumber, until she awoke suddenly to daylight and loud noise outside. She rose and walked into the living room where Sarah and Leli were peeking through the blinds.

"Oh no. The news." Leli quickly pushed Sarah back.

Tina stole a quick look. "Holy shit. Look at all those TV trucks. Channels 2, 6, 9, 13...Wow. Hey, there's CNN." Trucks lined the street. Several reporters and camera crews stood in the driveway and on the lawn. Tina backed off and sat down in shock on the sofa. "Unreal."

Within minutes, the doorbell rang; and Hans barked loudly.

"Oh, no. I'm not dressed. You guys handle this," said Tina as she left the room.

Leli quieted Hans, as she saw a police car outside and quickly opened the door. Lt. Johnston entered with another officer. Leli offered them a seat.

"Mom, it's the police."

Tina walked out into the living room dressed in jeans and a long-sleeved black top.

Lt. Johnston smiled. "Ms. Perry, this is Detective Suarez from our homicide division. We're here to give you an update."

Detective Suarez greeted the family. "Your story is now national news. We found Mr. Diaz's friend Ashley White at the airport desperately trying to change her ticket so she could leave town. She's been arrested."

"She confessed and said she planned everything, together with her other boyfriend Kyle Williams. She hired Nicholas Romano to kill you." said Lt. Johnston. "She also said Mr. Diaz gave her a lot of money and supported her lifestyle and drug habits. They sometimes did drugs together, and he didn't know about her boyfriend. She admitted she wanted you dead since Mr. Diaz often mentioned you, which made her jealous. She also said she paid the killer with money Mr. Diaz gave her for rent."

Tina stared in shock. Leli's and Sarah's jaws dropped.

Lt. Johnston continued. "Romano was arraigned this morning and charged with attempted first-degree murder. After your attack, Mr. Diaz told the officer he became aware of the crisis that morning after Ashley left the hotel room for an errand and forgot her phone. Mr. Diaz said he became upset when he read the texts between her and Williams where they discussed the plot like a joke. Mr. Diaz said at one point she called him her stupid sugar daddy who didn't have a clue, which made him angry. When Ashley returned, he confronted her about the texts, but she denied everything and refused to tell him about Kyle, which infuriated Artie even more. He told the officer he wanted to send Ashley home right then and there, but since he had to focus on his concert, he decided to stick it out until their plane left for Los Angeles. After he rehearsed that day, he said he worried you might be in danger but didn't want to call the police in case he was wrong. He drove to your house and waited in his car until you left. He mentioned he saw you were dressed up. Mr. Diaz followed you and said he notice a man behind you, so he parked his car but stayed distant. He said he wanted to make sure you were safe."

Tina shook her head. "That's just a crazy lie. When Nick attacked me, Artie just happened to be there. I still don't trust his motives and don't understand why he saved my life."

"We haven't totally ruled out his involvement. Now about his accident, a witness saw the car that hit him and wrote down the tag number. We arrested a drunk Windermere minor driving a BMW Z4 convertible. He and his friend were out drinking and when the driver got home, he left the car in his parents 'garage, the dented front bumper covered with Mr. Diaz's blood."

"I'm glad you got him," said Tina. She paused as she struggled to understand the entire story.

The two officers prepared to leave and promised to call with any updates.

"Don't let the media upset you," said Lt. Johnston.

The following day, Leli called Tina from the hospital.

"Hi Mom, how are you doing?"

"I'm better. Thanks."

"Artie had a setback."

"What happened?"

"He has developed an infection called MRSA from his wounds. The hospital has started intravenous antibiotics, but he's not doing well, still in a coma."

"Keep me posted."

Two days later, Lt. Johnston and Officer Vazquez returned to speak with Tina.

Lt. Johnston began, "Ms. Perry, we want to let you know that Kyle Williams has been arrested in LA. He confessed to helping Ms. White hook up with Mr. Romano to commit the crime. He'll probably be charged with conspiracy to commit murder and get extradited here. Please tell us more about your relationship with Romano."

"Years ago, I met him when he worked at his uncle's deli. He said he was an aspiring actor. We had a three-week affair, but I had no regrets due to my awful marriage. I ended everything after I found out Nick had a wife and family."

Officer Vazquez finally spoke. "The LAPD informed us he is a person of interest in several unsolved disappearances, rapes and murders. We believe he supported himself as a contract killer between acting jobs."

"I can't believe it," said Tina. "This boggles my mind."

"Oh, one more thing," said Lt. Johnston. "As officers led Ashley to jail, she shouted out to reporters that she's innocent. She'll probably be on the news tonight. Just be aware in case there's any trouble down the road."

"Thank you, Lieutenant."

"She is charged with conspiracy to commit first degree murder."

After seeing Artie in his present condition, Tina remained torn between avoidance and supportiveness for her children's sake, although this seemed to affect Sarah the most. Adam and Leli handled his accident with a stoic attitude, but Sarah wept every night. All Tina could do was to hold her daughter and rock her back and forth to comfort her. Sarah had placed Artie on a pedestal, and Tina did not argue with her.

A few days later, Sarah stayed next to Artie's bedside, while Luisa and Tina went downstairs to the hospital cafeteria for lunch. They stopped and looked at the board before getting into the cafeteria line. Today's special featured turkey with dressing and two sides. The cafeteria also sold sandwiches, fruit, and salads. After the women paid the cashier for their meals, they seated themselves with their trays at a small table.

Luisa began the conversation. "I know you, my brother, and your children went through hard times together."

Tina stopped eating and looked up at her. "That's an understatement."

"You want to know what happened to me, yes?"

"I do. The last time I saw you was when you went with us to Florida so long ago. You wrote you ran away with some guy."

"I left, because Luis and I fell in love. I knew Mama would never approve our relationship, because he was poor. In fact, Mama cut me off when I reached out to her, She said I was dead to her because of what I did, and she never wanted to see me again."

Luisa looked away for a moment. "We got along at first. When Joshua was born, I called Mama again, but she never called me back. Joshua died from crib death when he was four months old." Luisa paused and wiped a tear away. "Our marriage became difficult. Luis got drunk a lot and beat me. I ran away. I was ashamed. I thought I lost my family as punishment, because I was a bad sinner. After all, I hurt Mama so badly. When I returned to Los Angeles, I tried again to make up with Mama, but she told me she was still so angry and hurt at what I did, that she would not forgive me. I assumed Artie hated me too. Cut off from my family, I lived at a shelter, couldn't find a job and got hooked on drugs. I was broke. I turned a few tricks for some extra cash. Then, I got arrested one night. In desperation, I called Artie who bailed me out, and we reconnected. After that, I got clean and got a job as a housekeeper at Miss Pussycat's Ranch, the biggest cathouse in Pahrump and got room, board, and meals, plus my salary. I cooked and cleaned for the girls."

Tina gasped and her jaw dropped. "He mentioned you worked there, but I thought that was one of his lies. Why didn't we hear from you?"

"He would not let me contact you or the children, because I worked at the Ranch, but he visited me every few months and always helped me out financially. You see, I've always been very poor. My brother was the only person who cared about me. Now this tragedy. I'm all alone now."

"I found a receipt from the Ranch for big bucks right before we broke up."

Luisa hesitated. "Sometimes when he came to the Ranch, he had fun with the girls." She paused. "I'm sorry," she added abruptly.

Sadness washed over Tina's face as she shook her head. "That doesn't surprise me. She gazed lovingly at Luisa. "I'm sorry for everything you went through, and it must have been painful to have been cut off from our family."

"Very much so. It broke my heart. I visit Mama sometimes in her nursing home. She has Alzheimer's and doesn't recognize me, so I know she won't send me away."

"I remember you used to write poetry."

"I still do. In fact, I'm now a Poet Laureate."

"What? Really?"

Luisa smiled, opened her purse and pulled out a floral-bordered business card which said, *Luisa Diaz Hernandez, Poet Laureate of Pahrump*. "I write poetry for holidays and special occasions." After she handed the card to Tina, she took another bite of food. "Did Arturito ever talk about life in Argentina?

"Not really," said Tina. "He rarely spoke about his past, and it seemed something was wrong. He had nightmares and lost his temper easily."

Luisa continued. "Our family lived in the Palermo Viejo section of Buenos Aires. It was so beautiful there with the stately old houses, green trees and cafes. Mama taught piano at home. She loved to cook and sew and was so kind. We never saw Papa much because of his work. He was always too busy for us, but women called our house often asking for him. Poor Mama. She never mentioned it, but I knew he hurt her." Luisa stopped. Tina noticed the sadness in her eyes. "When Arturito was eight, and I was 12, something very bad happened to him. An old man bought the house next door. Everyone called him Tio, Spanish for uncle, because he was kind to neighborhood kids and gave them candy. Artie was a sweet little boy with such a sunny disposition. Everyone loved him, especially Tío."

She looked away for a second and continued, "Tio invited Artie over often for candy, and Mama told him if he didn't go, he was being rude, but my brother always looked sad when he came home. One day about two months later, we heard screaming and gunshots outside. When we ran to the window, we saw Tío dead in the middle of the street while another neighbor stood over his body, brandished a gun and screamed over and over again, 'You'll die in hell for hurting my son.' When police arrested him, I heard Papa tell Mama that he thought Tío might have hurt Artie too, but Mama told him never to mention that again. Artie changed after this all happened.

He gained weight and as you know, always joked around but never seemed happy."

"I sometimes wondered why he tried so hard to be funny and suspected it was to cover some past trauma," said Tina. "This explains a lot."

Luisa looked down and toyed with her bracelet. "He was so talented and as a teenager, he played in tango bars, because we needed money after papa disappeared. He also traveled when he was 16 and gave recitals around the country. He studied at the Buenos Aires Conservatory at the time, but the military government took everything away and left us with nothing. Then, another terrible thing happened. His best friend Manuel was also a piano student at the conservatory. Shortly before Papa disappeared, the police stopped the boys on their way home one afternoon and arrested Manuel for insurrection, but he resisted until one cop pulled out a gun and shot him dead in front of Artie. Miraculously, they spared my brother and evidently didn't realize whose son he was, or they would have killed him as well." Luisa hurriedly dabbed her tears away with a napkin.

"Awful," said Tina. She shook her head, got up, took her empty tray and plate to the drop-off window. Luisa followed her. "C'mon," Tina said. "Let's get back to the room in case he wakes up."

★   ★   ★

Leli visited Artie's room during her breaks and after her shift, she sat, knitted, and as she pushed their terrible conflicts aside for the moment, she told herself she had do the best job in her professional capacity to advocate for his recovery or otherwise, she could not face her own conscience. Her siblings and aunt also visited Artie daily. He stayed comatose.

Two weeks later on New Year's Eve, Leli and the other ER staff were deluged with auto accident and firework injuries. On her break, Leli went to her father's room, checked and adjusted the machine tubes. Artie suddenly stirred and opened his eyes for a second. Leli touched his arm to check his pulse, and his hand moved. She looked up to see Artie's eyes following her, which surprised her since he was so heavily medicated. She knew he obviously recognized her, and for a moment, her anger and resentment surfaced, but she pushed it out of her mind, smiled, bent down and touched his hair. "Happy New Year," she whispered in his ear before she left the room.

She told her family, which initially gave her siblings and Luisa some hope. However, that was the last time anyone saw him responsive; Artie lapsed again into unconsciousness. On January 9, he developed a fever. When Leli checked on him that afternoon, his forehead felt clammy, and his ankles were obviously swollen. She reviewed his chart and saw a significantly elevated white blood cell count.

When his attending physician Dr. Lewis stopped by, Leli expressed her concerns.

"His situation is serious and he isn't responding well to antibiotics," said Dr. Lewis. "I will call in an infectious disease consultant to see if we can switch him to another protocol."

"I'm comfortable with that," answered Leli. "I agree his current regimen isn't effective."

The consultant arrived a short time later, examined Artie, reviewed his chart and recommended an immediate more aggressive course of antibiotics.

Two days later, Leli and the family discussed Artie's labs with Dr. Lewis and the consultant. Results now showed elevated procalcitonin and indicated sepsis without response to the new antibiotic regimen, so the consultant placed Artie on another antibiotic course. The sepsis did not surprise Leli or Artie's doctors, because the severe injuries increased susceptibility to infection.

That evening, Tina called Sydney. "His condition is quite serious, and it doesn't look good."

"Do you want me to come fly out to stay with you?"

"Thanks, but I can manage. It's tough, but we're taking it one day at a time."

"I don't know if this is the right time to ask, but would you mind if we come visit next month and stay with you for a few days. We miss you, and I want to take Nathan to Disney World."

"I'd love to see you both. A visit would be great."

"I guess it's hard for you now dealing with all this."

"It was, but I'm doing better."

"How are you guys getting along with Luisa?"

"Fine. She's really a lovely laid-back person, so unlike Artie or Maria. I never really got to know her before, and I think she was stuck under Mama's wing if you know what I mean. Now, we get along very well. She stayed with Adam, now with me. You know she told me a lot about Artie's past. He was molested as a child and then saw his best friend murdered. Luisa also indicated their father was a womanizer and a jerk. And, did I ever tell you I saw Tamara's notes from that time Artie and I went together? She thought he had Asperger's."

"Sad, but nothing excuses Artie's bad behavior. Sorry. I'm not surprised about the Asperger's, though it's now called an autism spectrum disorder."

"True. I realize now that Luisa was not only the kindest, but the most normal family member and had such a rough life."

"She sounds resilient," said Sydney. "It's a shame you lost touch all these years, Glad she's back."

The following night before Artie died, his family said their goodbyes to him as he lay still and unresponsive, his skin grey with impending death. Tina sat next to her children to provide emotional support but had little interest herself in being there and watching him die. Leli called her rabbi, who had promised her to be there for the family if necessary.

Adam finally spoke up. "Dad wasn't religious, so why call a rabbi?"

Leli turned to her brother. "We could use some comfort right now no matter what he believed."

Tina sighed. "Kids, I hope you can resolve your issues with him and find eventual peace. He was very difficult."

"I'm okay now," responded Leli quietly. "When he arrived, I saw his sorry state. Although we fought a lot in the past, I forgive him and also myself, so my anger at him will not be my defining factor."

"You're forgiving him for everything?" asked Luisa.

"I'm not excusing his bad behavior. I forgave him, because I want peace. While I'll never forget how he treated us, I want to move on with my life."

Nobody else commented. Sarah and Luisa embraced each other and wept quietly.

Rabbi Berkowitz arrived a short time later and joined with the family.

"Rabbi," asked Tina. "What happens after we die?"

"We as Jews believe in an afterlife," the rabbi said. "In Hebrew it's referred to as *shemayim* for 'heaven' or *shel mallah* for the 'school on high', or *sheol*, the 'underworld'. We believe heaven welcomes all, regardless of faith."

"So do bad people go to hell?" asked Sarah.

"Judaism doesn't believe in a hell," said the rabbi. "Instead, we believe that a person who has done bad deeds is apostate, cut off from friends and family."

"What's heaven like?" asked Leli.

"Heaven can take many different forms, depending on a person's beliefs. Some believe it's a transitory place where souls will reunite when the messiah comes. Others believe the soul carries on in children and grandchildren. In addition, many people believe that the soul will resurrect with the body after death."

"Are there any special prayers for the dead?" asked Adam.

"In reform Judaism, there is no ritual per se, but we can say the *Shema*."

The family gathered around Artie's bed. The rabbi stood in their midst and prayed with his eyes on Artie.

You shall love Adonai your G-d with all your heart and all your soul.

Hear O Israel, the Lord is our G-d, the Lord is one. Blessed be the name of the

Glory of His kingdom forever and ever.

After the rabbi read the three sections of Deuteronomy which comprise the *Shema*, he gave Artie and the family a special blessing. The family was ready, and Leli called the attending medical team. While the rabbi prayed with the family, the physician and staff removed all life support. Artie was officially declared deceased at 11:05 PM.

JANUARY 2017

Funeral arrangements fell to Leli and Adam. Their father's immense popularity required a large venue, so they arranged to hold his memorial service at the Hollywood Bowl. Two days later, Artie was cremated and the following week, his three children and sister flew with his ashes back to LA. Tina excused herself from all further involvement.

In the meantime, Ben had been strangely absent, but a few days afterward, he called Tina, and they met for a drink after work. At the restaurant, they ordered an appetizer, a beer for him and a Margarita for her.

Ben seemed quieter and more serious than usual.

He stole a glance at Tina but then looked away. "Tina, we need to talk." He paused. "I need a break for a while. I'm sorry, but this whole experience has been too much for me."

She sat numbly and said nothing, while Ben stared at his plate as he twirled his fork. "I'm not breaking up with you," he continued. "I just need a step back. In the meantime, feel free to date other guys."

"You know, this is really disappointing. How do you think I felt going through this? I thought you'd be supportive to me at a time like this."

"It's not you. It's me. I just need time away for now."

Tina finished her drink and got up. "I'm going home, and I'm taking a cab." She got up and left the restaurant. Ben sighed and paid the bill before he departed.

At home by herself, Tina burst into a flood of tears, as if a dam within her broke. Through her heartrending sobs, she realized how deeply she wept over her unresolved conflicts with Artie and Ben's rejection. She had envisioned him as her strength and support, but that hope faded away. Later, the more that she thought about self-reliance, the more she decided strength and independence mattered the most. She knew that even without a relationship, she would allow herself to feel at peace. Relief flowed over her as she realized Artie would never hurt her again.

That evening, she saw that Leli had emailed her Artie's *Los Angeles Times* extensive obituary, and Adam called two days later. "You should have seen the crowd at his memorial service. Later, the four of us spread his ashes in the Pacific and had a quiet dinner with a few of his close friends. We're trying now to clean up his house and everything's a disorganized mess."

"Do you know how long you'll be there?"

"Not sure. When we're done, we'll sell the house. We quickly sold his piano. By the way, Mom." Adam paused and cleared his throat. "Dad's two Pomeranians are adorable. One is black and one white, and there's a gorgeous Siamese. They all need a home, so would you take them?"

"Son, you know I'm a softie and I love animals." She sighed. "How can I refuse? They can't go to the pound."

A week later, a large heavy package arrived addressed to Sarah in her own handwriting. Slightly puzzled, Tina put the box in her daughter's room. Luisa called that afternoon. "I have to stay here a while and take care of Mama. She's in hospice and not expected to live much longer."

"I'm sorry. It's so kind of you to be there for her."

"Thank you. She's comfortable. She sleeps most of the time and has stopped eating." Luisa paused. "It's a matter of days. I'll let you know when it's over."

"That must be so overwhelming for everyone to deal with both deaths at once. Mama could be difficult, but she helped us tremendously with the kids. I'm so grateful to her. I'm sorry about your strained relationship. If I'd known, I would have intervened."

"She was my mom, and I was happy to help her." Luisa hesitated before she spoke. "I-I need a favor. I'm staying now with a friend, since Artie's house is being sold, but after this, could I please stay with you for a while, while I try to figure things out? I have nowhere to go. I'll pay you rent somehow. I'll help you clean and cook, anything. I don't want to return to the Ranch."

"You're welcome to stay, if you don't mind hot sunny flat Florida."

"Thank you, dear Tina. I'm so grateful."

"I'm glad my children finally will have their aunt nearby. You're a good person, Luisa."

"Nobody ever told me that before. So are you."

Two weeks later, Tina picked up her children at the airport. Each toted a pet carrier.

"Artie died intestate without a will," said Adam.

"His estate has to go through probate," said Leli. "We probably have to go back to settle affairs, but it won't be for a while."

When they got home, Tina opened the carrier doors. The white Pomeranian Blanca cautiously ventured out, followed by black Luna. Angel the Siamese walked into the kitchen where Tina's two cats loudly hissed at her. Angel shot them a dirty look with her bright blue eyes, walked away and sat by the window, licking her chocolate paws. Hans, not wanting to miss out, ran to greet the two dogs, and they cautiously sniffed one another. Tina knew the pets' adjustment would take time.

The next morning, Tina saw that Michael Farswell had emailed her a friendly reply. He told her he lived in Brentwood, that their father had passed away ten years before and to stay in touch. Tina thought to herself how ironic that they had lived only a few miles apart for so many years.

Sarah retrieved and opened her package. She lifted Artie's old bandoneon out of the box and set it on the kitchen table to Tina's surprise.

"Why did you save that?"

"It's an antique Alfred Arnold, and I read that it's a fine instrument. I didn't want to leave it behind. Maybe I'll learn to play someday." Sarah gently caressed the bellows as she spoke as if she felt her father nearby.

MARCH 2017

Sydney and Nathan, now a college freshman on spring break, flew to Orlando for vacation. He resembled Sydney, and was tall with a trimmed beard and elaborate tattoos on his arms. They drove to a seafood restaurant for dinner. When Tina told her friend about her newly discovered past, Sydney laughed and said, "Now we have even more in common since you're part shiksa just like me."

"True, but I'm still Jewish, because it's passed through our moms." They pulled into the restaurant's parking lot. "There's more. Adam put together a family tree and did his DNA. It turns out he's also part Jewish on his dad's side. He discovered Maria's grandparents were Italian Jews, who immigrated to Argentina in the early 1900s and apparently became Catholic."

"No shit. Artie didn't even have to convert."

"Did I tell you Luisa is living with us now?"

"You didn't."

"She's very sweet and helpful. I'm trying to help her find an affordable senior apartment. In the meantime, she's staying as long as she needs to."

After they were seated at the restaurant, and Nathan left to use the men's room, Sydney's voice turned to a quiet barely audible whisper. "I forgot to tell you that LaRhea killed herself."

Tina raised her head. "Really?"

"Drugs. Overdosed."

"That's terrible. Does Nathan know?"

"I never told him. They don't have contact anyway."

Nathan returned to the table. "Let's go to Disney tomorrow. That would be awesome." "I'm for it," laughed Tina. "I need a break."

★　★　★

One evening, Cheryl stopped by. Since Sarah was at Leli's place and Luisa had retired early, Tina and her two friends watched TV by themselves, shared merlot, popcorn and rehashed their life experiences into the night, until the first morning light flowed through the window. The gentle fingers of dawn crept through the sky and touched the clouds, which burst into a dramatic red and orange sunrise.

"Oh, good lord," said Cheryl. "We have been chatting all night. Where did the time go?"

"It seems like a blink of an eye. That's what wine will do to you," Sydney laughed.

Tina had dozed off on the couch, her empty wine glass on the table next to her. Her blonde hair hung across her face as her head fell forward. When she heard the other women's voices, Tina startled and awoke.

"Oh shit. How long have I been asleep? It's morning already? Sorry. That was rude of me."

"That's okay, baby," said Cheryl. "You needed the rest."

Luisa came into the living room, dressed in her pajamas and robe. "Good morning," she said. "You've been up all night. Why don't I make some coffee?"

"Better yet, why don't we all go out," said Tina.

"Let me get dressed." Luisa retreated to her room.

"We had such a good chat, girlfriends," said Cheryl.

"We talked everything we endured," said Sydney. "Sometimes, I wonder where we go from here."

Tina sighed. "I feel a bit guilty, but I am so relieved Artie's gone. The only decent thing he ever did for me was save my life and father my kids. What a narcissist."

"Tina, you get the medal for having endured that schmuck for so long. Please don't feel guilty," said Sydney. "Everything he ever did was for his own glorification and for attention. Don't dwell on his traumatic past, because that was no excuse for his behavior."

Cheryl smiled. "We have grown and moved on to become three independent chicks."

"No more compromises," said Tina. "As we all said last night in our own way, enough is enough."

"If we meet someone, great," said Cheryl. "Either way, we won't be dependent on others for our happiness. We'll travel forward to create happiness in our own lives."

"Ready to move toward the next chapter?" laughed Tina.

"You know it," said Sydney.

Luisa appeared and the women hugged each other before they walked out the door to get breakfast.

★　★　★

I hope you found this story inspirational. According to statistics, almost half of the United States population has been in an abusive relationship with 49 percent of female victims raped by their perpetrators. If you're in a relationship with an abuser, please get help. Here are some resources.

Domestic Violence Hotline
1-800-799-7233
https://www.thehotline.org
National Center for Victims of Crime
1-855-4-VICTIM (855-484-2846)
United States Department of Justice
www.justice.gov/ovw/domestic-violence

Follow my abuse blog. https://mariehammerlingauthor.com

A huge thanks to my original editor Rebecca Augustine, and my beta readers and advisors, Laurel Forrar and Lynn Schiffhorst. Thank you to everyone who helped me with information for this project, Judith Segall, Judith Fabre, Sylvia Bartlett, Neil Lewis-Levine, D.O., Roxanne Baron, Rabbi Steve Cardonick, Norm Booth, Rosalee Hopard, Les Payton, Renee Ebert, Ginette Olson PhD.

Made in United States
Orlando, FL
04 November 2021